MW01703650

DARK WINDS RISING

Also by Mark Noce

Between Two Fires

DARK WINDS RISING

Mark Noce

St. Martin's Press New York

This is a work of fiction. All of the characters, organizations, and events portrayed in this novel are either products of the author's imagination or are used fictitiously.

DARK WINDS RISING. Copyright © 2017 by Mark Noce. All rights reserved. Printed in the United States of America. For information, address St. Martin's Press, 175 Fifth Avenue, New York, N.Y. 10010.

www.stmartins.com

The Library of Congress Cataloging-in-Publication Data is available upon request.

ISBN 978-1-250-07263-4 (hardcover)
ISBN 978-1-4668-8444-1 (ebook)

Our books may be purchased in bulk for promotional, educational, or business use. Please contact your local bookseller or the Macmillan Corporate and Premium Sales Department at 1-800-221-7945, extension 5442, or by email at MacmillanSpecialMarkets@macmillan.com.

First Edition: December 2017

10 9 8 7 6 5 4 3 2 1

Again
for Laurel

Beware those who dwell beyond
the north wind.

—CELTIC FOLKLORE

PART ONE

Spring, A.D. 602

I

Just when I thought it impossible, I find myself with child once again. Queasy beside my tower windowsill, I inhale the strong balsam breeze wafting over the castle. My knuckles turn white as I clench the stonework, trying to steady my nerves. *Breathe Branwen, breathe. Just a few more moments and the nausea will pass.* My stomach churns as I squeeze my eyes shut.

Footsteps echo up the tower stairwell. My serving girl gasps, rushing across my chamber to my side. She pats my shoulder as I swallow the bile rising in the back of my throat.

"My Queen, are you all right?"

"Fine, Rowena. Fine."

She knits her brows in worry, sensing my lie. The castle walls and the courtyard below spin in my vision. Rowena steadies me with her arm. I wave her away, breathing deep through my nostrils as the world comes back into focus. Sweat beads along my brow.

"Tell the King I'll be along shortly. I just need a few moments' rest."

Rowena hesitates, biting her lip.

"But . . . m'lady, everyone's waiting. The tournament cannot begin without you."

I hang my head. The tournament. It was my idea, after all, a chance to offer an olive branch toward our rival Welsh kingdoms. To gather former foes together in friendly competition. As hostess of the tourney, I ought to be at my husband's side to inaugurate the ceremonies. Why did these pangs in my stomach have to begin now?

Far below my window, the pavilions of canvas tents and fluttering banners dot the greens around the citadel. The din of a thousand bustling peasants selling their wares and drinking tankards of hard cider pervades the warm summer air. Woodsmoke and the aroma of roast pig permeate the castle grounds. The clang of practice swords resonates from the armory.

Rowena looks me up and down with a knowing smile. She has served as my lady-in-waiting since my teens. Now in our twenties, the two of us seem more like sisters than queen and servant. I cannot fool her.

"M'lady, I know a breeding woman when I sees one. You are with child. Another heir to the kingdom."

I shush her with a raised finger. Another heir indeed. Is that all anybody thinks a queen is good for? Breeding more little princelings and princesses? I take a deep breath. That's not fair. Rowena means well and has birthed two children of her own. Even though we are alone, I keep my voice low. Castle walls have ears and bleed secrets like water through a sieve.

"Not a word of this to anyone, Rowena. Not even the King. You know what happened before."

"You've had miscarriages, aye. But you've one healthy son already. Be thankful the Lord has quickened your womb again."

"Thankful? Do you remember what the clerics told me after my last mischance? They said bearing another child would probably kill me."

Rowena looks to her feet, not meeting my gaze.

"The clerics are not always right, my Queen."

I frown, wishing I could believe her innate optimism, but my last five years as queen have taught me that wishes do not lead to salvation. Only by taking matters into our own hands can anything be accomplished. And sometimes not even determination avails us anything in the face of overwhelming odds.

Blinking back the sting in my eyes, the heavy metallic taste in my throat subsides. My gut rumbles, but not as badly as before. I smooth the wrinkles out of my ivy gown, glancing in a bronze mirror as I pin back my raven locks in a loose chignon. A frown creases my cheeks. My face looks pallid as a dove's, but there's no helping that. Nonetheless, even after two husbands, one child, and several years as matron of a small kingdom, I still have an hourglass figure and the emerald eyes to match. I clear my throat as I head for the stairs.

"Come, Rowena. As you say, we cannot keep everyone waiting."

Descending the steps, we emerge from the dark stairwell into the bright sunshine of midday. I blink back the water behind my eyes. The green mountains surrounding the castle seem close enough to touch. Despite my uneasy stomach, the sights and smells of Aranrhod castle bring a smile to my face. The old Roman walls and tall towers of the citadel dominate the lone hill at the center of the valley, nestled in a green Eden within the aerie of the Welsh mountains. Ancient oak woods encircle the rolling fields of upland wheat and oats that make this tiny vale the breadbasket of the highlands. There is no safer realm in all the Welsh Lands, and no place I would rather be.

With the castle gates thrown open, we wander the sprawling encampment outside the keep walls. Green dragon banners loom prevalently amongst the tents, the traditional banner of Aranrhod and the flag of my husband's kingdom. A few dozen crimson and black dragon pennants also crown some of the tents, marking off the visiting guests. Red standards for South Wales and black ensigns for the North. A slight shudder runs down the spines of my feet. Those dragon banners bring back many memories, when some of these neighboring kingdoms called themselves our friends, and other times when they declared themselves our foes. Will the contestants in this year's tourney be allies or adversaries a year from now? It's anyone's guess.

But we cannot afford another war. Not amongst ourselves, not with the Saxons biding their time across the eastern border, waiting and watching for the Welsh kingdoms to snatch at one another's throats once more. Oft times I wonder who is worse, the Saxon barbarians or us.

Throngs of spectators crowd the open field west of the castle, already filling a natural amphitheater at the foot of the mountains. Half the onlookers form a semicircle around the horse grounds while the other half congregate around a large stage shaded by canvas overhangs. Dozens of armchairs line the dais, reserved for visiting nobility and their retinues. Rowena leaves me as I ascend the wooden steps.

An empty throne rests beside my husband's chair. He reclines in his own seat, one leg thrown carelessly over the chair arm. If not for my upset stomach, I might very nearly laugh. Despite his near thirty years of age, Artagan remains as much a boy at heart as ever. Half the kingdom looks on while he gnaws on a leg of mutton with the same unabashed abandon he had when I first met him. He has come a long way from a bastard-born hedge knight to rise as monarch of a free Welsh kingdom, but beneath that thin veneer of royalty, he is still the charming ruffian I fell in love with five years ago.

I recline in my seat beside him as he tosses a spent lamb bone behind his throne. I stifle a grin. Yes, a very thin veneer indeed. He leans down beside my ear with a half-smile.

"What kept you? The archers will start target practice on each other if we don't begin soon."

I shrug off his boyish impatience. Bowmen, swordsmen, horsemen, and other contestants stand arrayed in groups across the open field. They merely wait for me to raise my scepter and begin the games. I whisper in Artagan's ear, enjoying the tension as all eyes glance our way.

"A little anticipation makes a tourney all the more suspenseful."

"This was your idea, remember? What's the point? Everyone knows who will win. The North Welsh are best with a lance, the South Welsh favor the sword, and our people always win the archery. It's a forgone conclusion."

"Who wins doesn't matter. This isn't about festivities and games. It's about gathering together with the other Welsh rulers, trying to build friendships and alliances where there has been only mistrust."

"The Welsh kingdoms haven't been united since the days of Arthur, long before our grandsires were in swaddling."

My eyes suddenly narrow on the crowd. Artagan's talk of swaddling reminds me of our boy. I haven't seen him since I excused myself from breakfast. As though sensing my motherly alarm, Artagan points toward a knot of guardsmen surrounding Rowena. She holds my three-year-old son in her arms.

Rowena and Gavin wave at us from across the playgrounds, his shock of red hair making him stand out in any crowd. How two dark-haired parents like us begat such an auburn little angel I will never know. Artagan clears his throat, nudging me with his elbow. Time enough the events got under way.

I stand at the center of the stage and raise my ceremonial scepter, a hazelwood wand entwined with ivy and a bouquet of wildflowers. I nod with approval at the fine job Rowena did in creating my tourney baton. Hundreds of onlookers wait with bated breath as I hold my flowery stake aloft, as though I am some incarnation of Mother Nature herself. A thin smile creeps across my cheeks. I lower my scepter with a flourish.

The crowd roars as the contestants break into small groups. The swordsmen begin the melee with their blunt blades while the archers take aim at distant haystacks. Minstrels pipe merry tunes as the audience erupts into a thousand conversations, taking wagers, making bets, and grinning through teeth full of venison.

Collapsing back into my seat, I realize I haven't sat down a moment too soon. My pale limbs tremble as I lean my skull back against the headrest. *God, help me just to make it through the day.* All we need is for the hostess of the event to faint, and the tourney might be postponed or canceled. It's bad luck for a queen to pass out, and our simple country people believe in omens if they believe in anything. I clench my jaw, willing myself to smile and look serene. Artagan gives me a sidelong glance.

"You feeling well, Branwen?"

"Very. Just tired. Gavin woke in the night, and I wanted to rock him back to sleep."

He eyes me a moment before swallowing my fib. We don't keep secrets between us, so he shrugs and returns his attention to the games. Lying to him leaves a bitter taste in my mouth, but I can't explain everything to him just now. I simply cannot.

Farther down the row of armchairs and pincushions, two other groups observe the tourney. One couple rests under the black banners belonging to the North Welsh of Gwynedd, and a separate trio sits under the vermilion pennants of South Wales from Gwent. The Queen of the northern kingdom glances my way. Her black tresses and violet eyes complement her lavender gown. She watches me with a fickle smile.

Queen Olwen. Despite her having a few years on me, she still has the figure of a Welsh Venus. Her voluptuous curves and smooth voice have captivated men from one end of Wales to the other, including my husband in the years before I met him. I think Olwen bears a torch for him still.

I beam pleasantly back at her, uttering a few stifled oaths behind my forced grin. She nods back from across the pavilion, doubtless thinking the same black thoughts about me. Her quiet gray-eyed husband, King Iago, coolly watches the events, still as a lizard basking in the sun. It's an open secret that Olwen rules him in the bedchamber and thus rules North Wales from behind the throne. But we each have plenty of dark secrets in our pasts we would much rather leave behind us. More than once Olwen and I have been rivals, then allies, then rivals once again.

The crowd cheers as one of the bowmen in green scores a bull's-eye for the Free Cantrefs. Another knot of spectators boos when the horsemen under the black banners unseat several opponents in the joust. So far, each competition proceeds just as Artagan predicted. Our people gain laurels with the longbow while the North Welsh win on horseback. Meanwhile, the swordplay continues across the dusty green, the favored event of the South Welsh.

Far to my right, the plump King Griffith of South Wales leans forward in his seat, intensely urging on the combatants. His even plumper wife, Queen Cordelia of Cornwall, licks the honey from her fingertips as she finishes off another half rack of pork ribs. Beneath their scarlet banners, a third person sits in their midst, a boy barely in his teens. He pays no attention to either the games or the crowd. Young Arthwys, the Prince and future ruler of South Wales, glares at me across the multitude. Wild tufts of sandy hair fall across his stern eyes.

I immediately look away.

Although I bear him no ill will, I cannot blame the boy for hating me still. I was once his stepmother. Back during my first marriage, when my father betrothed me to the previous monarch of South Wales, Morgan the Hammer King. An icy shiver runs through me. Those were dark days indeed, full of dark memories. Both my father and my first husband now lie in their crypts, but those of us who survive must still live with the consequences of the decisions they made. Poor young Arthwys and I were merely pawns in their chess game of thrones, but I fear the day when Arthwys comes of age and wields the scepter of the South Welsh. He has the stony look of his dead father in his eyes.

I return my attention to the games, another bout of wrestling taking place in the center of the field. Despite the enthusiasm of the boisterous crowd, I find it difficult to concentrate. My stomach gurgles mercilessly with discontent, although whether from morning sickness or the nearness of my rivals, I cannot tell for certain. We sit on our makeshift thrones, watching the commoners bash themselves into pulp for our honor. The North Welsh on one side, the South Welsh on the other, and our Free Cantrefs stuck in the middle. Just like on the map. Perhaps it was folly of me, after all, to think anything good could come of this mindless blood sport.

Artagan sits on the edge of his seat, mimicking jabs and wincing with grief and pleasure by turns as the wrestlers have at it on the greens. I cannot hide my smile. He probably has half a mind to join them. Although he is brave and strong in battle, I sometimes fear his heart outweighs his head. Then again, I think I love Artagan as much for his flaws as for his virtues.

Amidst the fights, he speaks to me without taking his gaze off the field.

"Did you notice not everyone you invited has come to this gathering of lances and swords?"

"You mean the Kingdom of Dyfed?"

"Aye. Did they ever reply to your invitation?"

"No, not even so much as a raven to announce their refusal."

I hang my head. Wales has long been divided into a patchwork of various fiefdoms. North Wales, South Wales, and the Free Cantrefs, but it is the realm of Dyfed in the Southwest of the Welsh Lands where I was born and still oft times think of as my homeland. Although the people here in Aranrhod remain close to me as family, I cannot help but feel a pang of guilt for not being able to rule in the territory whence I was born.

But much of that remains out of my hands. Dyfed has been a land of chaos since my father died. For years now, his many bastards have taken turns claiming the throne there and feuding with each other. How ironic that I, his only legitimate heir, should rule as queen in a neighboring fief, not in the very shire in which I took my first steps.

In my dreams, I still recall the sound and smell of the sea crashing against the hill fort of Dun Dyfed. But those are only dreams, and I shall probably never again lay eyes upon that place for the rest of my days. Dyfed is as much a ruin as my own childhood turned out to be, a past to which I may never return.

The piercing cry of my son's voice suddenly draws my attention. Gavin moans in Rowena's arms, straining and reaching out for two swordsmen circling one another in the open arena. Rowena's face turns a shade of purple as she tries to restrain the boy in her grasp. Little Gavin is tall for his age, and has grown headstrong as any prince in Christendom. He whines, clearly wanting to join the swordsmen in the melee, oblivious of the danger. Just like his father. I shake my head. Heaven help me if I have to raise two brave and fearless boys, one my son and the other my husband.

I motion for Rowena to bring Gavin over to me. She deposits the wriggling toddler in my arms, his blue eyes enlivened by the spectacle of so many men-at-arms traversing the field at once. Part of me hoped Gavin might be a more bookish child like I was, but his father's blood clearly runs stronger in him. This fiery-haired boy was born to be a warrior.

He relaxes somewhat on my lap, but I still keep both arms around him as my son points and smiles at the combatants on the grass. My heart seizes a moment, imaging him a grown man years from now, having to face the perils of a real battlefield. I squeeze him tight in my embrace. Never. I'll make peace with the Welsh, the Saxons, or anyone else I have to if it ensures that no more wars trouble this country. I *will* find a way. I must. My baby should not have to refight the same battles his mother and father did.

King Griffith bellows across the stage as one of the swordsmen with a red armband falls back under the onslaught of two other contestants. Griffith rises from his chair, vociferating with spittle in his chestnut beard. His pink jowls shake with rage.

"Have at him, man! Mind your footwork! Watch him, watch him! That's it!"

The swordsman from South Wales begins urging his two opponents back again, swinging wildly under the commands of his king. Artagan and I exchange glances over our son's head. King Griffith is an honorable ruler, but the last few years of feasts and drink that go along with kingship have left him a soft, heavy drunkard. He pants through crimson cheeks, looking like he might topple over simply from his own strong speech and shaking fists. The battle royal in the sword pen continues amidst clanging blades and dented shields.

"Maybe I was wrong." Artagan winks at me. "We won the archery and the North won the joust, but the South Welsh look like they're in trouble in the sword competition."

My husband smirks at Griffith's growing agitation. Artagan palms his own sheathed longsword beside his throne. Unlike most of our woodland folk, who fight with longbows, Artagan has always been a master with the longsword. It earned him the nickname Artagan Blacksword in his youth, and rival kingdoms still refer to him as such. He still has enough spunk in his sword hand to probably best every challenger in the melee, but I'd prefer he not put it to the test. A king's place is at the head of a banquet or issuing edicts from a throne, not waving a blade in the face of every man he meets. Even though my beloved no longer lives day to day by his sword as he once did as a hedge knight, no amount of kingship will ever break him of his old habits.

This tourney has not turned out as I hoped. Instead of providing a friendly atmosphere of fun and trust, the rival groups only seem to antagonize each other all the more. Can this day get any worse?

My stomach gurgles again, making me wince. I need to excuse myself before I collapse and make a fool of myself. Why couldn't these pangs wait just a few more hours? Then I could retire discreetly to my bedchamber and while the day away in bed with my books. Reading legends about the fairy folk or old magic would do more to settle my nerves than any amount of herbals and fresh air.

King Griffith continues growling between clenched teeth as his champion falters under the blows of swordsmen with black and green armbands. It looks as though the South Welsh will not win their favored event after all. I might roll my eyes if all these noblemen didn't take sparring so seriously. Men and their pride. No better than overgrown boys with pointy sticks in their hands.

Griffith unsheathes his own sword and steps into the ring, grabbing a cleft shield from the mud. Heaving as though he might fall over, the monarch stands between his vanquished champion and the remaining two swordsmen. Both antagonists exchange looks, unsure what to do. Striking a king usually merits death by beheading. My pulse jumps in my throat. Damn Griffith for being such a haughty fool!

Artagan leaps forward from his seat, his blade still sheathed but at his side. The two kings eye one another as the remaining combatants back off. The crowds run silent. Artagan speaks loud enough for all to hear.

"What are you doing, Griffith? Let these men finish their fight without interference."

"Stand aside, *Blacksword*! If these men mean to sully the reputation of South Welsh swordsmen, I intend to teach them a lesson or two."

Artagan glances back at me as though looking for guidance. I merely shake my head. If Griffith wants to make a fool of himself, let him. Why did Artagan have to get involved? His stupid ideas about fairness and chivalry mean nothing to the vanity of lords and kings. Artagan sighs, speaking lower.

"Griffith, you are deep into your cups. Let us retire from this field together. We once fought Saxons side by side, let us not cross swords here over a few men in a tourney."

Griffith bristles at Artagan refusing to call him king. But when have kings ever recognized other monarchs as equals? Griffith aims his blade at Artagan.

"I'm not some old man to be trifled with, young pup! I fought Saxons while you were still at your mother's tit. Now stand aside while I teach these other sellswords a lesson, or I'll cut you down myself!"

Artagan tightens his jaw. Damnation. I rise, putting Gavin in Rowena's arms again. I can smell the liquor on King Griffith's breath from a dozen paces away. God help us, neither of them plan to back down. I've got to stop this, but how?

Queen Olwen and her husband exchange glances, looking on silently. They probably enjoy the spectacle of this tourney turning into a debacle. Artagan grips his sword, starting to pull it from its scabbard.

"This is *my* land, Southron. Lower your blade or I shall lower it for you."

Guards on both sides take up arms, but Griffith stays them with a raised palm.

"The rest of you stand down! If the Blacksword thinks he can best me, he'll have to bloody well do it himself."

I stagger onto the grass, lifting my skirts over my ankles so that I don't trip. I'll throw myself between the two of them if I must. I sway on unsteady feet, perspiration running down my back beneath the folds of my gown. I should be in bed, but I cannot let this confrontation between kings happen. Artagan will defeat Griffith in a heartbeat, but

Griffith will never quit. It will mean war, and worse, a bloodbath in my own front yard. Damn these prideful men! Their stubbornness does them courage in battle, but it makes for poor diplomacy.

As I reach Artagan's side, a horse whinnies loudly in the distance. All eyes turn as a pair of riders gallops headlong down from the mountain passes and into the thick of the crowd. Peasants curse and jostle out of their way as the two horsemen rear up their mounts directly before Artagan and me. Both heralds gasp for air, their mounts bathed in sweat. Each man bears a spear in one hand and a calfskin shield in the other. My eyes widen. I'd recognize such rawhide shields anywhere. These riders come from Dyfed.

The lead rider bends down in the saddle, addressing the crowd of kings and queens.

"We bear ill tidings from Dun Dyfed by the sea. Our fortress has fallen to the barbarians and we ask for aid."

Hushed murmurs break out amongst the crowd. Griffith and Artagan's showdown has been momentarily forgotten. News of barbarians on the move makes my skin run cold. I grasp one of the horses by the bridle, looking up into the faces of these worn warriors. Blood and dirt smudge their cheeks. They clearly have had a rough fight just getting here.

"Barbarians on our shores?" I ask. "When? How? Why would the Saxons break the truce now of all times?"

The lead rider shakes his head.

"I said barbarians, fair Queen. *Not* Saxons. Those who attacked us came on ships with black sails and animal-skin hulls."

My eyes narrow. What on earth does he babble on about? Saxons rarely use ships, and when they do, they're made of wood. The second rider explains.

"Their warriors had white lime in their hair and blue woad on their skin. The ancient enemy of our ancestors has returned from the northern wastes. Dyfed has fallen and all our kingdoms are now in peril! We were attacked by the Picts!"

I stagger backward, steadying myself on Artagan with one arm. Impossible. The Picts on our shores? Painted in white and blue like in the legends of old? They're a fairy tale, a bedtime story meant to frighten young children. They cannot be here now.

My gut betrays me as hot fluid rises in my throat. The tumult inside me will no longer be contained. I retch onto the grass, coughing up my breakfast of oats near Artagan's feet.

2

King Griffith paces in the main hall, scoffing before Artagan's throne.

"This must be some kind of trick! Isn't that obvious? The Picts could not have done this."

"Why not?"

Artagan stares down at the fat monarch. The other royal families gather in the central chamber of our castle, seated or standing around the otherwise deserted mead benches. Green-clad guards man the entranceways, keeping everyone else out of the main hall. The din of the tourney outside has ended, the stone archways of the keep and the fairgrounds eerily silent save for the dull hush of the wind. Gray clouds on the horizon blot out the afternoon sun, as though the mere mention of the Picts has chased the daylight away.

On my throne beside Artagan, I glance at Queen Olwen and King Iago across the floor. Neither say a word, but even their normally calm faces look unusually pale. Griffith continues to pace, his wife and stepson, Arthwys, seated nearby. The round king still looks half-peeved that he and Artagan didn't get a chance to cross swords earlier at the tournament. I bite my tongue, trying to exude a bit more diplomatic poise rather than vent my frustrations aloud. Headstrong oafs! Even with the threat of war and bloodshed on our very borders, these kings and knights still want to test each other's steel.

The two riders from Dyfed wait on foot, their clothes torn and besmirched from their journey. Each has brown hair and freckled cheeks, looking like cousins at least. The first one steps forward, directly addressing Artagan and me.

"My name is Sir Bowen and this is my brother, Sir Carrick. We have risked life and limb to reach here and call for aid. Many of our countrymen lie dying thanks to the treacherous Picts. If you do not believe our words, believe our wounds, inflicted by the barbarous sea pirates this day!"

Bowen outstretches his arms, his brother doing likewise. Both knights bear cuts and welts all along their exposed skin. Clearly, they have barely escaped with their lives after their run-in with the barbarians. Griffith holds up a thick palm, shaking his head.

"That's no proof! Anyone could've parried blows with you today."

Unable to contain my rising heat, I leap toward Griffith with a heavy finger aimed at him.

"What reason have you to doubt these men? What could they possibly gain by such a lie?"

Taken aback by my rising voice, King Griffith narrows his gaze on me.

"You were born in Dyfed, Queen Branwen, and it clouds your judgment. These so-called heralds might be in league with our enemies. If we ride to their aid, it would leave our own kingdoms defenseless. Did you think of that?"

"Dyfed may be a troubled kingdom, my lord, and many other things besides, but never have they aligned themselves with the Saxons or anyone else against Wales, and you know it!"

Griffith reddens at my calling him "lord" instead of "king." Once upon a time, he and his people united with us against the Saxons. Have a few years of kingship made him so distrustful of his Welsh neighbors, simply because they do not swear allegiance to his particular throne?

Artagan rises and places himself between us.

"Everyone, sit down! This is still my hall, and I will clear *all* of you from it if you cannot control yourselves."

Artagan eyes both Griffith and me as we retreat to our seats. I ball my fists at my sides. When my husband, of all the hot-blooded people in the world, tells *me* to calm down, I know I have gone too far. Nonetheless, hearing Griffith badmouth Dyfed sets something afire inside me. The people there have suffered so much in the past few years—war, famine, plague, and now this.

Lady Olwen clears her throat from across the hall. All eyes turn toward her as she crosses her legs beneath her skirts, reclining against the table behind her. Although she speaks loud enough for everyone in the room to hear her, she keeps her steady violet eyes on my husband and no one else. That northern Queen is still mooning over Artagan.

"I'm sure these two heralds mean what they say," she begins, "but let's all be reasonable. Picts? On these shores? No one has seen them venture out of their abode in the frozen North for generations."

Iago nods beside her.

"My wife speaks true. This so-called attack is a fairy tale, nothing more."

Bowen grimaces and moves toward him, but his brother Carrick holds him back. No man likes to be called a liar to his face. Gripping the arms of my seat, I cannot keep silent.

"The Picts were the fiercest enemies of the Old Tribes, whose blood lives on in most of us in this room. It was the Picts, after all, whose raids first forced the Romans to invite Saxon mercenaries here."

"Aye," Artagan adds. "Then the Saxons turned on ancient Rome and started carving up the island for themselves."

Griffith folds his arms as a mead bench sags under his weight.

"You forget the most important part of that story. Once the Saxons arrived, the Picts never showed themselves on our shores again."

"But we have driven the Saxons back," I counter. "For now, at least. Perhaps the Picts have come to seize an opportunity while both we and the Saxons maintain an uneasy truce."

Silence fills the hall, save for the drip of torches blazing along the stony walls. The overcast light dims in the high windows and arrow slits as clouds rumble outside. A storm is coming.

In some ways, I can't blame the others for not wanting to see the truth. Saxon armies coming overland from the east have proved bad enough in years past. And now Pictish raiders landing from the sea to the west and north? The Welsh kingdoms would be stuck between an anvil and a hammer. The four horsemen in the Book of Revelation might as well start riding the length and breadth of Wales. Saxons on one side and Picts on the other? Between two such threats, our people won't stand a chance.

Legend has it that the Picts dwell beyond the northern winds that buffet our coasts in winter. Many a bedtime tale oft ends with the warning to children to beware the bad things that dwell beyond the north wind. The possibility of encountering such boogeymen face-to-face suddenly seems all too unreal.

Artagan reclines in his chair beside me, sighing as he glances my way. The burden of kingship weighs heavy on his shoulders on days like today. Do we risk riding to Dyfed's aid while weakening our own defenses? What if the Saxons should find out and take advantage of our reduced strength? What if one of the other kings in this room betrays us? No easy decisions lie before us.

Nonetheless, something in my heart tells me that we cannot simply leave Dyfed to fend for itself. The people there are Welsh even if they do not swear allegiance to my husband. Dyfed and the Free Cantrefs both run strongest in the blood of the Old Tribes, especially when compared to any other province in Wales. Do we forsake the ancient bonds of our Celtic forebearers? I return Artagan's gaze with a pleading look. He knows what I think we should do, but I do not want to risk contradicting him in front of our rivals here. If only we had more time to talk, alone.

He looks me up and down, his eyes lingering a moment on the damp hem of my gown. The fabric still bears the stain from when I lost my breakfast on the greens. Blast my morning sickness for such ill timing! My gut still swirls even now. Artagan must know, or at least suspect my condition. Then again, men can be oddly blind to such things. God in heaven, why must everything go wrong at once?

Artagan raises his voice. I recognize the familiar tone, firm and beyond the point of compromise.

"If these two riders from Dyfed wanted to deceive us, they certainly could have thought up a better lie. Nor would they have come and humbled themselves before us unless the utmost necessity required them to. Whomever has returned to harry our shores, whether Picts or otherwise, I will go and find out myself. And I will not go alone. My men ride out with me at first light tomorrow. Have any of the other kingdoms the stomach to come with us? Or do they still fear the flicker of shadows in the night?"

My husband stares down the other two monarchs, both King Iago and King Griffith returning his gaze with steely glares. I wince slightly. Brave and forthright as he is, Artagan has never hid his intentions under a bushel. He ought to tread a bit more carefully when challenging other men's courage, especially if such men have thousands of warriors at their command.

Dark-haired, gray-eyed, lanky Iago rises to his feet. He offers an arm to Olwen, clearly intending to leave. His voice sounds cold as ice.

"These Dyfed riders run from their own shadows. They'll lead you on a fool's errant, nothing more."

Iago bows respectfully my way before leading himself and his wife outside. Olwen casts a long look back over her shoulder at my husband and me. Even when exiting a room, her curvy figure has a sultry movement that draws every eye upon her.

King Griffith takes his turn to rise, his plump queen and young Arthwys accompanying him. The rotund monarch frowns through his heavy, bearded jowls at my husband. A chill runs down to my feet. None of this has turned out as I hoped. Griffith sighs through his deep grimace.

"There was a time, Artagan Blacksword, when you and I saw more eye to eye. When the Saxons were our shared foes and things were simpler. I regret that those days have passed."

Without another word, the contingent from South Wales turns to leave. Arthwys gives me one last basilisk stare before stepping out under the archway with the others. Despite all that has befallen us today, his fiery eyes give me the most pause. May the Virgin help us if ever that boy becomes a king. Let us hope that Griffith will rule as steward over the South Welsh for many years to come. He may disagree with us at times, but at least he does not despise us.

The two heralds from Dyfed kneel at our feet, now that my husband and I are alone with them in the great hall. Artagan bids them to rise, never being one to stand on ceremony or courtly courtesies. Bowen beams at Artagan with renewed enthusiasm.

"You are a wise and good man to come to our aid. Thank you for believing us, King Artagan."

"I trust your honesty and sense of honor, but I did not say I believe you."

Bowen and Carrick exchange looks. Even I cannot help staring at Artagan. I must interrupt.

"But husband, you just said that you would ride to their aid."

"Aye, and I shall. Something foul is afoot in Dyfed, and I would find out what. I'm sure you men believe what you have told me, but I have my doubts. Pictish warriors are something out of legend, like monsters and magic. I have difficulty believing they've arisen suddenly after more than a century just so they could haunt our coasts."

Carrick speaks before his brother can reply.

"When you come with us tomorrow, my liege, you will see for yourself."

"I shall. But I hope to God you are wrong."

I turn to call out to my servants in order prepare rooms for our two weary guests. Both brothers look much alike with their chestnut mops and youthful grins. Bowen seems the more talkative, whereas Carrick chooses his few words very carefully. Nonetheless, something Carrick said gives me pause. When he called my husband "liege" and not "lord" or "king." I spin on my heels and call back to them.

"Sirs, we've had little reliable news of Dyfed these past few seasons. You neglected to tell us, whom you serve there? Who rules as king in Dyfed now?"

Both brothers pause, exchanging sidelong looks. Clearly, I've hit upon something they had rather not shed light upon. Artagan strokes his chin, scrutinizing our two guests. Not mentioning the current monarch of Dyfed seems an odd thing to omit. Bowen looks to the floor.

"My Queen, as you know, your late father reigned as king in Dyfed for many years, but when he died in battle against the Saxons several years ago, many claimed his throne."

"I know. Father had many bastards, but I was his only noble-born heir."

"And you are remembered fondly in Dyfed still, my lady. But many of your late father's base-born sons have sought to control Dyfed. In the last three years we have had half a dozen rulers proclaim themselves king, each besting the other until all of them were . . . dead."

Artagan and I exchange quick looks. Bowen cannot mean what he implies. I must have misunderstood. My gaze narrows on his freckled face.

"Sir Bowen, are you saying that *all* my father's bastard-born sons have perished?"

"Aye, Your Grace. Between internal feuds and this latest Pict ambush, we have no king in Dyfed now. The land is in chaos."

"But that would mean . . ."

I trail off, almost not daring to complete my thoughts aloud. Carrick steps in front of his brother and finishes my thought.

"That would mean you might claim the throne of Dyfed, Queen Branwen. You or anyone else with an army to back them. You understand now, perhaps, why we did not wish to bring this up."

Bowen steps forward, his shoulders tense.

"We need aid, true, but we do not wish to invite another dynasty to come in and claim Dyfed as its own. Please do not misunderstand us, wise King and Queen. We do only what we feel is best for our people."

The two knights seem to sag under the weight of their burdens. Their calfskin shields and spears hang low in their arms. I put a palm on each of their shoulders and smile cordially.

"We all do what we must for our people. I am a child of Dyfed, and

I promise you that we come as allies, not conquerors. You have served your people well, and are surely weary. We can talk more of this tomorrow."

The warriors nod, doubtless relieved that they can rest after such a perilous day of barbarians and kings. My servants take them to fresh quarters as Artagan calls out for the castle seneschal. The light begins to fade in the arrow slits lining the hall. We have much work to do and many troops to summon on the morrow. Artagan slumps in his chair as the pair of us sit alone in the great hall. He parts his lips to speak. I fear he will ask me about the scene earlier on the lawns when I was sick. I do not want to have to lie to him again.

"Those two Dyfed men seem honorable," I begin, "but they are wrong about one thing."

"And what's that?"

"One of my father's bastard-born children still lives."

"Who?"

I smirk at Artagan as his eyes narrow on the lone figure entering the hall. One-eyed Ahern, loyal seneschal and grizzled defender of the castle, he has served me since before the last war with the Saxons. He lost one eye to the barbarians and ever since has worn a patch over the empty socket, but never has it prevented him from keeping Aranrhod safe. He stands at attention with spear and shield in hand.

"You summoned me, my King."

"Well, I'll be damned," Artagan replies, covering his mouth.

"Sire?"

I stifle a laugh before trying to enlighten my seneschal.

"Ahern, you have served this household for years, but you are also my half brother."

"Born on the wrong side of the blanket, aye, my Queen. What of it?"

Artagan winks at me before turning to my kinsman.

"How would you like to be King of Dyfed, Ahern?"

"My liege?"

"Never mind."

My husband and I cannot repress our mirth, grinning from ear to ear. Poor Ahern. He has dedicated his whole life to soldiering, but he much prefers to take orders rather than give them. Much as I care for him, I don't think he has the right temperament to rule, nor would I want him to have to run the entire realm of Dyfed when I need him here at my side as my loyal seneschal and steward. A throne would be more a curse than a blessing to him.

I rise from my throne. The darkness reminds me that Gavin will soon have to go to bed. I excuse myself, planting a kiss on first Artagan and then Ahern's cheek. Let the two warriors plan out the details of corralling their knights and bowmen. I have a castle to run.

Passing by the castle chapel, I can almost hear the scratching of pens on parchment as a few resident clerics scrawl away at the small but growing collection of manuscripts we keep within the priory. I first started our library collection with the books of my mentor, the late Abbott Padraig. Although he has long since perished under the Saxon scourge, his memory lives on in the life of his books and the great wisdom and stories recorded in their pages. I smile, thinking of the balding monk and all the things he taught me as a youth, both in the healing arts and in how to live a good life. Every day his passing stings a little less, but his memory remains emblazoned within my heart as strongly as ever.

So many graves mar the chapel yards across Wales, so many great figures lost in the struggle to preserve the Welsh Lands from barbaric invasions. The Abbot who first taught me to read. My husband's mother, Lady Annwyn, who instructed me in the Old Ways of magic and other ancient wisdom long since lost from our foremothers amongst the Old Tribes. And my own mother, Queen Vivian, slain by the Saxon menace when I was but a child. But those dark days are long past us, or so I've thought.

Upstairs in one of the ancient tower chambers, I find Rowena with a small herd of children running about her skirts. Her two little girls, Mina and Mora, twirl a rolling hoop across the floor. Several tiny straw-stuffed dolls litter the floorboards. In the corner, Gavin and another toddler arrange a small army of miniature wooden soldiers painted in green and black. Their toy spearmen and knights collide as the two boys crash their armies together in a mini-Armageddon. Rowena shrugs her shoulders at me as I enter the boisterous children's room of chaos and toys.

My eyes linger on the small dark-haired boy playing with my son. Young Cadwallon is the same age as my Gavin, and the two have been constant companions since birth. They look so opposite, my son with his fiery hair and Cadwallon with his charcoal mop, and yet at heart they play and fuss as though they were brothers. I frown despite myself, knowing it dangerous to let these two boys get close. Cadwallon may be my foster son, but he is no ordinary boy. One day Gavin and he may find themselves enemies when they grow up.

Rowena whispers in my ear.

"Cadwallon's mother is here. She's waiting outside. Shall I let her in?"

I start, surprised even though I should not be. She is his mother, after all. How could I not expect her to look in on her only son? I nod to Rowena as she opens the stairwell door.

Olwen steals quietly into the room, unnoticed by the quartet of noisy children playing across the chamber. Rowena gives me and the northern Queen plenty of room, tending to the scattered jacks and knucklebones strewn all over the floor. I speak low so that only Olwen can hear me. We watch our children playing with their toys.

"I thought you'd be gone by now," I begin. "Your husband has little mind to stay."

"With nightfall coming on, he will wait. Better to leave at first light. How fares my son?"

"Cadwallon grows strong. Well cared for and reared with the other children of the castle. Just as I promised, when you first sent him here, three years ago. Would you like to see him alone?"

"No, let him play. He seems quite involved with your own son."

Olwen bites her lip, blinking back the water behind her eyes. She watches Cadwallon play, the children oblivious of us standing across the bedchamber like a pair of motherly statues. Even with her eyelashes glistening with tears, Olwen still looks like a carven figure of a goddess. I know I should pity her as she looks longingly at her only child, but in her low-cut gown and perfumed tresses I cannot forget all the things that have gone before between us. She has tempted men and used them for her own purposes, but I'm sure others whisper the same about me. How can she and I be so akin in some ways yet so different in others? Olwen has always remained a mystery to me.

She clears her throat to steady her voice. It must irk her to show any weakness before me. She wipes a tear from her cheek, pretending only a bit of lint landed in her eye.

"How ironic that of all the people in Christendom, I can trust only you with the care of my boy."

"He can stay as long as he likes. Unless of course you wish to take him back with you."

Olwen levels her purples irises on me.

"You know I can't do that. Cadwallon is my boy, but he is not Iago's son. My husband may eat out of my palm at times, but even I would not trust him should I bring my natural child to live at his court."

"Does he know who the father is?"

Olwen flashes a cat's smile.

"Tired of the rumors that Cadwallon is your husband's bastard?"

"We both know that's not true."

My skin flushes hot, knowing she enjoys scratching that old wound. The fact that Artagan was her lover before I met him. She probably still thinks I stole him from her. And now our children must grow up in the mess we've made. So many secrets we share, Olwen and I. How we have fought and been forced to ally from time to time to save our own skins. Olwen examines her fingernails as though unconcerned about our conversation.

"Fostering my son has advantages for you too. So long as you have him, you know I will keep the peace between our kingdoms."

"So long as you keep Iago under your spell. Do not think I don't see the game you play, Olwen. Despite our mutual . . . *history* . . . you know that Aranrhod is the safest place for your son. And one day, when he is grown and Iago no longer useful to you, you'll put your own boy on the northern throne."

Olwen tilts her head back in a silent, mock laugh.

"Why, Branwen, what an imagination you have. Must I remind

you that I've saved both *your* life and your husband's when you needed me most?"

"Only because it suited your purposes. And because you're still in love with him."

The North Welsh Queen glares at me, her lavender eyes smoldering like hot coals. How strangely God works. He made Olwen and me antagonists yet gave us each the ability to read the other's soul like an open book. I almost can't blame her for loving Artagan still. *Almost.* He is a good man, but he is *my* man. Our children play happily a few paces away while Olwen and I stare one another down. Cadwallon's babyish voice perks our ears.

"Mumma?"

The small boy stares at Olwen across his field of fallen toy soldiers. Smart for his age, Cadwallon has seen Olwen only half a dozen times since coming to live at Aranrhod, but he clearly remembers her. Olwen swallows the lump in her throat at hearing her child call out to her. She presses her lips tightly together, failing to control a trembling hand as she strides over and touches the young boy's cheek. Cadwallon wraps his arms around her skirts and presses his head to her hip. Olwen kneels down to embrace him, hiding her face from me as she hugs the child who has been forced to live apart from her.

Gavin glances at me with a puzzled look, his playmate no longer beside him and their wooden figurines. My son is perceptive as well, and he watches Olwen closely as she kisses the boy he considers his brother. I give Olwen and her son a moment, pretending to pick up scattered toys.

She rises and pats Cadwallon on the head, stifling her sniffles as she fakes a smile and heads toward the door. Part of me wants to say something to comfort her, something that might make everything all right. But of course there is nothing I can say. Olwen pauses on the threshold and whispers my way without sparing me another glance.

"I trust you'll continue your exemplary treatment of my boy. Oh, and congratulations. It seems you are with child once again. I wonder whether Artagan knows."

My cheeks burn hot, my lips suddenly lost for words. She retreats down the turret steps with a half-grin on her face. I bite my fist as I watch her go. That nosy shrew! Just when I start to let down my guard, Olwen shows me her fangs once again. After I threw up on the lawns this afternoon, she must have guessed my predicament. I grind my teeth with half a mind to go after her. Instead I silently fume until her footsteps fade down the stairwell.

Without turning around, I call out to Rowena and the children. My tone brooks no argument.

"Time for bed!"

The children whine as Rowena tries to pull them away from their playthings. Gavin cuddles onto my lap while the other little ones chant in unison. *Song, song, song.* I sigh, knowing it will take more effort to fight their demands than to sing them an evening lullaby. Even in my own castle, the children rank higher than me, it seems. I clear my throat and hum a soft lai, one that my mother used to sing to me. I don't have a good singing voice, not as full throated as my husband's, anyway, yet the children demand another and so I sing a second ballad about lords and ladies at a courtly dance. One by one, the children's eyelids start to sag with sleep.

After I finish, I leave Rowena with Cadwallon and her girls as I pick up Gavin and head for the door. He squirms within my grasp, still clutching a small wooden knight in his fist. We trek back down the steps and across the dark courtyard, heading toward my own tower where my husband and I keep our solar chamber.

All runs quiet, most of the castle inhabitants doubtless already tucking themselves into their beds for the night. Only the clack of my shoes on the cobblestones sounds through the darkness. It seems unusually dark in the central yard tonight, all of the torches snuffed out and the braziers smoldering with dowsed ashes. I'll have to talk to Rowena about that tomorrow. We shouldn't waste precious fuel on needless fires, but I do like to keep the courtyard lit at least a little. It's a small matter, of course, and can wait until morning.

Gavin is already fast asleep in my arms. His heavy breathing stirs my cheek. A few paces from the entranceway of my tower stairwell, an odd clicking sound stops me dead in my tracks. A short snap like a coiled spring perks my ears. I turn around to see a lone figure silhouetted against the castle ramparts, looking down at me. My eyes widen. Aside from this stranger, there are no guards in sight.

He cocks a crossbow in his arms, his silent shadow taking aim as I stand paralyzed with fear in the courtyard below. Gavin still nods innocently against my shoulder. I part my lips to cry out, but I know that as soon as I do, the assassin will loose his arrow and all will be over. I have only a moment before the inevitable happens. The dark figure shifts his aim, pointing the bolt in his crossbow not at me but at the little boy in my arms. He has come for my son.

3

A falcon's cry pierces the night air. A mass of wings and claws descends on the assassin's weapon, tearing at the bowstring just as the bolt lets loose. The man in the shadows curses as the bird of prey throws off his aim. A feathery dart whistles through the darkness, scratching my cheek before embedding itself in a wooden pillar behind me. Hot blood runs down my jaw.

Atop the battlements, the winged raptor continues to caw and menace the man with the crossbow. Even in the blackness, I recognize the shriek of the aerial creature. Vivian! My hunting falcon.

Without a moment to spare, I duck into the tower entranceway and scale the steps two at a time. Gavin stirs in my arms as I jostle him over the threshold of my bedchamber. I slam the door shut and throw the latch. My heart drums against my ribs. For the first time in what seems an eternity, my voice returns to me.

I scream.

Within moments, half the garrison appears on the castle parapets. Bowmen and guards crowd the courtyard. From my darkened solar, I peer down into the yard, not daring more than a glance in case the assassin should take a shot at my upstairs window. Artagan and Ahern emerge from the main hall with torches in hand and their weapons drawn. My husband snaps at Ahern.

"Why the devil aren't the braziers lit? It's black as pitch out here."

"Something's afoul, my King. None of the guards I posted are on watch."

"I swear that scream sounded like Branwen."

I call out to my husband and kinsman. Even though they cannot see me, they instantly recognize my voice. I only hope I'm not too late.

"Artagan! Ahern! On the eastern wall, a man with a crossbow. Hurry!"

The shuffle of weapons and footfalls murmurs throughout the darkened citadel. My falcon cries out again, somewhere under the dim starlight. Heavy footsteps rumble up the stairwell. A fist bangs against the locked door.

I flinch, still clutching my sleepy child in my arms. My birch wood bow hangs on the wall. I've half a mind to grab it, but I do not want to put Gavin down. A hand knocks again on the door.

"Branwen! It's me! Open up."

I heave a sigh of relief, recognizing Artagan's voice. I throw the hasp and let him inside. Two of his most trusted knights follow close on his heels, gray-bearded Sir Emryus and broad-shouldered Sir Keenan. The two knights slam the door shut behind them, illuminating the room with their torches as they search out every nook and cranny. Emryus nods toward Artagan.

"The room is safe, sire. We'll stand watch outside."

I call out to Sir Keenan, glancing at the wedding ring on his finger.

"Keenan, make sure your wife and children are safe. I left Rowena just moments ago."

"I passed their chambers first, my Queen. My family is unharmed."

I nod, swallowing the lump in my throat. Praise the Lord. Rowena, Keenan, and their two little ones are like family to me. The two knights bar the door behind them as they leave to stand watch outside our tower steps. Artagan holds up my chin to the flickering torchlight. His eyes narrow on the bloodstain across my cheek.

"Branwen, you're bleeding! What happened?"

"Just a nick. It could've been much worse. Did you catch him? The man who attacked me?"

"Ahern's leading the search now. Even though he has only one eye, he's got a bloodhound's nose. He'll find the fiend who did this."

Artagan grabs a cloth and washbowl, dabbing the dried blood along my jawline. I wince as he finishes. Laying Gavin down in his cot beside our bed, I keep my voice low to prevent waking him. My little son sleeps fitfully in his tiny bed. Artagan holds me close as I speak into his ear.

"It was an assassin, Artagan. But he didn't come for me. He wanted the boy."

"Gavin? Are you certain?"

I nod, my hands starting to shake. It all happened so fast. A few horrid moments. The cocked bow, the menacing black figure, and then the cry from my hunting bird. I lean my head against Artagan's chest, his body emanating warmth through his thin tunic. My own flesh feels cold as frost.

As the daughter of a king myself, I survived several assassins in my youth, but I was a teen at the time. What black-hearted monster would try to kill a child? And to what purpose? My little boy couldn't harm or offend anyone. I clench my hands, drubbing them against my husband's broad chest.

"This was planned, Artagan! Someone nearly killed our boy and maybe me. If it hadn't been for my falcon, the assassin would have succeeded."

Clenching my teeth and wringing my hands by turns, I oscillate between fear and anger as I explain the story to Artagan. Several times he has me repeat key elements of what I remember. The dowsed braziers, the crossbow, and the arrowhead aimed not at me but at our son. Artagan growls as he paces the floor, his naked longsword in hand. His blue eyes blaze like fiery embers. He looks fit enough to strangle a wild boar.

A knock comes at the door again. Artagan opens it a crack, his sword hand ready. Ahern steps inside with something wrapped under his arm. He bolts the door behind him.

"The assailant is dead, by his own hand. Looks like poison."

"Damn it, Ahern! I wanted the culprit alive. He can't tell us anything dead."

"I did recover this, my liege."

Ahern uncovers a crossbow. The blood in my veins turns to ice as he holds up the assassin's weapon for us to see. Just having the evil thing in the same room as my son gives me tremors. I instinctively put myself between the spent weapon and my sleeping boy. Ahern grimaces.

"Crossbows are rare and expensive. Neither we nor the Saxons use them. It probably comes from the continent across the sea."

"You think the assassin was a foreigner?" Artagan asks. "A mercenary?"

"Perhaps, my King. Hard to tell. The bow looks torn and wrecked—"

"My falcon," I interrupt. "Vivian attacked when the assassin let loose his quarrel."

Ahern's good eye widens into a full moon.

"Your hawking bird came to your aid? I've ne'er heard of such a thing. Even the animals come to the defense of Mab Ceridwen, it seems."

The seneschal crosses himself, closing his one good eye as he bows toward me. Mab Ceridwen, the local pet name the commoners have for me. It means Fairy Queen in the Old Tongue, and although they speak the title with reverence, I don't think I'm half the sorceress they seem to believe I am. Peering closely at the crossbow, I smell a pungent odor between the gears and springs.

"Animal fat. The bowman greased his weapon recently. Vivian probably smelled it and it reminded her of prey. I let her hunt for bats and field mice after nightfall."

Artagan shakes his head with a smirk.

"Call it magic or luck, but either way that bird shall have want for nothing the rest of its days. Food from the kitchens, a warm nest, and a roost full of male falcon suitors if she is so inclined."

I smile at my husband. Even in the throes of the terror I've seen tonight, he still manages to lighten the mood. Just think, my spotted she-falcon, all fat, happy, and surrounded by a nest full of sharp-beaked chicks. A fine reward indeed for any winged beast.

Ahern gives me a sidelong glance with his single eye, as though still convinced I willed Vivian to my rescue through some sorcery. Doubtless, word of this will spread to every servant and field hand in Aranrhod by morning. Whatever the explanation, God's providence seems to have spared me and my child this night.

Artagan and Ahern continue going over plans to have their guards scour the grounds tonight, just in case any more assailants lurk nearby. I recline on the bed beside my sleeping boy.

Gavin's chest rises and falls in a peaceful slumber, blissfully unaware of the dangers he has encountered this night. Whatever Artagan or Ahern plan to do, I know I shall not sleep a wink. I will keep watch over my son, like a hawk over her young. Many hours of darkness await and I will need them. Time to mull over the numerous possibilities. But who in Christendom would dare make an attempt on my son's life?

I take down my longbow from the wall and clutch it close to my chest as I watch over Gavin. Whether the next day, next month, or next year, I will find out who did this, and they will taste the steel of my arrowheads before I am through.

"I want to see him."

Ahern frowns at my request. We stand alone down in the dungeons of the castle. A cool draft pervades the murky, damp cell walls that drip with green lichens. Few shafts of dawn light penetrate this deep under the fortress. The seneschal hesitates, holding the end of a sheet over a corpse on the stony floor.

"The poison has disfigured him, Your Grace. It's not a pretty sight."

"Just do it, Ahern. I have to see for myself."

He sighs before pulling back the grimy sheet. A faceless cadaver blotched with crimson fuzz and blackened flesh buzzes with flies. The carcass lies still as a slab of butchered meat on the cold ground. I put a palm over my nose to stifle the smell. Ahern paces nervously beside me.

"My lady, the King and his retinue ride for Dyfed within the hour. If we do have a run-in with the Picts, I must prepare my men."

"Just a few moments, Ahern. Then you can see to your duties."

What with all the turmoil of last night's events, the possibility of Pictish raiders on Dyfed's shores suddenly seems such a remote threat. A killer was right here, in my very own castle. I shudder, trying not to think of all the terrible things that might have happened last evening.

Pacing around the rotting body, I try to make out the soiled clothes. Simple woolens and leathers, nothing out of the ordinary for a Welshman or a Saxon traveler. The crossbow itself suggests a foreigner, but any man anywhere is capable of using a foreigner's weapon if he should somehow get hold of one. I sigh with exasperation. This dead man only raises more questions than answers.

I glare at his faceless corpse. Who are you, you son of a bitch-dog? Who paid you? And why did they want to harm my son, of all people?

Nothing comes to mind. Just the repeating mantra in my head: *dead, dead, dead.* I'm glad this stranger is dead. He came to kill my son and possibly myself. Did he ever think I would be looking over his cold corpse instead? I nod toward Ahern, who promptly covers the body with the stained shroud.

Only the dead man's hand protrudes from beneath the sheet. Strange purple markings mar the wrist and left palm. A prickly feeling rises along my spine, although I know not why. It's just a dead hand, after all.

I trail Ahern back up the dungeon steps. Passing through the underbelly of the castle, the architecture of its many centuries of inhabitants shows through the ground in sections. Like rings of a tree.

Huge megalithic stones mark the period of the Old Tribes, archways and aqueducts from the Romans, and icons of saints from the first Christian missionaries. Much stonework has been repaired and other portions buttressed with timbers, thanks to the hard work of our people over the past few years. Although we lack the knowledge of the ancients in construction, our smiths and masons still retain the know-how to restore the wonders that our forebearers built. What little wisdom we have we must pass on to our children. The Saxons and other barbarians have robbed us of enough of our heritage over the centuries.

In the main courtyard, Ahern and I part ways. He sees to his men. Scores of archers prep their longbows and stuff their leather satchels with provisions. My husband is nowhere to be seen, yet I know he must be preparing to depart. A sudden yearning to hold Artagan close overtakes me, to smell the scent of his skin and run my hands through his tousled black hair. He will soon ride into peril again, as he has many times before. No matter how often he rides away, I never get used to it.

Across the yard, Carrick and Bowen crowd around Ahern, their voices too low for me to make out their words. Ahern purses his lips, nodding his head as he listens closely to them. Both warriors pat his shoulders before joining my husband's companies of archers arranged along the front gates. Sir Bowen's voice carries as he bids farewell.

"Think it over, Sir Ahern."

I sidle alongside my half brother, keeping my voice nonchalant yet low.

"What's that all about?"

"Nothing," Ahern grumbles. "Those two knights are good men, but they fret about anyone other than a Dyfed man sitting on our late father's throne."

I perk an eyebrow. These Dyfed knights may very well prefer someone like my brother on Dyfed's throne now that he is the last living son of our deceased father. But surely Ahern wouldn't consider such a thing. To rule a rival kingdom, possibly against my husband and me? He has always been my loyal guardsman and seneschal. He wouldn't wish things otherwise, would he?

I decide against asking him, quickly shaking such odd thoughts from my head. Ahern sees a pair of soldiers fastening on their bedrolls wrong and goes over to chastise them. Ever the veteran soldier. I cannot help but frown with approval.

Excusing myself from the boisterous courtyard full of soldiers, I slip off toward more familiar haunts across the inner keep. Scaling the steps to the rookery, I slowly open the door where the castle's hunting hawks are kept. I tiptoe inside, careful not to disturb the birds of prey as they sleep in their roosts. I stifle a yawn, rubbing my eyes. A sleepless night watching over my son has done my body little good, but I need answers now more than I need rest. Answers that only the dead man down in the dungeons can possibly provide.

A lone falcon at the end row squawks my way. I smile at the brown-spotted bird as she stares up at me with one black-marble eye. Her mottled feathers bear marks from last night's attack, but otherwise she looks fit and scrappy as ever. I put on a leather glove and gently pet the she-falcon's mane.

"Thank you, Vivian. I named you after my mother, and you have proved as wise, caring, and brave as she was."

Vivian squawks again in reply, cocking her neck as she gazes up at me. Almost as if she understands. Perhaps I fool myself. I've spent so many hours hawking and hunting with my favorite bird that it oft times seems we are of one mind. But how could a bird, or any creature, for that matter, truly comprehend human speech? Nonetheless, I owe this falcon my life and the life of my babe.

She paws at my gloved hand with her formidable talons. I smile, noticing how long and thick her claws curve, claws that have taken down large prey many a time in the forest.

My cheeks suddenly sag, that familiar cold feeling creeping into my bones. The talons. Of course. My eyes widen. How could I have been so blind? Suddenly, the disparate details of last evening's attack coalesce in my mind. The crossbow, the strange marks on the dead man's wrist, and now the talons. I give Vivian a quick peck on the cheek.

"Thank you again, my soaring huntress. That's two debts I owe you."

I descend the steps double quick. I must be careful how much I reveal to others. My heart beats faster with every step. The danger to my family remains more prevalent now than ever. I must tread carefully in order to set things aright.

Ahern runs into me in the courtyard, his face set in a stony frown. The rest of the archers assemble in the main yard, hundreds of them stretching in long lines out the open main gates. A few riders stand ready at the head of the column, Artagan and his knights among them. Ahern still looks grim.

"Brother, whatever disturbs you so?"

"Just my pride, my lady. The King readies to march, but he has ordered me to stay behind in order to look after you and the castle."

I put a hand on the seneschal's shoulder. Poor soldier, worried he will miss all the excitement. Most men would see it as an honor to remain behind and guard the queen, but Ahern was born for battle. He will only see this as further evidence that the King thinks him an old, one-eyed warrior past his prime. I gently squeeze my half brother's arm.

"Let me talk to him, Ahern. You're the only one he trusts to look after me."

He nods as I stride toward the head of the column of green-clad troops. Artagan rears his mount, a large black stallion named Merlin. The old warhorse sniffs my palm as I rub his neck. Both Artagan and I have had many adventures with this faithful stallion. It belonged to my first husband before he died. I hold Artagan's hand as he looks down from the saddle.

"You're leaving Ahern behind. He thinks you believe him unfit for battle."

"Because of his one eye? Quite the opposite. I want him guarding you and our son like a wolfhound."

"I know. I'll smooth things over with him. How long will you be gone?"

Artagan shrugs. He grins, giddy as a shepherd boy readying for an adventure in the hills. Why do men always get to have all the excitement while queens and mothers must stay at home to keep watch over the castle? But Artagan rides possibly to war, and if the rumors are true, the bloodthirsty Picts are waiting for him. Artagan leans down and presses his lips to mine.

For a long moment I cup his face between my hands. He still kisses me with the same longing he had when we first met. When I belonged to another man, another husband. My heart smarts, the back of my eyes tearing up. If only the two of us could stay in one another's arms forever, wrapped in our warm bed with our son sleeping peacefully nearby. But the lives of kings and queens are rarely so tranquil.

Artagan draws his longsword, shouting out to the few hundred bowmen awaiting his command. Bowen and Carrick ride out in front as scouts, while Emryus and Keenan hang close to Artagan's side. Sir Keenan blows a kiss to Rowena and their children watching from a nearby tower. She keeps Gavin and Cadwallon near her as she waves back.

The King digs his heels into his steed, leading the column of fleet-footed archers down into the green dales that lead to the western passes in the mountains. I stand beside the front gates, watching until the last soldiers disappear into the misty distance. A lump rises in my throat. Not just because my husband has gone, but because I have not told him all the truth. About last night or the child quickening inside me.

I grab Ahern by the shoulder, ducking into a side entranceway. I draw a deep breath, trying to clear my mind. A long trial lies before me, and I need all of my faculties if we are to survive this. Ahern furrows his brow at my suddenly serious tone.

"We need to talk."

"My lady?"

I peer down each corridor, making sure we are quite alone.

"One of your guards has gone missing, correct?"

"How did you know that? He was the one who relieved the other guards last night, or so they say. He must have been paid off by the assassin, but I've yet to locate the missing man."

"That's because your guardsman is already dead. He's lying in the dungeon under a sheet."

Ahern gives a start, blinking furiously with his good eye.

"What? That's impossible."

"Your missing guardsman, was he left-handed?"

"He drew his bowstring with his left, aye. How did you know that?"

"The body in the dungeon has calluses and marks on the left hand, as a left-handed archer would have."

"But the body in the dungeon is the assassin's!"

"No. The assassin I saw last night held his crossbow right-handed. Furthermore, whoever the assassin was would have scars all over him from Vivian. My falcon has very long, very sharp talons. The body you have down in the dungeon neither has the scars from a bird of prey nor was he right-handed."

Ahern's cheeks blanch white.

"But then that would mean . . ."

"That the assassin is still alive and among us."

Just saying the words aloud makes my flesh run cold. Ahern gulps, looking like he has swallowed some bad food. Unfortunately, the cold logic of what I've said still holds true. The assassin didn't take any poison last night to avoid capture and torture. Instead, he caught up with his paid-off guard and forced the poison down his throat. Possibly with a subtle drink or otherwise. I bet the welts on the dead man's wrist came from a struggle with the assassin, but only once he realized he had been double-crossed and was dying. In other words, when it was already too late.

"We must post more guards outside the children's room," Ahern begins. "Rowena is with your son and the others, yes?"

"Not just yet, Ahern. If we do that, the assassin will know we're on to him. I have another plan that will require all of your skill. But you're not going to like it."

"I am seneschal of the castle and defender of its queen. I'll do whatever you command."

"I knew you would." I smile. "Now we must move quickly, but quietly, understood?"

I whisper in his ear, detailing my plot as quickly as I can. Ahern grimaces by turns, but each time he tries to speak I shush him and press on. When I finish, he hangs his head.

"This is either the most brilliant or most foolhardy thing you have ever asked me to do, my lady."

"Maybe both," I admit. "Can I count on you, brother?"

He nods his head. We part ways without another word. Time is of the essence, and unless I am very much mistaken, our assassin will keep a keen eye on us. He probably will wait for cover of darkness before striking again, but should we give away our hand too early he might strike sooner. Everything hinges on what happens in the next turn of the hourglass. I know what to do, but I still wish to God I knew who was doing this to us and why.

Entering the castle chapel, I search the pews for Father David. The church seems deserted. A voice echoes off the archways behind me.

"Lady Branwen, come to offer your latest confession?"

I smile at the bald-headed priest. Father David smiles back. A true believer, his hands and bare feet bear many a callus and blister from his years spent wandering and preaching in the wilds. I trust this cleric more than most, holy men or otherwise.

"I fear my confessions would only shock you, Father David."

"Nothing shocks the Lord, my child. He watches all and forgives all, if only we have the courage to ask."

"Actually, I wanted to ask you a favor, Holy Father. A favor, and to keep a secret."

Father David raises an eyebrow before bowing toward me in reply. I heave a sigh, knowing that I risk not only my life but also the lives of those I love. But a queen must sometimes risk her all in order to save all.

4

Ahern grunts beneath the hood of his cloak.

"I still think this is a bad idea, your ladyship. We should turn back."

"Just keep your eye on the road."

Seated beside Ahern at the front of the wagon, I tug my hood down so that it hides my face. A rumble of thunderheads and a light sprinkle of rain make it all the more reasonable for me to conceal myself under a large cloak. The high walls and tall towers of Aranrhod shrink behind us as our cart wends its way up the switchbacks into the mountains.

A few other oxcarts dot the trailheads on the otherwise deserted greens. All the better. It makes us look like just another merchant's wagon following the trade routes between kingdoms. Nothing to draw any particular attention, especially from the watchful eye of an assassin, wherever he lurks within Aranrhod's keep. I glance back under the canvas cover of our wagon where several barrels protrude.

Rowena looks up at me from a mat of straw, hidden in the center of the covered cart. Four little children lie asleep beside her in the hay. Mina, Mora, Cadwallon, and my beloved Gavin. Rowena puts a finger to her lips as she whispers.

"I gave them each but a few drops from the medicine bottle. Just enough to make them sleep."

I nod at her prudence. The last thing we need is for one of the children to make noise and draw attention to us. Fortunately, the guards never gave our everyday cart a second look, and they certainly did not recognize that their queen and seneschal rode in front with long hoods draped over their eyes.

Turning into the mists, our wheels groan as we traverse the first mountain passes. Enveloped by the fog and rain, we talk more freely now that our wagon lumbers along quite alone on the winding road. Only the most desperate of merchants would travel the roads during a brewing thunderstorm. Ahern shrugs off his hood, letting the rain pat against his beard.

"I still don't understand, my Queen. Won't they notice we've left?"

"Eventually, but not for at least another few days. I left Father David in charge of the castle. He will give the impression that we all are keeping close together in the children's tower for better safety."

"I still say you should've let me bring an escort, at least few armed men."

"That would've been practically an open declaration that we're no ordinary travelers. If the assassin was clever enough to steal into the castle in the first place, he'll be clever enough to recognize a royal escort of guards. No, secrecy will get us much farther than force of arms."

"Besides," Rowena chimes in, "the roadways are much safer nowadays since King Artagan's knights have cleared the highways of bandits."

Ahern turns away, frowning as he slaps the reins on the two oxen that pull our cart.

"Bandits don't worry me. We're heading west into Dyfed. There are supposed to be Picts there now, remember?"

I scoff at my half brother's eternal pessimism.

"It's also the last place anyone will look for us. The order was mine and the responsibility is mine, not yours."

I crawl into the covered portion of the cart, tugging a wool blanket over me. Best to catch a few hours of rest in our rumbling wagon bed while I can. Let Ahern sulk by himself. My eyelids sag heavy as church bells, my lack of sleep quickly catching up with me. How strangely the Fates weave our lives together. Despite having a castle and queenship, I find myself hiding in the back of a straw-filled wagon on a rough road in the wilderness. Time will tell whether my decision proves foolish or wise.

I awake to the sound of crying. Blinking my eyes open, darkness fills the back of the cart. Little Mora moans until Rowena suckles her at the breast. Youngest of the bunch, Mora still needs her mother's milk. The other children roll about in the straw, gnawing on cuts of cheese and bread. It must be after nightfall, but all the children have awoken.

I did not think this journey into the wilderness with young ones would be easy, but we had no choice. Gavin was in peril, and if we left any of his playmates behind, the assassin might have slain one of them, mistakenly thinking he was targeting the young prince. After all, an arrow in the dark or a cup of poison is not discerning amongst its victims.

Ahern still sits at the reins as our chariot slogs through the muddy highland passes. Cranky as he gets, his stouthearted loyalty makes him a dependable guard and guide. Lying in the hay, I nestle closer to Gavin and stroke his gorgeous auburn hair, shiny as polished copper even in the dimness.

It churns my stomach just to think of someone trying to harm him. Through the canvas folds of our cover, I speak to Ahern over the rain. Swirling winds howl through the unseen peaks in the darkness.

"Ahern, did you question any of our guests before they left Aranrhod? Iago, Olwen, or Griffith and his wife?"

"Nay, they had already departed just before dawn."

"You just let them go?"

"Had to. They're monarchs in their own right. If we tried to detain them for questioning, it might have started a war. First thing a guardsman like me learns is who is above the law and who isn't."

How damned convenient. So any one of our visiting rulers could easily have let an assassin in with them and their entourages. Even if we knew the assassin and the culprit slipped out with them at dawn, we would have had to risk war in order to take him by force. The North and South Welsh contingents certainly had the ability to have set an assassin upon my son, but does that mean one of them did?

Iago is ruthless, but Olwen should know better. I have her own son in my care. Although I'd never lay a finger on the boy, she must know he would be as good as a hostage in my household if conflict ever arose between the Free Cantrefs and the North. Then again, Olwen is just wily enough to try anything. But I cannot see what she or Iago would gain by my son's downfall.

And what of King Griffith? He and Queen Cordelia have their flaws, but never would I suspect them of such treachery. Young Arthwys certainly has his reasons for wanting to hurt me and mine, but he is still just a boy. Too young to plot with assassins against me, right? Maybe I'm being too naïve. It's a dark world we inhabit.

Rowena sidles up next me, little Mora falling asleep at the breast. Gavin, Cadwallon, and Mina chuckle with glee as they roll around the bed of the swaying wagon. To them, this rocky road seems like some marvelous adventure. Little do they know the peril I have put them all in. Rowena whispers in my ear so that Ahern cannot hear us.

"M'lady, a question has taxed me mind of late. Pardon my impertinence, but I must know."

"Ask away, Rowena. I keep no secrets from you."

"It be about the baby, Your Grace. The one you're but a moon or two along with."

My shoulders tense. I'd tried to push such thoughts to the back of my mind. I try to sound calm.

"What of it?"

"Well, ma'am, why keep it a secret from the King? A child is a blessing."

I hang my head, a knot forming in my throat so thick I can barely whisper.

"Because, Rowena, I've not decided whether to keep it or not."

Rowena gasps.

"M'lady, you cannot mean that! You wouldn't take a bitterroot potion, would you? To quell the life inside you before it grows?"

"Many women of the Old Tribes did so, and some womenfolk still do. I don't think I'd survive another pregnancy, Rowena. What good am I to a newborn if I'm dead? Or to my husband and son, for that matter? I've a kingdom, a people to protect. I can't look after any of them if I end up in the graveyard before my time."

"You don't know how the birthing will go, my Queen. Perhaps this time it'll go easier."

I shake my head. The last two miscarriages alone were brutal enough. I honestly thought my womb was past childbearing, although I am still plenty young. Of all my pregnancies, only Gavin's came to proper fruition. He is my one gleaming exception in a series of otherwise dismal failures. All the reasons I've given Rowena may or may not be good ones, but they're not my only reservations. I sniffle back the tears, trying to keep my voice low. How can I explain to Rowena the fear that grips my heart?

"Rowena, what good is it to bring another life into this cold-hearted world? A place where grown men attempt to kill children still in the cradle. A land where Saxons try to wipe us out and sometimes our own Welsh barons. I cannot promise to keep even my husband, my son, or myself alive. Is it right to bring another life into all that danger?"

Rowena sighs, her shoulders sinking low.

"What is written, is written, m'lady. We do not know what's to come, that's all in God's hands. We've both good husbands and healthy children. Let us take what happiness we can in this life while we have it. Worry is all you'll have if you let it eat you up, m'lady."

I look away. Darkness pervades the landscape. Give up worrying? *Worry* is what has kept me alive these past years. Worry has kept my mind sharp and one step ahead of those who would've killed me. And now they want to slay my only son. No. Worry is a companion I cannot afford to rid myself of. I shall need it to the bitter end. Rowena means well, but she does not understand.

Nonetheless, I know she will keep my secret. But I must come to a decision soon, otherwise my swelling belly will betray my condition within a few moons. Nonetheless, I will think no more on it tonight. Not tonight. My limbs suddenly feel heavy as lead. Despite my restful nap, I feel weary as a rain-soaked lamb.

My son tugs at my sleeve, restless and no doubt wanting a song or some such, but I've no voice for lullabies this evening. Instead, I stroke his head as I tell a bedtime story to him and the other young ones. The timbre of my voice more than my words reaches them, the kind of comforts toddlers seek. Racking my weary mind for a tale, I relate brief stories about Artagan and me: how we first fell in love and fled from an evil king, then how we saved our people in our many adventures against the Saxons. For a while, I lose myself in my own memories, my heart smarting as I think on my husband. My beloved Artagan, how I wish I could enfold myself in your arms on this stormy night.

One by one the children gradually nod off again. The combination of darkness and the cradlelike motion of the rocking cart puts them all back to sleep. I soon find my own eyes closing, but I know I must relieve Ahern. Even the most stouthearted of men cannot go forever without rest.

Laying my head down in the straw again, I close my eyes. Strange dreams percolate through my thoughts and the tapping of the rain. My mother works at the loom with me on her lap, humming a soft lullaby. Her song fills me with an inescapable warmth and wholeness. I am very young, my hands small against the strings of woven wool. I wish her tune and the lavender scent of her robes would last forever.

But the dream twists and blurs. Alone on a barren, rocky plain, a lone figure beckons me across the expanse. I squint my eyes, now much taller and older, as I am now. A woman with long flowing hair like my mother's holds me with her stare, but it is not my mother. Lady Annwyn aims her finger at me, yet I cannot tell if she does so accusatorily or to single me out for some purpose. I try to speak but find myself completely robbed of my voice. I can neither move nor talk. Darkness falls.

Before I know it, birds twitter in the morning sunshine. I blink back the perspiration from my eyes. I've not dreamt of my mother in years. As for Lady Annwyn, what was she trying to tell me? Whatever it may be, I have the distinct feeling it is something important.

I sit up with a start, rubbing my eyes. Has the night already fallen away from me? I turn to check on Ahern but find him snoring beside me. Rowena sits at the reins, taking a turn directing the oxen. The tired beasts low heavily after a ceaseless night of toil. We must have crossed the divide into the hills of Dyfed. The uneven trail jounces the bed of straw beneath me. Roads in the westernmost provinces of Wales have always been rougher and less maintained with wear.

I crawl past the slumbering children toward the front of the cart. Gnawing on a cut of dried beef, I share my meager breakfast with Rowena as she keeps a hand on the cattle's traces. Golden light pervades the clouds. The recent storm must have broken in the night.

"Any sign of anyone in front or behind us?" I ask.

"None as far as I can tell. Except a few horse prints in the mud, trampled nearly flat."

"Probably Artagan's knights, and his archers following close behind. They make good time."

"M'lady, the King will probably not be pleased to see you when we catch up with them."

"No, I don't think he will, but I must convince him that I was right to do what I did."

"I hope so. It looks like they're still half a day ahead of us on the trail."

"I wish these oxen moved faster. I would have brought horses, but steeds are expensive and it would've given us away as something other than humble merchants when we left Aranrhod."

"My Queen knows what she's doing, I suppose."

Rowena and I exchange sidelong glances, before letting out a laugh. Maybe some of what Rowena said last night does hold true. What's written, is written. We can only roll the dice and muddle through as best we can.

Just when I'm finally starting to breathe easier, Ahern sticks his head between us.

"We've got trouble."

He points toward the mountains behind us. Rowena slows the cart as we descend into the foothills. The upper peaks to the east still have lingering clouds stuck to them. Far behind us on the edge of the horizon, a figure looms in the mountain pass. My pulse hammers in my throat. I squint, trying to see better.

"What is that back in the pass behind us?"

"Not sure," Ahern replies. "But it's no beast alone. Only man rides on horseback."

My eyebrows narrow. A rider? Maybe another traveler? But why would anyone other than us have journeyed through the mountains in a rainstorm? Unless our ruse has not fooled anyone. Unless the lone figure half a league behind us is following our trail. My voice trembles.

"Ahern, you don't think that it's . . . ?"

"Him? The assassin? I don't plan to wait around and find out."

Rowena bites her lip.

"But if he's on horseback, he'll catch us sooner or later. Two tired oxen will never outpace a horseman."

"We're trying to catch my husband's army with cattle," I counter.

"But they're mostly on foot," Ahern interjects. "And probably slowed by the rain. Rowena's right. This rider will catch us before we reach the safety of the King's army."

One of the children starts to cry. Rowena halts the wagon and crawls back into the straw. We've four younglings starting to wake up. They'll be hungry and restless, and will only slow us down more. God help me. I was a fool to think I could just steal away into the wilds toting children with me. But what other choice did I have?

I grab my birch longbow from the hay, digging around for my quiver of arrows. Hopping off the wagon, I string an arrow to my bowstring and trot a few paces to the rear. Ahern comes after me, toting his shield and spear with him.

"What in the blazes do you think you're doing?"

"I'm not waiting for the inevitable without a fight. The assassin is still one man. You and I make two warriors for him to deal with. Send Rowena on ahead with the children in the cart. You and I will lay an ambush for this horseman when he catches up."

Rowena leans out the back of the cart.

"I'm not leaving you two. Besides, I won't get far with four squalling children."

The children start to whine and wail. It tugs at my heartstrings to hear such pitiful moans, but we've no choice left. I plant my feet firmly in the narrow roadway, waiting for the distant figure. Ahern turns to Rowena.

"Just put as much distance between us as you can. The Queen and I will catch up after."

Rowena reluctantly slaps the backs of the oxen with the reins. It takes the better part of an hour for the grind of the wagon wheels and the murmurs of the children to fade down the path to the west. Godspeed, Rowena. Godspeed.

But of course, it won't much matter. If Ahern and I cannot stop this mercenary ourselves, Rowena and the children won't stand a chance. My jaw tightens as I try to clear my mind. I won't allow any harm to come to my son or any of the other children. I simply cannot.

Ahern and I take up positions in the shrubs on opposite sides of the road. Between his spear and my arrows, one of us has to land a killing blow on the assassin. But this killer was smart enough to nearly slay my boy once before, smart enough to leave a corpse behind in place of his own, and smart enough to figure out that I secretly left the castle with Gavin. Will he expect me to lay an ambush for him? We'll soon know. I've staked everything on this.

The landscape turns gray and cold over the next hour. I had forgotten how quickly the weather changes in Dyfed. Storms come off the sea without warning. What looked like a promising morning has clouded over again. The first tendrils of fog move across the heaths and foothills. I nearly start to nod off when the clack of horseshoes down the road perks my ears.

Taking aim at the empty trail, I listen as the cantering horse nears.

Several twists in the path come straight again near the thickets where Ahern and I wait. Once the rider turns the last corner and comes into view, it should be too late for him to react. The clacking of hooves looms louder in the glade. I draw back my bowstring, trying to steady my breath for the shot. More fog rolls in through the hills, but I can still see at least a dozen paces in any direction. It's now or never.

The horse rounds the bend, trotting down the path. My eyes suddenly widen as sweat rolls down my temples. The steed's saddle is empty.

I peer over my shoulder, knowing that our ambush has been found out. Darting quick glances every which way, the incoming mists and whistling wind only obscure more of the downs surrounding me. Ahern cries out from the brush across the way.

A dark figure looms in the gray vapors, thrashing through the undergrowth with Ahern. I aim my bow but cannot discern more than two shuffling shapes in the briars across the way. No! I cannot let this mercenary kill my brother while I sit by and do nothing.

I sprint across the path and into the brush, searching for the two combatants. More groans emanate from Ahern as his silent attacker battles through sedge and brambles. The clang of steel rings through the mist.

Rounding a bend in the labyrinth of thorn bushes, I find a massive man towering over Ahern. My kinsman lies sprawled in the dirt. Ahern clutches his broken spear, blood covering his beard. I loose an arrow into the assailant's back, but he merely spins around as though pricked with a sewing needle. What kind of man is this?

I draw another arrow and thread it onto my bow. The assassin glares at me through the mists, but his face is placid and still. Only then do I realize he wears a mask. A steel mask with a pair of broken antlers protruding from the helm. I'd know that battle mask anywhere. But it cannot be! The man who wore that mask is long since dead. The Hammer King, my first husband. My *dead* husband.

My voice suddenly sounds small, like that of a child.

"Morgan?"

The masked man does not reply, darting straight for me. I loose another arrow directly into his chest, but he hardly loses a step. Charging like a bull, he grasps a war-hammer in one hand and a spent crossbow in the other. I ready a third arrow, but this Minotaur of a man is nearly on top of me.

A hunting horn blares through the fog, stopping the masked assailant dead in his tracks. The horn sounds again as the thunder of hooves rumbles through the glade. A hundred voices cry out in the gray fogbanks.

"Mab Ceridwen!"

My heart stops. The battle cry of the Free Cantrefs, my namesake. Mab Ceridwen! Green-clad archers pour into the thickets, a lead horseman with a longsword in the vanguard. Artagan charges headlong astride his stallion.

The masked assassin flees into the mists, faster than I imagined any man on foot could move. Perspiration drenches my tunic. Did I imagine things? Was that masked man really my former husband, King Morgan? But no. The Hammer King is long since dead. He perished on the battlefield years ago. I was there when it happened.

Artagan rears up his mount before me, scooping me into the saddle without a word. We return to the main road, where Sir Emryus and Sir Keenan tend to Ahern's wounds. Scores of archers line the trail, encircling the wagon with Rowena and the children. Air comes back into my lungs. Gavin and the others are all right.

Ahern has blood all over his shirt, but he sits up well enough as Emryus and Keenan dab him with bandage cloths. I turn toward Artagan in the saddle, my mind brimming with questions.

"How did you find us so quickly? How did you know?"

Artagan ignores me, aiming a stern finger at his two Dyfed scouts, Bowen and Carrick.

"Report!"

Bowen replies, still breathing hard.

"No sign of him. The bugger must have caught his horse and made a break for it. He's damned fast."

"Damnation! Enough of this. Rally the men. We've wasted enough time as it is."

Bowmen line up and begin jogging westward. Rowena embraces Keenan while Emryus helps each of the children into the saddles beside various knights. Emryus holds Gavin on his own steed. At least the boy is safe.

Artagan still won't look me in the eye, even with me astride his horse and the two of us in the same saddle.

"Artagan, what's going on? You're not going after him? That was the assassin!"

Artagan turns his stern azure gaze my way. I've never seen him so angry before. His nostrils dilate with every breath.

"Whomever he is, he's like a hare hidden in a briar patch. We'll never find him in all this fog. My men have wasted enough time double-backing to get here!"

"What made you turn back in the first place?"

"I always keep a couple riders in the rear, in case of an ambush. They spotted Rowena's wagon, and it didn't take a scholar to figure out what must have happened."

My husband doesn't look happy to see me. I glance over his shoulder at our son in the saddle with Sir Emryus.

"You plan to take the children on horseback and not in the wagon?"

"That damned thing will only slow us down," Artagan snaps. "Things are in a bad enough mess as it is, and that'll be quite enough questions from *you*!"

He turns and yaws into the stallion's ear. Before I can reply, we gallop headlong into the mists, trailed by half a dozen knights and at least a hundred bowmen jogging at a steady pace. I clutch Artagan around the middle to steady myself, but I have half a mind to strangle him in my grip.

He has had enough of me, has he? Maybe I deserve more than a slap on the wrist, but I damn well did what I had to in order to keep our son alive. If only I could make Artagan understand. But there's no time to discuss anything as we charge headlong into the foggy moors. In trying to save the children from an armed madman, we've ended up in a cavalcade heading into battle, possibly against Picts or worse.

I crane my head close to my husband's ear as we sit astride his black warhorse.

"Artagan, listen to me. I did what I did to protect our son. We had to slip away in disguise."

"A lot of good it did," he retorts hotly. "And I thought I was supposed to be the rash one."

I bite my lip a moment, ignoring his comment. I struggle to get the next words out.

"The man, the assassin, he wore a . . . a mask."

"A mask?"

"Like the one the Hammer King once donned."

Artagan slows his steed's pace, turning in the saddle to look me in the eye for the first time since this entire debacle began. He opens his mouth to speak, but thinks better of it. My husband simply wags his head.

I reexamine the silhouette of the assassin in my mind, but every aspect of him reminds me of my deceased former husband. The man in the thicket had the right physical build, tall and powerful, yet adept and fast on his feet. Few men could have matched such a warrior in any age. If not Morgan, then who? I shake my head, finding it more and more difficult to disregard what I saw.

"It was him," I continue. "At least, it looked like him."

"You must be mistaken," Artagan replies. "Morgan is dead. It's just someone with a similar war-mask."

"It's the same mask! I know it."

"Then someone must be using the Hammer King's old mask."

"But who would have it? Presumably he was buried with it."

"I presume very little with certainty these days."

Artagan sighs, wearying of this debate. Exasperated, I sit back in the saddle behind him, my arms still entwined about his middle as we ride Merlin through the mists. The long column of mounted warriors thunders through the fog around us.

Despite it all, a worse, nagging fear tugs at my mind. We may be well away and safe from the assassin for now, but whoever attacked Ahern and me, his mask certainly belonged to no stranger. I shake my head, wondering if I truly am mad. It's all so impossible! Nonetheless, I cannot deny what I saw in the thicket. That unique metal mask, the war-hammer, and that superhuman strength. My former husband, the Hammer King, has returned from the dead.

5

The open moors give way to a lone hillock surrounded by several clumps of woods. Mists still obscure most of the downs, but the hilltop overlooks the surround like the humped back of a sleeping leviathan. At its summit, a ring of ancient standing stones keeps watch like megalithic sentinels. A crossroads of several trails passes beneath the foot of the hill. Something about the snaking way the mists congeal along the craggy monoliths makes my spine tingle. I've oft heard of this place but never seen it. One of the most ancient ruins in all of Wales: Ogham Stone.

Artagan halts our horse, ordering his men to make camp at the foot of the hill. His exhausted bowmen halt in their tracks and drop their dusty satchels. They exchange wary glances as they rest in the shadow of the standing stones atop the mound.

Artagan dismounts from Merlin, offering me a hand to help me down from the saddle. He still hardly deigns to look me in the eye. Both of the Dyfed scouts, Bowen and Carrick, raise their eyebrows before dismounting their steeds. Bowen slowly approaches the King.

"King Artagan, do you intend to make camp *here*?"

"For the night. We're in the heart of Dyfed and my men need rest.

I don't want to reach the sea tomorrow and find my soldiers worn out by the march if should we encounter any barbarians."

"But, sire, this is Ogham Stone. No one spends the night here. These grounds are haunted."

"Which makes this the perfect place to pitch camp. Whomever is marauding these lands, be it Picts, Saxons, or other Welshmen, they'll all keep clear of these ruins. It's the safest place in Dyfed right now."

"Except for the spirits," Carrick murmurs.

Artagan laughs, overhearing the knight's comment.

"They once said Aranrhod was haunted before we rebuilt it," the King begins. "But a brave woman taught me otherwise."

He glances my way, the first look without malice Artagan has shown me all day. The King walks away to help right several canvas tents with his men. I know not whether to smile or frown. Artagan has never been one to keep hold of his anger for long, but even if he forgives me for bringing the children and myself along, he still probably thinks it a foolish idea. I clench my jaw. Does he still not see I had no other choice?

A few dozen beige tents pop up along the dew-ridden greens. Several knots of watchmen take up positions near the woods and across the plain, but none linger near the hill itself. Half the men kindle small campfires in the clearing, erecting pup tents over their bedrolls in the tall grass.

I gaze up the slopes at the dozen-odd boulders on the heights, each rock impossibly old with weathering and lichens. Notched runes carved in stone display the script of the Old Tribes, known as Ogham. Few know how to read such signs anymore, but in my youth at the monastery by the sea, the monks seemed to both revere and curse the unfathomable learning of the ancients. The clerics said that they knew just enough of the Ogham to know it was best left alone. They pronounced it *Owum*.

Artagan's tent stands nearby, his dark silhouette cast against the canvas behind the glow of a lantern. I stomp through the weeds and catkins toward his rawhide shelter, but I cannot escape the prickly feeling of the tall standing stones behind me. As though the rocks quietly watch me.

I duck into Artagan's tent to find him working his longsword with a whetstone. Ahern sits on a bedroll nearby, wrapped in pink-stained bandages. My gaze darts to every corner of the tent, my heart tensing.

"Where's Gavin?"

Artagan sharpens his blade without looking up.

"With the other children in the next tent," he says. "Both Emryus and Keenan stand guard. Rowena's with them."

I breathe easier. The little ones must be tuckered out from a long day in the saddle. At least they are safe.

Artagan shifts his jaw as he runs the whetstone down the long length of his blade.

"You put the children in danger, Branwen. *Our* son! You knowingly put our son in harm's way."

His blue eyes glare up at me, our gazes meeting for the first time. All the breath goes out of me. He has never snapped at me so before others or in private. But instead of being cowed, my skin runs hot and my mouth tightens. Does he think I want to endanger our son and the other children? Does he think I realistically had any other choice? A damned assassin is on the prowl, and I am doing the best I can.

Ahern averts his gaze, probably pretending he can't hear us even though he lies but a few paces away within the very same tent. Most certainly wishing he wasn't present in this spat between my husband and me. I grind my teeth.

"I did what I had to, husband. Might we discuss this later? I'm tired."

Artagan catches my glance toward Ahern and nods his head, his gaze focusing on his blade once more.

"Fine," he says. "But we've not finished discussing this. I simply do not wish to wash our dirty clothes in front of others."

I bite my tongue. Let it go. At least he has the foresight to put this argument away and deal with it later. Spats so rarely occur betwixt my husband and me, which makes his words smart all the more. I wait a few moments for the heat to fade from my chest, for my breathing to ease. An old trick Lady Annwyn taught me, a way to curb the demons that anger breeds in the blood.

Although Artagan no longer seems as stern as he did a few moments ago, he still appears to pay me little heed. Even Ahern doesn't look my way, slumped on a stool, nursing his hurts. A pang of guilt seizes me. I haven't even tended to him since the attack in the thickets. Between the assassin, the children, and Artagan, my mind hasn't had room for much else. I put a palm on my half brother's shoulder.

"Are you all right?"

"Nothing that won't mend," Ahern says, faking a smile. "If the King hadn't showed up when he did, I'd have been mincemeat."

"Did you tell him?"

Artagan puts his whetstone down, hissing through his teeth.

"That the Hammer King's come back from the grave?" Artagan interrupts. "Maybe our scouts were right about those standing stones being haunted. They've got you and Ahern seeing ghosts."

I frown at my husband. For the first time in my life, he genuinely doesn't believe me. Ahern seems too embarrassed or ashamed to speak up, maybe both. I stomp my foot, having no intention of backing down.

"I know what I saw, Artagan! He had Morgan's mask. Even a warhammer in hand."

"Branwen, the Hammer King died at the Battle of Bloody Fords, fighting the Saxons! I was there, and so were you. A thousand men saw him die that day, Saxons and Welsh. It can't be him!"

"I don't know how it's possible, but you have to believe me . . ."

My voice trails off in a pleading tone. Why can't I make him see? Artagan puts down his sword and comes toward me, wrapping his arms around me. He speaks soft and gentle as though we were alone.

"My love, I trust you in all things, but if the Hammer King has really returned, then why now and why like this? He was a *king*, my dear. Why not reclaim the throne of South Wales? He has a son, Arthwys, there still. And why of all things does he sneak about like an assassin, not trying to kill you or me outright, but our baby boy? Do these things sound like the man you once knew as King Morgan?"

I look away, unable to answer him. My first husband could be both kind and also cruel, but he always had his pride. It certainly doesn't sound like the old Morgan, sneaking about like some sellsword. His body was buried with pomp and ceremony in Caerleon, the capital city of South Wales. Every logical faculty in my mind tells me that Artagan is right, that the man I saw couldn't possibly be my dead husband. And yet my heart tells me that it was no apparition in the briar patch that bloodied Ahern and nearly killed me. Something stalks the moors tonight, still hunting for my son. But how do you kill a ghost?

I walk away, shaking my head. I have no answer for Artagan, but I cannot accept what he says. This is no hired assassin looking for pay. This killer knows us well, and he comes in the form of the deceased Hammer King.

If someone else is parading around dressed as the Hammer King merely to terrify me, then who might it be? Reason dictates that it is the only conclusion possible. But the warning in my heart tells me that anything—*anything*—is possible.

Inside the children's tent, Gavin is fast asleep beside the other young ones. Even Rowena snores in the corner while two knights keep watch outside. I lie down on a mat beside Gavin, listening to the wind burr through the tent canvas and open grasslands. The breeze whistles eerily through the nearby standing stones, making odd resonances that sound almost like a child's voice, just faint enough to be on the edge of hearing. I shut my eyes and coil myself around my slumbering son. Whatever befalls us, we will endure it together. I clutch my longbow and dagger close to my side. My last thoughts linger on my husband and my boy. I will not let harm come to either of them. I *will* not.

At daybreak, the thud of ax heads and the braying of horses rouse me from my bedroll. Peeking out the tent flap, I spy dozens of woodsmen felling timbers by the tree line and hauling them back to camp. Other archers trade their longbows for spades and dig lengthy pits in the soil.

I rub my eyes, blinking back the sleepiness from my vision. My husband's soldiers are entrenching.

Gavin stirs in his sleep beside me, his faint breath like butterfly wings brushing against my arm. Both Emryus and Keenan have gone, but a lone guard stands watch outside the tent. I rise to step outside when I see the longsword in his hand. Artagan himself stands watch.

I kiss his neck, wrapping my arms around him while he keeps a keen eye on the surround. I rise on my toes, so glad to feel him in my embrace. Since Gavin's birth and all the trials of kingship, Artagan and I have not had as much time for each other as we once did. I miss the mornings when we did nothing but lie in one another's arms in a warm bed. Will those blissful dawns ever return to us? We've so many worries, so many cares now. I nuzzle his neck, feeling his strong muscles beneath his tunic. He smells like woodsmoke from the campfires.

A few shafts of golden light penetrate the clouds. Green dragon banners fly over the encampment while bowmen erect spiked barricades. Diggers form a perimeter trench around the circle of tents. I speak low in Artagan's ear, so as not to awake the children.

"Planning on staying awhile?"

"We're in hostile country now. The Romans always built a fortified camp when in new territory. That's how they conquered most of Britain."

"All except for the Picts," I remind him.

He nods, the name itself making him shiver slightly.

"Aye, except for them."

He turns toward me with a kiss, but I can tell by the look in his eyes that his mind has already ventured many miles away from me. Artagan was such a jovial, carefree hedge knight when I first met him. I don't think he ever wanted to be a king, but fate thrust the mantle on him and he has had to think for an entire kingdom ever since. His hawkish gaze surveys the woods and moors as though expecting some imminent trouble.

"Still glad you came along?" he asks. "You and Gavin are no safer here than at Aranrhod."

"We're always safer together. Always."

My voice sounds comforting and calm, although I fight hard to keep Artagan from knowing how defensive and worried I really am. I rub his brows, wrinkled with heavy thoughts. Artagan tries to play the part of a coolheaded soldier, but it doesn't become him. I know he remains a hot-blooded Celt under that kingly exterior. He needs my calming touch now more than any words I can give him. I wonder if he knows how deeply I love him. Deeper than the roots of the mountains or the bottom of the sea. Deep enough to swallow my own pride and worries when I know he needs me most.

A strange din slowly rises from the heaths and scattered woodlots to the west, like a flock of birds murmuring just beyond the rise. Artagan and I exchange looks as the sound looms closer. Several guardsmen hear it too and look up from their work along the barricades.

A throng of peasants on foot appears all along the western marches, many of them women and children and elders. Some tote baskets on their backs while others hang bindles from walking staffs. A few of them herd a handful of sheep or hogs, but the majority have nothing but what they carry. A few bear bloodied bandages across their brows and arms.

My eyes wax into half-moons. There must be at least a few hundred of them. Although women of every age appear in their ranks, I hardly spot a man between sixteen and sixty. They stagger as though having traversed many leagues of hard travel. A lone figure leads them, wearing a dark cloak with white trim. The attire of a nun.

"Refugees," Artagan remarks. "They must be villagers from Dun Dyfed by the sea. Whoever attacked the old capital has driven out the inhabitants."

"Those poor people," I reply. "Word must have spread of your army here. We must give these people shelter."

"Shelter? Half my men don't even have tents. How are we supposed to provide for such a multitude?"

I grasp his hand, entwining his fingertips with mine.

"We have always found a way, you and I. Please, Artagan. I was born in Dyfed. Even though I am your Queen of the Free Cantrefs, these too are my people. They need our help."

Artagan sighs as though weighed down by invisible stones.

"I'll have my men split their rations with them. We'll do what we can."

I plant a kiss on his lightly stubbled cheek. There is no more honorable man in Christendom than my man. He turns to give orders to his knights.

Rowena arises and tries to herd the children together as they go about investigating the camp. Mina and Mora stick relatively close to the tent, but Gavin and Cadwallon are in their element. The two boys eagerly palm bows and daggers cast aside by the soldiers. They gaze wide-eyed at woodsmen constructing the defenses. I turn to grab both toddlers by the wrist.

But something gives me pause. The lead nun from the refugees catches my gaze. The holy woman and I lock eyes, her fair hair somehow familiar despite a shock of white woven through it.

"Una?"

"Lady Branwen."

She bows toward me. I stride over and embrace her. Her blinking eyes seem to smile with surprise. It takes an effort to breathe enough air into me. I never thought to see Una again this side of paradise.

"Una, what brings you here? It's been years since you took to the holy cloth."

"A nun's life differs much from a queen's lady-in-waiting, but I enjoyed both very much."

I smile until I notice Rowena from the corner of my eye. She holds one daughter in her arms while standing close to the other. Her gaze never wavers from Una. Both women once served as my ladies-in-waiting, until a man came between them. One took the habit and the other married him.

Their choices in life have aged them differently. Rowena has grown plump with children while Una has grayed slightly and turned skinny as a rod in the service of God. I swallow for a moment, lost for words between the two women. We lived close as sisters in the old days, but the flinty stares between the two of them dowses any hopes that things might go back to the way they once were.

Both Rowena and Una glance at Sir Keenan across the camp. The man who unintentionally drove them apart. He smiles as he works with the other lumbermen, unaware of the stares of his wife and his former mistress. Una and Rowena nod curtly to one another.

"Una."

"Rowena."

I try to break the unnatural silence as the wind howls through the standing stones on the nearby hill.

"Have you left the cloister, Una? I thought your order allowed their sisters to leave only under exceptional circumstances."

Una puts a hand on my shoulder, her cheeks starting to sag.

"The cloister was destroyed. As was the monks' abbey nearby. Both pillaged and sacked by the Picts."

A leaden weight sinks in my throat. The nunnery *and* the monastery, both destroyed? Many clerics called those refuges home. The pride of Dyfed and all Christians in Wales, those two holy sites housed hundreds of priceless books. Many original copies handwritten by generations of monks and nuns now forever lost. More knowledge, history, and irreplaceable heritage gone! And how many innocent holy men and women died cruel deaths? I shut my eyes. The End of Days has truly come upon us all. My voice quivers.

"So it's true, then? The Picts have really returned from the northern wastes?"

"I saw them myself. Painted in blue, howling like demons from hell. They spared no one in their path."

Una glances back at Rowena, almost daring her to defy her word. Rowena says nothing, unusually cool for her normally sunny countenance. Lost in my own thoughts, the whinny of horses jars my focus back to the present.

Artagan mounts his steed. His knights and most of his men have already grabbed their arms. Word of the massacre by the sea has clearly reached their ears. Artagan has his longsword drawn, barking orders at his men and looking like he could take on a pack of wild hounds himself. So much for the coolheaded general. Once Artagan's blood is up, the only thing that can sate it is more blood.

Instinctively, I lift Gavin into my arms. He starts to squall and cry, but I pay him no heed as I rush toward Artagan. If only my little boy would keep quiet a moment, but oft times there's no reasoning with a toddler. It takes an extra effort to think clearheaded, knitting my brows as I stand beside my husband's horse.

Artagan could be riding right into a trap. Who knows how many Pictish barbarians await him at the coast. The King orders Ahern to remain behind and command the camp. Ahern nods, too bloodied and spent to argue. Artagan gives him a few last orders.

"I'll take two hundred bowmen with me and leave a hundred with you to guard these people."

"Understood, my liege."

I interrupt, raising my voice so that Artagan will hear me over Gavin's whining moans.

"You plan to attack them, don't you?"

"And grind them into the ground!" Artagan growls.

I shake my head. He's thinking with his sword now, not his head.

"Artagan, did it ever occur to you that the Picts might expect this? They pillage the monastery and cloister only a few dozen leagues from where your army has encamped. It's a perfect trap!"

"They're the ones backed against the water. I'll drive the devils into the sea!"

"But you don't even know how many of them await you. What if you're outnumbered?"

Artagan says something back, but I do not hear. Gavin screams, deafening me to all else. Ever the saint, Rowena appears and takes him from me. He struggles in her grip, wanting her to set him free, but I cannot let him wander the camp, what with moving horses and troops hastening about. Artagan shouts some last bit that I barely catch over the wind.

"... innocent men and women have died today. Their only crime was that they were Welsh. Today, it's our turn to stain the sea red with *barbarian* blood!"

He yaws into the ear of his stallion, Merlin whinnying loudly before galloping headlong into the West. Half a dozen knights and two hundred archers follow close behind. Glancing from my son to my husband, my body and soul threaten to tear themselves apart. I should stay behind and guard Gavin. That assassin remains at large somewhere in the hinterland. But Artagan has his battle-rage on him and will listen to no one if he encounters overwhelming odds today. I'm the only person who has a chance of reasoning with him. How can I protect my son and still keep his father alive with so many perils threatening us all at once? I've only moments and must make my decision quick.

Ahern, Una, and Rowena all stand nearby, the closest thing to family I have outside of my husband and my son. The three of them give me sidelong looks, still taking in all the commotion swirling around us. Warrior. Missionary. Caretaker. Each of them has unique strengths, but together they are stronger. I lean in close to them, raising my voice so that they will hear me over the din.

"I leave you three in charge. Secure the camp, but above all protect the children. They are the key to all of this. Our future, our hope. I'm trusting you with the life of my son, heir to the crown."

The three of them exchange looks, still trying to grasp the enormity of what I have just laid upon them. But there is no more time to explain. Ahern bellows after me as I grab my longbow and mount a spare pony.

"Where in thunder do you think you're going?"

"To make sure my husband doesn't lose his life or his throne before my son comes of age!"

I dig my heels into the pony's flanks, bolting toward the open moors to the west. A faint dust trail hangs in the air where my husband's army has gone. Their rear guard remains just within my vision as they traverse the undulating downs. I urge my mount on faster until the noise of the camp fades behind me, and I smell the first salty hint of the sea.

A fierce headwind buffets my cheeks. The elements seem to swell in tandem with the maelstrom rising inside me. What have I done? Taken my family into the perils of the wilds. And chosen others to guard my son while I attempt to save my husband.

I've even endangered Olwen's boy by bringing him along. If anything should happen to him, it would mean war between the Free Cantrefs and the North Welsh for sure. But I have already made my cast and must wait for the dice to fall. Too late for second guesses now. I never was the type of noblewoman to stay by the hearth while the men rode into battle, anyway. As my father always used to say with the shake of his head, the blood of the Old Tribes runs strong in me.

As the sun moves through the sky, I seem to lose ground. Artagan's men disappear completely from view. He must be driving them hard. My pony slows her pace, panting fiercely as we finally find a hill overlooking the sea. The scent of ash and cinders fills the air.

Far below, along the frothy crags and sandy beachheads, columns of black smoke rise along the shoreline. Charred ruins smolder where the monastery and cloister once stood, overlooking the endless waves of blue water extending far to the west. In the distance, the dark silhouette of the hill fort, Dun Dyfed, looms at the end of the peninsula. Its stone walls crawl with scores of blue-painted figures. Like some strange plague has infected the rocks of the old stronghold itself.

I catch my breath, not having seen my birthplace since I was sixteen. My father wed me to the Hammer King and I never came back. By the time I'd run off and married Artagan, I never thought I would lay eyes on Dun Dyfed again. Now smoke billows from the countryside. Dozens of fires crackle amidst burnt-out hovels from the ruined villages.

The clang of steel and the roar of mingled voices reverberate farther down the shore. Dozens of black ships line the shallows, anchored with mooring lines tied to stones. Each vessel bears black or crimson sails, the prow of every boat emblazoned with an evil eye painted on either side. The symbol of the Picts.

I clutch a hand to my throat. Until this moment, I didn't truly believe it. The boogeymen from the old bedtime stories have returned to harry our shores once again.

Hundreds of blue-painted warriors clash with the green-clad bowmen of the Free Cantrefs. Arrows whistle through the air while slingstones thud against timber shields. In the heart of the fray, Artagan and his knights cut a swath through the throngs of screaming, raging barbarians. A trail of bloodied blue bodies lies in their wake. Artagan lifts heads from shoulders, his longsword deadly as a scythe amongst the barbarians. Inspired by his example, his men chant a rallying cry behind him. *Blacksword, Blacksword!* My husband and his famed dark blade look fierce enough to conquer the gates of hell itself. No wonder his men love him.

But it does no good. From my vantage, I see that at least twice as many Picts grapple with Artagan's men. The azure barbarians slowly bend the line of Free Cantref troops back until the green crescent of archers can barely keep the Picts from encircling them. Artagan has bitten off more than he can chew, and the Picts know it.

My pony neighs as I put my heels to her, charging down the switchbacks and onto the bloodied sands. I have to make Artagan see reason and pull back. If not, the Pictish raiders will turn this battle into a massacre, and take my husband along with it.

The first lifeless bodies I pass make my mount rear up. Sweat pours down my temples, my heart drumming in my ears. The dead Picts don't even look human. As the tide washes over their corpses, the blue woad doesn't leach from their pale flesh. Instead, the swirling cobalt designs seem actually *etched* into their skins, as though they were born with these ungodly blue markings. Several of their mouths hang open, displaying filed teeth, sharp as saws. Many have white lye greased into their hair, making it stand on end.

These Picts go nearly naked into battle, save for a loincloth and weapons. Most carry clubs of bone or wood, while others hold spears with stone heads. I blink at several motionless bodies in the surf. Dozens of warriors among them are women!

Drawing back my bowstring, I guide my pony forward with only my legs. I've only ever tried this in practice, and never when Artagan or anyone else was looking. But I need both hands for my bow. Loosing several arrows into the crowd, I wound multiple warriors as my pony charges into the fray. I must reach Artagan before it's too late. Before we all die here.

Emryus twirls his quarterstaff and Keenan his broadax, the pair of them clearing a path for my steed. They battle on either side of me, oblivious of the danger. Only when Artagan turns around to swing his sword does he hold back. His gaze widens when he glimpses me, Pictish blood running down his hair and longsword.

"What the hell are you doing here?"

"Saving your behind! You're about to be outflanked on either side. You have to retreat, now!"

Artagan merely growls in reply, running two more Picts through with his blade. More Free Cantref archers encircle us, trying to defend us as they launch their last arrows into the crowd of Picts. They down dozens of shrieking barbarians at point-blank range. Nothing but death itself gives these blue-faced barbarians pause. Sometimes not even that, it seems. The deafening clamor of battle claws at my ears. I wince, loosing arrows until my quiver runs empty. There are simply too many wildlings on every side.

A hunting horn dangles from Artagan's mount. I know the signal to fall back: three toots. Artagan may scold me for this, but he can take it up with me later. If we ever get out of this mess.

I grab the bugle and blow three times. Artagan glances back at me with betrayed eyes. His men start to fall back.

We find ourselves in a running battle all the way back into the foothills overlooking the beach. Despite their fury, the Picts slow their pursuit once the remnants of our tiny army reaches the high ground. Even the barbarians know better than to try to attack us uphill.

Panting hard, Artagan, Emryus, and Keenan all exchange looks with me. Bloodied cuts and nicks mar every face. Bowen and Carrick stagger through the throng, both limping and leaving bloody footprints in their wake. Maybe half the archers Artagan took into the fight still number among us. Judging by the circling buzzards overhead, I'd wager that we slew at least double our number amongst the Picts.

Artagan snatches the hunting horn back from my hand, too out of breath to rebuke me. Before I can think of anything to say, a figure down on the strand catches my eye. Between the two separated armies, in the carnage of bodies in no-man's-land, she smiles menacingly up at us.

Ropes of greased lye hair lie piled atop her scalp. Her middle-aged face might be considered almost pretty if not for the swirling teal tattoos on her cheeks and brow. A necklace of finger bones rests on her heaving, sweat-soaked chest. Black war paint circles her eyes. She lifts up a bone spear and shouts a trilled war cry, the rest of her followers replying in ululating tones.

My blood runs cold. Her savage stare and bloodied hands leave no doubt in my mind while she glares up at us from across the battlefield. This must be the fabled Queen of the Picts.

6

A Pict rider approaches, his white steed speckled with blood. I instinctively reach for my longbow as the horseman nears camp. Artagan stands beside me while scores of Free Cantref warriors pick up their spears and bows. Many still nurse bloody wounds and bruises. From our vantage on the bluffs, the dark silhouette of Dun Dyfed stands out in the distance. The setting sun turns the sea the color of beaten copper, so bright it makes my eyes water.

Carrion crows and gulls argue over the carnage of rotting bodies on the beaches far below. Thankfully, we do not camp downwind of the battlefield. The hooves of the lone horse clack louder as the rider halts before us. He carries the long white bone spear of the Pict Queen.

For a herald, he seems unusually quiet. He stares down at Artagan and me without saying a word. My skin crawls under his flinty gaze. Muscled and tall as a gladiator, the rider has the soft cheeks of a boy. Despite his serpentine woad tattoos and unnaturally white hair, his yellow eyes set him apart. Even for a Pict.

Our bowmen clench their drawstrings as the silence lengthens. I nock an arrow on my bow, never taking my eyes off the strange horseman. Why has this barbarian come to us? Just to take a closer look? Artagan takes a step forward, nearly nose to nose with the pale steed. He aims his longsword at the Pict.

"If you've come to surrender, you best drop your spear and get on with it."

His men guffaw as Artagan smirks my way. I almost shake my head. Ever the carefree hedge knight at heart, he would laugh at his own funeral. Our bowmen relax their grips on their bowstrings, but I still clutch my arrow tight. The Pict looks down at me and my husband without so much as blinking his eyes.

The barbarian croaks out a single word.

"Sab."

Artagan and I exchange looks. Does this savage not even speak proper Welsh? The Pict growls slightly louder, this time pointing with his ivory spear toward the battlements of Dun Dyfed in the distance.

"*Saab.*"

Wrinkling my brows, I glance toward the dun where the Picts hold the fortress. Sab? Sab what? This broad-shouldered beggar makes no sense. Artagan looks agitated as well, gripping his sword tight. If this savage doesn't start talking sense quick, someone will put an arrow in him. I wish Artagan would step away from the brute. The Pict thumps his chest.

"Bal. *Baal.*"

He points at Dun Dyfed again.

"Sab. Sab!"

My eyes widen. I point at the Pict, then the dun, repeating his mantra. I make sure to lengthen the vowels like he does in his strange manner of speech.

"Bal. Sab."

He nods, ever so slightly. Artagan blinks at me, looking as befuddled as an ox. I take him aside.

"*Bal* is his name. *Sab* is either someone or something he wants to take us to."

"Go with him? To Dun Dyfed alone? It's crawling with Picts."

"I think he offers us a truce, a chance to talk."

"Or he takes us to our deaths! Branwen, these Picts have no honor."

I lower my voice, keeping one eye on my husband and one on the mounted Pict.

"What choice do we have? We've camped on the bluffs since the battle but have only created a stalemate. We don't have the numbers to attack them again. They seem equally wary of crossing swords with us after the losses they took."

Still visible in the growing darkness, well over the half the bodies down by the surf bear the blue markings and pale greased hair of Picts. But our own force numbers barely a hundred men now, most fatigued by travel and battle. Artagan frowns at Bal before glancing back at me.

"And just whom do you think we will *talk* to if we go with him? This oaf doesn't even speak our tongue."

"They must have someone who can speak to us. They probably just didn't want to risk us taking that person captive or worse. It's what I would do if I were in their position."

Artagan sighs, sheathing his longsword in its scabbard slung along his back.

"If someone told me yesterday I'd be walking into a Pict camp at sunset, I'd have thought them mad."

"But you won't go alone. I'm coming with you."

Artagan shakes his head. I put my hand on his arm. Brave as he is in battle, my love has no tact for diplomacy. Alone, he would just as likely come back on his shield, probably after taking half a hundred Picts down with him. He needs me with him.

I rub his tense shoulders, faking a smile to try to put him at ease. It doesn't work. I lean close to his ear so that only he can hear me.

"You'll need me to negotiate. Don't you remember the legends of the Picts? They don't follow kings and warlords like us. They always follow a queen."

Artagan raises an eyebrow. Either he doesn't remember the old stories or he doesn't believe me. He would rather hack off this Pictish herald's head than parley with their queen or any other barbarian leader. But he will come, because he trusts me and my judgment. I only hope

I have not miscalculated. If I am wrong, our heads will likely adorn spits outside Dun Dyfed by nightfall. No one ever said being a monarch was easy or without risk.

I nod to Bal. He seems to understand and leads Artagan and me toward the dun. Our bowmen murmur behind us, but Artagan raises his hand and calls to them.

"Wait and keep watch. If we do not return before sunrise . . . you damn well better rescue us."

He winks at his men, keeping up his devil-may-care attitude. Only when we walk out of sight, alone with our Pict guide, does Artagan level his troubled gaze on me. I take his hand in mine. At least we still have our weapons. Whatever our fate, we will meet it together.

Bal says nothing, not even sparing a glance back to make sure we accompany him. In the waning blue light after sundown, we thread our way through the switchback trails, past the tall grass in the dunes. Artagan leans down close to my ear, his voice low and rough.

"Did you have to blow that damned horn, Branwen? You ordered the men to retreat against my wishes!"

His anger takes me aback, suddenly recalling the end of the battle earlier.

"I saved your life!" I retort. "I'm sorry I stepped on your toes, but there wasn't time for niceties."

"I nearly had those blue-painted beggars on the run."

"You nearly had you and your entire command surrounded. I apologize for usurping your authority on the battlefield, but not for saving your hide, beloved."

He gives me a sidelong glance and for a moment I fear he will raise his voice. I love him more than life itself, so can he truly blame me for doing everything in my power to keep him safe and sound? Instead of growing cross, Artagan's features soften as he threads his arm through mine.

"You were right, and I probably bit off more than I could chew by attacking the Picts head-on, although it certainly threw the bastards off balance."

I squeeze his hand in mine.

"I nearly lost you in our war with the Saxons. I couldn't bear anything happening to you now."

He flashes his typical cocky smile of pearly teeth.

"I'll strike a bargain with you, my headstrong wife. If you're willing to make it up to me, I think we can put this minor discord behind us."

"Make it up to you, how?"

He reaches around and squeezes my bottom. My eyes go round like hens' eggs as he grins back at me. Even in the shadow of the Picts, his libido remains healthy as ever. I swat his hand playfully, my spirits rising despite being near the enemy camp. A faint grin spreads across my lips. Even after years of marriage, my beloved man still manages to surprise me.

If Bal hears us at all, he makes no move to eavesdrop, whether he knows our tongue or not. His silence for some reason unnerves me. These Picts seem as otherworldly as wraiths.

Thoughts of little Gavin suddenly come to mind, his rosy hair and soft cheeks. I pray to God that I have not just made him an orphan by rushing to meet with these blue-painted warriors. I take a deep breath, pushing such thoughts to the back of my mind. I need my wits sharp if Artagan and I are ever to walk out of Dun Dyfed alive.

The craggy, black outline of the rocky hill fort looms closer. My birthplace. An ancient fortress built by the Celts, what it lacks in polish it makes up for in impregnability. Backed up against the cliffs on one side, the landward end of the castle faces a narrow isthmus connected to the mainland. The perfect enclave in which to hold off an invading force. My first husband, the Hammer King, besieged my father's realm here until I agreed to marry him. How long ago that all seems.

I still cannot believe the barbaric Picts, of all people, have conquered the place. Dyfed must have truly grown weak of late, its guards few and sloppy in their work, for this fortress to fall so easily. But the Picts were always renowned for their deceptiveness and stealth in the old tales.

The first Pict guards sneer and hiss at us when we cross into the fort's defenses. Men and women with clubs and slings eye us suspiciously. Bal leads us past their bonfires toward the heart of the fortress. My pulse thuds in my ears, but I keep a stoic face. Artagan and I no longer hold hands, keeping our weapons at the ready. A handful of half-naked warriors bare their sharpened fangs at us as Bal escorts us inside the main hall.

I stifle a rising knot in my throat. Maybe Artagan was right. We should never have come here.

The old hall looks nothing like it did when my father ruled here. The mead benches and wall hangings are gone, replaced with smoky peat fires pitched right on the cobblestone floor. Hunks of meat roast on spits in the murky dimness. In a few short nights, the Picts have befouled this ancient stronghold of the Old Tribes. It looks more like a cave now than a proper feasting hall.

Bal rides his horse right into the central gallery, dismounting as though in a stable instead of a throne room. He lets his mount wander at will, grazing amongst scraps on the ground. I wrinkle my nose at the stench of defecation from side corridors. A horse has more breeding than these people. At least animals know not to shite where they eat.

The she-warrior I saw during the battle sits cross-legged on my father's old throne. Her hair stands in a topknot, her eyes shut as though in a meditative trance. Her eyelids flicker but do not open. Bal halts and gestures toward her.

"Sab."

He takes his place beside her, flexing his fingertips along the tall bone-white spear. The rest of the Picts in the room no longer pay us any heed, gorging themselves on meat and drinking the last stores of ale from the castle's vaults. The Pictish Queen opens her eyes, staring straight at us. Her eyes do not look the same, one a grayish-hazel and the other an icy blue. Other than her lips and eyelids, not a muscle on her body moves.

"I am Sab, Mother of my People. In the olden days, your kind would've called me Queen of the Picts."

Artagan's gaze narrows on her swirling blue facial brands.

"You speak our language? How?"

Sab closes her eyes a moment before glancing my way.

"You're not the first children of the Old Tribes to be my . . . guests."

Something about the way she says "guests" makes my stomach turn over. I step forward, my hands clasped to my longbow to keep from trembling. I summon all the queenly confidence I can into my voice.

"We came with the understanding of a truce. To talk."

"So you did." She smiles. "The first to do so, I might add. Must have been your idea, no? All the Welsh *men* I've sent emissaries to try to cut off my messengers' heads instead."

She glances at Artagan as though guessing his previous intentions. In truth, Artagan probably would've sent Bal back in pieces had I not been there to counsel him otherwise. But Sab's perceptive stare does little to calm my nerves. I clear my throat, trying to get to the point of our meeting.

"Queen Sab, why have you come here? Why have you invaded Wales and slain so many?"

Sab shuts her eyes again, clicking her tongue.

"The Emptiness has pushed us here."

"The Emptiness?"

Her multicolored eyes flash open again, reflecting my silhouette and Artagan's in each pupil.

"The Emptiness has come again. It makes our lands in the North barren, cold as death, an endless expanse that leaves behind only . . . emptiness."

My eyes narrow suspiciously. She seems serious. Emptiness? Even when we find a Pict who knows our tongue, she still speaks in riddles. Whatever this Emptiness may be, a storm or a monster, this phenomenon seems to have rendered the Pict homelands in the frigid North uninhabitable, for the time being, at least. And now they have come south to covet our green lands and make them their own.

Artagan shuffles his feet, furrowing his brows. He looks agitated, uncomfortable with the Pict Queen's ambiguity. She replies to our questions but does not truly answer them. She talks, but we do not understand. Artagan jabs a finger at her.

"Is this what we came to talk about? Your *Emptiness*? I'd sooner cross swords with you again than listen to this inane babble."

Sab flashes a wicked smile. Out from behind her throne a young woman emerges, clad in barely enough animal skin to make two napkins. Her bare skin has fewer tattoos than either Sab or Bal. She slinks around the Queen's throne, her voluptuous curves and generous bust flecked with sweat from the peat fires. She rubs her naked legs together, adjusting her topknot of dark locks. Her eyes focus on Artagan. Her irises have the same odd multicolors as the Queen's.

"I like this one, Mother. He's a fighter. Can I keep him?"

The youth reaches out as though to touch Artagan's lips. He steps back, unsure at first what the young woman intends, but I read her thoughts all too clear. My flesh buzzes hot. I step between them, fletching an arrow to my bowstring without raising my weapon. I clench my bow until my knuckles turn white, the flames in a nearby grate rising and crackling to match my fury. Sab's eyes narrow a moment, noticing how the blaze responds to me. The young temptress beside her merely steps back a pace, eyeing me sulkily as the hearth fire subsides.

I expected to parry words, maybe even a little violence, but not a scantily clad vixen. The young Pict hisses at me like a cat. Sab nods toward the girl.

"My daughter, Ness, only means to compliment you, Queen Branwen. She's very picky about whom she considers a worthy mate."

I clench my jaw. A worthy *mate*? If this Pict harlot wants something to prick her so bad, I've got a dozen arrows in my quiver willing to oblige her. Artagan is *my* husband. He gives me a quick nod, putting a hand on my arm. My husband wants no part of Ness's advances, and I know it. He's a worthy man, which makes my ire for Ness rise all the more. I struggle to keep my tone calm.

"He's spoken for. And how do you know my name?"

"Oh, the famous Mab Ceridwen and her Blacksword are spoken of with awe amongst the Welsh and Saxons everywhere, even reaching our ears in the far North," Sab replies. "When I saw the two of you on the battlefield today, I doubted you could be anyone else."

Ness circles us, her bare feet treading far too close to Artagan for my comfort. She sniffs him like a bitch-dog in heat. Ness gradually returns to her mother and leans against the throne. Bal stands silent as a boulder, neither looking our way nor ignoring us. I get the feeling he could snap us in two if Sab asked him. Despite his fearsomeness, he has the beardless face of a teen. With a behemoth of a warrior on one side and her sultry she-devil on the other, Queen Sab sits calm as a coiled viper in my father's old seat.

I take a deep breath, trying to clear my thoughts. Sab did not call us here just to have her daughter ogle my husband. Or to speak about some mysterious Emptiness. The Queen seems too smug, too calm. Already she inhabits this castle as though her people had dwelt in it a thousand years. She won't reveal anything of use to us so long as she feels in control. I clear my throat.

"Despite incursions by the Romans and Irish, we Welsh are mostly descendants of the Old Tribes. The Picts and the Old Tribes were deadly enemies in the ancient days. Before we drove you away."

Her smile fades, her stiff cheeks looking unamused for the first time since we arrived.

"Yes, your forebearers pushed us into the far North, but neither you nor the Romans nor the Saxons could defeat us completely. You seem to know an awful lot about the old tales."

"I was schooled in my youth at the monastery your brigands burnt down yesterday. And for a short time was tutored by one of the last of the Old Religion, the Lady Annwyn."

Sab's eyebrows perk up at mention of Annwyn's name. So she has heard of Artagan's illustrious mother. Although a pagan, Annwyn knew much of the Old Wisdom, most of which is now lost. We had so little time together before she died. If only I could have learned more from her. Sab leans forward in her chair, eyeing me with a keen stare.

"You learned from Lady Annwyn, did you? Her name too was known far and wide for her knowledge with the Old Ways. How would you like to learn more of the Old Wisdom she knew?"

"She was a wise woman and mother to my husband, but alas she has long since died, and much of her wisdom, I'm afraid, died with her."

Sab gives me a wry smile.

"Not entirely lost. Although rivals, the wisdom of the Picts mirrored that of the Old Tribes. Together we knew the secrets of healing, of divination, and of many mysteries forgotten by the world of your monks and priests. I could teach you such things."

Ness frowns, leaning down close to the Queen.

"Mother, don't waste your time on this plain-looking Welsh woman. She is not worthy."

Sab shushes her without a glance, steepling her hands. Ness sulks behind her, casting long glances at Artagan. The Queen speaks cordially but firmly.

"Let us be blunt. Your forces cannot dislodge us from here. It would cost a thousand lives to breach this castle, with cliffs on one side and a narrow approach on the other. But you and your brave Blacksword have surprised us with the ferocity of your green-clad warriors, and I doubt we could venture far from Dun Dyfed now without finding your arrows in our backs every step of the way."

"In other words, we are at an impasse," I reply. "Neither one able to defeat the other."

"For now. I suggest a continued truce. My people will keep to the shores around the dun while yours remain inland and out of bow shot."

Artagan steps forward to interrupt, his fists clenched.

"You harry our lands, slay innocent women and children, and expect us to make peace with you!"

"I expect you to recognize the reality of the situation," Sab replies, glancing at Artagan like a child in a temper tantrum. "I will hold up our end of the agreement, and raid no further into Welsh territory so long as you both agree to my single request."

"Which is?" I ask.

"That you, Queen Branwen, come to me each day and talk with me."

I blink my eyes incredulously.

"That's it? Just to talk?"

"Like you once did with Lady Annwyn. You and I can talk each day with words, or our warriors can draw each other's blood instead. The choice is yours."

Artagan and I draw back a few steps, whispering to one another.

"Smells like a trap," he says with a grimace.

"If they wanted to trap us, they could do it right now," I reply. "This is an opportunity, Artagan."

"For what? To chat with a murderess?"

"All she wants to do is talk. Think about it another way. Every day I come to her is another day we can rebuild our forces, gather more troops from afar, and seek allies. We can keep the Picts penned up in Dun Dyfed, and all we have to do is let their queen exchange a few words with me. This will buy us time without the loss of a single soldier."

"It also gives *them* time to repair their ships and maybe get reinforcements of their own."

"I didn't say this was without risk. They're playing their game and we are playing ours. It's a double-edged blade, but it's a gamble we have to take. Besides, think of what I might learn if Queen Sab knows something of the Old Wisdom."

"Branwen, our people spent generations ridding our lands of Picts in the ancient days. My mother may have known the Old Wisdom, but she would never have trusted a Pict."

I sigh at his stubbornness. Can't he see that everything in life does not fall simply into categories of good and evil? Harsh as these Picts seem, they differ from other barbarians, like the Saxons. Straightforward and rough, the Saxons make no mystery of their intentions. They want land and loot, and to drive our people into the sea. These Picts, however, act much more indirect in their mannerisms, fighting us to the death one day and asking to talk the next. We must learn more about them if we are ever to deal with them successfully.

Queen Sab clears her throat, clearly tired of Artagan and me whispering back and forth. I stare Artagan down until he hangs his head. Whether he likes it or not, he knows I am right. I turn to the Pictish Queen.

"We would be honored to accept your offer, Queen Sab. Beginning tomorrow I will ride to Dun Dyfed each day, and in return our forces shall impose a truce on one another."

"Agreed," she replies. "We shall honor the terms, but do not attempt to play us false, Queen Branwen. Should you forget to come to us, even for a single day, we shall consider this accord null. We are a patient people, but Picts do not easily forget . . . or forgive."

"I understand. See you at noontide tomorrow, my Queen."

Sab nods to Bal, who escorts us from the main hall. As he mounts his horse, I glance back to see Sab watching me closely. Her daughter runs her tongue over her lips as she eyes Artagan. I link my arm with my husband as Bal guides us out into the dark night, the thunder of the sea rumbling against the cliffs far below the citadel walls.

Once outside the battlements, Bal halts his horse without a word and lets us wander back on our own. After a few dozen paces, I glance back to see that he has vanished into the evening fog. Artagan and I lengthen our strides across the dunes. My heart lightens with every step we put between us and the smoky, dank abode the Picts have made of Dun Dyfed. Although I will have to return tomorrow, at least I can keep that half-naked girl, Ness, from laying her paws on my Artagan.

My husband walks silently beside me, lost in his own thoughts. Sab has doubtless given him much to ponder, but what part of his mind will he follow in his next move? The brash hedge knight, the plotting general, or the benign king? I suppose when it comes down to it, he will trust my judgment, as he always has. My smile broadens as I clutch him closer, our arms still entwined.

A half-moon emerges from the cloud cover when we return to camp, illuminating every bowman and pony in a silvery hue. Artagan immediately mounts up and orders his men to make ready to march. Sir Keenan stands beside the King's horse.

"I feared we'd never see either of you again. What happened, sire?"

"We've a temporary truce with the Picts," Artagan replies. "We ride back to Ogham Stone tonight."

Both Bowen and Carrick leap to their feet, hastening toward us.

Despite their limps from their wounds, Bowen sounds hot enough to go straight back into battle.

"A truce! You made peace with those demons? We asked you here to help rid us of the barbarians, not invite them to stay!"

Gray-bearded Emryus steps between the two Dyfed knights and Artagan.

"Mind your tone, Dyfed man. You're speaking to a king, and the Blacksword at that."

Carrick tries to hold his brother back, but Bowen's voice continues to rise.

"You've made a pact with the devil, King Artagan! Once the Picts gain a foothold, they will continue to infest the countryside until they are in every kingdom in Wales."

Artagan growls as he turns his mount directly toward Bowen. Merlin's nostrils flare right in the Dyfed men's faces, forcing them to take a step back. Artagan sounds ready for a fight himself.

"I'm no happier about this arrangement than you! But facts are facts. The Picts already have a foothold and we cannot dislodge them, they're dug in like ticks. But we bloodied them today and they won't venture far from their ships. We need time to muster our full forces. Queen Branwen has negotiated this truce with the Pict Queen, and so long as she continues to meet with her, it will buy us the time we need to defeat these invaders."

All eyes fall on me. A mix of silent awe and maybe even fear lingers on the faces of these brave warriors. Do they think me a traitor for parleying with the enemy? Some, like Emryus and Keenan, look more like they pity me, seeing as I must now spend more time amongst the Pictish barbarians. Others, like Bowen and Carrick, glare with open hostility, as though offended by my presumption that the invaders who have ravaged their kingdom can be negotiated and reasoned with. Artagan seems put off himself, barking orders at his men as they form up for a night march back to our encampment at Ogham Stone.

I mount my pony without looking back at any of them. What's wrong with everyone? We should be celebrating our success. We have not defeated the Picts, but we have checked their progress and isolated them within a single hill fort. Imagine the trouble my husband and his warriors would have gotten into without me! Most of them would probably either be either dead or captured by the Pict Queen. How prideful a bunch of knights with spears can be! I've accomplished more with a few well-placed words than they could with a hundred soldiers.

None of them understand the magic of words. Words have the power to inspire warriors against overwhelming odds, to broker peace between enemies, and to sow discontent amongst friends. Swords and spears alone do not make a leader great. My weapon shall be my tongue.

PART TWO

Summer, A.D. 602

7

I awake just before dawn within the privacy of our tent. The encampment runs still. I stretch out my limbs as a yawn spreads across my cheeks.

Artagan rolls over in the blankets beside me, spooning close. Even half-awake, I can feel his roused manhood prodding my tunic. My eyes widen into half-moons. I love my husband like a second self, but even in his sleep he's like a hound in heat. Artagan sleepily cups my breast as he nuzzles my neck in the predawn light, much of the encampment still quiet and asleep.

His vigorous thighs rub beside me and his strong muscles do make me wet, but the sudden thought of my pregnancy stills me to the core. If I let him put his hands all over me, he is sure to notice the subtle changes in my body. Even a man should be able to discern a breeding woman when he has his lips running down her naked skin. I'm nearly three moons gone with child, if I counted right. In another moon or so, I'll start to show for certain. I won't be able to hide my secret much longer.

Artagan sleepily moans in my ear. I hate to disappoint him, but I can't let him slip off my garments for a quick romp.

Still, I want to make things right between us, to rekindle the intimacy we've always shared. Reaching beneath the blankets, I run my hands down under his belt. Fortunately, his sleepiness makes him pliable.

Eyes still shut, he groans pleasurably as I pet and stroke him. He fondles my bosom, his breath quickening and his lips pursing with enjoyment. I move my hands faster around his throbbing loins until his wet heat spills onto the grass between us. He gasps and presses his sleepy mouth to mine.

"What a sweet dream," he whispers. "I adore you, Branwen."

I kiss him back, cleaning my sticky fingertips on the blades of grass. My goodness, how deft I've become with my hands. I roll my eyes. For a queen, sometimes I swear I'm no better than a common harlot beneath the sheets. But my husband doesn't seem to mind. He droops an arm over me, cuddling close as the first beige hues of sunrise illuminate our tent canvas.

Gavin sleeps quietly within his blankets on the far side of the tent. By now the clang of blacksmiths' hammers and the chop of woodsmen's axes fill the camp. The machinations of this small makeshift settlement come to life. I rub my eyes, smelling smoke from a thousand campfires. It's getting crowded around Ogham Stone these days.

Outside the tent, the walls of a timber keep have begun to rise. Ahern shouts at the mix of Free Cantref soldiers and Dyfed laborers working together to erect the palisade defenses. I flash a wry grin as I watch him. Although he has been in my husband's service these past few years, he too was born in Dyfed like me. Ahern seems in his element as he berates and praises the workmen by turns. Every laborer obeys promptly, for fear of my one-eyed brother's temper. Within a few days, he has started to raise the skeleton of a proper wooden keep. Give him a fortnight, and I bet Ahern could construct a cathedral.

Gavin snores peacefully in his blanket. I watch the sun rise over the standing stones atop the hill. Despite the growing multitude of Dyfed refugees around our camp, none have dared set foot on the ancient tor. The hillock looms like a grassy island in the heart of a hundred ramshackle tents and wicker hovels. Each day more huts sprout like mushrooms at the foot of the hill.

Artagan rises and offers me a goatskin of water. Not the usual cup of mead or mulled wine to start my day. Does he suspect that another child quickens inside me? No. Artagan thinks a little spirits do a breeding woman good. But his mother taught me that the Old Wisdom forbade such drinks for women heavy with child. Just one of the many such mysteries observed by the wise women of the Old Tribes, knowledge that has nearly vanished in recent generations. Perhaps today I shall learn a few more of those mysteries from Queen Sab. Perhaps.

Artagan looks down at our son, stroking a stray lock of Gavin's auburn hair while the boy sleeps. He loves our boy so much. What if Artagan knew I had doubts about birthing another one? How could he understand the fear of bleeding to death in childbirth? How could any man? Artagan keeps his voice low, so as not to wake the child.

"I've sent Emryus and Keenan back to Aranrhod to gather reinforcements. We'll need more men in the days to come. I've also got Bowen and Carrick scouring the countryside looking for more refugees and Dyfed spear-men to join our cause."

"How many survivors have come here to Ogham Stone?" I ask.

"At least two thousand people by last count and more every day. Why do they come?"

"Like a shipwrecked crew, they cling to any dry land they see. We're the closest thing these people have to protection now. There is no one left to lead the Kingdom of Dyfed."

"Ahern's got the bit between his teeth. He'll have this new keep built in another moon if nothing stops him. Who knew the old soldier had the heart of a master builder?"

"It would be nice to have a roof over our son's head, instead of living in tents like wanderers in the Bible."

I look to my feet, knowing I will have to ride more than a league in the saddle today to reach Dun Dyfed before noon. I'll probably have to eat my breakfast on horseback. My heart contracts like a clenched fist, realizing that Gavin may not yet awake before I have to go. Will he cry or simply go about his day without me? Both thoughts give me little comfort. Still, one trepidation remains heavy on my mind. I speak close to Artagan's ear.

"What news of the assassin?"

Artagan shakes his head.

"None. He seems to have vanished. The beggar hasn't shown himself once since we camped at Ogham Stone."

I frown. Artagan's words should give me comfort, but instead they only curdle my stomach. I wag my head.

"Something doesn't add up. This assassin went to great lengths to ensnare our boy back at Aranrhod and then pursued us relentlessly across the wilderness. Now that we've camped at the foot of some standing stones, he suddenly gives up the chase? I don't believe it."

"The people here both fear and revere Ogham Stone. Some say the old rocks have power."

"So if Morgan's ghost has come to kill my child, the power of the stones somehow holds him at bay?"

Artagan grimaces.

"The Hammer King is as dead as a dung heap. And it was no ghost that pursued you and Ahern into that thicket a few days ago. The assassin ran away from me and my soldiers. Seems like the actions of a living man to me."

I look away, still unconvinced. Maybe my first husband isn't as dead as Artagan wants to believe. But if not King Morgan, then who would parade about in his old war-mask, striking at innocent children? If only there was a way to be sure. Morgan's body lies entombed in Caerleon. I could ride there and be back again within two days. But no. I have to meet with the Pict Queen and cannot miss even a single rendezvous with her or else risk our entire truce falling apart. Besides, the inhabitants of King Griffith's realm aren't likely to let me dig up the grave of one of their most revered rulers just so that I can sleep better at night.

I aim my index finger at my husband.

"I want at least several guards, trusted men, watching over Gavin at all times while I'm gone."

"I'll guard him myself. No harm will come to him. Funny to think I'm the knight and king, but it's my wife who rides away into danger while I stay behind to mind the child."

I beam back at him.

"I was never the kind of woman to stay home and tend the hearth fires, anyway. Take care of yourself."

"You too, my love."

He kisses me long and lovingly, one hand cupping my cheek. Half of me wants to surrender to his embrace, to forget about the troubles of the world, to retreat to the safety of our bedchamber and castle. But no fortress in the world can keep out assassins or barbarians indefinitely. No, the only way to give our family a peaceful future is to pursue our difficulties head-on. I heave a sigh. My bones feel weary just thinking of the lonesome ride I must make today.

Artagan clasps my hand in his, his fingertips almost unwilling to let me go. I kneel down beside our boy's bedding and press my lips to Gavin's warm little head. He stirs in his sleep but does not wake.

Saddling my pony, I walk her up the slopes of Ogham Stone. The eyes of a thousand peasants and woodsmen in the dales below watch me as I ascend the forbidden hilltop. Something about the way the wind whistles through the rugged boulders calls to me. Curse or no, I must see these stones for myself, even if no one else will.

Despite the clamor of the encampment spread out below, the summit of the hill seems unusually quiet. A dozen slabs of ancient rock encircle me, with many more shards of rubble half-hidden in the overgrown grass. The wind stills.

Celtic runes dot the edges of each rock face. I reach out to touch one, hesitating before pressing my fingertips to the worn grooves. My fingers buzz with sensation as I run them along the cold stone, my forearms rippling in gooseflesh. To think, some man or woman of the Old Tribes carved these signs into the rock hundreds of generations ago. But why? And what for? Curse or no, these bluish-gray boulders do have power. The unbroken view of the mountains to the east and the open moors to the west fills my blood with the tingling sensation of a thousand needle pricks. My pony whinnies, disturbed by the silent watch stones.

I close my eyes and press both hands to one slab. I say a silent prayer. *Keep my boy safe. Ancient ancestors, if you can hear me, watch over my son and husband. Let no harm come to them or our people while I am away.* I kiss the chilled stone and make the sign of the cross. Like many folk in Wales, I find nothing wrong with praying to our Christian God while at the same time beseeching the spirits of the Old Tribes. In heaven's eye, all divine love is one.

I mount my pony and yaw into her ear, galloping headlong down the slopes and toward the western heaths. Una and Rowena wave to me as my mare pounds the rough trail with her hooves. The scent of salt and kelp from the nearby sea rises on the breeze as the campfires and crowds surrounding the tor shrink behind me.

Gnawing on some waybread and dried jerky in my satchel, I urge my mount along the trackless moors toward Dun Dyfed. The journey seems much briefer than it was yesterday. Maybe because the route is familiar now. Or because the place in which I was born will forever call to me.

In my daydreams, memories of my former teacher and mother-in-law bubble within my thoughts. Annwyn sits with me beside the hearth in her old chambers at our castle in Aranrhod. We keep our palms raised over the flames, making the fire rise and fall. One of the basic elements of nature: fire, water, earth, air. Hints of shadows dance within the blaze, figments of my imagination or the shades of things to come, I never knew. Perhaps if my lessons with Annwyn could have continued I would have learned what powers dwell within me. But then she died, leaving my tutelage under her at an abrupt end before it had really begun. Now all I am left with are tidbits of knowledge and a few parlor tricks. I'm no mistress of magic as Lady Annwyn was.

But Sab is no Annwyn. Even in my optimism I know this. She is a Pict, the dark side of the same moon from which my ancient foremothers amongst the Old Tribes originated. Yet she may be the last link with that archaic past. My last chance to grasp at some of the wisdom Annwyn tried to impart to me.

As though by magic, the dark outline of Dun Dyfed appears along the horizon. I blink, drawing in a deep breath as my mind settles on the present once more. The broad-beaked longships of the Picts lie moored in the foaming tide. My pony's pace slackens.

More crows circle overhead, continuing to pick at the remnants of the battle along the beach. Yesterday, war and death pervaded the landscape. Today, the windswept moors seem calm and pacific. I can almost hear the chants of the monks who used to make their rounds by the abbey. But that monastery and cloister are gone now, I remind myself. Destroyed by the Picts. However cordial I must behave toward Sab, I can't forget what she and her people are capable of. I must not forget that they can smile one day and rip out my beating heart the next.

Bal sits astride his pale stallion, as unsurprised by my presence as he is of the sunrise. I trail him inside the walls of the dun. Much of the garrison lies asleep, male and female warriors entwined together from last evening's revelries. White bones litter the grounds.

We stop outside the main entranceway to the great hall. My eyes linger on the shape and arrangement of bones. Some seem too long for sheep, others not large enough for cattle. My eyes narrow on a small pyramid of skulls near the archway. Human skulls.

My skin turns cold as ice. The barbarians haven't dined just on animal meat but also on the remnants of people. It suddenly dawns on me that many of the missing bodies on the strand were not carried away by crows or gulls. My gorge rises in my throat. The Picts have eaten their own dead.

Sab laughs softly to herself, leaning against an archway with her arms folded. She dismisses Bal with a lifted finger. The boyish behemoth retreats to a rocky outcrop, where he keeps watch over us like a silent hawk. Sab smirks at my wan face.

"You do not approve. We do not believe in wasting good meat. Your people were not so different from us long ago."

My stomach churns. She must be lying; my ancestors could never have lived like this. Like savages, like animals. I circle around her and the heap of bones, toward the western wall that overlooks the cliffs. The surf thunders against the cliff face, a light film of spray covering the precipice like dewdrops. Sab sidles up beside me, just the two of us and the roaring ocean for company. I force the confidence back into my voice, an old trick I have learned as a queen these past few years.

"Even the Saxons do not desecrate their own dead. Nor did Annwyn ever tell me of our people doing such things."

"Maybe she hadn't gotten around to mentioning it. Or perhaps she kept secrets from you."

"And what of your secrets, Queen Sab? Is that what you've asked me here to discuss?"

Sab shakes her head with a smile, pacing the rocky walls with me.

"You distrust me, and you are right to do so. My people must seem like something out of an evil fairy tale to you, no? But would it surprise you to know that you are just as much a legend to me?"

"Me?"

"Is it so surprising? My people sail forth, for the first time in generations, into lands ruled by Saxon chieftains and Welsh warlords, but all of them *men*. Lo and behold, I find a queen amongst them, a woman ruling in the style of the Old Tribes. You, Branwen, have far more in common with us than you do with your Saxon foes or your Welsh neighbors. At heart, you are one of us."

My eyebrows rise. Does she merely seek to flatter me or does she truly believe what she says? Artagan is king of our people, but I have always ruled as an equal beside him. Am I really like a queen of the Old Tribes to this woman? Never have I heard such straightforward talk from another queen. She does not tiptoe around the truth as I did when younger or use her sultry wiles as Queen Olwen does. Lost for words, I walk beside her.

"We share the same enemies," she continues. "The Saxons and even rival Welsh kingdoms. We have much to gain and to learn from one another. That is why I asked you here."

"For an alliance? Our people were killing each other only yesterday."

"Hot-blooded men make war. It's up to coolheaded queens like us to make the peace. I saw the way you handle your husband. The Blacksword is a brave leader, but it was his rash idea to attack us yesterday, and not yours, yes?"

I bite my tongue. Sab takes my silence as answer enough.

"So you cleaned up his mess," she adds. "Well-intentioned as he was, he might have had much less bloodshed on his hands had you and I met first."

I stop, turning quickly on her.

"But you first attacked this castle, and burnt down both the abbey and the nunnery. Many innocents perished. Those are not the acts of peace."

Sab raises her hands in supplication.

"Too true, but I hope to make you understand. We were driven here ourselves, by the Emptiness. To find a home for our people. No one would give us such a home willingly. You know that as well as I."

I shake my head, my temples starting to ache.

"I still don't understand. What is this Emptiness of which you speak?"

Sab smiles placidly, like a sage with a student.

"It comes strongest when there is cold and darkness, and this year it is very cold and dark in the far North. Many of our people died, the Emptiness made the land barren and cold. No crops grew, no game to be found. So we follow the will of the Emptiness as it pushes us south. But we do not come here because we wish to spill blood. We come only to live, to escape the darkness and nothingness. That is the Emptiness of which I speak."

I blink, trying to take in all she says. So her people are refugees themselves, looking for greener pastures, a place to escape the barrenness of their homeland. They do look thin as scarecrows. Little wonder they eat their own dead to survive. Still, I cannot easily forget the destruction of the abbey and the cloister. Maybe these barbarians deserve some pity for their circumstances and backward ways, yet they are still savages at heart. And dangerous ones, at that.

Nonetheless, arguing with this Pict Queen will not accomplish anything. She sees herself as the steward of her people, much as I do in my own kingdom. We both have our own families and our own kin to look after. Although I do not condone her methods, I cannot fault her motivations. She watches over her people as a mother. Somehow, I must channel her efforts to preserve her people into a peaceful venture, not the bloodshed we saw yesterday.

"You are right about one thing," I begin. "The Saxons are both our enemies."

"The Saxons," Sab says, spitting as though the name were a curse.

"When they first came, we tried to learn their tongue and make peace. But did you know they use the same word for *woman* as they do for *slave*? After that, we knew there would never be peace between our people and theirs."

"My people do not trust you, not yet, at least. Helping us fight the Saxons, however, would go a long way toward convincing my people that your intentions are good."

Sab strokes her chin.

"I must think it over and discuss it with my people. We've no love for the Saxons, but my people distrust yours as well. Letting us remain here in Dyfed would convince us that *your* intentions are equally good."

I smile politely back. Sab knows the ways of queenship well. Nothing comes free.

"I too will think it over, and relay what you have said to my husband and my people. Fair enough?"

Sab nods. It's not much, but possibly it's a start toward peace. Letting the Picts remain in perpetuity at Dun Dyfed will not go over well with most Welsh, particularly the people of Dyfed. But another army on our side against the Saxons would be worth its weight in gold, especially if these Picts fight our foes as ferociously as they did our own warriors yesterday. We have a truce with the Saxons that has lasted for the past three years, but no one expects it to last forever. Sooner or later the Saxons will break their word, and an army of Picts might be just the weapon we need to defeat the Saxons once and for all. Like using fire to fight fire. No one ever said a queen's decisions would be easy.

"You remind me much of the late Queen Vivian," Sab murmurs.

I pause in my tracks, my skin running cold.

"You knew my mother?"

"By reputation. Fair of face, dark of hair. She too had dealings with the Picts, long ago."

I blink, trying to regain my composure. I rarely discuss my mother with anyone, especially a stranger and potential rival. Still, I sense that Sab knows more than she lets on. What dealings did my mother, of all people, ever have with heathen Picts? She never spoke of such things to me, although I was quite young when Saxon swords took her from me. I eye Sab cautiously, trying to sound more like a diplomat than a spooked child.

"Then perhaps you and I can bridge the gap between the generations of mothers who came before us."

"Perhaps." She smiles noncommittally.

Sab leads me around the battlements, where Bal squats and watches us. She nods toward him. He leaps down and fetches his horse. Sab turns to me with a smile.

"I think we've given each other enough to think over for today. I look forward to meeting with you tomorrow. Perhaps we can talk more of the secrets of the Old Tribes."

I bow slightly in reply. I'd certainly cross another field of bones to learn more of the mysteries of my ancestors. Time will tell whether Queen Sab can unlock some of that forgotten knowledge for me. In the meantime, my continued visits will ensure the peace between our camps. One day at a time.

Sab retreats to a stretch of open flagstones in the courtyard where her followers have laid out a slain deer. Her breathing stills as she stands over the creature, meditating as though quite alone. I stay behind a moment to watch.

The Pict Queen kneels over the lifeless carcass, raising an obsidian dagger in one fist. She plunges the stone blade into the animal's skin, folding back the hide as she delves deeper into its steaming guts. This creature cannot be more than an hour dead. My stomach turns over as the shamaness digs her arms up to her elbows inside the doe's corpse, her forearms caked in a deep vermilion hue. She pulls out the long rope of bloody entrails from the dead beast and spreads the crimson innards across the ground, her blank, trancelike gaze roving over the stinking remnants. Her eyes start to flicker until only the whites of her eyeballs show beneath her fluttering eyelids.

Whatever manner of black magic this is, I've no desire to see more. The Queen's manservant, Bal, motions for me to follow him, probably thinking I've dawdled too long. Perhaps I've glimpsed something I shouldn't.

Bal leaves me with my pony outside the walls of Dun Dyfed, the same massive bone spear in his hand. I have half a mind to ask him about it. An unusual weapon. I reminds me of what I might imagine a giant's toothpick to look like. But he disappears into the defenses of the dun once more without comment. Such a quiet creature, but I doubt Sab would keep him around if he were not deadly as well with that pale spear.

Sab's mention of my mother has put me off balance. But perhaps that is what the Pict Queen intended. Her words seem harmless enough, but something in my gut roils nonetheless. My mother was a peaceful, upright woman. Even my boisterous father, God rest him, could find no flaws with my mother. Yet having truck with Pictish barbarians hardly sounds like the kind of thing a queen of Dyfed would have engaged upon. I'm probably being ridiculous to trifle over such a small detail, but Sab's words about my mother stick like a thorn in the back of my mind. What sort of dealings did my mother ever have with the Picts? Unfortunately, neither she nor anyone who would know the answer walk among the living now.

I shake such troublesome thoughts from my head. Time enough to sort out such mysteries another day. Plenty of work remains afoot today as it is.

At least I did not have to stomach the sight of Ness today. The skulking harlot never appeared, praise the Lord. I gallop at an even pace into the eastern groves as the sun bronzes over in the western sky behind me. My visit has already borne one valuable fruit. No one in either camp has died this day, and if things grow from today's seed, perhaps I can prevent bloodshed from continuing here in Dyfed. I laugh to myself, alone in the rolling downs. Today was a good day.

When I arrive on the outskirts of the encampment at Ogham Stone, dusky hues of orange light filter through the standing stones atop the hill. The outer walls of the palisade already stand upright with the green dragon banners of the Free Cantrefs flying over them. At least a few dozen more dwellings and tents have appeared on the lawns. Bowen and Carrick must have found more survivors and brought them to camp.

Spring blossoms on the trees have faded and the early summer nights have begun to warm. Just in time too. Living in tents out in the open would prove untenable in a colder time of year.

Dismounting outside the palisade, the scent of pine sap and freshly cut wood permeates the darkening air. My journey back from Dun Dyfed took even longer than I thought. Oddly enough, no one comes out to greet me. Inside the timber walls, a large open fire pit burns with snapping oak logs. I spot Artagan amidst a crowd gathered around the flames. The flickering hearth casts long shadows across his face. By the firelight, he looks like he has suddenly aged a dozen years. My palms begin to sweat. Something has gone amiss.

Artagan looks up at me as I enter the circle of his knights, Bowen and Carrick among them. He still says nothing, not even a friendly greeting. My eyes dart around, fearing something terrible has befallen us. Yet Rowena stands across the way with all the children around her skirts, including Gavin. I glance back at Artagan and see Ahern beside him, his single eyelid sagging heavy as he grimaces into the flames. I can no longer contain my astonishment at their strange behavior.

"What's the matter with everyone? It's quiet as a crypt in camp."

Artagan picks at the dirt with his sword, not meeting my gaze. Ahern looks away, and even Rowena won't reply. She shushes the children as they play about the tents. Una's voice rises outside the keep walls, leading a small service of women singing hymnals in the evening light. Their voices sound strangely mournful, their somber tune without any musical accompaniment. I put my hands on my hips, raising my voice.

"Isn't anyone going to answer me?"

Artagan raises his eyes, pursing his lips as though tasting something bitter in his mouth.

"A messenger arrived this afternoon, on horseback. He came from South Wales."

"Aye, and what of it? Has King Griffith changed his mind about aiding Dyfed in its time of need?"

"Not quite. He had some other news for us."

Artagan sighs and clenches his jaw, his voice a mix of anger and grief.

"Saxons crossed his borders this morning and attacked several villages. They're moving inland toward Caerleon. Our truce with the Saxons is over."

8

Except for the chirp of crickets and the crackling hearth logs, the entire encampment runs silent. I steady myself by placing my foot on one of the warm hearthstones surrounding the bonfire. My eyes cloud over as I gaze deep into the ruby flames. God help us. The Saxons have returned.

I still can't quite believe it. Three years ago we fought a costly war against the Saxon hordes, both sides losing heavily. My mother, father, first husband, and countless others all met their deaths at the hands of Saxon savages. And now those same barbarians hunger for Welsh blood once more. I shut my eyes, clenching my fists. This cannot be happening all over again.

Artagan paces the fire, dismissing everyone but Ahern and myself. Rowena makes a move to take the children with her, but I stay her hand. These grave matters concern even my three-year-old son. He might as well stay and learn that there are real monsters that go bump in the night, and that they wear Saxon helms and bloody beards.

Little Gavin looks up at me, the firelight flickering in the sheen of his azure eyes. He only understands that his mother and father look frightened. Gavin juts out a pouty lip, so I lift him into my arms, holding him close. His tiny heart races against my chest.

"Emryus and Keenan have sent word from Aranrhod," Artagan begins. "They've rallied a few hundred more bowmen to the castle, but I've told them to stay put. I wanted them here to help us keep the Picts at bay, but with Saxons on the loose, there's no telling where we'll need our warriors in a few days' time. I'm afraid we may not even be able to linger here long if we are needed in the East Marches."

I incline my head, a low heat rising through my veins.

"But we cannot abandon Dyfed in its hour of need! If we leave now, our truce with the Picts will end, and they will ravage these lands in our absence."

"What choice do we have?" Artagan replies. "If we do not gather our forces to defend the Free Cantrefs, we may lose our own kingdom while dawdling here in Dyfed."

He frowns, turning away from me as he continues to pace. Does he consider trying to save my birthplace and its people mere dawdling? I open my mouth to speak, but Ahern puts a hand on my forearm. He motions over his shoulder at several onlookers at the edge of the firelight, Dyfed knights including Bowen and Carrick among them.

I nod back at Ahern, taking in his silent meaning. I am raising my voice too loud. What we discuss in our inner circle should not circulate openly, even amongst our allies. There is too much at risk, and too many loose tongues in a camp full of this many refugees. What I wouldn't give to have some castle walls around us now, not just tent canvas and a few timber spikes.

Ahern turns to me, trying to refocus the three of us on the task at hand.

"How many Picts did you observe in Dun Dyfed?"

"Hard to say," I reply. "They're scattered all over and some deep within the castle. At least a few hundred warriors."

"Any new ships? Have they gained any reinforcements?"

I shake my head. Artagan stops pacing.

"Bowen and Carrick saw two Pict ships while patrolling the shore," Artagan recalls. "But both were heading out to sea."

"That's good!" Ahern interjects. "It means they may even have a few less warriors than before."

Artagan and I exchange grimaces. It makes little sense for Queen Sab to deplete her forces, even by just two ships. So why would she willingly do so? Perhaps she has grown overconfident in the defenses of Dun Dyfed, thinking that she can hold the fortress with only a skeleton force. But then where are those two ships going? I take several deep breaths. Too many unknowns, too much that we still do not understand.

"First thing's first," Artagan begins. "We need to send riders to King Griffith and learn more about the Saxon threat. Perhaps he exaggerates his losses. We need to know whether it's only a few raiding parties or a full-scale invasion taking place in the East Marches."

"We should send ravens to King Iago in the North as well," Ahern adds. "To find out whether the Saxons on his borders have shown any aggression."

Artagan nods in agreement. I want to speak up, but Gavin grows heavy on my shoulder and I do not wish to wake him. I gingerly hand him to Rowena, who takes him in her arms and returns to our tent. I sigh, knowing what I must do.

"You and Ahern should rally our troops while I keep the Picts content at Dun Dyfed by continuing to meet with Queen Sab every day, as per the terms of our truce."

Artagan shakes his head.

"Like hell. You would be defenseless if I have to leave to counter the Saxons."

"The people who have come to Ogham Stone will be defenseless too if you and your men leave, but perhaps I can buy them time by continuing to meet with Sab. You can't spare any troops against the Picts if the Saxons attack, but you can spare me."

Artagan turns his back, pacing again. He is such a stubborn man sometimes. He knows I'm right. It's what a wise monarch would do. Why garrison a few hundred warriors to keep the Picts in check when he can accomplish the same thing with a single emissary? In other words, me.

But Artagan won't let me risk myself like that. He won't ask me to do something he wouldn't do himself. It makes him a brave hedge knight and beloved of his men, but it also makes him a foolhardy king. Even in chess, sometimes a king must risk his queen in order to win the game. Only the game we play now is one of life and death, with half the kingdoms in Wales hanging in the balance.

I have to convince him somehow, before he does something rash. The people of Dyfed will perish if Artagan and our small army leave. But our own kingdom at Aranrhod may fall under siege if we do not return there and gather our strength. I sigh, lowering my head.

"What if I can convince the Picts to fight for us, against the Saxons?"

Both Artagan and Ahern look up at me as though I just hatched a rotten egg.

"Branwen, we were just killing them yesterday," Artagan says.

"Queen Sab has no love for the Saxons. She might consider coming in on our side if we allow the Picts to make their home at Dun Dyfed."

Ahern leaps forward, nearly nose to nose with me. I flinch at such unusual aggression from my half brother. He talks through clenched teeth.

"You would sacrifice the castle of our forefathers to those . . . those . . . *things*? You and I were both born there, my Queen. Our father and all his fathers before him ruled from the throne on which that Pictish demoness now sits!"

I glare back at him, refusing to back down to either him or my husband.

"We cannot survive without some sacrifice! What do you suggest? We do not have enough troops to defend both Dyfed and the Free Cantrefs, especially with Saxons in the East and Picts in the West. We've made enemies enough amongst the barbarians. It's time we started making some allies."

Ahern growls and stalks off into the darkness without another word. Never have I seen him so agitated with me. Artagan shrugs, just the two of us beside the fire.

"That went well," he remarks.

"What would you have me do?" I reply. "We've nothing but bad choices before us. I'm merely selecting the lesser evil."

"You certain of that?"

"How can you say that? Would you rather have the Saxons as allies?"

Artagan shakes his head.

"Of course not. We both know the Saxons would rather see us all dead or as slaves first. You've given me good reasons for your plan, but not the real one. Care to tell me now that it's just the two of us?"

My eyes narrow, my mouth half askew as I try and summon an angry retort. But my anger quickly fades. Artagan knows me better than I know myself. I lower my head.

"I fear what may happen to our boy if we leave Ogham Stone."

"You really think some mystical magic in a bunch of rocks will keep him safe?"

"I can't explain it! All I know is that our son was hunted and nearly killed by an assassin day after day until we arrived here. Since then, not one single attempt has been made on his life. If we leave the safety of Ogham Stone, something evil may befall our son."

"You don't know that."

"I know it in my heart."

Artagan grunts in frustration as he circles the fire pit. I'm being unreasonable, and I know it, but I cannot help myself. There is some piece of the puzzle I'm still missing. For some reason, our presence at Ogham Stone seems to be keeping the assassin at bay. Until I know what that reason is, it makes sense to keep my son in the one place his potential killer will not go.

I rub my shoulder, my joints aching from the day's ride. Come dawn, I shall have to arise again and make the journey back to Dun Dyfed. To maintain the peace, to protect my people, and to keep my little boy safe. I stifle a yawn. All I want to do now is lay my head on a straw pillow and sleep.

My husband sighs. He gazes into the dancing flames with that far-away look that tells me he has much on his mind. My husband will likely stay up half the night wrestling with the same questions, over and over. He tenderly touches my cheek, brushing back a stray lock of my raven hair.

"All right. You continue meeting with Sab, see if she'll help us fight the Saxons. I'll keep my soldiers here at Ogham Stone as long as I can, at least the next few days. It will take that long for Ahern to ride to Caerleon, assess the situation, and report back."

"Thank you." I smile back at him. "Having Gavin here, with you watching over him, puts my greatest fears to rest."

"Just one more thing. Let's keep this idea of letting the Picts stay at Dun Dyfed between ourselves for now. I'm not saying we won't agree to it if the Picts come in on our side against the Saxons, but in the meantime I don't want Bowen or Carrick catching wind of this. I'm trying to rally as many Dyfed men to our standard as I can right now, but they'll balk if they think we'd negotiate away the old capital of their kingdom."

I nod my head. He is right, of course, but I tire of keeping secrets. Especially since I cannot blame the people of Dyfed for their attachment to their ancient castle. Dun Dyfed has housed their chieftains and kings since the days of the Old Tribes. Many of my ancestors called that ancient hill fort their home. How many of them would turn over in their graves if they knew I contemplated giving it away to the Picts? But these troubles can wait for another day. I must lay them down for the evening and rest.

The vehemence in Ahern's voice returns to my mind. I've never seen him so wroth before. As though I like the idea of a Pictish chieftess sitting on our dead father's throne any more than he does. A throne that, by all rights, Ahern could lay claim to as the sole surviving male heir. Born on the wrong side of the blanket or not, that matters little in places where the blood of the Old Tribes runs strong. Perhaps my half brother longs to be more than a seneschal and guardsman. My eyebrows rise.

But that doesn't mean he would betray me. I shake my head, ashamed that I could even entertain the notion. Artagan and I have no designs on Dyfed; we merely wish to push out the Pictish invaders that threaten all of Wales. As for Ahern, he has ever been a loyal soldier to me.

Except for that one great misstep of his years ago, when he betrayed me into the waiting hands of my enemies.

I shut my eyes. That was long ago, and Ahern repented his actions, even confessing to Artagan so that I and my unborn babe might be rescued. Ahern spent many a long day in the dungeons after that before returning to my service with redoubled loyalty and dedication. Still, I cannot blame the man if he wishes to forgo the life of a seneschal to become a king. He might very well seize power due to the simple fact that he *can* seize it. Since when have men anywhere needed more a reason than that? But this is Ahern we're talking about. I try to picture my one-eyed kinsman atop Father's old throne. Somehow, the image doesn't quite fit.

Taking a deep breath, I remind myself that I am a queen. Sister or no, I ought to use my head and take precautions. Ahern has experience as an envoy and messenger, so it makes the most sense that I should send him to South Wales to treat with King Griffith. Sending him on this mission is the prudent thing to do.

Best not to put off until tomorrow what can be accomplished now. I stride over to Ahern's tent, folding back the flap without announcing my presence. He gives a start, reaching for his spear until he sees it is me. He lowers his weapon but still keeps a hand on it. He gives me the slightest of bows.

"I'm tired, my Queen, and was preparing for bed."

"I shan't keep you, brother. I have an errant for you tomorrow. At dawn you must ride to King Griffith's court in South Wales and press our cause there."

He wets his lips as though choosing his words carefully.

"I'm no diplomat, my lady. Surely there is someone else more qualified."

"But there is no one I can trust. Not like mine own kin."

His gaze searches mine. I mean every word I say. He is my kin and I do trust him. Ahern grimaces, doubtless knowing that much work lies before each of us now.

"As you wish, Your Grace. I leave at first light."

I nod in reply, turning to go. His hand on my shoulder stops me in midstride. I keep my back to him.

"You will look after Dyfed while I am away, my Queen?"

I raise an eyebrow, still not looking him in the face. Does he mean that I should look after the people or his future throne? Perhaps both. I clear my throat, glancing back at him out of the corner of my eye.

"I will do my duty, just as I expect of everyone else."

He nods in reply as though lost for words. I cannot tell whether he disapproves of the mission I have laid out for him or if he is merely fatigued. With a yawn he retires inside his tent.

I tread softly through the grass as it tickles my ankles, making my way across the encampment toward my own tent. Come dawn he will ride out of camp while I doubtless still slumber. I wonder whether he will glance back at the green dragon banner flying over my tent, and whether he will see me as a sister or as a queen.

More than a week has gone by, and every day I return to the dun. For a land in peril, everything seems eerily quiet. Ahern has not yet returned from Caerleon, even though he should have come back days ago. Nor have we received another rider from King Griffith or a single raven from King Iago. The entire world could be afire for all we know. Or perhaps nothing of consequence has happened at all. Either way, we simply do not know.

A gray dawn emerges in the east as I mount my pony. Artagan paces beside me, wearing a rut in the earth. Waiting like this makes a natural fighter like him restless. He clutches his sword as though afraid it might grow dull if he doesn't put it to use. Yet I cannot help feeling a measure of relief despite all the uncertainty. Not one danger has approached our ever-growing encampment of refugees, and not a single attempt has been made on my son's life since coming here. I don't understand it, but I've come to trust the magic of those standing stones atop the tor. As though from atop that ancient summit, the old spirits watch over my boy. As though he were one of their own.

I ride for Dun Dyfed, passing the morning journey quickly. Day after day, I have sat with Sab, discussing fragments of our pasts, each of us somewhat reserved with the other regarding our many secrets. We've even spent hours meditating, something Sab insists was important to both of the Old Tribes and the Picts in the olden days.

As I come within sight of Dun Dyfed, a speck on the horizon catches my eye. Another ship with a black sail diminishes in the distance. That's the third ship that has left Dun Dyfed in the past fortnight. But why and wherefore? Dozens of Pict longships still lie anchored along the shores, but I wonder how many more may have left. Perhaps Sab has sent them home to gather the remnants of her people in the far North, trying to escape the Emptiness that devours their lands.

Bal escorts me to Sab's main chamber, where she already sits cross-legged in a trance. Each time I enter the fortress, I peer down side corridors and peek at the throngs of Picts congregating along the walls. I never glimpse more than a few dozen of them at once. Ancient tunnels and vaults beneath the castle teem with voices. No telling how many more barbarians lurk in the underbelly of the castle.

Alone again, Sab and I sit in a tower solar overlooking the cliffs. It takes me a moment to remember. The stripped walls and bare floors look so different without the bedstead and stools that once crowded it. This was my childhood bedchamber.

Sab opens her eyes, a large bowl of dark water on the floor between us. Seated on the cold stones, we gaze down at our reflections in the black mirror of seawater. The Pict Queen touches the surface with her finger, sending perfect ripples across the water bowl.

"Both our ancestors would meditate for hours before a trance. Peering into the bowl of water, they would see things if they had the will and ability to see them."

"What would they see?"

Sab shrugs.

"It's different for everyone. Some see nothing at all. Others, the future, the past, or things happening now in places far away."

"What do you see, then?"

"Not much. I have another way I prefer to scry the secrets of the cosmos. I will show you another time perhaps."

The memory of her cutting open that deer carcass the other day resurfaces unbidden in my mind. A tiny knot forms in my chest. As though sensing my apprehension, Sab smiles behind her soothing voice.

"But first, let us see if the water chooses to speak to either of us today."

She closes her eyes, still as a gargoyle. I sigh, wishing we could discuss more regarding the Saxons first, but that will have to wait. Each day Sab promises that she will bring her people around to waging war with the Saxons but explains how they are tired of fighting and worn-out. In return, I allude to our interest in allowing them to stay in Dyfed, *if* they should help us in our standoff with the Saxons. Little progress has been made either way, but at least my daily visits have kept the peace. So long as I come, our truce holds true. Both sides have respected the lull in the fighting despite their mutual distrust.

I close my eyes, sitting cross-legged like Sab. At first, the rush of the sea outside the window fills my ears. I smell washed-up kelp drying out on the beaches. The subtle dampness of the sea air moistens my lips. My breathing stills as I pass out of thought and out of time, allowing myself simply to be. Without concerns or worries, without plots and plans. Just to be.

My eyelids flutter and I find myself leaning over the bowl. The sound of the sea has stopped. Everything turns still, except the dark liquid in the bowl. My cheeks flush hot as the water stirs and mingles with crimson and gold hues, one moment black as obsidian and the next as bright as stained glass.

A woman's voice slowly grows louder, her cries and grunts setting my teeth on edge. My own silhouette appears in the reflection. I see my face from afar, a face with eyes squeezed tight. The image of myself screams, my dark locks soaked with sweat. Several hands hold me up from either side as my swollen belly heaves with every shout. Blood runs down my skirts and onto the floor. I pull away from the water bowl, knocking it over as I tear at my own hair.

Suddenly, the room turns cold again, the gentle whoosh of the surf outside returns. I prop myself up on my elbow beside the spilled water.

Pawing my gown, I find no blood, just damp perspiration. Sab has not moved, her eyes fluttering open as she sits across from me.

"You are with child."

I sit bolt upright. Did she see the same vision in the bowl? That's impossible. But I saw it. Me, in labor pains, screaming my life out. And the blood everywhere, on the ground, on my hands. I swallow hard, my arms trembling. I saw my death.

Wiping the sweat from my eyes, I try to calm my breathing. Sab flashes a wry smile.

"You have the Gift. You saw something, a glimpse of things to come."

"You saw my birth pangs? Is that how you knew of the baby?"

She shakes her head.

"It doesn't take a shamaness to see that you are with child. You're probably two or three moons along? Even menfolk will be able to tell in another moon or so."

I turn to the side, not wanting to look her in the eye. Am I so transparent? Can every woman tell my secret? I feel naked before the Pict Queen, as though she can look into my heart. This is not what I expected when we sat down by the scrying bowl. I try to steady my voice.

"Have you seen into the future before?"

"Rarely," she admits. "The shadows of things to come are usually murky at best."

"Then that fate can be changed?"

Sab's eyes narrow.

"Your husband doesn't know, does he? Is it not his?"

"Of course it's his!"

She holds up her hands innocently.

"A mother's blood is all that matters. So it was for my people as well as yours."

I rise to my feet, brushing the wrinkles out of my tunic. I was the one who wanted to delve into the secrets of the Old Wisdom in the first place, but now I've seen too much. No woman should know her own fate, especially if she has no means by which to alter it. But there is always the bitterroot potion, isn't there? If I put it off much longer, I may find myself too far along and perish anyway. And even if I carry my child to term, will the baby live? I did not see that far into the vision, only my bellowing and the blood. I waver, slightly unsteady on my feet. Sab rises to balance me with her arm.

She feels oddly cold to the touch, those blue snaking tattoos along her arms making my skin prickle. I've never seen her skin paint so close before. More like sea monsters and dragons than serpents, they almost seem to writhe as her muscles move and contract. She calls for Bal before turning back to me.

"You are too weak to ride. Spend the night and rest before returning to your camp."

I shake my head.

"No, I'm fine, truly."

She smiles at me like I am a headstrong child.

"If something happens to you, it would bode ill for our truce."

"If I do not return by sundown, I assure you my husband will put an end to the truce himself."

Sab's smile fades. Perhaps I should have phrased it a better way, but the truth is the truth. Much as Sab's and my relationship has improved these past weeks, no amount of negotiation will move my husband if I go missing. Sometimes Artagan is more like a force of nature than a man. My presence is the only thing that can calm him once his blood is up.

"Very well," Sab replies. "Perhaps we should take a respite from our sessions. One day will put nothing amiss, no? Rest tomorrow in your own camp, and you may return the next day. I will keep our end of the truce until then."

I nod my head, grateful for her flexibility. I could use a day of rest. All this riding back and forth has taken its toll. Sooner or later these daily jaunts on horseback may have an ill effect on the child. If I choose to keep the child, that is.

The memory of my screams returns, the vision from the scrying bowl making me sweat anew. I know in my heart that the future I foresaw cannot be altered. Neither the pregnancy nor my death can be avoided. I shake my head, trying to clear my thoughts of such ill forebodings.

Bal sees me to my mount, and within a turn of the hourglass I ride alone, far across the moors in the fading light. A rising wind chills my sweat-soaked skin. Just before dusk, the wooden keep and campfires around Ogham Stone loom in the distance.

I ride slowly into camp, trying to collect my thoughts and allow the color to return to my cheeks. If Artagan sees me worn-out and pale as a ghost, he certainly won't let me keep riding to Dun Dyfed to treat with the Picts. Then our truce with the barbarians would meet an abrupt end indeed.

Something nags the back of my mind. Not since that first day have I seen Sab's vixen daughter. Not that I mind, of course, but it strikes me as odd. Perhaps the harlot has chosen to avoid me during my visits. If so, all the better. I still have half a mind to put an arrow in her after the way she fawned over Artagan. Maybe Queen Sab has seen fit to separate us. When it comes to such matters, Queen Sab has a truly perceptive mind. Ness and I would probably test the bounds of our newfound truce sooner rather than later.

I dismount and wend my way among the tents. Several peasants recognize me, bowing their heads as I pass. Many of them murmur "*Mab Ceridwen*" under their breath. Do even the commoners in Dyfed refer to me as such now? The very same pet name my subjects in the Free Cantrefs call me by. I suppose my daily efforts to keep the peace with the Picts may have something to do with it. But from what Rowena tells me, my lone jaunts to the standing stones atop the tor seem to have become popular gossip amongst the camp. No one other than myself dares to go up there. I nod and smile back at the refugees who bow my way, still unsure how to feel about such undeserved reverence. What have I done that any queen in her right mind would not also have done?

Inside the ever-growing keep of wooden timbers, I stable my pony before joining Artagan and his men around the central campfire. Gavin shouts merrily as he and little Cadwallon try to snatch glowworms in the grass. Rowena's little girls, Mina and Mora, cackle as the boys tumble over one another in their efforts to ensnare the tiny glowing bugs. A broad smile spreads across my cheeks.

I too once chased fireflies in my youth on these very moors, following the flickering lights as though they were tiny pixies. How remarkable that my son should repeat the same pastime I enjoyed as a child, even though I've never mentioned it nor remembered until this very moment. Artagan wraps an arm around my shoulder as the two of us watch the children dart after the iridescent lightning bugs.

A horse whinnies outside the palisade. Several guards call out to the rider, and my ears perk up, hoping that Ahern has returned to us. Instead, the bowmen escort a stranger into the keep and allow the traveler to dismount. Cloaked in a large white fur, I cannot make out our visitor until the person stops before me and lifts their hood. I falter back a step as my eyes go wide. Queen Olwen.

She flashes an uncharacteristic grimace, but even her twisted frown cannot mar her fair complexion and hourglass figure that draw the gaze of every man in camp. But why has she come, and come alone without guards or a train of attendants? Artagan and I exchange looks. Before either of us can speak, Olwen bores into us with her violet stare.

"I have been replaced as Queen in the North, ousted by some harlot upstart who has put a spell over my husband. She and her Pictish friends have taken over our castle in Gwynedd. The little tart calls herself Ness. I believe you know her?"

A leaden weight sinks in my throat. Suddenly, the past few weeks, the raid into Dyfed, and my meetings with the Pict Queen all merge together in my mind, leaving me with one undeniable conclusion. Queen Sab has played me for a fool.

9

At dawn, our army prepares to march on Dun Dyfed. Smoke rises from the dowsed hearth fires across the vast encampment beneath Ogham Stone. Within the ring of standing stones, I watch from atop the hill. My pony shifts her weight nervously beneath me. I pat her side. *Save your strength, girl. We've a hard road ahead.*

My writing hand aches from penning messages throughout the night, inking notes for riders and ravens. Correspondence to our forces at Aranrhod, our Gwent neighbors in South Wales, and anyone else who will listen. I stifle a yawn as I rub my eyes. I will feel awake enough once the march begins. A few hours of sleep will have to do.

Under the red sunrise in the eastern foothills, another contingent of several hundred bowmen joins our camp. Sir Emryus and Keenan lead the reinforcements from Aranrhod, jogging double-quick. Green dragon banners flutter in the early morning breeze. Every so often I note a female archer amongst our green-clad columns. Unlike most Welsh armies, our Free Cantref warriors have always counted a few spear-wives in their ranks. I smile with grim satisfaction, clutching my birch bow in hand. The Picts aren't the only ones with woman warriors.

Hunting horns blare as the archers march out of camp, my husband's half dozen knights leading the way on horseback. Scores of spear-men in dun-colored tunics line up beside them. Dyfed foot soldiers. At least Bowen and Carrick have managed to rally some of their countrymen to join us. Rarely since the days of the Old Tribes have spearmen from Dyfed and archers from the Free Cantrefs fought side by side.

I kiss my palm before pressing my hand to one of the standing stones. *Watch over us, old gods and new. We will need all the help we can get today.* My mount seems only too eager to descend the hill of ancient watch stones, nervous as always beside the ancient ruins.

I join Artagan in the forward ranks as the army disentangles itself from the encampment. Elders, women, and children cluster within the half-built keep. It will offer them some protection, but we cannot spare a single soldier to protect them. Our warriors must succeed today, or their kinfolk will have no defense should our enemies seek retribution.

Olwen nudges her white filly in front of me, barring my path. I clench my jaw as I move my pony off the main trail, allowing the rest of our soldiers to march past. The former northern Queen aims a stern finger at me.

"You deliberately endangered my son by bringing him along on this little adventure."

I open my mouth to speak, but she cuts me off.

"We'll discuss that later! We've little enough time as it is. Where are the children now?"

I make no move to answer her. The ungrateful woman! I've looked after her boy and my own these past three years, keeping them safe and sound with Rowena's brood. Now we must leave the protection of Ogham Stone, although I am still unsure why these ancient rocks have mysteriously kept the assassin at bay. But I won't let anyone know the children's whereabouts. It's for both my son's good and hers. The assassin might not distinguish between the two boys if he strikes again, possibly thinking it safer to dispose of them all. Even though my son has auburn locks and her boy is dark of hair. I fold my arms as I stare her down. I wouldn't tell her where the children are if the Pope himself threatened to excommunicate me.

Olwen's mare paws at the earth, sidestepping nervously. I fight back the urge to take a riding crop to the beast and send both Olwen and the horse out of my path. The Queen leans down, close to my ear.

"Your handmaiden and that nun have both gone missing. I know you sent them somewhere with the children."

My eyes widen. Damn her nosy ways! I doubt anyone else in camp noticed Una and Rowena's absence, but Olwen has a sixth sense for clandestine affairs. She could ferret out secrets from nuns under a vow of silence. I nudge my pony nose to nose with her mount, our mares snorting in one another's faces.

"You've trusted me these last three years with the safety of your son. Trust me a little bit longer."

"I merely want to see my boy! Do you think I would betray the children's whereabouts?"

"You would if you went to recognize them, even if inadvertently. An assassin hunts them."

"Who?"

I hesitate. Anything I say she will consider a lie, anyway. I might as well tell her the truth.

"My former husband, King Morgan."

"The dead Hammer King?"

"Him or someone who wields his old war-mask."

Olwen looks me up and down, like my mind has suddenly addled. I cringe as she looks down her nose at me, half skeptical and half full of scorn. She thinks me either mad or a liar, or probably both. Ironic. Some people immerse themselves so deeply in a world of lies that when they actually hear the truth, they can no longer see it.

But Olwen and I cannot banter all day. The rear guard of Artagan's small army passes us as they march into the western moors, their green dragon banners snapping in the breeze. We have a war to fight, no thanks to Olwen and her recently subverted husband. But I hang my head, knowing that part of the blame falls on me as well.

Queen Sab played me like a pawn, all the while using her daughter Ness to sink her hooks into the North Welsh kingdom. In many ways, this Pictish Queen has wrought more havoc than ten thousand Saxons ever could. She has planted the seeds of our destruction by taking power in the North. Unless we act quickly, she will turn Welshman against Welshman in a bloody civil war.

I gallop to the head of the column where Artagan and his knights ride. My husband gives me a quick glance. His normally jovial smile and cocky countenance have vanished. Today he is all warrior, a king, a killer of men. He nods my way, knowing I will not be kept out of this coming fight. Besides, we need every bow we can get.

Artagan alone knows where I have sent the children. Although I know he disagrees with me, he still trusts my judgment. My only hope is that I can outwit the assassin who stalks my boy. Until now, I have kept Gavin at my side or my husband's. Hopefully, the assassin believes Gavin rides with us.

Cantering my mare beside Artagan's stallion, the rumbling hooves of our cavalcade crack like thunder across the moors. Nonetheless, I keep my voice low so that only he can hear me.

"Do we have anything resembling a plan?"

"We've four hundred Free Cantref archers. And Bowen and Carrick have rallied nearly three hundred of their Dyfed countrymen to join us."

"Seven hundred soldiers. Will it be enough?"

"It has to be. What choice do we have?"

Artagan yaws into his mount's ear, spurring Merlin forward. The rest of the column picks up its pace behind him, the warriors on foot jogging faster. I glance back over my shoulder at the snaking column of green-clad troops, half of them toting longbows. The rest heft broad spears and rawhide shields. All veterans, all descendants of the Old Tribes. On any other day, I would bet my last copper on the valor of such troops. But the citadel of Dun Dyfed awaits us beside the sea. It will cost a thousand lives to take that old stronghold. More than we can spare. Brave as our people may be, Artagan and I may merely be leading them to their doom.

But my husband is right. We have no other choice. Yet we've defied the odds before, mayhaps we will again. God willing.

The fogbanks thicken across the moors as we approach the coast.

Mists obscure the horizon, reducing my vision to less than a bowshot in any direction. The perfect conditions for an ambush.

My forearms prickle as the whoosh of the surf murmurs through the gray vapors. The cries of gulls and the scent of salty kelp fill the air. We have nearly arrived but still cannot see a thing. Artagan sends out several scouts in each direction, but once they descend into the fog, they do not return. I swallow hard, thumbing my bowstring like prayer beads. Olwen rides up beside me in the mists.

"You grew up in this pea soup?"

"What are you doing here? Battle is no place for someone worried about chipping her nails."

Olwen hisses back at me. I thought she stayed behind at Ogham Stone. She may have ridden the length of Wales to warn us about her husband's alliance with the Picts, but that doesn't mean I trust her. Olwen remains with us only because our purposes suit her own. Today will be bad enough with Pict barbarians in front of me without having to worry about Olwen putting a knife in my back.

Her dark tresses hang in straight perfect sheaves, so unlike my own frizzy raven locks. In her spotless white gown, she looks like she rides to a ball, not a battlefield. She clutches a small dagger on her belt. I flash a wicked grin. I half-hope she tries to wield that little toothpick against the Picts today. Those blue-painted warriors will give her a surprise she isn't likely to forget.

The black outline of Dun Dyfed emerges before us as we halt outside its defenses. Artagan speaks in hushed tones, ordering his men to deploy for battle. A long line, three men deep, forms behind us. I crane my ears for any hint of the enemy, but their lookouts have not blown their horns to sound the alarm. Sweat chills my skin. They will wait until we come right up to their walls before they reveal themselves, like snakes coiled within their lair.

Artagan raises an eyebrow when he sees Olwen in our midst. He probably wonders as much as I do of what use she could possibly be on a battlefield. Perhaps she comes merely because she still bears a torch for him. But that ship has long since sailed, and it would be sad indeed if she doesn't realize it. Artagan takes my hand and gives is a kiss. I smile, despite the impending battle, glad to have his love and to have him near me. He turns his gaze on his soldiers, all business once again.

His poise and countenance today could not be more different from when we first clashed with the Picts a fortnight ago outside Dun Dyfed. He was all red eyes and fury then, barreling down on foes with all the wrath of a young knight. But today his gaze is cold and calculating, probably determining in his mind what troops to place where. Having to decide who will die and whether such sacrifices will bring us victory today.

And I always thought I was the tactician and he the valorous one. Perhaps I'm rubbing off on him. Although I know I could still find the headstrong hedge knight under his skin if I but scratch a little, Artagan has truly begun to transform into the tactical persona of a king. Ready to lead his men from the vanguard if need be, but, more importantly, laying out battle plans for his troops with the cool, passionless logic required to win battles. In his own way, I suppose he has also rubbed off on me. Despite my best-laid plans, I've found myself more often than nought having to improvise, and my decisions of late have been a bit more ruled my emotions than I care to admit.

Artagan turns to me in the saddle.

"Branwen, command the archers from here," he says in a gravelly voice. "Try to soften their defenses before I lead the main assault, but wait for my signal."

My heart stops, thinking of Artagan in front of his men and first into danger. But I steady my trembling cheeks. He needs me to be strong today, to show no fear or doubts. I nod toward Olwen.

"What about our shadow here?"

"Just keep her behind you. We may still need her, if we're ever to get King Iago back on our side."

I grab his arm as he turns to go, pressing my lips to his. Artagan's hard cheeks soften a moment under my touch. I cling to him, knowing I may never hold him in my arms again.

"Be careful, my love."

He flashes his old familiar grin.

"Hey, it's me."

That's what worries me. He dismounts and leads his men silently into the mists, toward the foot of the hill fort defenses. His warriors creep noiselessly amongst the mossy rocks and dune grass. Our only hope is to take the Picts by surprise and overwhelm them before they know what hit them. But Queen Sab is a crafty viper. She will not give up easily.

The archers with me silently nock their arrows and wait for my command. I put an arrow on my bowstring, wiping the dew off my sleeve. These pervasive mists bead every skin and fur with droplets of moisture. Olwen sidles up beside me, whispering beneath the wind.

"I don't understand. Why attack Dun Dyfed now?"

I grimace at Olwen standing so close to me, but I know that the only way to shut her up is to answer her question.

"The Pict Queen may have fewer forces since she sent her daughter to seduce your husband. She may not yet know that you have ridden to our camp and told us what happened at Iago's court. Our only hope is to catch Queen Sab off balance and attack her here at Dun Dyfed before she can gather her strength. Once she unites her forces with the North Welsh, she'll be too formidable for us even if we rally every soldier we have."

"But what if Sab has guessed your plan and her warriors are waiting for you up in that dun?"

"Then God help us."

A bird call whistles over the moors. Not the common seabird caw, but an inland thrush like we have deep in the forests of the Free Cantrefs. My ears perk up. It's Artagan's signal.

I draw back my bow, ordering my bowmen to angle their shots high. I do not want any stray arrow to hit Artagan or his men. Time to make it rain death over the crags of Dun Dyfed. I release my arrow as I shout to my warriors.

"Archers, loose!"

The twang of bowstrings hisses through the moors. A cloud of black arrows rises like a deadly flock of birds over the citadel. Moments later the clatter and thud of arrowheads hitting stone and wood reverberates within the hill fort. If the sting of a few hundred feathery darts doesn't alert the Picts to our presence, nothing will.

Artagan's men roar as they charge forward, their mingled voices surging up over the first line of stony defenses. Only glimpses of Dyfed spearmen and Free Cantref warriors show through the passing mists before the fog obscures them completely. I press my lips together and say a quick prayer for Artagan. *God, spare my love from harm this day.* I string another arrow onto my birch wood bow.

Olwen nudges me.

"What's happening? I cannot see a thing in this sea mist."

I shush her, craning my ears. Something has gone wrong. The usual clang of battle, the din of clashing men does not echo across the moors. Instead, a deadly silence pervades the surround. What the hell is going on up there? I urge my horse forward in front of my bowmen.

"Archers, make ready to charge."

Several bowmen exchange looks, but nonetheless they ready their bows or draw short-swords and spears. Whatever has happened, Artagan needs help and he needs it quick. Olwen snaps at me.

"What are you doing? Artagan gave you no orders to charge."

"I know what he said! Shut up, girl, or stand aside!"

I shout over the gusts of wind rustling my wild locks.

"Free Cantref warriors, forward!"

"*Mab Ceridwen!*" they chant in reply.

I spur my pony forward, headlong into the defenses of Dun Dyfed. My thighs grip my mount's flanks tightly as I aim my bow, intent on driving an arrow straight into the heart of the first Pict I see. I was born within the walls of Dun Dyfed, so perhaps it's fitting that I shall die here as well. Whatever fate has befallen Artagan, I intend to share it with him.

My mare whinnies loudly as she leaps over the first stone wall. A maze of rocky bastions radiates out from the center of the citadel. The mists swirl thickly around me, blinding me to all else except the roar of bowmen following close behind. Charging deeper into the ring of breastworks, I glimpse signs of the Picts everywhere. Piles of bleached bones, smoldering campfires, and strange runes chiseled into the stonework that mar every corridor and passageway. I dismount my pony, the narrowing passages growing too constrictive for a rider to pass.

My heart races as I peer down every corner, stalking toward the archways of the main hall. My arrow quivers on my bow, my fingertips ready to release it at a moment's notice. Baritone voices well up from deep within the castle. My eyes narrow as I step into the main hallway alone. Not a single Pict has assailed me yet. What is Queen Sab waiting for?

Footsteps jostle up a tunnel leading to the hall. I aim for the archway as a shadow looms over the threshold. The lone figure calls out, holding his hands over his head.

"Stay your hand, my Queen!"

I lower my bow, squinting at the man with an ax emerging from the shadows.

"Sir Keenan? What's going on? Where is my husband? Where are the Picts?"

He shrugs. Rowena's husband is a brave and loyal knight, but has never had an abundance of wisdom with words. I peer down the other passages leading to the main hall, wrinkling my nose at the lingering stench of feces and peat smoke. Gray-bearded Emryus emerges from another archway, his quarterstaff in hand.

"My lady." He bows. "We've secured the main keep and have men searching out the tunnels below the castle, but it will take some time. The underground cellars are extensive in places."

"What do you mean, Sir Emryus? What will take some time?"

"To secure the fort, my Queen. So far, it seems to be free of Picts."

"You mean the enemy is missing?"

Another voice echoes from the main archway.

"They're gone! Queen Sab gave us the slip."

Artagan marches into the main chamber with his longsword sheathed across his back. A dozen warriors march behind him. He steps around piles of manure on the cobblestones, fanning swarms of flies away from his face. The Picts have truly made a pigsty of the fortress.

Despite his frown, I rush forward to wrap an arm around him.

Both of us are whole and unharmed. Whatever has happened today, I will count that as blessing enough. But Artagan does not look so relieved.

"Once again, Sab remains one step ahead of us," he fumes. "Her ships are gone. They probably set sail no more than an hour ago. The castle hearths are still warm."

"But why would she leave? This fortress is near impregnable."

"She must have ferried more of her warriors into Gwynedd than we thought. I doubt she had more than a skeleton force manning the walls of Dun Dyfed the last time you visited."

I look to the floor. Artagan doesn't mean his last comment as a rebuke, but I cannot take it any other way. I had not the foresight to realize Sab was depleting her forces from the castle, and she did it right under my nose. I should have been more perceptive, more observant. But I could never tell how many Picts remained within the dun. They always skulked about, more down below the main keep than aboveground.

Bowen and Carrick enter the hall, cheering with several Dyfed spearmen. The Free Cantref warriors, by contrast, remain silent. Sir Bowen raises an eyebrow when he sees Artagan's unusually stony countenance.

"Why so glum, brave King? We've retaken Dun Dyfed from the Picts!"

"Only because they let us have it," Artagan snaps. "We needed to defeat Queen Sab before she could join forces with her new allies in the North. My guess is that her ships sail for King Iago's castle as we speak."

"Then the Picts are fools!" Bowen replies. "Dyfed is free once more."

Artagan shakes his head. Bowen and Carrick exchange looks, still not understanding the weight of the situation. I step between the King and the Dyfed men, trying to explain.

"Sab is not like a Saxon chieftain. She does not seek to directly conquer us and hold territory. She intends to carve us up, one kingdom at a time, by setting us against each other, and all the while the Picts and Saxons grow stronger on our borders."

The normally silent Carrick steps forward, his brows furrowed.

"But surely this is a victory today, is it not, my lady? We've retaken the castle without losing a soul."

I shake my head, raising my voice for all the soldiers gathered in the hall to hear.

"We've won the castle, but we may have just lost the war. Look what Sab has done to us! We've drawn our forces away to the west, far now from any Saxons or Picts. The barbarians have made us weaken our defenses to the east and north. As soon as Sab unites with Iago's army, she will set Welshman against Welshman by raiding the other kingdoms. Meanwhile, South Wales is already under attack by Saxons while we're sitting out here by the sea, a hundred leagues away from the settlements we need to defend from the barbarians. No, my brave knights, today is no victory but merely the beginning of a long defeat. There are dark winds rising against us."

My words gradually sink in, every warrior in the hall suddenly lost in his own somber thoughts. I could kick myself for my ignorance. I was blind not to see this coming, but who else could have foreseen it? No Welshman or Saxon would've given up a prize like Dun Dyfed, but Queen Sab has the cunning of an altogether different magnitude.

She might have bled us dry during a siege, but she would probably have lost in the end. Now her people are safely at sea, en route to the north. Within a week she will have a few thousand northern horsemen to back up her bloodthirsty Picts, and many a defenseless Welsh homestead will pay the price for our blunder today. How in God's name have all our carefully laid plans come to this?

Something catches my gaze.

A piece of torn parchment lies on my father's empty throne, where Queen Sab sat mere hours ago. I glance down at the water-stained page, just a few lines of text and a small hand-painted icon of a female figure. Probably penned by a long-dead monk who spent his life copying tomes of ancient history at the abbey. It makes my blood boil to think of all the books the Picts destroyed when they sacked the holy monastery. Taking treasured papers like this and using them to wipe their arses. Barbarians indeed.

But something about this tiny scrap of vellum draws my eye. The small icon looks like a noblewoman, a crown atop her head and with long dark tresses. I lift the page and read the fragmented words:

And the young Queen Vivian led her people away from the land of the Picts. Her followers came into Dyfed, where she wed King Vortigen where they have dwelt ever since . . .

My gaze narrows. It's a passage about my mother. I turn over the soot-covered page but find no more. I reread these unfinished lines over and over again. Finding this tattered inscription was no accident. Sab left this here on my father's old seat for me to find. But why?

It raises more questions than answers. My mother, Queen Vivian, lived near the land of the Picts once? No one ever spoke of such a thing to me. Not father nor my tutor, Abbot Padraig, God rest his soul. Yet Sab wanted me to know this. It was her parting gift, so to speak, yet I cannot decipher the meaning behind it. Perhaps she thinks I know more of my mother's past than I actually do. It appears as though this bit of text ought to convey some profound meaning, at least to someone who does know what my mother was doing living near the Picts long ago. Whatever Sab's game, this sheet was left behind out of malice. I sense it as thick in the air as the stink of dung that pervades this befouled castle. Perhaps if I can get to the bottom of this story about my mother, it'll at least give me some understanding of what goes on behind Sab's lifeless eyes. Why she does the things she does and what she hopes to gain. By such small measures wars and kingdoms are gained or lost.

But everyone who knew my mother in her youth has long since perished. And with the abbey destroyed, I've little hope of finding any record to illuminate this mystery. There must be some place in Christendom left that still maintains books containing the answers I seek. But where?

I almost instinctively turn toward the eldest man in the room. Graybearded Sir Emryus. I hand him the parchment.

"Sir Emryus, what do you make of this?"

The old bard strokes his beard a moment as he contemplates the words on the page.

"I'm afraid I'm of little help to you, my Queen. I know many a legend and song by heart, but ne'er have I heard one about your mother's youth. I always assumed she was raised in Dyfed, but evidently she must have lived near the Old Borderlands in Hen Ogledd once upon a time."

"Old Borderlands?"

"As you know, the Welsh Lands once extended much farther to the north and east than they do today," Emryus begins. "Entire kingdoms that have since been engulfed by the Saxon hordes. But even when your mother was young, there would've been a few Welsh realms that still directly bordered the lands of the Picts to the far North. I can only assume that the late Queen Vivian must have been there at some point, or at least that's what this scrap of parchment seems to allude to."

"Thank you, kind sir.

"I only wish I could be of more assistance."

He bows and moves away. His words linger in my head. The Old Borderlands. Lost realms of old Welsh kingdoms, somewhere to the northeast. What would my mother have been doing there when so young, and what of the Picts who lived nearby? Evidently, Sab knows much more of my mother's past than I thought. It is certainly disquieting to have an almost complete stranger like Sab reveal secrets about my own mother. *Oh, Mother, if only you were here now to help me.* So many answers she might give me. But I hang my head, knowing in my heart that wishing will never bring my mother back.

I stuff the tiny scrap of text inside the folds of my cloak and pace the hall. I wander closer toward my husband, his brow furrowed in deep through. Something else ails him as well.

Upon noticing me, Artagan takes me aside. The other warriors murmur amongst themselves. He leans close, not looking anyone directly in the eye as he whispers in my ear.

"We need to do something, Branwen. Whether or not our cause is lost, I will not go down without a fight. We must think of something quick, before things sour between us and the Dyfed men."

"Sour? They're the only loyal allies we have."

"Aye, but Bowen and Carrick think I want to claim Dyfed's throne. They've got their capital back, but no king. Bad as the Picts were, they did give us a united purpose with the people of Dyfed. That purpose is now gone."

"But the Picts will be back sooner or later."

"You know how short the memories of most men are. I give it a fortnight before Bowen and Carrick ask my army to leave. When that happens, we will be even weaker, with fewer warriors to resist the Picts and the North Welsh when they come."

"Then we need more allies, something to rally others to our banners and keep Dyfed confident in our alliance."

"There's no one left to ally with."

"What about South Wales?"

"The South Welsh are under attack from Saxons as it is, asking *us* for help. They'll not send reinforcements against the Picts while Saxons still harry their borders. Don't forget, the South Welsh and the Free Cantrefs have fought against one another more often than they've fought on the same side."

"Leave those worries to me. I'll ride for Caerleon today and meet with King Griffith."

"Are you mad? You're the only one in my household of Dyfed blood. Your presence is one of the few reasons these Dyfed knights even trust me at all. If you go, something's bound to go wrong sooner or later."

"You said yourself they'll probably ask you to leave in a fortnight no matter what. Besides, Ahern hasn't returned since you sent him to King Griffith. He's my half brother and of Dyfed too. I have to find out what happened to him. He might be in some kind of trouble."

"Which gives me less reason to let you go alone in the first place."

"Then send an armed escort with me. We don't have much time left, Artagan. Your army needs you here to hold it together. Let me try to talk some sense into King Griffith. It's our only chance. We *need* more men."

Artagan frowns, contemplating my proposal. He knows I'm right, but as usual doesn't want me anywhere near danger. But what place will be safe once Sab and her new army are set loose on Wales?

Olwen enters the hall, holding a kerchief to her nose as she sidesteps several small dung heaps. I groan with frustration. Even on the eve of a battle she continues to dog my steps. What does she want now? She stalks over to me, leaning in too close for comfort.

"A rider just arrive outside the gates, from Ogham Stone. She says her wagon was attacked on the road to Aranrhod."

"She?"

"It's your nun friend, Una. She says her wagon was ambushed by a lone rider who wore the horned mask of the Hammer King."

My cheeks blanch as I hold a hand to my lips. The assassin has struck again. My God, the children.

10

We stand in the morning mists that pervade the main courtyard of Dun Dyfed. The three of us with our cloaks bundled close against the cool breeze. My husband, Olwen, and I. Artagan hisses through clenched teeth.

"Christ wept, woman! You put the children in danger *again*? I thought they were supposed to be safe where you were sending them."

I grimace, trying to remain calm. It irks me to discuss this in the presence of others, especially in front of Olwen. The northern Queen seems to haunt my steps of late. Wherever I go, there she soon follows. She folds her arms, her lips hinting at the thinnest of smiles while my husband and I have our spat. I've half a mind to swat her across the face with my longbow.

Artagan's gaze darkens.

"I love you more than life itself, my dear. But sooner or later I fear you must choose whether to be a mother or a spear-wife. I do not think you can be both."

My jaw tightens.

"I am a queen, so I can and *must* be both mother and huntress if need be."

Artagan raises an eyebrow, unconvinced. Olwen butts in, as though anyone wanted her in this conversation.

"Some queens tend the hearth and raise their children whilst others put them in the care of servants while they attend to affairs of state. I know of no queen who has the stamina to do both."

I spin on my heel to face her.

"Then you've yet to see a woman of the Old Tribes do it!" I reply, before turning back toward my husband. "Don't make me choose between my children and my throne, Artagan."

My husband's eyebrows narrow, his eyes looking hurt.

"You misunderstand me, dear wife," he says in a soft voice, his gaze falling. "I'm merely trying to look after you. I would never make you choose one life over another. Life simply is the way it is, that's all."

I swallow a lump in my throat, suddenly feeling like the villain now. My beloved man only means the best, even if he doesn't see that his words still hint at an ultimatum. As though a woman cannot lead her people and tend to her children all at once. But my forebearers of the Old Tribes did as much, and their blood runs in my veins. I know I can be both a mother and a warrior-queen. I do not have to choose one over the other! Heaven help me, I will have both or perish trying.

Striding forward, I plant a soft kiss on my husband's cheek. He responds by wrapping his arms around me. He whispers in my ear.

"Be safe, Branwen. Bring both our son and yourself back to me."

I nod, my dry throat suddenly robbed of its voice. Artagan kisses me tenderly upon the lips, and for a moment I forget all else. He knows I've set my mind to go and does not bother trying to dissuade me from it. In many ways, he is a better man than I deserve. We each do what we must in trying times like these, and Artagan and I will weather these perils as we always have. Together, as equals.

Olwen peers at me from the corner of her eye. She stalks away without another word. The sight of Artagan and me so tenderly embracing seems to have robbed her of her voice as well. My gaze narrows as she disappears into the fog.

Outside the fort, I find my mount waiting for me.

I don a large sky-blue cloak to hide my ever-swelling belly. I cannot keep my pregnancy hidden for much longer. My thighs ache in the saddle as I dig my heels into my pony's flanks. No time for comfort. Artagan wouldn't even let me ride if he knew my condition. But my son is in peril somewhere out there and I have to find him. I have so little time.

A dozen bowmen on horseback ride a few lengths behind. Artagan must have put an escort of guards at my disposal, but I fear they will only slow me down. I've ridden the length and breadth of Wales before with no more than my bow and God's good grace. Perhaps I've pushed my luck. Maybe I will not come through this latest trial unscathed. But what mother ever really has a choice? I would trade my life for Gavin's in a heartbeat. The thought suddenly makes me come up short, halting my mare.

Here I ride at a breakneck pace to find my son, all the while endangering the child growing in my womb with all this jostling about. And to take the bitterroot potion now would probably spell death for both the child and myself. I suddenly realize that I have already made my choice. All along, delaying the inevitable, because in my heart of hearts I cannot bear the thought of harming the life within me. Even if it means my own death. I wince. The unbidden image of myself broken and bleeding after childbirth flashes through my mind. I draw a deep breath, swallowing hard. If that is my fate, so be it.

My guardsmen halt and exchange glances, wondering why I have suddenly stopped. A cool wind whistles through the heather that blankets the moors. Another pair of riders catches up with our small retinue. The green banners of Artagan's army still linger in the distance beneath Dun Dyfed. My eyes brighten at the sight of Una, but my smile quickly fades when I see Olwen galloping beside her. May the Virgin help me! Will that woman never leave me alone? My voice comes out harsher than I intend.

"Una! What's she here for?"

Unperturbed, Olwen halts her mare between us.

"My son is endangered too. Not you, or anyone else, will stop me from finding him."

I grip my mare's reins all the tighter.

"I ride on a dual purpose, Olwen. First to find my child, and then to treat with King Griffith at Caerleon to see if he will join our side in this conflict against the Picts. This is no journey for a king's mistress accustomed to pillowed litters and a warm bed."

Olwen jabs her finger close to my nose.

"*You* are the one who put my boy in danger in the first place! Now I will accompany you until you show me where he is and I can be assured he is safe."

Una, Olwen, and I sit quiet a moment in our saddles. The Free Cantref warriors give us a wide berth, their mounts nervously swishing their tails. I make a wry face at Olwen. Very well. I've little chance of getting rid of her, anyway. If she chooses to ride into harm's way with me, then be it on her own head. She is concerned for her child, after all, and I can hardly blame her for that. I give Una a knowing look as I reply to Olwen.

"Una hasn't told you, then? Good. Then she has fooled you as well as she did the assassin."

"What are you going on about?" Olwen snaps.

I nod toward Una, giving her permission to let Olwen in on our little secret. Might as well, especially as Olwen has no intention of letting us leave without her. Una clears her throat.

"The assassin did indeed attack my wagon on the road back to Aranrhod. I escaped because he was interested only in the passengers in my cart."

Olwen raises her voice until the cords show in her neck.

"You mean you deserted the children?"

"Nay, my lady. I did not have the children, just a handful of sheep hidden beneath the blankets in my cart. The assassin did not realize his mistake until it was too late."

"But then where are the children? Where is my son?"

"With Rowena," I explain. "He should be safely at Caerleon by now. Una's cart was a diversion. A decoy. Rowena took another wagon with the children, heading in the opposite direction in the dark hours after Una had left."

"Then my Cadwallon is safe?"

My heart suddenly grows heavy as I exchange looks with Una.

"If Rowena has already reached Caerleon. That's where we ride to find out. Griffith may have his disagreements with us, but he is an honorable man and would shelter my boy as he once did myself when I was younger. But the assassin has merely been tricked, not deterred. The ghost of the Hammer King will strike again now that he has realized his mistake. We ride posthaste."

I kick my heels into my pony's sides, yawing in her ear. Without a word, Una, Olwen, and my guards follow as we traverse the trackless moors to the southeast. Doubts plague my mind as the sun crosses the sky, rising past its zenith. Should I have sent guards with Rowena? But I couldn't. It would have attracted too much attention and undone our ruse before it began.

On top of it all, I've risked Una's life to divert the assassin. Artagan still doubts that Morgan has mysteriously risen from the dead to hunt our child, and I'm sure he is right. But he did not see the Hammer King when he cornered Ahern and me in that thicket. This killer is no ordinary mortal.

And what of my half brother? We've still no word since he rode to Caerleon. Ahern should have returned by now. What could possibly keep him? Nothing good. My temples throb from all the conflicting thoughts ruminating in my mind. War with the Picts, raids by the Saxons, and the northern kingdom turning traitor to Wales. All the while my brother goes missing and my son remains in mortal danger. It's enough to make my heart race faster than the tread of my pony's hooves. I urge her on. *Faster, my girl. Faster. We've so little time.*

The hours wane with the setting sun as our steeds splash through the fords along the rivers of South Wales. Undulating downs give way to woodlots and fields of budding rye. Every village we pass looks deserted, but the patchwork of well-tended fields tells me that the peasants have not fled. They merely hide within their hovels. Does even a small company of riders scare these commoners nowadays? Such have the past years of conflict taught our people. To fear any armed cavalry, whether they be Saxon or Welsh.

Finally, the ancient stone towers of Caerleon loom in the distance, their crimson dragon banners glinting brightly in the setting sun. Red-tile rooftops surround the castle, encircled by the town nestled along the banks of the river. Boisterous boatmen unload their produce along the docks. A crumbling amphitheater and a moss-covered aqueduct attest to the legacy of the Roman legions who first build the fortress that became Caerleon all those generations ago.

Butterflies flutter in my stomach. I've not see Caerleon since I was a teen, when first betrothed to the Hammer King. I wed and bedded him here, losing my maidenhood and for the first time answering to the title of Queen. How long ago it all seems, and yet my fingertips tremble as though I were still a mere girl of sixteen.

Hailing the watchmen on the outskirts of town, my bowmen put out word that the Queen of the Free Cantrefs has come to treat with King Griffith. Townsfolk in the cobblestone streets murmur as we pass, *Mab Ceridwen* on many of their lips. I might smile if the faces of the shopkeeps and fishwives did not look so serious. Even here, in the heart of Griffith's realm, rumor of my unusual deeds and namesake has reached the ears of the common folk.

The blood of the Old Tribes does not run as strong here. Many of the citizens inherited the aquiline noses and tan skins of the Roman legionnaires. Nonetheless, Caerleon has more citizens than any other settlement in the Welsh Lands. Thousands of people all congregate together in the old city, sporting the latest styles that their merchants have brought back from the continent across the sea. Men wear long hose breeches instead of the kilt tunics of the Free Cantrefs. Women pile up their hair in tight buns or lazy chignons, their skirts twirling with eye-catching warm reds and topaz. The dyes sold amongst the wares of Caerleon seem a far cry from the homespun woolens and fur tartans worn in Aranrhod or Dyfed.

Inside the gates of Caerleon, I dismount and enter King Griffith's main hall. A score of armored men-at-arms line the chamber walls. Their chain mail and steel helms glimmer under the torches, their red cloaks vaguely reminiscent of ancient Rome's long-lost legions.

Olwen and Una wait beside me in the eerily silent hall, our guards posted outside the entranceway. Griffith's throne is empty. Other than the guards, we stand alone in the colonnade of ancient pillars. None of the men-at-arms look us in the face, their gazes blankly focused elsewhere. I don't like this. My hand itches to grab an arrow from my quiver. A small voice echoes across the stone-tiled gallery.

"Mama!"

Gavin rushes out between the columns, his outstretched arms grasping my waist as he buries his face in my tunic. I touch his copper hair, pressing my lips to his soft cheeks. The insistent grip of his small hands assures me that this is all real. My boy, safe and sound, and in my arms again. He nuzzles close to my stomach, unaware he has his ear pressed against his younger sibling who swells inside me.

The other children enter the main hall, followed closely by Rowena and King Griffith. Olwen sinks to her knees and wraps her arms around her son. Dark-haired Cadwallon quickly puts his arms around her neck. Even though he rarely sees her, every boy remembers and longs for his own mother. Cadwallon follows Gavin's lead as he too presses his face against Olwen's skirts.

I bow before Griffith. The fat king smiles stiffly through his bearded jowls. As he turns his back to ascend his throne, Rowena flashes me a nervous glance. Something has gone amiss since she arrived here in Caerleon, but she dares not speak of it in front of Griffith. God bless her, though. Without giving herself away, Rowena has put me on my guard. I glance back at my bowmen clustered outside the hall. If only Griffith's guards didn't stand between me and my archers.

Queen Cordelia enters and takes her seat, licking some white powder from her fingertips. Probably cake or some such. She makes a great effort to squeeze into her smaller throne beside her husband.

Last, Prince Arthwys enters. For a moment, I do a double take. The young teen's broad shoulders and angular face look so much like his deceased father's. However, Arthwys has sandy hair and no beard where Morgan once sported locks dark as sackcloth. One glance from the young man's cold gray eyes sets my blood pumping fast. My former stepson still bears me more malice than ever, the ill will in his stare almost palpable. His livid glare must have something to do with Rowena's warning. Everyone in the chamber exchanges courteous smiles, but their grins seem fake as they shift glances from one face to the next. Griffith clutches the arms of his chair with his sausage like fingers, his young ward perching behind him like a hawk.

"You've put me in a difficult position, Queen Branwen."

I bow slightly again. An extra dab of courtly courtesy will not hurt. I must endeavor to stay on Griffith's good side if I'm ever to convince him to join us. But I sense another threat under the surface, only I have no idea what. As though my fate and the fate of my son may hang in the balance. What I do in these next few moments must be done with careful tact.

"I thank you from the bottom of my heart, gracious King, for sheltering my son and the son of Queen Olwen."

I elbow Olwen. She catches my drift, taking a bow and thanking him likewise. Griffith does not return our smiles.

"You give me no warning," he continues. "Instead I find your lady-in-waiting at my doorstep with four children, two of whom are heirs to two of the greatest kingdoms in Wales."

"If you will allow me to explain, King Griffith—"

He holds up a meaty palm to silence me.

"Your handmaid told me about the assassin. Let me assure you, Queen Branwen, your former husband has not risen from the dead to hunt for your beloved son. King Morgan lies interred in his crypt in this very city! I find your pretext for sending your boy here both preposterous and insulting to the memory of a former South Welsh king."

Griffith's voice booms off the rafters. Arthwys never takes his eyes off me. It requires little imagination to guess how he feels, especially with me accusing his dead father of trying to kill children. The Hammer King who died in battle against the Saxons became both a hero and martyr to his people. If only the commoners knew the warmongering Hammer King in private like I did. Arthwys certainly knows what kind of man his father was, which makes me all the more certain that he has turned into the spitting image of King Morgan. I can at least comprehend Arthwys's sentiments, but what has Griffith so riled? I decide to play somewhat dumb until I can learn more.

"Forgive my hasty actions, wise King. As a mother, I was merely concerned for my son and foster son. Someone has indeed tried to harm my boy, so I sent him here in the hopes that I might outwit the killer, knowing that none would dare to hurt a guest of the honorable King Griffith."

Griffith shifts uncomfortably in his chair. He does not entirely believe me, but at the same time his sense of honor and pride recognizes the need to protect my son. In all Wales, the relationship of a host and guest is considered sacred. Most of all for kings. After all, who would respect a king who could not protect guests and subjects in his own hall? Griffith leans forward in his seat.

"No one would dare harm your son under my care. I can assure you of that, my Queen. But you are here now, so you've no need to ask my continued protection. Yes?"

I wet my lips with my tongue, trying to choose my next words carefully. There is something in our conversation I'm still not seeing clearly. I've little doubt that the assassin could still strike at my son no matter how many guards Griffith posts around Gavin's bedchamber. After all, the assassin first struck at our home in Aranrhod. On top of all this, I must somehow convince Griffith to aid us in the coming conflict with the Picts and North Wales. But I can cross only one bridge at a time. I must be patient. I force a smile.

"Of course, my King. I ask only to stay a few days and rest. I've had a weary journey. I understand that my guardsman, Ahern, is here. I'd like to speak with him."

Griffith leans back in his chair, shifting his jaw from side to side.

"He is not here."

"What do you mean?"

"Your kinsman went to Caerwent to see the Saxon threat for himself. He has not returned."

A chill runs through me. Caerwent. The sister citadel to Caerleon, a full day's journey to the east. During my first husband's reign, Morgan made Caerwent his capital and fortified it with an army the likes of which Wales had never seen. In those days, it seemed that the high walls of that fortress could never fall. But since Morgan's death, the

Saxons have sacked Caerwent once, and although the South Welsh later retook it, the old citadel remains a ruined shadow of its former self. The common folk say the castle at Caerwent is cursed.

Rowena flashes me another look. Whatever warning she has tried to give me, it must have something to do with Ahern. I yawn, feigning a bit more fatigue than I perhaps feel, although the journey has certainly left me famished. Whatever further questions I would like to press Griffith about can wait. The King graciously excuses me, clapping for a servant to show us to our quarters. I feel Arthwys's heavy stare on me as I exit the hall.

When we reach the tower solar overlooking the river, I post several of my green-clad archers on the stairwell. Griffith may have guards aplenty in this citadel, but I don't trust anyone outside my own entourage right now. Olwen retires to a neighboring chamber with Cadwallon while Una excuses herself so that she may join the evening vespers in the castle chapel.

Rowena and Una exchange silent looks. Despite their loyalty to me, their mutual distrust remains high as ever. If only I could make them see each other as sisters like they once did. But their love for the same man will remain a barrier for the rest of their days.

Gavin plays with Rowena's girls in the corner, oblivious of all else but the small wooden toys Griffith's household has provided for them. I kneel down on the floor with him, my little boy cackling with glee as I take hold of a mounted timber knight and pretend to make it ride around his. My goodness, how my Gavin loves tiny wooden soldiers. My hearts stops a moment, thinking how my boy might someday have to ride real horses into battle, facing very real enemies with their long spears and knives.

But thankfully those days are a long way off. In the meantime, it's my duty to leave him a more peaceful realm than I inherited from my parents. I give my son a quick squeeze, the boy squirming under my smothering embrace. I rise to my feet, quietly watching him carouse with the other children.

Checking the lock on our bedchamber door, Rowena makes sure we are quite alone. She moves to the window, pacing beside the panorama of the riverfront and the crimson-tiled rooftops of the city below. I've rarely seen her so tense.

"Griffith is lying to you, m'lady. Though I do not know why."

"Did Ahern not go to Caerwent as he says?"

"He did, but only because the King banished him from the city."

"Why would he do that?"

"Griffith's guards caught Ahern breaking into the catacombs beneath the chapel. He was trying to open the Hammer King's tomb."

The hairs rise along my skin. Ahern could have only one reason for taking such a risk. He wanted to see whether Morgan is indeed entombed beneath the cathedral. He wanted to know for certain whether the Hammer King is really dead, or if he is actually the assassin who has been hunting my son. I grasp Rowena by the wrist.

"Did he see for himself whether or not Morgan is in his coffin?"

Rowena shakes her head.

"I don't think so. The guards caught him in the act. Griffith has posted a dozen men to watch over the tomb since then."

I begin to pace. If Griffith wanted to prevent thieves from defacing the Hammer King's casket, he would not need more than a couple guardsmen to do so. But a dozen soldiers? Griffith is clearly hiding something. He does not want anyone getting near that crypt, and he suspects that if Ahern almost succeeded, someone else might try again.

My temples throb as I hold a hand to my head. This only raises more questions than answers. Artagan sent Ahern here to evaluate the Saxon threat. To see whether only a few raiding parties or an entire invasion was happening in South Wales. We still don't know for certain. Presumably, the Saxons are fighting Griffith's forces near Caerwent, but it seems odd that King Griffith remains here at Caerleon when his army is elsewhere. I stop my pacing beside Rowena.

"How did you find all this out, Rowena? You've only been here a day or two."

"The kitchen servants wag their tongues a lot here, m'lady. Kings and knights never think their bondservants are listening, so they don't bother to silence them. I tried to find Ahern the moment I arrived, wanting to confide in someone I could trust. That's when I learned from the cooks about a Free Cantref herald banished from the city for breaking into the Hammer King's mausoleum. It had to be Ahern."

I nod with a grin. Rowena is worth her weight in gold. She risks the perils of the countryside to save my son and help bring him here. Then she learns more secrets in a few nights than I might have after a week of snooping around. I grasp her by the shoulder, giving her a kiss on the cheek.

"Rowena, you are better than I deserve. The sister I never had."

My handmaid smiles, returning my embrace with a hug. She glances back at the children as they play with their toys across the room. She keeps her voice low.

"I'm glad you're here, my Queen, but what do we do now? That assassin's still on the loose and will show up here sooner or later."

"We need South Wales as an ally, against both the Saxons and the Picts. But before I can convince Griffith, we need to find out what happened to Ahern, and how to stop the assassin before he strikes again. There's only one way to get to the bottom of this. We have to open up the Hammer King's tomb ourselves."

Rowena stands silent a moment, swallowing hard.

"But, m'lady, won't that sour King Griffith against us if we disturb the Hammer King's tomb?"

"It would, *if* he finds out. So we must make sure he does not."

"But there are a dozen guards watching the crypt at all times."

"Not only that, Morgan is probably entombed in stone, which means you and I won't have the strength to open his coffin. I'm willing to bet that Ahern was discovered as soon as he took a hammer to it."

"So between the guards and immovable stone, how are we supposed to do all this quietly?"

I sigh, glancing at my feet. This won't be easy, yet it's a greater risk if I do nothing at all. I have to make Rowena understand. I look her straight in the eye.

"We need to do three things first, and you're not going to like any of them."

Rowena raises a skeptical eyebrow.

"I take it that you intend to sneak into the crypt this very night?"

I sigh, trying to explain myself as best I can.

"First, we need to trust Olwen, to both watch the children while we're away and to swear we were with her the whole evening. Second, we need to steal a few vials from the castle apothecary, some *dangerous* vials, so to speak. Third, we will need Una's help."

Rowena frowns at this last part. She would risk betrayal by Olwen and palm a few unsavory potions before she would put her fate in Una's hands. But I trust both Rowena and Una entirely, and I need them to work together this night. Personally, I'm more doubtful about Olwen in the long run, but she will help us so long as her purposes and ours remain in line. I've no intention of telling her where I go or what I'll be up to, but she'll agree to play her part if she wants me to continue to watch over and care for her son when all these troubles are over.

My lady-in-waiting still looks pensive, her brows furrowed with worry. I give Rowena's hand a squeeze. She gradually nods her head. I know that no matter what occurs tonight, she will stay the course with me to the bitter end.

Warming my palms over the fireplace, the flames rise and fall under my eyes. Rowena glances at me out of the corner of her eye, never having grown quite accustomed to the way hearth fires flicker or goblets of water tremble around me. Yet she has the good manners not to say so. Nonetheless, she crosses herself before exiting the chamber so that she can go about the tasks I have set for her this evening.

The sky turns purple outside as the sun sets beyond the western hills. We've little time and much to do. Once the children are abed, I'll speak to Olwen while Rowena purloins the necessary ingredients from the apothecary's vault. Getting word to Una may prove a little problematic, but I will simply have to wait until she returns from evening vespers.

Someone pounds on the door, giving both Rowena and me a start. What the devil? More fists bang on the timber entranceway before Olwen's voice seeps through the planks.

"Branwen! Open up! Quick!"

I unlatch the lock, finding a pair of my guardsmen trying to restrain the former Queen. I wave them away, giving Olwen a moment alone with Rowena and me. Her violet eyes look wild with fright.

"He's struck again! The blackguard is here, in the castle!"

I try to shake some sense into the woman.

"Who? Who, Olwen?"

"The assassin! He left this embedded in the door of my chamber."

Olwen holds up a large dagger, its hilt gilded and carved with intricate knot-work. Clearly such a finely crafted weapon could belong only to a nobleman. My eyes widen as Olwen places the dagger in my hands. The blade drips with blood.

II

"Post all of our guards on the stairwell. Wait for me until I return. Say nothing of this to anyone!"

Olwen looks at me like I have suddenly sprouted a second head. She doesn't understand, and who can blame her? Things have been set in motion that can no longer be stopped. I hand the bloodied blade back to her.

"Hide this. Don't get rid of it, but keep it until we need it."

Olwen stammers, shaking her head.

"Branwen, someone has just tried to kill our sons! And you want to hush it up?"

"If the assassin wanted our boys dead, he would have simply struck. He would not have left a bloodied dagger."

"What are you saying?"

"I'm not sure myself. Only that something is afoot. Something has changed."

"We must tell Griffith, so he can protect us! Someone tried to harm our boys, now we must keep them safe with all means at our disposal. It's that simple!"

"This is anything but simple, Olwen! We don't even know whose blood this is! The assassin has made several attempts on my son's life, and now he simply leaves behind a bloody knife for the fun of it? No. I don't understand it myself, but we must keep our heads. I don't trust anyone outside our own guards right now. Everyone else is suspect. That includes Griffith and his men."

Olwen breathes fast and heavy before regaining her calm. Maybe my words have shaken some sense into her. Or maybe she simply doesn't want me to see her unhinged. I ball my hands into fists to keep them from trembling. I too want to roar like a mother bear protecting her cub, but what good would that do? We are caught up in a chess game of life and death, and I refuse to be played like a pawn again. We need to stay clearheaded.

Rowena returns with something bulging under her skirt. She nods as we exchange quick looks. Good. She must have fetched the materials I need from the apothecary. I turn to Olwen, gripping her by both shoulders.

"I'm putting my son's life in your hands, as you have often put yours in mine."

"Where are you going?"

"Never mind that, I'll return shortly. I need you to trust me, Olwen."

She swallows, looking me up and down. We've been adversaries over the years more often than we've been allies. We ruled rival kingdoms, resisted the Saxons, and loved the same man. But tonight both our boys' lives depend on our mutual trust. Surely, she understands that. Olwen straightens her posture.

"I will watch over the children tonight and guard them with my life. You have my word. But whatever you're planning, Branwen, do it fast. It had better work."

I repress a frown, my lips twisting into a sour face. I suppose we've struck as amiable a compromise as we ever will. She would rather run to Griffith for protection even when he clearly cannot keep us safe within his own castle walls. But at least my bowmen are here, and they are loyal to a man.

But how could the assassin have gotten by them? And why only leave a bloody knife? Whose blood is even on that blade? Killers don't typically leave a warning. Unless the killer really is Morgan, risen from the grave. Perhaps he simply wants to terrorize us first before slitting our throats. A shiver runs down my spine.

Every fiber of my being wants to run back into the bedchamber and wrap my arms around Gavin once more, but I fear that if I do, I may never have the courage to let go again. Instead, I peek into the room as he plays with the other children, blissfully unaware of the peril he is in. Sleep well, my little darling. Mother will not let anything harm you tonight. I promise.

Setting my jaw, I descend the shadowy stairs with Rowena. My green-clad archers congregate around the entrance to the tower, their longbows polished and strung for a fight. If anyone does return to the tower this evening, he will taste the steel arrowheads of Free Cantref warriors.

Rowena and I steal through the dark corridors of the castle complex, most of the inhabitants already abed. Crickets chirp as the moon rises through the clouds overhead. Rowena hands me a bundle of clothes. I thread my arms through a dun-colored robe, the kind that a nun would wear. I pull the hood down over my face as Rowena whispers beside me.

"M'lady, it's still not too late to turn back."

"You spoke to Una, I gather?"

"Aye." She frowns. "She's waiting for us."

"Good. We have to do this, Rowena. Everything hinges on it."

Rowena opens her mouth to speak again, but the castle chapel looms before us. A dozen red-caped guards linger outside the entrance. The sole archway leading into the crypts below the church, and Morgan's grave.

Una appears beside us, silent as a wraith. She hands both Rowena and me rough hempen rope to tie around our waists. Her voice barely registers above a whisper.

"Let me do the talking. Keep your hoods low. You're supposed to be subservient brides of Christ."

Even in the shadows, I can sense Rowena's shoulders tightening. She has no taste for taking orders from Una, but we've no time to argue. We follow Una single-file toward the guards. The guardsmen tell jokes and pass a jug between them as we approach. They fall silent when we stop in front of the church. The head guard puts a palm in front of Una.

"Chapel's closed, Sister. No one enters. Orders of the King."

Una attempts to walk around him, unfazed.

"I was in the chapel not an hour ago for evening vespers. I still have work to do."

"Work?" the guard bellows. "At this hour?"

"The work of God, you foolish man of the world! Now step aside."

The guard's voice turns grim.

"No one may pass."

Una doffs her hood, clasping a crucifix in one hand. She bores into the soldier with her dark gaze, aiming a disapproving finger at him. He flinches as though her fingernail were the tip of a knife.

"We pray for the souls of the departed. Souls like yours that have spent their life spilling blood and now rely on the prayers of the holy to beseech God to lift them from purgatory toward paradise. Think well on it, soldier. When you pass into the next life, all that may stand between your soul and eternal damnation might be the prayers of a few barefoot nuns like me."

The guardsman swallows hard. His companions seem equally sobered, putting down their wine jug. Their gazes collectively fall to the floor. Each warrior has surely slain men and broken many a commandment for love of king and country, but they nonetheless fear the lake of fire of which the priests preach.

I wince at the thought of such a dismal afterlife. It seems too cruel to be anything other than the invention of spiteful priests, but nonetheless the people clearly believe it and so do these men. Thinking on my own sins, I prefer to dwell more on God's forgiveness and the promise of paradise. Maybe the Old Ways that Annwyn stuck to made more sense, souls being reborn with each new generation, seeking to continue to grow and learn lifetime after lifetime.

But I shake my head. This is not the time to contemplate such weighty matters of life and death. We've work to do.

The head guard motions for us to enter. He eyes each of us as we hide our faces beneath our hoods. I start to sweat. If any of these men should recognize me, our ruse is at an end. Foolhardy queen that I am, I should not have come. But I have to know who is really down in that crypt. It was my decision to do this, and I must see it through.

The guard looks me over before allowing me to pass. I sigh with relief. The lead guardsman calls after us as we shuffle into the dark church.

"Do not take too long, Sisters. Or the king shall have my head and send me quicker to the next life than I wish."

His fellow guards laugh, but it is a forced laugh. They seem just as nervous as we do. Perhaps we all risk our lives this night.

Once inside the nave, Una leads us behind the altar, where we descend narrow, winding steps into the dark. I blink against the pitch-blackness but cannot discern anything from within the dim crypt. A rush of cold, dead air prickles my skin. Although I cannot see anything, I instinctively know that I am surrounded by the dead.

Una kindles a torch with the tinder and brand in her hand. She must have hidden it beneath her robes. She lights another set of torches for both Rowena and me. The three of us descend deeper into the stony vaults, our orange torchlight illuminating the mausoleum of stone walls. Each paving stone bears an inscription, a name and the memory of the bones that lie behind it. With every step, I know that I tread over the remains of long-dead ghosts. Even behind the stonework and shadows, I feel their ancient eyes upon me.

I talk to keep my mind off the skeletons entombed behind every cold slab.

"That was brilliant the way you got us past those guards, Una."

Rowena interrupts, crossing herself as we tread through the catacombs.

"Even those dimwits will grow suspicious if we take too long. I doubt we have half a turn of the hourglass before they come to remove us, whether we are nuns or no."

Una snaps at her without a backward glance.

"I told a lie so that you could come here and disturb the dead! That's two sins in one night I will have to do penance for. Worry not so much about your mortal life. It's only a matter of time before we end up just like the men and women interred in these tombs."

All three of us cease talking. Only the sound of our footsteps echoes off the narrow stone corridors. How many generations of Christians lie buried in this dim complex? Probably some burials date back to the Roman period when followers of Christ were persecuted by the Empire and forced to conduct their rituals belowground.

Una halts at the end of an archway over a large stone funerary box, its surface chiseled with Latin inscriptions and the Chi-Rho. My knees start to tremble, the coldness in the floors seeping right up through my feet. By the glint of our torches, a name emerges from the dusty stone slab: MORGAN SON OF MEURIG, KING OF GWENT. Una's voice barely registers above a whisper.

"This is the Hammer King's crypt."

I clutch my torch close, keeping it between myself and the limestone coffin. As though my former husband might leap out of his crypt and wrap his hands around my throat. Rowena seems to sense my thoughts.

"Do you really think he's the one hunting your son?"

"Let's find out."

"But how? It would take a dozen strong men to lift that slab. You'll never get it open!"

Without a reply, I extend my hand. Rowena fishes out several vials of fluid, purloined from the castle's apothecary at my request. I remove a small flask from my garments and begin to combine the potions. Rowena throws up her hand.

"M'lady, those are just commonplace substances. Why do you need them?"

As I add each vial to the mix, the liquid in the flask begins to bubble. A misty broth rises from its surface. I talk over my shoulder as I work.

"Commonplace potions alone, yes. But Lady Annwyn taught me that in the right order, even the most mundane cordials possess rare magic. Magic that only the women of the Old Tribes learned to unlock."

Una stands over me, her voice trembling for the first time.

"Mistress, whatever black arts you're using, what do you hope to gain by them?"

"Either my former husband is trying to kill my son or he is not. I must know what's inside that coffin."

Adding the final ingredient to my potion, it nearly boils over as it glows with an iridescent green tint. Both Rowena and Una back away as I gingerly clasp the volatile elixir in my hands. I stand over the stone sarcophagus. A sickening flush rises up through my veins, as though I stand upon a precipice. I clench my jaw. No time for doubts now. Whatever happens, I must risk opening Pandora's box and accept my fate.

I pour the glowing emerald liquid around the edge of the cover stone. It sizzles as the potion drips along the seam of sealed masonry. Smoke rises from the rim of the crypt, as though the devil himself might soon emerge.

A low rumble thunders within the limestone coffin. Several large cracks spread across the slab, branching out like lightning bolts. A puff of putrid air escapes from within the fragmented sarcophagus. The cover of the stone coffin has been broken, undone by the potion eating away at its mortar. The three of us stand silent before Rowena breaks the stillness.

"What do we do now?"

I wipe the sweat from my brow.

"The top slab is still too heavy for us to lift, but together we might remove one of these cracked pieces. Just enough to glimpse inside."

Una looks at me with wide eyes.

"And what do you expect to find?"

"If Morgan's body is there, it means he couldn't be the assassin. But if he's gone, then we know he must somehow still be alive."

Rowena clutches my arm.

"What if he *is* in there, but he's a ghost . . . the one that's been haunting your son?"

A tremor rises up through my bones. I struggle to steady my voice.

"Then only God can help us now."

I wrap both arms around a loose fragment of the coffin lid. About the size of a small, flat boulder. I can hardly budge it. Rowena and Una get on either side of me, all three of us taking hold of the shattered piece of stone. I count to three before we heave with all our might. Each of us strains until the cords in our necks show, our torches flickering on the floors behind us. I grit my teeth as sweat runs down my temples.

With a groan, we push the chunk of rock over the lip of the coffin. It hits the ground with a heavy thud that echoes throughout the catacombs. If the guards aboveground didn't hear that, they must be as deaf as the skeletons down here with us. We probably have only a minute or two before they come down into the crypts and find us.

A cloud of dust permeates the coffin. I waft away the gray mist, coughing as the sulfuric fumes of the stone-breaking potion sting my nostrils. No living person has laid eyes on the interior of this sarcophagus since the day Morgan was laid to rest. The Hammer King. The man who was my husband, then my enemy, and perhaps my enemy still. I place my hands on the edge of the coffin and lean in to take a look.

I blink, pawing around inside the dim confines of the crypt. Una grabs a torch and holds it over my head. My skin turns cold. The coffin is empty.

The heavy clank of chain mail reverberates down the corridor, voices filling the dim passageways. Torches flash from every side as guardsmen encircle us with their short-swords and glaives. Rowena and Una raise their hands over their heads.

I stand still as a gargoyle, dumbly staring into the vacant crypt. Morgan is not there. I choke down the bitter bile in the back of my throat, trying not to retch. Morgan lives.

The lead guard approaches me with a set of manacles in hand.

"All of you are under arrest."

Even when he claps the irons on my wrists, I do not look away from the hollow tomb. I shut my eyes. All is lost, all is lost.

At daybreak, King Griffith comes storming into the dungeons, his heavy tread echoing off the stone floors. I sit up on my cot, a thin beam of daylight streaming in through a high arrow slit. As dungeons go, the cells at Caerleon are not bad, almost tolerable. Almost.

Griffith halts in front of my cage, waving his guards away. His bearded jowls shake as he pounds his fist against the bars.

"You desecrated the grave of one of our most honored monarchs!"

"There was nothing to desecrate. Morgan's not there. But you knew that already, didn't you?"

Griffith gnashes his teeth. I pace the length of my cell. Where they've put Rowena and Una, I can only guess, but they must be isolated in a cage similar to mine. Wearing only the ill-fitting nun's robe from last evening, my swollen belly protrudes like a small hump beneath my garments. I must be closer to four moons along by now. I gently rub my subtly ripening stomach. Griffith's eyes grow wide as chicken eggs.

"My lady, you are with child?"

"My husband doesn't know yet. Otherwise, he wouldn't have sent me to treat with you. Nonetheless, I'm sure once he learns that his pregnant wife and son are imprisoned within your castle he shall arrive here shortly . . . along with his army."

Griffith's cheeks pale. Despite his anger, he knows that Artagan will come for me no matter how many Picts, Saxons, or Welsh stand in his way. Odds be damned. I repress a smile. Sometimes my husband's reputation for recklessness provides me with a most useful bargaining chip. Griffith narrows his gaze, trying to look stern, but I can tell that my words have taken the starch out of him.

The King aims a fat index finger at me.

"You have still damaged a king's grave."

"An empty grave. You built a king's monument without a king inside it."

"My people need a hero, someone to inspire them, and the Hammer King's memory does that."

I fold my arms. Griffith does have some wisdom. He is not the dashing warrior my husband is, but his people must be inspired nonetheless. He has given his people an ideal, not with himself but by revering the legacy of his predecessor. Morgan's memory reminds the people of South Wales that they were great once and can become great again. How ironic that Morgan's reputation should inspire such honor in people. Few people knew Morgan as I did. Was he ever truly honorable? More like cunning and relentless, but history is written by those who survive, and both Griffith and I intend to survive. I take a step closer toward him, choosing my words carefully.

"It would certainly damage morale in Caerleon to learn that the Hammer King's revered tomb is empty. Their monument to their hero, a mere hollow shell. But who really knows this? You and I, and a few guards? It's still a secret. With some simple repairs to the crypt and several paid-off guardsmen, it could remain a secret."

Now Griffith takes a turn to pace, glancing at me from the corner of his eye. He understands that my offer is both a means at reconciliation and a threat. Repairing the crypt will restore prestige to his catacomb, and keeping the secret will keep his people's morale up in these trying times. A secret he now needs me and my household to keep private. Griffith stops, leaning his face nearer the bars.

"You would keep this secret?"

"If you let me out of this prison."

"What about the repairs to the tomb? It will be costly after the witchcraft you did to it."

"I am a queen with some means at my disposal. My kingdom can spare a few coppers as a gesture of goodwill between our realms."

Griffith strokes his beard, considering my offer. It allows him to keep his precious honor and his city's pride intact, all the while enabling me to get out of this cage without starting another war. But something in Griffith's searching eyes leaves me unconvinced. I swallow, trying to keep up my mask of calm. Trapped like a bird in a cage, I have nothing but my wits to protect me and my unborn babe. Griffith taps his brow.

"One thing I do not understand. You think Morgan lives, and hunts your son, yes?"

"I know it now."

He shakes his head.

"I too was at the Battle of the Bloody Fords, remember? I saw Morgan die. The Saxons took me captive. I watched as they dismembered the Hammer King's corpse. They made trophies of his arms, legs, head, his . . . extremities. They burnt the rest. So you see, Morgan has no body, yet I found a way to honor him nonetheless."

I wag my head. Griffith did not see the assassin in the thicket that day Ahern and I encountered him. I stick my head between the bars, nearly nose to nose with the King.

"That's not possible! I've seen the assassin. His build, his hammer, his mask. It's Morgan."

"Then it must be a ghost, because the Hammer King is dead!"

He scoffs, looking away. I wonder if he believes what he says. He may have seen Morgan die, but I saw him come after my boy not two moons ago. I don't know how those two things could both be true, but somehow they are. Somehow I must convince him. If he does not trust me enough to believe Morgan hunts for my son, he will never trust me enough to form an alliance with us against the Picts. I must put my best chess piece forward in order to earn a victory here. I clear my throat.

"Gracious King, please send one of your guards to Lady Olwen. She has something I think you should see. Something that may convince you better than any of my words."

Griffith raises a skeptical eyebrow but nonetheless calls for one of his guards. After acceding to my request, he sends his guardsman off. Minutes later the soldier returns with something wrapped in a bloodied cloth under one arm. The guard pants out of breath as he hands the concealed object to his King.

Griffith frowns as he unwraps the bloody dagger. His eyes widen when he recognizes the make of the blade and its polished handle. Well-crafted South Welsh steel. This could have belonged only to a well-to-do nobleman like the Hammer King. I choose my words with care, knowing that this is the moment to make my point. If I do not convince him now, I never will.

"Does that look like the handiwork of a ghost, my King? It was embedded in the door behind which my child sleeps."

Griffith blinks in disbelief.

"This happened in *my* castle?"

"An assassin has followed me here to Caerleon. One who knows the castle well enough to sneak past your guards and mine."

Griffith clenches his fist around the hilt until his knuckles turn white. He does not want to admit that I am right. Only someone like Morgan would have had a blade like this. Only Morgan would have known all the secret passages within the castle. He once ruled over

Caerleon and Caerwent, after all. Griffith examines the tarnished steel.

"Whose blood is this?"

I shrug. If only I had more answers to give him. Nor do I know why the assassin tried to hurt my boy twice before, and this time merely left a crimson dagger to taunt us. Of course, if Morgan is indeed a ghost, perhaps he can sense our fear. Perhaps he merely savors the taste.

Griffith lowers the blade. Without looking at me, he paces toward a sunlit arrow slit. A shaft of copper light cuts across his face.

"If I let you out of your cell, where will you go? I doubt you'll linger in Caerleon now."

"I make for Caerwent. My kinsman, Ahern, went there last before he disappeared."

"The Saxons are there! My men hold the castle, but the countryside to the east is crawling with barbarians."

"Which is exactly why I must go there and see for myself."

"You still think the Picts who have Iago's ear are a greater threat than the Saxons?"

"I don't know, but I intend to find out. The answer lies at Caerwent."

"As do God knows how many Saxons. You would risk such peril?"

"These are perilous times. We must risk much if we are to survive."

Griffith sighs.

"Then you will not go alone. It would shame me to my dying day if a queen heavy with child braved the dangers of the Saxons while I sat at home behind thick walls. When do you plan to depart?"

It takes me a moment to gather my wits. Does he jest? I very nearly stutter.

"I plan to leave right away."

"Then we make for Caerwent and the peril of the Saxons posthaste."

12

I grab my third bun from the basket on the table. A serving girl deposits another bowl of piping-hot stirabout in front of me as I down my second mugful of milk. My rumbling stomach hungers for more. I seem to have become a bottomless pit of late.

Sitting in the central mead hall of the castle, I devour another plate of eggs while a servant refills my cup. Rowena, Una, and Olwen sit opposite me, nibbling at their meals while the children make a mess of their breakfasts. Gavin and Cadwallon launch spoonfuls of porridge across the table at one another, cackling behind their tiny makeshift catapults. Olwen chides them both, but they always seem to find another spoon. Rowena's little girls keep putting their palms into their pudding, smearing it across the table.

Grabbing Gavin by the wrist, I drag my squirming boy over to my side of the table and plop him on my lap. He struggles against me with his stout, meaty arms, his thrashing subsiding only when I begin to spoon-feed him his stirabout myself. The child inside me somersaults, making the bile rise in my throat a moment. But at least Gavin is calmer now, greedily devouring the breakfast I spoon into his little gullet. I smile down at my hungry boy as I wipe some stray oats from his chin.

I hear Griffith's footsteps before I see him. His heavy tread rattles the bench under me. After a cursory glance, I devour another handful of fresh berries. Griffith certainly keeps a well-stocked table, I'll give him that. The King clears his throat, dispersing his servants. I understand the gesture. He wants the two of us to speak alone. I nod to Rowena, who nudges Una and Olwen. The three of them herd the children to a mead bench several table lengths away. Gavin slides off my lap to join his companions. The boys' boisterous voices and the girls' laughter reverberate off the rafters. Griffith sits down opposite me, the bench groaning under his weight.

"The horses are saddled, my soldiers ready to depart. Your wagon has been prepared."

"Wagon? I already have a mount."

"Aye, a mountain pony. Barely fit for a peasant but hardly appropriate for a queen, let alone one so far along with child."

My eyes narrow, my skin growing hot. Griffith raises a placating hand.

"Please, this request comes from your own lady-in-waiting. She insists that a woman in your condition should not mount a horse. Bad for the baby, she says."

I flash Rowena a glance across the room. She shrugs sheepishly, no doubt guessing the words that pass between the King and me. She is right to insist, of course, but a wagon will only slow me down. It's hard to feel much like a warrior-queen when astride pincushions in the back of an oxcart.

Griffith stabs a sausage with his knife.

"I don't claim to be an expert in womanly affairs, but it would certainly bode ill for both our kingdoms if the Queen of Aranrhod miscarried while in my care. Agreed?"

I frown, nodding reluctantly. I don't mind their concern so much as I do the lack of choice I seem to have in the matter. It still amazes me how once a woman becomes a queen, her body no longer belongs to herself but to the kingdom at large. The only heirs who can sit on Artagan's throne after him will come from my womb and no one else's. Such is the power that all queens have wielded since the days of the

Old Tribes. But with such sway comes a heavy price, the need to produce offspring for the greater good of the realm.

Gavin and Cadwallon merrily chase one another around mead benches, earning frowns from the servants dodging out of their way. I pat my round belly and the life inside me. Whatever will become of my beloved boy and his unborn sibling? Will they have to sit on thrones, lead armies, or submit to arranged marriages as I have in my time? It's hard to imagine Gavin as anything other than the cherub-cheeked princeling I adore. He is just a boy, but already some cold-blooded assassin seeks to snuff out his life before it has even begun. Does the same fate await the infant growing within me? I sigh. If my vision of childbirth holds true, I doubt I will ever live long enough to get to know the babe growing inside me.

After finishing my bowl of porridge, I stuff a few more buns into my robes. Who knows when I will find my next full meal on the road? The Saxons have likely stripped the countryside bare.

Rising from my seat, I pull Griffith aside with a gentle hand on his arm.

"Good King, you've been a lord and ruler in Wales longer than most."

"That's a kind way of saying I'm getting old and fat," he replies with a cordial smile.

"I did not mean it that way, Griffith. Instead, I was curious what you might remember of my mother . . . when she was young."

"Queen Vivian?" he replies with his eyebrows raised. "I knew her not when she was Vortigen's wife. Sadly, we never got the chance to meet. Why do you ask?"

I shake my head, trying to hide behind a sad smile.

"Nothing. I was just curious."

Griffith scratches his beard a moment.

"My clerics have some histories recorded from older manuscripts, here and at Caerwent. I'll ask them to see if any reference the late Queen of Dyfed."

"Thank you, Griffith. My memories of her are so few. I suppose I look for any scrap of knowledge about her life that I can nowadays."

He calls aside a passing servant, giving him orders to send for his clerics to search their tomes for any word about Queen Vivian of Dyfed. I thank Griffith again, still wondering what if anything his scribes might possess that would be of any use to me. It seems if I am ever to discover what my mother was doing near Pictish territory in the days of old I will have to ask Sab herself about it. The mere thought makes my skin crawl.

Outside in the castle courtyard, my dozen archers sit astride their small mountain ponies. Several of the bowmen's feet hang barely a few hands above the ground. Griffith's guardsmen exchange grins. They doubtless consider our small Free Cantref mounts little better than dogs with ponytails. But these lowlanders have never seen one of our stout upland ponies traverse the side of a mountain in a thunderstorm. I doubt any of their thoroughbred horses could withstand such a test.

Griffith mounts a well-muscled bay. The stud whinnies under the King's immense weight. The sight of it makes me wince. They must have found the strongest beast in the kingdom to hold his prodigious girth. I would have put money down that Griffith could no longer mount a horse. Griffith blushes red in the face, looking almost as amazed as I am that he can still keep himself in the saddle. Several of the children snicker behind us. I chide them with a quick hiss.

I should not mock Griffith, even in my mind. I look no better as I step into my hay-filled wagon. A quartet of horses stands tethered to the front. I take up the reins and place myself on the front lip, trying to keep my composure like some queen charioteer. Instead, I look more like a peasant girl in the back of a donkey cart. Barefoot and pregnant. So much for looking regal.

Gavin, Cadwallon, Mina, and Mora all pile into the back of the wagon. To them, this is all just another marvelous adventure. I fake a smile, playing along with their game of make-believe. What kind of mother am I? Leading them into danger, toward a place where my kinsman has disappeared and Saxon barbarians roam at will. But what safer place is there for them? Picts linger in the North, and an assassin stalks our steps. If our fortunes do not change for the better, soon every child in Wales will suffer our enemies' wrath.

Rowena and Una sit on opposite sides of the cart, keeping the children between them. It also gives them an excuse not to talk to one another. Olwen mounts her white filly, looking down her nose at my hay-stuffed wagon. Let her. I may look like some farm girl in a jaunting car, but at least I am still a queen in truth. I have a husband and a home to return to. Let Olwen have her pretty white horse. Aside from that and her young son, the poor thing doesn't own so much as a pot to piss in.

Griffith leads a column of red-caped soldiers out the castle gates. A few hundred infantrymen in jangling chain mail and steel helms march down the old Roman road toward the eastern woods. Hundreds more guards line the battlements of Caerleon, watching us go. If only Griffith would march more of his troops outside his walls. But the threat of the Saxons on his eastern borders has him curled up in his shell.

Imagine what we could do if Free Cantref archers fought alongside South Welsh swordsmen. Griffith's troops and ours might actually stand a chance against Queen Sab and her Picts. But Griffith won't do that. Not so long as the Saxons have Caerwent besieged. Caerwent, the last place in Wales I should be heading, and the one place my destiny seems to be leading me toward. The Fates truly work in mysterious ways.

As we pass beneath the tall towers of Caerleon, a sickly chill runs through my bones. I look up at a pair of dark eyes boring into me from one of the highest parapets. A figure with his hands on his hips, silhouetted blackly against the morning sky.

Arthwys.

The young Prince stands still as a gargoyle. I can almost feel his eyes smoldering a hundred lengths away. His father once looked at me that way, silent and menacing. On the night I fled his castle forever, with Artagan and a stolen horse. Morgan hunted me for years after. Perhaps he hunts me and my son still.

A dark tremor runs through my mind. Could the young boy be impersonating his dead father? If anyone has the build and the means to obtain Morgan's old war-mask, it might be him. But no. I quickly dismiss such foreboding from my head. He is still a boy, after all. But perhaps at sixteen he is old enough to be a killer. Yet I feel that if it had been Arthwys underneath Morgan's old mask I would have somehow sensed it. Odd though that may seem, I still trust my gut in matters of such importance.

Despite the perils ahead, it lightens my heart to know that Arthwys will remain behind. The thought of the young Prince in our cavalcade would have given me many sleepless nights. Though only a boy, I cannot convince myself that Arthwys is an innocent child. He carries his father's seed of darkness within him.

A gray sky rumbles overhead. Our mixed caravan of South Welsh soldiers and Free Cantref archers winds its way toward the foggy sun. The roads will be wet and muddy. I bite my lip. Damnation. Can't my journey across this godforsaken land be advantageous for once? Would it anger God if my travels across Wales went according to plan for a change? I heave a heavy sigh.

Perhaps I am being unfair. Rough as our country is, mountainous and full of rivers and thick woods, its very topography has helped protect us against barbarians in the past. Soggy weather and boggy terrain may inhibit Saxons and Picts, but to the Welsh it's just another day at home.

By midday, a torrential downpour halts the column. We encamp at the edge of the woods, utilizing the dripping canopy for cover. Droplets hit the roadway so hard it seems as through the mud splashes the treetops. Men and horses alike stand with grim faces in the shadows, waiting for the cloudburst to end. The children take no heed, however, sticking out their tongues to catch fat drops of rainwater. I smile and do the same. It tastes clean and cold.

Perhaps my little boy and the other children are wiser than so-called adults like me. Where we see hardship, they see an opportunity to have fun. Fun. Have I completely forgotten the word? I suppose a queen and a mother has little room for such things.

Gavin chuckles as the rain plasters his red locks to his forehead. I cannot help but smile. He reminds me so much of Artagan when he grins like that.

I draw Gavin close to me, my son still bright eyed and grinning despite his frigid cheeks. My heartstrings constrict at the thought of Artagan so far from us now. I hug Gavin all the tighter.

Our company keeps a decent pace between rain showers, but eventually a new storm front stops us in our tracks. We bivouac under a tall stand of oaks near the old Roman road, spending a wet night beneath soaked blankets and tents. Half the soldiers stand on guard at any given hour, wary of both the nearby Saxons and highway bandits. I remember a time when bandits wouldn't have dared strike a king's entourage within his own realm. But it seems that those prouder, safer days in South Wales are long gone.

Sleep comes to me slowly as I lie coiled on the ground with Gavin in my arms. The baby in my womb stirs. I put one hand on my stomach and another on Gavin. My two sleeping babes. I smile through a groggy yawn. Our nest of quilts steams with damp warmth amidst the downpour. The tapping of droplets on broadleaves fills my dreamless slumber.

At daybreak, little more than a grayish glow hints at sunrise. Another overcast day. The thick slop of horses' hooves slipping and suctioning through the muddy thoroughfare announces our presence to every startled deer and rabbit. Birds stir in the trees. So much for stealth. In this godforsaken muck, even a child could hear us coming. And I doubt the Saxons will be less watchful than a rain-soaked child.

Atop my makeshift chariot, I slap the reins against the workhorses' backs. Cakes of mud stick to the timber wheels, the uneven road jouncing the wagon until my tailbone stings. In the back of the wagon, the children gnaw on a breakfast of hard bread. The women rub the children's cold palms by turns to keep them warm. I yaw into the ears of the draft horses tugging our cart. Saxons or no, the sooner we reach the shelter of Caerwent, the better.

When the caw of crows reaches my ears, I know something is wrong. An icy feeling wends its way up my spine. The forested roadway breaks before a large clearing, the blackened silhouette of Caerwent's crumbled towers looming across the plain. Ravens circle high overhead.

Griffith draws his sword, ordering his men to form ranks. They spread across the overgrown greens, looking over their shoulders as they advance. A misty stillness pervades the grassy fields. Not a single signal or halloo comes from within the fortress of Caerwent. Not a single watchman patrols the broken walls. I hand the wagon reins to Rowena and pull my birch wood bow from the straw. I've only half a dozen arrows in my quiver. It'll have to be enough.

This castle was once the strongest in all Wales. Now its stonework cracks with age, its battlements crumbling in gaps as though gnawed upon by giants. Years of Saxon assaults have taken their toll. Masonry battered by catapults. Timber supports blackened by fiery arrows. The ages have reduced Caerwent to a hulking shell. But where is everyone? The Saxons? The Welsh? Even in decay, Caerwent's thick walls provide a prize no general would dismiss. Ancient walls are still better than none at all. Griffith orders our company to halt. He points his sword down at the grass beside my wagon.

"My men will secure the castle. You and your women should stay here."

"So we can be picked off like sheep? Nay, we stand a better chance if we stick together."

"If there is any danger ahead, my men will flush it out."

"I thought your army held Caerwent still. Where are they?"

"I received a raven from them but a week ago. We're wasting time, Queen Branwen."

He puts his heels to his horse's flanks, the beast neighing wildly under his broad girth. Red in the face, Griffith leads his men forward himself. I have touched his pride, and I cannot blame him for getting cross. We have ridden barely two days from his capital and found the borders of his own land deserted. No king should be caught so unawares within his own fiefdom.

Rowena's girls begin to fuss in the back of the cart. Their mother returns to them, trying to shush her daughters. Una does the same for Gavin and Cadwallon. Olwen comes forward and takes the reins as I draw back my bow.

My protruding belly nearly gets in the way as I draw back my bowstring. My cheeks burn hot, but what can I do? I probably look as silly as a cow caught in a blackthorn vine. Halfway into my pregnancy and

I'm feeling more awkward than ever. But I can still shoot straight. For now. Olwen represses a half-smirk beside me.

Her grin quickly fades as we approach the shadow of Caerwent's outer walls. She whispers barely loud enough for me to hear.

"If Griffith's army has gone missing, then where are the Saxons?"

"I think we're about to find out."

Olwen pales as we near the citadel's western gate. Griffith's men push open the large timber doors, filtering into the defenses. Their rattling armor and heavy tread murmur throughout the complex. These South Welsh may be brave, but they lack the stealth of our Free Cantref bowmen. My dozen-odd green-clad archers form a crescent around our wagon, their eyes scanning the woods behind us. Griffith charges inside the citadel, brandishing his sword overhead. Olwen halts our wagon at the foot of the open gates.

Drawing my bowstring, I pull back an arrow to my jaw, my hands starting to sweat. The first foe that sticks his head through the castle entranceway will get a mouthful of steel arrowheads. Mingled voices shout from inside the walls, but I cannot make anything out. My fingertips tremble along the bowstring.

Griffith emerges from the castle gates, his blade sheathed. He waves both arms over his head, the signal that all appears well. I lower my bow with a sigh, but I keep an arrow nocked just in case. I call out to the King.

"What happened?"

"See for yourself."

He motions over his shoulder. Olwen slaps the horse's reins as our wagon rumbles inside the citadel walls. The stench of rotten meat wrinkles my nose.

Scores of men lie head to foot in the courtyard, some wrapped in blankets and others dressed in little more than tatters. My skin turns cold. Rowena and Una instinctively cover the children's eyes. Only when some of the soldiers stir do I realize that most of these men still live. Just barely. Olwen does not seem as convinced, halting the wagon inside the walls.

"Are they dead?"

"Sick," Griffith answers her. "More than half the garrison has the blight."

I swallow hard, putting down my bow and rubbing my round stomach. Arrows will not protect my unborn child from a pestilence that can be neither seen nor touched. But it certainly has a smell. An odor of overripe cheese and sulfur permeates the interior walls. The monks in Dyfed told me as a child that the devil himself smells of sulfur. My palate runs dry. The devil has indeed come to Caerwent.

Olwen tugs the reins hard to one side, trying to turn the wagon around. The horses whinny, struggling to turn in the confined space of the courtyard. Her eyes widen as she grabs me by the shoulder.

"We have to leave! Before the children and all of us take down with the plague!"

I open my mouth, but no words come out. My brow beads with sweat. I'm inclined to agree with her, but what can we do? If the Saxons lurk nearby, then the woods or the open road will afford us little better protection than the walls of Caerwent. Nonetheless, my skin begins to crawl, imagining the unseen blight that breathes in the dank spaces between the castle walls. I've seen people perish in many ways, but death by plague is one of the worst.

Before I can think of a reply, Griffith rides his steed between us and the open gates, barring our path. His voice brooks no argument.

"No one is going anywhere! We're already exposed. Fleeing will only spread the pestilence. We stay put, all of us."

Olwen puts her hands on her hips.

"I'd sooner take my chances with the Saxons! I'm still a queen, daughter of a king, and I'll not endanger my child by remaining here another minute."

"You *were* a queen!" Griffith growls. "And you are in *my* kingdom, under the protection of *my* guards. Restrain yourself, your ladyship, or I shall be forced to have my men restrain you."

Olwen lurches forward like a maddened mother hen, but I stay her with my arm. She looks me in the eye as I shake my head. For once, I feel much the same as her, but it will do no good to contradict Griffith in front of his troops. There's no sooner way to start bloodshed than to defy a king in front of his own men. Besides, Griffith might be right. We're exposed anyway, so what would fleeing accomplish?

Still, I glance back at Gavin and Cadwallon. They are so young, their cheeks still baby soft even at three years of age. Would God strike them down before they've even had a chance at life? Bad enough we have barbarians and assassins to fret about. Now a plague visits the land. I shut my eyes. Sometimes I think God has forsaken Wales altogether.

I turn to Griffith, trying to put as much authority into my voice as possible. A queen shouldn't squeak like a scared little girl, even if she does tremble inside. I'd rather face a thousand Picts right now than spend one night in a castle riddled with a pox, but what alternative do I have? I point at a nearby tower.

"My King, we should secure one of the larger towers. I've seen contagions before, and if we can isolate ourselves somewhat from the infected, it may help prevent the spread of the disease."

"It *may* help?" he replies with a raised eyebrow.

"Please, sire, we must try. For our own sakes. For the children."

He glances at the boys and girls in the back of the cart. Griffith sighs before surveying the throngs of enfeebled men sprawled across the courtyard cobblestones. His shoulders sink.

"As you wish, Queen Branwen. Your knowledge as a healer earned you the namesake of Mab Ceridwen for a reason. My guards are at your disposal. Cordon off one of the towers, but I will stay with the ill men here. I am their king and I should share their fate, whatever befalls us."

I nod, biting my lip. Despite his flaws, Griffith is an honorable man and a just ruler. Such a rare quality in most leaders these days, amongst both the Welsh and the barbarians. It shames me to not stand beside him, but I have my own children to think of. Those born and unborn. I lead our wagon toward the tallest tower, making arrangements with Griffith's guardsmen before the King has time to change his mind.

My footfalls echo up the tower stairwell, as though a ghost walks ahead of me on the stone steps. The hairs rise along my forearms. I've not set foot inside this castle since I was Morgan's queen. Ghost or no, perhaps he will come here, his former stronghold. I doubt plagues scare ghosts much, but they might just ward off an assassin. Then again, what made the assassin restrain himself when we encamped beneath Ogham Stone? I still have no answer for that. My head begins to ache. Too many mysteries for me to attempt to solve just now.

Una and Rowena set about sweeping out the interiors of the tower chambers. I post all of my archers at the foot of the stairs, relieving Griffith's guards to tend to their duties. After all, someone should stand watch over this castle. Has the blight truly been so bad that the garrison could not spare a single man to stand as lookout?

I suds a bucket of soap and begin scrubbing the floors. My knees ache and my swollen belly makes every brushstroke doubly tiresome and awkward, but these tasks must be done. Olwen folds her arms, looking at me skeptically as I clean the chamber floorboards.

"Kindle a fire in the hearth, if scrubbing doesn't suit you," I say, without giving her a glance. "We must purify these chambers as best we can if we are to isolate ourselves from the plague."

"I still say we should put as much distance between us and this cursed castle as we can!"

"And have Griffith's men or bandits hunt us down on the open road?"

"I'd rather take my chances."

Her words set my teeth on edge. Can't she stop her gums from flapping for just a single turn of the hourglass? I too would like to flee South Wales with my child in tow, but it simply isn't an option. Besides, I still am no closer to convincing Griffith to ally with my husband's army against King Iago and the Picts. I cannot return to Artagan empty-handed, not when our people so desperately need a miracle to save us.

I rise to my feet, glaring at Olwen. My foaming scrub brush drips in my hand. I have half a mind to wash out her mouth with these bristles. She eyes the suds on my brush as though guessing my intent.

When I return to my washing, Olwen loses interest and stalks away. I pause over the washbowl, expecting to glimpse my reflection in the dank water, but instead the suds begin to swirl like a nautilus shell.

My trancelike stare into the water pot deepens, and I'm unable to look away as the bowl froths over. Within the clear dark center, the water stills like a mirror as hazy images take shape. My skin grows cold and damp.

Artagan appears in the reflection, slumped lazily on Dyfed's throne, Father's old chair. He abruptly rises to his feet, his face stern as he argues with someone. I cannot hear the words, but both Bowen and Carrick appear beside him, clearly discussing something in a heated manner with my husband. The vision quickly fades into the swirl of soapy eddies. I sit back from the washbowl as steam rises from the water and dissipates in the breeze.

Blinking back the sweat from my eyes, I glance around the room. None save myself seem to have noticed the vision. But I know what I saw. Artagan, not as he was or will be, but as he is right now. Are things already falling apart back at Dun Dyfed, the restless Free Cantref and Dyfed warriors snapping at each other's throats like so many bored hunting hounds? How odd that the visions that once came to me by firelight with Annwyn now appear in water since my meeting with Sab. As though the Picts evoke a new element within me, something colder and darker than that in which Annwyn instructed me. Like a dark wind rising from the inside out.

Before I can give voice to my thoughts, Una rushes in through the solar doorway. She quickly curtsies, placing herself between Olwen and me. I hold a sudsed palm to my forehead, replying with a bit more sass than I intend.

"Una, not now, please."

"But my Queen, it's your kinsman Ahern! He's here. He has the plague."

The scrub brush in my hand tumbles to the floor.

13

He lies on a church pew, arms folded over his chest as though prepared for burial. His torso rises and falls almost imperceptibly. The castle chapel overflows with coughing soldiers, lying head to foot across the stone floors. I reach out to touch him, my hand stopping just above his eye patch.

"Ahern."

His good eye flickers open. His neck and limbs do not budge, his gaze darting from side to side. He grimaces, as though he doubts he hears my voice. I kneel beside him, clasping his hand.

"Brother, it's me."

He shakes his head, his voice raspy as a toad's.

"Leave. You should not be here. It's not safe."

His stare travels down to my swollen abdomen. He gasps, closing his eye. Now he knows. Ahern stifles the phlegm in his throat. I press my lips together, trying to keep my composure. I've not seen him this ill in all my life. His voice barely registers above a whisper.

"The last time you were this far gone with child, I was in the dungeons at Aranrhod."

I force a smile, my eyes starting to water. What a witch I've been, sending Ahern on this errant because I feared claiming Dyfed's throne might prove too tempting for him. Now he lies here dying, and all because of me.

"I remember. Artagan imprisoned you for trying to betray me. What a silly oaf you were."

"I justly deserved far worse punishment. Perhaps God has seen fit to rectify my penance."

He brings a fist to his mouth, turning away as a violent coughing fit overtakes him. He withdraws his palm from mine. Even now he tries to protect me, not wanting to risk passing along the blight to myself or my unborn child.

Part of me knows I should return to the tower. Every moment I remain in this chapel full of sick men, I risk contracting the same infection. But I've only one adult kinsman left in all Christendom. Few men or women have known me as long as my one-eyed brother. I have so little family left.

His coughs gradually subside. Without glancing back at me, he remains on his side

"Go. I will not be the cause of your death or your child's."

I scoff at his indignance.

"Och! Since when do queens take orders from their guardsmen? Besides, I came to Caerwent to find you."

"It is not safe. Plague. Saxons. You should never have come looking for me."

"The rest of Wales is not much safer. Picts. Treacherous King Iago. But where are the Saxons I heard had besieged this castle?"

"They were here when I first arrived, but most keep to the woods now. For better cover."

"How many of them are there?"

"God knows. More than enough."

Coughing overcomes him again. I pat his back, but he waves me away. His ailment has certainly not diminished any of his stubbornness. Poor man. Sent on a mission to treat with King Griffith, then banished to Caerwent, only to catch the plague just as it overcomes the garrison.

And what of all those Saxons lying in wait in the woods? I was certain this was nothing more than a raid by savages bent on pillage. Nothing more. King Griffith has always been an overly cautious general and prone to exaggerate. But now it seems that indeed a full invasion force has laid siege to Caerwent. And as such has dashed all my hopes of diverting any of Griffith's army to aid us against the Picts in the Gwynedd. I hang my head, my limbs suddenly heavy.

Una waits by the entrance to the church. She stands in the archway, surveying the rows of suffering soldiers with a long face. If not for her loyalty to me, she would probably have long abandoned my entourage and returned to her work as a nun. Praying to God and tending to needy souls, such as these. Thankfully, she chose to come to the church to say her midday prayers, else she would not have seen Ahern. Else I would not have even known he lay here suffering while I ensconced myself in a castle tower.

A knot forms in my throat as I rest my head in my hands. The world slowly crumbles around me, and all I can do is watch it fall apart. I pound my fist into my open palm. There must be something I can do! Some way to see through this descending darkness. But my mind runs blank. I've no idea what to do or where to go from here.

Ahern begins to snore. Whether he fakes it or not, I cannot tell, but I decide to leave him in peace. He needs his rest one way or the other.

Una approaches, holding a calfskin-bound book in hand, open to a page about midway through.

"My Queen, the clerics here received word from King Griffith of your interest in any writings pertaining to Queen Vivian of Dyfed."

"Aye, I asked the King as much."

"The vaults of books are few here nowadays, but the local parson found this one tome containing a short inscription regarding your mother's early years. I have the passage here, if you wish to view it."

I nod and thank her, reaching out for the open book in her hands before she has even finished speaking. My eyes quickly traverse the page full of Latinate text. It takes me a moment to gain the thread of the story, many other facts and tales involved don't seem to concern my mother at all. But then my eyes alight on a short passage listed within the larger history.

For a time the Welsh in the lost Kingdom of Hen Ogledd fought both Saxons and Picts in the borderlands, and the Saxons and Picts fought one another as well. When the king there perished in battle and his Dyfed wife died soon after of a broken heart, their only heir and daughter, Queen Vivian, took the leadership of her people in this far northeastern realm.

I pause a moment, taking in the full meaning inscribed on the tallowed page. My mother lost her parents when she was younger than I am now. Her father, a king of a lost eastern Welsh fiefdom, and her mother born in the western mountains of Dyfed who must have then once lived with her husband in the East. My grandparents. The short description doesn't even list their names. A young woman in a failing kingdom surrounded by enemies, it appears that my mother had to lead her people during a tumultuous time against impossible odds. Why did I never hear of this before? Why did neither my father nor my long-lost mentor, Abbot Padraig, see fit to even so much as mention this to me? I read on, desperate for some explanation regarding what became of my mother after her parents died.

A Pictish queen approached young Vivian and offered an alliance against the Saxons, else both their realms might be destroyed. Reluctantly, Queen Vivian agreed to this pact, even though she bore little love for the Picts. Their shared enemy amongst the Saxon hordes was greater. But on the day of battle, Queen Vivian led her meager forces and her entire remaining people away, abandoning her kingdom far to the east and forsaking the Picts to their fate against the encroaching Saxons. Queen Vivian led her people safely into the West, where they joined with King Vortigen's realm in Dyfed—a place where her mother's people once dwelt. After her marriage to King Vortigen,

Queen Vivian never heard or saw more of the fate of the Picts from that day onward.

I swallow hard, reading on but finding the story diverging upon disparate topics about harvests and realms in other ages. No more about my mother or her youth. I return to the previous page and reread the lines about Queen Vivian's flight from the Old Borderlands once more.

Could this be true? My mother led her people to safety, but at the cost of her Pictish allies? How little these few lines tell me about what my mother thought or how she felt at that tender age. A teenage girl thrust into a position of power, much as I once found myself. She saved her people by fleeing the Saxons altogether and marrying a Welsh king who lived behind the safety of the western mountains. My father, King Vortigen. But what became of the Picts near the Old Borderlands? Surely nothing good if they stood little chance against the conquering Saxon armies. Little wonder Sab bears me ill will, if my own mother reneged on the Picts in order to save her own subjects.

But people only ever spoke well of my mother. She was kind and gentle, a woman of a peaceful disposition. Was she truly capable of such a coldhearted decision, necessary though it may have been? And something more of this tale remains obscured by shadows. Sab's loathing for me has a personal edge to it. Somehow she must be directly connected to this episode from my mother's youth. But how? Sab herself would've been but a small girl at the time. Enlightening as these pages have been, there's something crucial missing from it. Some piece of knowledge I'm not seeing.

I return the book to Una. More unanswered questions spring to mind, but no solutions present themselves. Perhaps it's mad of me to worry over such a trifle when surrounded by an army of plague-ridden soldiers.

Una and I return to our tower. The Free Cantref archers nod to us, glancing nervously over their shoulders at the wheezing South Welshmen scattered across the courtyard. An invisible death pall hangs over all our thoughts.

Upstairs, Olwen sulks in a corner, screwing her eyes up toward the rafters. I'm in no mood for her antics and walk past her, trying to ignore her. The children splash through thin puddles as Rowena mops up the last of the floorboards. Olwen aims her finger at me like the tip of a crossbow.

"Keep us isolated? Quarantined, you said? You'll infect us all, now that you've been visiting your sickly cycloptic brother!"

I stare Olwen down, my eyes burning with green fury. For an instant, she returns my defiant stare, and I wonder if the two of us will come to blows. Alas, we both have the breeding of queens in us and know better. Still, I'd like to take a broomstick to her when she speaks so thoughtlessly. I came here to save my brother, and with God as my witness, somehow I shall.

Olwen turns away and we retreat to our respective corners of the room with our sons in hand. I hum a soft lullaby to Gavin as he lays his head in my lap. Olwen plays knucklebones with Cadwallon in the corner, making him chuckle. Neither of us deigns speak to the other.

Gavin's breeches feel damp under my hand. I pull back his trousers to find that he has wet himself. I bite my lower lip, knowing full well that Gavin knows how to use the latrine by now. With pouty lips, he looks up into my face. My little boy is scared. Even though he may not fully understand, he knows we are hunted, that we are in peril. I press my lips to his brow. My sweet child, you should not have to deal with such difficulties so young. I fetch a fresh tunic and wrap him in my arms, gently rocking him against my chest.

Just as Gavin starts to rest complacently in my lap, Rowena leaps to her feet. Her startled girls start to whimper anew, but their mother ignores them. Rowena stumbles to the tower windowsill, pointing at the green fields and woods beyond.

"M'lady, look! The woods, they move!"

I raise a skeptical eyebrow. How can woods move? My temples start to throb. I've already snapped once this morning, I don't want to do it again. I try to ignore her, but Rowena grabs my wrist.

"My Queen, see for yourself! The trees are moving."

With an exasperated sigh, I rise to my feet and saunter to the window ledge. At first the quiet fields and misty oak groves look like nothing out of the ordinary. Then my eyes widen.

Scores of treetops within the forest canopy sway from side to side, as though advancing through a sea of branches. Bare wooden trunks filter through the wolds, making the skin of the canopy seem to ripple. The woods do indeed move.

Una and Olwen join us at the window.

"What in heaven's name . . . ?" Una's voice trails off.

A quavering ram's horn sounds through the woodlots, drawing the attention of every guardsman posted along the castle walls. Griffith paces the battlements himself, his wide form visible across the keep. He draws his sword as a second quivering bugle call booms through the dells.

My palms start to sweat. I recognize the sound, although I've not heard it in some time. That's no hunting horn. It's a Saxon battle trumpet.

Guards shuffle about the battlements, readying shields and spears as Griffith shouts orders to his men. Those still able to stand, that is. Even the sick men look up from their makeshift bedrolls, craning their ears toward the barbaric sounds emanating from the woods outside Caerwent.

I descend the tower with my bow and quiver, dodging bustling solders who take up positions along the main defenses. Several of my green-clad archers accompany me. I order the rest to stand guard by the tower. I don't want anybody to leave or enter the bedchamber where I keep the children. We've enough perils to deal with as it is.

Griffith grimaces when he sees me approaching the eastern parapet.

"This is no place for a lady, let alone a breeding woman."

"I'm neither a lady nor a woman. I'm a queen. I've never flinched from the Saxons before and I shan't start now."

I plant my feet shoulder width apart, putting an arrow on my bowstring. I don't draw the twine back, though. Else, Griffith might see how ungainly I appear when I try to move a drawstring around my belly. Perhaps I'm a touch farther along than I thought, maybe five moons heavy with child now. My body betrays me, feeling heavier and more sluggish each day. But I've not time for such concerns now with the Saxons outside our walls.

Several more toots from the ram's horn reverberate from the trees, the woods still shaking as though every other tree uprooted itself. Those "trees" moving about must be Saxons' spears and pikes. But how many of them are out there? There must be at least a thousand of them for the woods to shake like that. My heart clenches like a balled fist. The Saxons will not spare a single soul within the walls of Caerwent if they take the castle by force.

Griffith growls behind clenched teeth, shaking his head.

"I don't know who's worse, you, my lady, or the Saxons. At least they aren't ruled by their women's whims as we are."

I ignore the tone in his voice, keeping my eyes to the woods.

"How many men do you have fit for duty, my King?"

"Not enough. The few hundred I brought with me, but the rest of the garrison has the blight."

"I wish those savages would stop tooting that tiresome horn of theirs." I wince.

"Strange that the Saxons don't show themselves. Why all the bluster? Why don't the cowards come out and fight?"

I blink the sweat from my eyes. Griffith has a point. Why don't the blackguards show themselves? Saxons rape and pillage, but subtlety has never been one of their attributes.

My fingers tighten their grip on my birch-wood bow. I wish Artagan were here. Wild and crazy as he gets in battle, he always exudes calm and confidence before a fight. His cockiness infects those around him and makes waiting for the shock of battle a little more tolerable. Besides, he's the best swordsmen born since the days of Arthur.

Although months have passed, it seems only yesterday I lay in Artagan's strong arms, snug and restful within our castle bedchamber at Aranrhod. Warm, in bed, our son resting safe and sound just down the hall. Where did all those tranquil days go? If only I had known how good my life truly was, how I should have cherished those moments of happiness like so many jewels embedded in my heart. *Dear God, if you deliver me and my boy from this, I swear I shall never again venture more than a day's ride from Aranrhod. Well, just so long as my kingdom doesn't need me to do otherwise.*

The blaring ram's horn suddenly stops, the shifting woods growing still and quiet. Like the hush before a storm breaks. Not a man inside the citadel speaks.

A lone rider breaks from the woods. He rears his horse, waving a large battle ax overhead, his bushy blond beard flowing behind him. A Saxon if ever I saw one. I squint at the horseman as he gallops around the castle walls, shouting in his barbaric tongue.

"What is that ruffian doing?"

Someone shuffles up behind Griffith and me, his voice low and gruff.

"It's a Saxon message," Ahern says. "He shouts it out every day, vowing death to every Welshman inside Caerwent who does not surrender."

Turning around, I see Ahern bracing himself against a pillar atop the parapet steps. I frown seeing him on his feet, his single eye bloodshot and his chest heaving from exerting himself on the stairs. I steady him with both arms.

"You should be abed, brother."

Ahern waves me away, but I keep one arm beneath his elbow nonetheless. We probably look a comical pair, one with a missing eye and the other round as cauldron. Griffith presses his face close to Ahern's.

"You certain that's what he's saying? If he does it every day, what's the point?"

"I lost an eye to the Saxons, but I've fought them long enough to recognize a barbarian's curse when I hear one," Ahern replies. "As for why he does it . . . why do Saxons do any of the evil things they do?"

The Saxon rider circles the castle, shaking his ax as he rages at the silent guards manning the battlements. He is brave, if somewhat stupid. Doubtless some local chieftain. A Saxon war-chief must look brave before his men in order to hold sway over them. His warriors probably look on from the woods now, sharpening their knives in the shadows. My eyebrows suddenly perk up.

"Ahern, when did this Saxon rider start this ritual? The exact day."

My half brother scratches his scalp.

"Not long after I arrived, the day some of the garrison first took down with the plague."

"You're certain?"

"Of course, did I not just say as much?"

I smile at my testy kinsman, his lack of sleep doing little to improve his temperament. I turn toward Griffith, directing his gaze toward the forest.

"Odd, don't you think so, King? The very day the plague strikes, the Saxons start their taunts."

"For once, your guardsman's right, my Queen. There's no reason why the Saxons ever do anything."

Griffith leers back at Ahern from the corner of his eyes. After banishing Ahern from Caerleon for trying to steal into Morgan's tomb, he likely hasn't much patience for my half brother. Then again, I did the same thing, and yet Griffith does not seem to have cooled toward me. But I never claimed to be an expert in menfolk or their whims.

Especially such thick-headed men as these. Even Saxons have reasons for what they do, foreign though they may seem to us. I learned that when Saxons first tried to steal me on my betrothal day as a youth. I've done my best not to underestimate them since. I try to steer Griffith's attention back to the problem at hand.

"I still find it odd that the Saxons would lay a siege and then retreat to the woods, showing hardly one of them to us at a time."

"Perhaps they took cover for protection against archers?" Griffith replies.

I shake my head.

"Against Free Cantref warriors maybe, but your South Welshmen favor the sword and close combat. The Saxons know this from years of warfare. They wouldn't fall back into the woods for no reason."

"You think they fear to approach because we have the plague?"

"I think *they* have the plague. And just like us, no longer have men fit enough to wage war."

Griffith and Ahern exchange looks. The King puts his hands behind his back.

"That's quite a presumption, Queen Branwen. Nonetheless, we cannot afford to let down our guard so easily."

I sigh. The fat king is as overcautious as ever. It makes him a fine defender of castles, but he has no aggression when in the field. My husband wouldn't sit still behind tall walls. He'd have rooted out the Saxons from the woods even if he had to do it all by himself. I fold my arms, refusing to give in to Griffith's skepticism.

"Then I will lead a sortie into the woods and prove it to you."

Griffith's mouth hangs open. Ahern nearly stumbles backward down the stairs. Soldiers along the battlements murmur amongst themselves as Griffith shakes his finger at me.

"But you're a woman . . . with child! You can't be serious?"

"If your men fear to go where a pregnant woman dares to tread, then you had best stay with them behind your walls."

I turn my back and march down the stairs to the main courtyard, my archers gathering around me. Although my palms tremble, I keep a straight back and a confident demeanor. I walk a dangerous line, trying to shame Griffith on one hand but not insult him enough to make him throw me in a dungeon. He must see for himself that the Saxons can no longer threaten his borders. Only then can I possibly hope to enlist his help against the Picts and King Iago in the North.

Many dangers lurk behind every decision I make or do not make. Perhaps it is preferable to risk death by plague than fall into barbaric hands. But a queen doesn't have the luxury of always playing it safe. Sometimes she must risk everything she holds dear if she hopes to keep it.

Griffith calls out after me, but I ignore him. Ahern hobbles beside me. I can tell by his wide grimace that he heartily disapproves of my plan, but he does not question me openly in front of the others. Instead he curses under his breath, using his spear like a crutch. He joins my retinue at the castle gates, adjusting his patch. My good, stubborn brother. He would follow me into the fires of hell if I set my mind to do so. Maybe I already have.

By the time my small company of archers stride halfway into the greens outside the castle, I hear the rumble of hooves behind us. Griffith leads a small contingent of guards on horseback, although whether to accompany me or return me to the castle keep, I do not know for certain. I spare a passing glance at the citadel tower. *Rowena, look after my boy. If I'm wrong, you and Una will be all Gavin has left.* Lord knows, I wouldn't put him in Olwen's hands.

The lone Saxon chieftain sees us, rearing his steed again as it boxes the air with its hooves. He digs his heels into the mount's flanks and charges straight for us. I freeze in my tracks, suddenly feeling like a fool with my bowstring drawn before my wide belly. My skin grows cold with sweat. Perhaps I've made a grave error.

My bowmen draw back their longbows. The mere sound of Free Cantref archers pulling their strings taut seems enough to give the Saxon war-chief second thoughts. He spins his horse about, bolting for the cover of the woods. My men loose a couple arrows after him, nearly clipping the yellow braids from his hair before he descends into the forest.

Although my men are only on foot, I order them into the woods. Griffith's horsemen canter after us. Whether or not he plans to take me back to Caerwent, Griffith has now cast his lot with me. He will have to help rather than hinder me should we run into any Saxons in the brush.

Ahern hobbles beside me, but I fare little better, weighed down by the child within me. We follow my bowmen into the dark shades of the wood. They shout a throaty *Mab Ceridwen* hurrah that makes my skin ripple in gooseflesh. Though only two dozen men, they are brave as were their forefathers. The knights of Arthur's day and the warriors of the Old Tribes would smile with approval seeing that their descendants still have such courage in their hearts.

But a baritone roar answers us back as a score of Saxons clad in furs and iron helms surrounds us. My throat stops up, not able to utter even a scream. I've led my warriors into a trap. God help us.

The blond Saxon on horseback urges his savages on, howling as they grapple with my outnumbered guardsmen. Ahern coughs into his fist before summoning his last reserves of strength. He hurls his spear through a Saxon's throat, spraying us both with hot blood. I loose an arrow into the crowd of Saxons, but they are too many.

Griffith's cavalcade charges into the groves, trampling the barbarians under their horses' hooves. The fat king nearly slumps out of the saddle twice, but he keeps his seat as he swings his sword down upon the helms of his long-bearded foes. The lead Saxon and his warriors break ranks before fleeing deeper into the woods. Several of Griffith's horsemen and my archers chase after them, howling amidst their pursuit. Griffith steadies his mount, glaring down at me.

"No wonder Morgan couldn't keep you as his bride. Do you disobey Artagan's commands as often as you do mine?"

"A queen *gives* commands, she does not take them. And Artagan keeps me as his wife because I desire it to be so."

I plant a hand on my hip, giving him a hard stare. What business is it of his if I choose to go my own way in life? I'm not the scared little girl I was when the Hammer King first took me to bed all those years ago. Besides, we've no time to fret about niceties and decorum. The cries of battle and Saxons still haunt the woods.

Ahern staggers up beside me. At first I think him wounded, but then he wheezes through his teeth and leans against a tree. He should be in bed, not in the thick of a swordfight. I cannot fault his loyalty, though. He shakes his head, wiping the dew from his brow.

"We should never have come into these woods. We must regroup back at the castle, my Queen. There are doubtless more Saxons hiding in these groves."

"I'm counting on it," I reply.

Ahern blinks his lone eye incredulously at me. Griffith likewise looks at me as though I've lost my wits. My remaining archers and Griffith's score of knights gather around us, having given their barbaric foes a good chase into the forest. I dart ahead, wending my way between the trees. Griffith's exasperated voice echoes behind me.

"Where in Christendom is she going now?"

"We best go after her," Ahern replies.

I clench my jaw. Do they still not understand? Could they possibly be so blind? We encountered only a few dozen Saxons. Since when do those bloody savages do anything in such small numbers? They prefer large sorties, a hundred men at least. It takes a Welsh mind-set to fight a little war in small groups, and the Saxons certainly haven't the craftiness necessary for that. No. The Saxons would never fight with such small numbers by choice.

The trees open onto a small open glade. I pause in my tracks. A stench like rotting cheese makes me wrinkle my nose. The footsteps of my companions halt abruptly behind me. I fold my arms and stare smugly back at Griffith and Ahern.

Scores upon scores of Saxons lie strewn about the undergrowth, coughing into their fists and sweating feverishly beneath their animal-skin coverlets. Many of them stare in wide-eyed fear at the sight of us. Few of them can crawl more than a few paces. Ahern stutters beside me, still defiantly lug-headed to the last.

"What are these beggars doing just lying about?" my brother asks. "Why do they not run or fight?"

"Because, you fool, they have the plague!" I scoff. "The whole Saxon army is just as immobilized as the garrison at Caerwent."

The Saxons are spent. It's difficult to conquer a kingdom when your own troops are too sick to stand. Even barbarians must understand that.

Griffith looks down at me from the saddle, his eyes glazing over with a look difficult to discern. When he nods my way, I finally understand. Kings are loath to admit their wrongness, so I suppose a simple nod is as much as I should expect from Griffith. Even with his overly cautious gaze, he finally sees the Saxon forces for what they are: sickly, unable to even defend their own. They will not threaten his borders so long as this blight persists. They put up a good bluff, hiding in the woods where even their wounded could wave a few spears and make their numbers still appear strong. The woods move now only with the sounds of their slow retreat.

Which means that Griffith's forces back at Caerleon a day's ride to the west, healthy and far from the plague, are free from the burden of defense. Free to accompany their King anywhere should he choose to go on the offensive. Preferably with me against the Picts.

A broad smile fills my cheeks. I feel hopeful for the first time in a long while. But my grin quickly fades as something convulses down below my gut. I glance down, my skin suddenly growing pale. The baby within me moves.

Stumbling backward, I lean a hand against a tree. Ahern and Griffith both rush to catch me. My insides turn over again. *No, it is too soon. Far too soon.* The child cannot come, not now, not yet. I collapse to my knees, clenching my teeth as the pressure swells and contracts inside me.

14

My innards pinch together, the pain between my hips surging anew. Rowena and Una hover on either side as I squat on a stool, a cool breeze wafting over the tower windowsill. Sweat pours down my brow, my damp forelocks plastered to my head. I breathe short and fast through clenched teeth.

The guards who carried me in bar the door behind them, standing watch on the tower stairwell outside. My vision swims in a fog of peat smoke from the nearby hearth fire. I hear a child's whimper between the walls.

"Where's Gavin?"

"The children are fine," Rowena assures me. "They're with Olwen."

I cringe. Olwen? Motioning to get up, the cramps in my gut intensify. I fall back into my seat. Una prods me with a bucket.

"Best make water if you can."

"Una, I don't need to pee."

"Just try, Your Grace. It may help alleviate the pain."

Heaven help me. I color at the thought of dropping my skirts in front of both women, but they have seen plenty more from the birthings of other women. I do as Una says. The pressure around my belt begins to ease almost immediately. My breathing slows, the tremors still lingering within me but gradually fading. Like an echo dissipating in a tunnel.

Una puts a hand on my shoulder.

"Better?"

"Aye."

"'Tis as I suspected. False birth pangs. Making water or lying on your side can help alleviate them."

I wipe the perspiration from my hairline, feeling like a childish dolt.

"I should've known. I rarely felt them when I was pregnant with Gavin."

Rowena frowns, wagging her finger at me.

"You led armed men into battle against the Saxons, m'lady! What did you expect? All that excitement and the blood rushing inside you. You're lucky you didn't go into labor right then and there!"

Una nods in agreement.

"Rowena is right, my Queen. You cannot do such things as you are accustomed to. Not at least until after the child is born at the proper time. It's still too early for the babe to come forth."

I frown at her words, reminded how much her reasoning sounds like Artagan's. Perhaps I ask too much of myself trying to be both a mother and a spear-wife. Rowena grimaces at Una.

"The Queen is a midwife herself! She needn't be told she could lose the baby if she pushes herself too hard. Both she and I have had babies of our own, *we* know what to expect."

Una's gaze narrows, her cheeks coloring at Rowena's slight. As a nun she certainly has never borne a child herself. I shut my eyes. Just when I thought the two of them had made amends, they're at one another's throats. Una leans in, almost nose to nose with Rowena.

"I've delivered many a child at the nunnery! Many a lost mother shows up on our doorstep there, I assure you."

Rowena glares right back at her, hands on her hips. I push my arms between them.

"Enough! Bad enough we've Saxons and the plague to contend with without you two snarling like wildcats!"

My two ladies-in-waiting pace along opposite sides of the chamber.

My shoulders sink as I lean back against the cool stone wall, exhausted in mind, body, and soul. Una tries to change the subject.

"What of the Saxons in the woods, Your Grace? The soldiers say the brigands have the blight just the same as we do."

I nod in reply.

"Aye, we scattered them good, took some prisoners, and left a few dead who refused to be prisoners. But they're still out there, like a pack of wounded wolves. They'll sulk in their lairs so long as the plague lasts."

"At least the threat of a siege has temporarily lifted." Una sighs.

Rowena folds her arms, frowning at the nun.

"Little good it does us! Especially if we are just as like to catch the plague ourselves."

"The clerics in the chapel pray to God every day for salvation," Una begins, "and they alone have yet to contract the affliction. Perhaps you would do well, Rowena, to do the same."

"Pah! Those soup eaters probably keep to their prayer cells simply to avoid contact with the dying."

"Soup eaters? Those clerics dedicate their lives to the sick and infirm!"

I roll my eyes as the two women clench their jaws, ready to spar again. What has gotten into them of late? They've got their blood up, hot as young knights in a tourney. If I didn't love them so much, I'd take a switch to both of them this instant.

My mouth suddenly twitches with the hint of a smile. Something Rowena says sticks in my mind. *Soup eaters?* Now why would the clerics, of all men, be immune to the blight? They've surely been exposed as equally as the soldiers. So what do they do different? Prayer may play a part, but a tingling feeling tells me there is something more afoot.

The soup! Of course, how could I have been so blind? The truth has been there, staring us all in the face this entire time. I start to laugh, drawing looks from Una and Rowena. They exchange glances, both a little pale, probably thinking I've become unhinged. Rowena's voice squeaks like a tiny mouse.

"Have I missed something, m'lady? What humors you so?"

"I have to hand it to the pair of you. Even in discord you two are better than the brightest minds in Christendom."

"I still don't follow," Una replies in turn.

I repress a smile, realizing than neither woman sees the obvious truth.

"What have the soldiers been fed? Rations are low, probably rotten bread and salted meat, aye?"

The two of them nod in reply. I go on, failing to repress my grin this time. They *still* do not see.

"And what do the monks eat? The soup. Onion or garlic I don't doubt, it grows wild in Wales this time of year."

"Forgive my dull wits, my Queen," Rowena replies, "but I still don't understand."

I rise to my feet. It's not necessary that they understand just yet. So long as we act quickly, we have a chance to save this garrison, and maybe turn the tide of this conflict in our favor.

"Both of you, hasten to the kitchens! Fetch every able-bodied soul you can. We've picking to do."

"*Picking?*" the two women say in unison.

"Onions, garlic, leeks, anything growing wild at the verge of the forest. And we'll need a vat, a big vat for soup."

I pace the floor, trying to manage the figures in my head. We need to gather enough to feed the entire garrison. The rains have been plentiful of late, and the wild onions and garlic in particular should be sprouting everywhere. Rowena blocks my path.

"Pardon, m'lady, but how will we stop a plague with *soup*?"

"Broth, girl, broth! We need every green growing, wild thing we can put in the broth."

Una steps forward.

"Clerics eat such things, but the soldiers won't, Your Grace. They consider green things peasant food."

"They'll consider it salvation once I'm through with them. Now, go. We've little time!"

Each of them shrugs before hastening from the room. We've little time indeed, but if I'm right, we may have just saved hundreds of men from untimely deaths. Better yet, we can keep the children safe and healthy as well. Of course, if I am wrong, we'll all be in our graves in a fortnight anyway. If the blight has its way.

Griffith shakes his head with a smile. He slurps another bowlful of yellow-green broth, chewing on the vegetable rinds floating in the stew. I lean against the castle wall with a satisfied smirk as the soldiers in the courtyard drink the same piping-hot brew. Ahern sits nearby as well, the color returning to his cheeks as he drinks his stew. Already he looks fit enough to fight a bull. What a change for the better the last few days have been for us all.

King Griffith's lips smack together as he sighs, steam rising from his mouth.

"I'll be damned, Lady Branwen. You truly are the *Mab Ceridwen.* Only someone blessed by the Fates could have wrought such a miracle."

"It's old knowledge, long forgot, is all. Wise women of the Old Tribes knew as much."

"It's magic, whatever it is! In two days' time, nearly every man in the fortress has begun to come around, all thanks to you."

I laugh. Magic? Does he think me a sorceress simply for applying a good dose of common sense? Albeit perhaps not as common as it was in the ancient days. I try my best to explain.

"Lady Annwyn, God rest her soul, told me a story about when the Roman legions invaded Britain. By the time they reached Wales, many of their men began to drop like flies. Their eyes sunken, their skin pallid, some even losing their teeth."

"Just as my men were here in Caerwent, when we first arrived."

"And just like those Roman soldiers, your men had low rations, little more than breadcrumbs and dried meat. The blight they caught is no mere infection but rather a condition. When the body lacks green things in its blood, it starts to die. The women of the Old Tribes knew this and fed their warriors such stews so as to keep the wasting sickness away. A *scourge,* they called it, or *scurvy* for short. But the Romans conquered nonetheless, and such ancient wisdom has very nearly disappeared from the Welsh Lands."

"But not from you, my lady. We owe you a great debt. You have saved my army."

I turn to him, my face suddenly serious. Now is the time, the opportunity I have been waiting for. It's now or never.

"Now I ask you, King Griffith, to help save *my* army. To save my *people* from destruction. My husband's small force stands alone against the might of the Picts and the treacherous King Iago. Shall we stand alone forever?"

The broad-faced King knits his brows in thought, the full weight of my request making him frown through his bushy beard. His blank gaze wanders the battlements as he sinks deep into thought. I dare not rush him. Such decisions are not weighed lightly. Perhaps he does owe me mightily for having saved his men from the blight, but monarchs can be fickle. All hinges on this. Without his help, we will be mincemeat before Iago and Queen Sab's combined armies.

Does Griffith still think the Saxons a threat even in their current plague-ridden state? They do not know the secret of the plague, which it turns out is not a plague at all. Merely malnutrition at its worst, but still deadly enough to kill those too ignorant to see it for what it is.

Griffith's frown deepens and my heart begins to sink. He remains cautious as ever, even with the danger of the Saxons on his doorstep temporarily lifted. Our gazes travel to our feet, neither one of us able to look the other in the eye. Griffith heaves a sigh.

"I'm sorry, my lady, but—"

I cut him off, not wanting to hear the truth but unable to keep silent.

"You won't help us, will you? Even with all of Wales at stake?"

"Risk my army and my kingdom for the sake of all Wales? All the bickering, stubborn, independent-minded free folk who hardly heed their kings, let alone each other? No."

I bite my lip, my shoulders sinking. I have lost all, my mission here in South Wales a failure. Griffith clears his throat, drawing my gaze toward his face.

"For Wales alone, of course not. She is too divided and treacherous a nation. *But* . . . for the Mab Ceridwen . . . well . . . that's a different story."

He flashes a broad smile and my heart rises within me. The jovial blackguard! He almost had me believing that he would forsake his friends in their greatest hour of need. I beam back at him, unable to contain my mirth.

Near a full moon has passed. Perhaps too much time. But pebbles gradually join together to create an avalanche. And so I too have an avalanche, a torrent, a rising tide behind me, and I intend to make the ground shake.

Atop my mare, I trot slowly at the head of Griffith's army, my belly ripe and round as a melon. Crimson dragon banners snap in the breeze amidst the steady tromp of two thousand foot soldiers, their polished shields and grieves glinting under the late summer sun. My ladies-in-waiting finally relent and allow me to mount a pony, only so long as I promise to keep her at a snail's pace. My ever-rounding belly swells beneath my garments with a full six moons, or more, of child inside me, my light-azure gown streaming behind me like bands of gossamer in the wind.

Griffith rides beside me, putting an ox horn to his lips to announce our presence. His bugle call echoes off the green hills and rolling downs of the valley before us. The circle of Ogham Stone looms in the distance, the green banners of my husband's army encamped just where my messenger raven asked them to be. I cannot help but smile with approval.

The wheels of my plan have been set in motion. We shall soon see what Queen Sab and King Iago think when they encounter an alliance of green and red dragon banners. The Free Cantrefs, Dyfed, and the South Welsh have not fought on the same side in some years.

Squinting into the late afternoon sun, I ride into camp and dismount before the throngs of temporary hovels and canvas tents. My namesake of Mab Ceridwen passes from the lips of the soldiers and camp followers nestled beneath the small tor of Ogham Stone. A familiar voice speaks in my ear.

"Looking for a bed to spend the night, fair lady?"

Artagan flashes his cocky half-grin, his opal eyes as full of mischief as ever. I wrap both arms around his neck, pressing my lips to his, despite my swollen abdomen between us. His balsam scent and strong arms surround me. I press myself ever harder into his grasp, afraid that this may be only a dream. For far too many moons we have been apart. Never, never again do I wish to be parted from him for more than a day, nay, even an hour. May God be my witness. My husband runs a palm over my stomach.

"When were you planning on telling me? After the child is born and learns to walk?"

"I told you with the message raven!" I say, feigning indignation. "Or have you forgotten those reading lessons I gave you so long ago?"

He scratches his head sheepishly.

"I seem to recall a different sort of lesson, one with you atop me."

I repress a grin, reddening from ear to ear.

"Hush! It's that hound dog attitude of yours that got us with this one." I pat my womb for good measure.

Artagan's gaze softens as he stares into my eyes, his arms wrapping around me.

"You and I?" he whispers. "Another young one? Truly?"

I nod my head, suddenly robbed of my voice as the water rises behind my eyes.

"Yes, my love. Another little addition to our family."

He smiles back at me, blinking back a few budding tears of his own. The miracle of life still manages to surprise us both. Another lovechild grows inside me, another part of Artagan and me that will always link the two of us together. For the moment, we are not king and queen but simply man and wife. Two people in love, their world centered round the newborn who will soon join our lives forevermore. I sniffle a touch, my cheeks stinging with mirth. Despite all the trials that came before, now that I see Artagan's love in his eyes, I've never wanted this child more. Our child. Another small part of us soon to be brought into the world.

Before either of us can say more, little Gavin gallivants past me and into his father's arms. Artagan lifts him high into the air, the young boy cackling amidst his father's attentions. The two play-wrestle in the grass, as comfortable with one another as though they had parted only yesterday. My eyes water even more at the sight of our little family reunited again. I turn away, wiping my lashes lest Artagan tease me for being so motherly. But even a queen should be entitled to her own emotions from time to time, should she not?

Heading toward our tent, we pass a pair of men wrestling bare-chested while a crowd of Dyfed and Free Cantref soldiers cheer them on. I blink before I recognize Bowen of Dyfed and Keenan of Aranrhod as the combatants. Several purple bruises and welts mar their forearms and necks. I abruptly turn toward Artagan.

"What's this all about?"

"Blowing off steam." He smiles. "Our archers and the local spearmen kept getting into spats. Both camps grew restless as roosters in a henhouse. I even had Bowen and Carrick bickering with me at one point, griping about everything from the food to whether our intentions in Dyfed were as pure as we claimed."

"So you decided a wrestling match would resolve these issues better than words?"

"These men are warriors. If you don't let war dogs hunt, they'll start snapping at each other."

I glance back at the wrestling pit and, sure enough, both men grin and clasp one another's shoulders after the bout has finished. I shake my head. Menfolk are truly a species unto themselves. Rivals near beat each other to a pulp and suddenly they become lifelong friends. Still, I admire the way Artagan has unified the men. Such a solution truly would have never occurred to me in a hundred years.

The encampment bustles with activity as the soldiers hone their blades with whetstones. Wives and sweethearts try to steal a few last moments together with their lovers behind tent canvas and wicker huts. And who can blame them? None know what tomorrow brings.

Once inside our tent, we feast on fresh game hens and barley broth as the sun sets. The scent of woodsmoke permeates the small timber keep where Artagan has made his headquarters. A few pieces of furniture deck our otherwise spartan tent. A few chairs, a tabletop, some flagons of wine, and a simple bedstead. Artagan must have sent for these or had them built by local artisans. Small touches to make this tent dwelling feel a little bit more like our bedchamber back home. I put a warm hand on his sleeve as he and our boy eat at the table beside me. Artagan gnaws on his dinner, grinning at me with bits of chicken stuck between his teeth. I chortle through my nose. Mighty king or no, he still makes me laugh like at a court jester. Our little boy follows suit, giggling with us.

Yet a sudden wave of melancholy overwhelms me.

I put a finger to Artagan's lips, unable to refrain from interrupting him. My own voice overwhelms me, the words flooding from my lips like an unexpected torrent. I've put this off for too long.

"It's all been my fault," I begin. "Despite the things we've gained, I've risked much trying to save us and our kingdom, and I've put the life of our son and the child inside me in danger more than once. I can only ask that you find it in your heart to forgive me, husband."

Artagan blinks at me, surprised by this outburst of guilt.

I hang my head in candid repentance. Yes, I may have had my reasons for everything, but that doesn't entirely justify the risks. How hollow would our lives be now if I had secured peace or an alliance but lost our children in the process? Artagan reaches forward and lifts my chin.

"You are the *Mab Ceridwen* of my heart, and whatever you choose to do I will always trust you, Branwen. Always."

My eyes start to brim over.

"I love you, Artagan."

He smiles and puts his lips on mine.

"No tears, my love. From now on we do everything together, eh? No more divide and conquer. We'll meet our challenges hand in hand."

"Agreed." I beam back at him, squeezing his palm.

Gavin rattles his plate, either trying to get our attention or attempting to weed the vegetables out of his meal. Perhaps both. With one arm, Artagan scoots our son across the bench and puts Gavin between us. Our little boy murmurs contentedly at his food between the warmth of both his parents. A weight seems to lift from the bellows of my lungs, as though for the first time in a long time things are exactly as they should be. Our hunger takes over as the three of us devour the chicken until only bones remain.

After supper and the dismissal of the servants, Artagan invites the various leaders of our combined army to a council of war. Ten of us ring a large outdoor fire pit: Artagan's knights and those of Dyfed, as well as Griffith and myself. Olwen and young Arthwys also join us. I'd rather sleep with a snake in my bed than invite them to a secret council meeting, but at least I have the tact not to say so. War and alliances do indeed make strange bedfellows.

Artagan stokes the fire logs with a stick, gazing into the sparks as he addresses our council.

"Sab and Iago have not been idle in the North. My scouts report that the Picts have marched on the northernmost Free Cantref lands and subjugated them. The entire northern half of Wales is now under their sway."

A brooding silence falls over the small gathering. Olwen gasps, lowering her gaze. Although a former queen of the North by marriage, she was born in the northernmost Free Cantrefs, where her long-dead father once ruled as King Urien the Old. A twinge of sympathy for her rises within my breast. Her violet gaze suddenly fixates on me.

"This never would have happened had we not dallied in the South these past few weeks!"

I clench my jaw, balling my fists at my sides. All my budding sympathy for her vanishes in the smoke of the fire. My voice booms over the timber palisade.

"If we hadn't gone south to Gwent, Griffith's army would be half dead of the plague instead of here at our side! And my son and yours might very well have fallen prey to the assassin who stalks us!"

Artagan holds up his hands. Olwen and I both hold our tongues, but just barely. Why did she include herself in this council of war, anyway? Probably because she still sees herself as the rightful queen of the North. She knows that *if* we win, when this is all over, we will need someone the North Welsh still trust. Someone to try to make peace with the other kingdoms. But that's all a big *if* right now.

Even now, she still has no gratitude despite all I've done for her. Protecting *her* child, fighting to regain *her* kingdom. If not for our mutual foes, I'd just as likely expect to meet her at the end of an arrowhead. I suddenly find the thought of riddling her with arrows darkly pleasing.

And what of the assassin who seems to have strangely vanished? Not since we discovered that dagger embedded in our door at Caerleon have we seen hide or hair of him. Does the magic of Ogham Stone once again keep the villain at bay? Perhaps.

My stomach turns over, the babe inside me restless. Why of all times, oh Lord, do I have to be heavy with child now? While our kingdoms fight for their very existence! Why?

Perhaps Queen Sab has already won. Already she has what she wanted, one half of Wales at war with the other half. North against South. Welshman against Welshman. Cousin against cousin. No matter who wins, she will have revenge for the ancient blood feud between the Picts and the children of the Old Tribes. That blue-painted she-wolf and her temptress of a daughter will turn the Welsh Lands into a graveyard before they're through.

Griffith raises his voice, drawing my attention out of my own inner thoughts.

"We should let them come to us! Fortify ourselves here at Ogham Stone, and we will have the defensive advantage."

Several conversations break out at once. Bowen and Carrick argue that Dun Dyfed would offer a better defense, while Keenan and Emryus speak in favor of Aranrhod. Griffith stomps his foot, kicking up dust. He clearly favors a more southerly bastion near his own domains.

I shake my head. Hiding behind walls again will not help. Ever cautious, Griffith would build himself new fortifications. He would sit and wait for his enemies to come to him, breaking themselves against his defenses like waves against a rocky shore. But I doubt Queen Sab would be so stupid. No, she thinks like neither the Welsh nor the Saxons. She prefers to move sideways, always keeping her opponents off balance.

Glancing at Olwen, a thought engenders itself in my head. She once made herself queen of all the North, and she certainly didn't need any army to do it. Glancing around the fire, I briefly eye each knight and king.

Unable to restrain myself any longer, I lob a handful of pinecones into the hearth. The pop and crackle within the flames momentarily overwhelm all conversations and arguments. All eyes turn on me as the embers die down once again.

"Queen Sab is not like most opponents," I begin. "She will not try to besiege our castles or meet our army in the open, if she can avoid it. She's far craftier than that. If we hole up at Ogham Stone or somewhere else, her army will simply move around us, laying waste to the countryside as she goes."

Artagan nods in agreement.

"My Queen speaks true. Sab struck at Dun Dyfed when we least expected it and likewise abandoned it just before we could concentrate our forces against her. She is shifty. I doubt she will come to us simply because we want her to."

Arthwys smirks, folding his arms as he glares at me across the flames.

"What would you have us do, then? Cower in fear before a woman enemy?"

Ignoring Arthwys's attempt to bait me, I glance again at Olwen before turning my level gaze on the dark-eyed teenage prince.

"We must exploit Sab's weakness. King Iago."

Most of the nobles around the campfire laugh, all except Arthwys and Olwen. Iago has been a rival king to many of these noblemen, and few consider him a friend. King Griffith shakes his head with a grin.

"'Tis a good jest, my lady, but what advantage, pray tell, do we have merely because King Iago marches with the Picts?"

"More than half of Queen Sab's army is made of North Welshmen," I reply. "Unlike Sab and her Picts, King Iago *is* predictable.

We must merely find something he wants, and we shall draw his army to us."

"Something he wants?" Ahern asks.

"Aye. We should do something that even Iago and Sab cannot ignore, something that will force them to meet us in open battle. We should muster our armies and invade North Wales."

Silence pervades the group. Nothing but the snap of kindling murmurs from the fire pit. Artagan turns toward me.

"You mean to take the coastal road north and cross into Iago's domains?"

Before I can answer, Prince Arthwys interrupts.

"'Tis folly! No one, not us nor the Saxons, has conquered Gwynedd since the days of the Romans!"

"The boy is right." Griffith grimaces. "North Wales is surrounded by the tallest mountains in the Welsh Lands, its approaches covering barren moors and rocky rivers. The North is a natural citadel. We could never hope to take it."

My eyes narrow on Griffith and the young prince.

"We don't need to conquer the North, nor should we try. Merely our presence alone on Iago's borders will be threat enough. He cannot afford to ignore us if we march on his lands."

A small smile forms on Artagan's lips. He nods.

"I see. Conquest is not our goal, but merely to draw Iago and Sab's forces onto a field of our choosing. Whatever Sab wants, she will have to abandon her plans should we invade the North. Iago and his men will kick and scream until Sab lets them rally to defend their lands and homesteads. It is a wise plan, my love."

He beams at me with his azure gaze, admiring me the way he might a wise sage. Before I can smile back at Artagan, Griffith folds his arms beside me. The shadows of the firelight deepen the dark bags under his eyes.

"It is indeed a bold plan, but a risky one at that. If Sab and Iago do not go for it, our own lands will be defenseless."

"They'll take the bait," I reply. "If they don't, they risk us razing the Northlands to the ground."

I try my best to sound confident and calm. Thankfully, my sweating palms are hidden within the folds of my gown. The plan I offer indeed has many perils, but surely these men see that we have no other real choice. Not if we intend to defeat the Picts without destroying ourselves in the process.

We must somehow defeat Sab without getting our own warriors butchered. Otherwise, the Saxons will overwhelm us just as soon as we rid ourselves of the Picts. Our conflict with Sab is anything but simple. Even if she loses, she may still draw enough blood to mortally wound the free kingdoms of Wales. It seems that she might get her vengeance upon us either way.

PART THREE

Autumn, A.D. 602

15

A fell breeze chills my skin, the babe stirring within me. My navel has popped out and I know my days run short as I near the end of my term. Soon the birthing will come upon me. A few weeks more at most. And likely my death with it.

I've not spoken a word of my vision to anyone, not even Artagan. Bloodstains and the cries from childbed haunt my dreams enough as it is. What good would it do to tell him, anyway? Such foreboding would only poison our last days together, and I would rather feel Artagan's warm caresses as he sleeps beside me and our son each night. No pity or sorrow will cloud his glances. Instead, a perennial hope for an ever brighter future shines behind his eyes. I love him dearly, but he is a man, after all, and succumbs willingly to such unbounded optimism. Women, especially mothers, know better.

As I sit up in our tent, my husband and son lie asleep beneath the coverlets. The dim thunder of the nearby seashore murmurs in my ears. A thick fog obscures the sunrise. We have journeyed ever northward each day with our army, with neither sight nor sound of our enemy. I almost wish they would appear, simply to end the tension that tightens each day within my chest. Another few days of this and my heart shall burst asunder. I'd rather face my foes head-on than withstand this damnable waiting game.

Where have Sab and Iago gotten to? They wouldn't simply let us march up to their borders unchallenged. Would they? No, they have to come and try to stop us. They have to. Otherwise, our own lands in the South will indeed lie undefended should the Picts and North Welsh strike there. Heaven help us if I am wrong.

I pace outside the tent flaps in the gray dawn. Perhaps I have forgotten something, something important. Iago and his forces may have already withdrawn into their citadels at Snowdon and Mona. If they do that, all we can do is lay a siege, and in the barren crags of the North we would be just as likely as the enemy to starve to death. But if what Artagan's scouts report is true, then Sab and Iago's forces have scattered themselves across the northern Free Cantrefs of Powys while attempting to subdue the villages there. That would mean the enemy has ranged too far from their northern holdfasts to reach their castles in time. They will have to make directly for the coastal road and try to intercept us first. Or so I keep telling myself.

The morning mists part over our encampment, revealing the green and red dragon banners of our alliance. About two thousand green-clad archers and a thousand more Dyfed spearmen surround our tent in a wide crescent. Another two thousand of Griffith's swordsmen have their tents pitched across the sandy coast road. Near five thousand souls all told. Hopefully, it will be enough. It has to be. There simply are no more troops to be spared from Aranrhod to Caerleon.

Several years ago we gathered a host twice as large to face the Saxons. But we suffered severe losses and have not had time to replace those who fell defending our homelands. A few years of intervening peace have not given our population nearly enough time to recover. Ever more are our warriors needed against the threats of Saxon and Pictish barbarians. And each season there are fewer and fewer of us left to defend Wales. Perhaps the brooding old priests are right, and the End of Days is truly upon us.

Arms surround me from behind. I flinch and nearly cry out before recognizing my husband's familiar scent. A hint of sweet pine sap and woodsmoke. The smells of a man who spends many days outdoors and in the field. I relax in his arms as he nuzzles my hair, his voice soft beside my ear.

"How fares my love and our little bundle inside you?"

"The child is restless. I think I've only another fortnight or two before my time comes."

"Your shoulders are tight as a knotty oak, my sweet. What troubles you so?"

Only Artagan could ask such a question. What with a war against the Picts, memories of an assassin, and a nearing birthing all weighing me down. If only I had his gift for living in the present, somehow able to put off thoughts of worry as he does. I merely kiss him in reply.

He smiles as our lips touch.

"Do you remember our first kiss, my love?"

"Aye." I beam back at him. "That and the many after."

I press my cheek against his chest, closing my eyes as he holds me. He rests his chin atop my head. Most of the encampment still slumbers, leaving just my husband and me awake while all the world sleeps. My voice warbles out scarcely above a whisper.

"I'm scared, Artagan. Mayhaps more than I've ever been."

"More than when your first husband tried to kill us? Or the Saxons? Or anyone else, for that matter?"

"I'm serious, love. In some ways, Sab and the Picts scare me more than the Saxons. They are so different from us, almost more animal than human. And I cannot forget that assassin wearing Morgan's helmet, hunting for our boy. Promise me, Artagan, no matter what happens to me, that when the child comes you will look after the newborn babe and Gavin. Promise me you'll let no harm come to them."

Artagan draws back, still smiling as he plants a kiss on my brow. His arms feel warm as I snuggle up against his sternum, clinging to him as a drowning woman to a piece of driftwood. Heaven help me, I'm shivering like a child afraid of the dark. But there's no one else here to see but Artagan. He strokes my hair, his soothing voice in my ear.

"Hush, my love. No harm will come to you or our children. You birthed our boy just fine and you'll fare just as well with this next child. As for the Picts, don't give them another thought. Yours was a good plan to take the fight to them. I think you surprised everyone, including me, with your battle strategy. When did you become such a war-chief?"

I shrug.

"I only do what I must. Build a castle, barter peace, fight a war. A queen has little choice. She must make do, or she will soon do without."

Artagan guffaws slightly under his breath.

"Well, give neither Sab nor Iago another thought. Your tactics have brought us this far, and now I have a plan of mine own once we encounter the brigands."

"You do?"

I back up a touch and eye him closely.

"Aye, of course I have a plan," he replies, with a half-feigned smirk of consternation. "Why look you so surprised?"

"Because you are brave and honest and a great leader of men amidst the chaos, but when it comes to looking ahead, your plots oft involve far more improvisation than well-laid plans. Although, truth be told, you're becoming a better strategist day by day."

He flashes his familiar cocky grin.

"Improvisation, eh? If you're referring to that time on the King's Road, I knew what I was doing the entire time."

"You were outnumbered ten to one by Saxons! You barely survived by the skin of your teeth."

"I saved your life, though, didn't I?"

I frown, not deigning to reply. My husband has more luck in his little finger than all the saints in Christendom, but that doesn't mean he can walk through fire at will. One of these days, his reckless good luck is bound to run out. Artagan rubs my shoulders, gently trying to assuage the tension in my muscles.

"Trust me, Branwen. I've a stratagem of my own, and I aim to turn the tables on Sab and her would-be allies whenever they decide to show themselves. You do trust me, my Queen, don't you?"

A knot forms in my throat. What can I say? I've entrusted him with my heart. I would follow him through the fires of hell and back. My love for him goes far beyond paltry words like "trust." I'd give anything at this moment for the two of us to be home again, in our bedchamber at Aranrhod. I look down, trying to blink back the water behind my eyes. Artagan lifts my chin with his hand.

"Branwen, you trust me, yes?"

I nod, sniffling slightly. Artagan presses his lips to mine, his warm breath thawing the morning chill on my cheeks. I stroke the dark stubble on his jaw, shutting out the rest of the world as I close my eyes. A small hand tugs at my skirts.

"Mama."

Gavin smiles up at me. My little darling. Was I wrong to bring him so near to danger? But that assassin still lurks out there somewhere. Surrounded by an army, my son could find no safer place in all of Wales, even if we are on the very brink of battle. I'll not let Gavin leave my side for a single day. Not until this is all over. If indeed it ever ends.

My son grins up at me with a blanket in one hand. I suddenly notice that he is naked from the waist up. My eyes narrow. Where did his nightshirt go? It's cold enough outside to freeze beer, and my boy offs his shirt as though it were a midsummer day. Early autumn winds blow swiftly off the nearby sea, but Gavin only smiles as his chest ripples in gooseflesh. Another hot-blood, just like his father. I kneel down and wrap Gavin up in my shawl.

"Darling, you'll catch your death of cold in this weather."

Gavin smiles, and points at Artagan.

"Dada."

Artagan has doffed his own linen shirt, bare chested and fair skinned as our boy. His nipples perk in the cool sea air. He pinches Gavin's cheek.

"That's my little Celt!" Artagan beams. "A warrior-poet, born for the misty morn."

My two boys giggle, despite one being a toddler and the other my husband. I shake my head. Artagan really is no better than a child himself at times. I chastise the pair of them with half-feigned indignation.

"Get your clothes back on over your heads, both of you! No better than a pair of heathens!"

The two smirk, their grins mirror images. One being dark of hair and the other auburn. I stifle a smile myself. My two boys. They thread their arms through their linens, but I still wrap a fur tartan around each of their shoulders for good measure. My King and Princeling might be mighty warrior-poets, but I swear they'd freeze to death on a wet day if I wasn't there to cover them up.

Someone clears her throat behind us. My shoulders immediately tense. Olwen folds her arms, one eyebrow raised as she watches us.

"Don't let me interrupt your family moment."

I level my gaze. Doesn't she have her own son to tend to? Maybe if she'd been more of a family woman herself, her own husband would not have been lured into the arms of another. My tone runs cold.

"What do you want, Olwen?"

"We've a war on, remember? Or at least we're supposed to. Still no sign of Sab or my husband. Looks like your plan has all come to naught, *Mab Ceridwen*."

She pronounces my namesake with more than a light mocking tone. I ball my fists at my sides, but Artagan puts his hands on my shoulders, trying to sooth the knots out of my muscles. It's never a good sign when my hot-blooded husband is the one trying to get *me* to calm down. Is my wrath for Olwen so obvious? It would seem so.

By now most of the encampment's inhabitants have awakened, smoke trails filling the sky from morning campfires. Soldiers banter as they roast their breakfasts of gruel and fresh game. Enough woodsmoke fills the air to ensure that every Welshman in North Wales can tell where our army camps. Surely Sab and Iago must know where to find us by now.

Trying my best to ignore Olwen's violet stare, I unroll a large map on one of the makeshift tables erected in Artagan's tent. Rowena takes Gavin off my hands, feeding porridge to each of the children for breakfast. God bless her. It's hard enough to be heavy with child and watch a toddler, let alone having to be a queen in a time of war.

Artagan and Olwen both join me as I pore over the chart. My round belly bumps the table. Jesus wept! I can hardly lean over a tabletop, so how could I lead an army into battle? When the fight comes, and it will, I shall have to be looking on from a distance. Artagan and the others may take up the battle standard, but I can hardly waddle, let alone wield a bow or spear against the Picts.

Which probably means I'll be stuck at the rear of the army with Olwen. I grind my teeth. She would be the last person to consider going into battle. Her ladyship wouldn't want to rend a fingernail or muss the rouge powder on her cheeks, I suppose. Some women are meant for pincushions, and Olwen is such a woman if I ever saw one.

Centering the chart on the table, I place a palm on either side of North Wales. Faded ink indicates the large crescent of mountains and squiggles of streams that intersect the landscape of the North. Olwen frowns beside me, rapping her knuckles across the parchment.

"This is hopeless!" she scoffs. "The North is impregnable. I should know, I've been its Queen these past few years. Mountains bar every invader, leaving only two narrow approaches, one along the north coast and the other where we are along the western shore. A narrow passage either way that our enemies can block up indefinitely. You're leading us into a bloody massacre, Branwen!"

I clench my jaw, not deigning to look at her smug face.

"Have you a better idea? Or do you expect your husband to stop cuckolding you and just give you your queenship back?"

Olwen's eyes burn with a purplish fire. Artagan steps between us. If not for him, I'd take a switch to Olwen before she could blink. Trying to keep us focused on the task at hand, Artagan strokes his chin while he ponders the map.

"Strange that with such a barren, mountainous kingdom, Iago manages to keep the best horses and cavalry in Wales," he muses.

Olwen taps the outline of a large island off the coast of the Northlands.

"That's because the Isle of Mona is fertile, very unlike the rocky coasts of the mainland. The island is a breadbasket with enough grain and pasture to feed Iago's entire kingdom."

Artagan's eyebrows rise in astonishment.

"Then North Wales truly is the most perfect realm for defense. A good food supply for Iago's horses and rough terrain on his borders to thwart his foes."

I bite my tongue until a bitter, metallic taste rises in my mouth. Even Artagan starts to see things Olwen's way. The North is indeed a natural fortress. The Isle of Mona holds all their foodstuffs, but in order to get near it an army would have to cross impenetrable mountains and then approach via a narrow coastal defile that Iago and Sab's army would certainly be guarding. My shoulders sink. Perhaps my stratagem is truly hopeless. We cannot possibly hope to defeat Iago's men on their home ground.

But we don't need to conquer them. That would bleed both our armies dry, anyway, and I do not wish to see any more Welshmen die than necessary. No, we need only draw Sab and Iago to us. And then what? My mind suddenly runs blank. I turn to Artagan, trying to summon the last reserves of confidence into my voice.

"You said before that you had your own plan, my love. A way to defeat Queen Sab?"

"Aye, but first we need her to come find us."

"She'll come, she has to. We're on the edge of their hinterlands now. If Sab and Iago don't move to block us soon, we'll be near the heart of his kingdom within a few days."

Artagan smiles.

"Iago won't let us get that far into his territory uncontested. He'll show up."

Olwen scoffs, exhaling sharply through her teeth.

"My husband might, but Queen Sab? Heaven knows what that heathen chieftess will do."

For once, I cannot disagree with her. Olwen has a point about Sab. She is anything but predictable. But we cannot delay confrontation with her any longer. Time is on Sab's side. The longer we postpone battling her, the more time she has to weaken Wales. Every day her barbarians pillage and burn our villages while the Saxons look on across the border, biding their time. We must strike the Picts, and we must do it soon.

An ox horn sounds across the encampment. My skin ripples with goose bumps. Griffith's bugle call. He would not use it this close to enemy territory unless some danger was nigh at hand.

Artagan, Olwen, and I duck out under the tent flaps. Griffith stands outside, lowering his horn as an armorer fits chain mail and bracers on him. The fat monarch points toward a quartet of riders galloping headlong across the greens toward us. My husband's scouts. Emryus, Keenan, Bowen, and Carrick.

The four knights halt their panting mounts a few paces from our tents, plumes of steam rising from the stallions' dilated nostrils. The riders' chests heave in and out, equally out of breath as their steeds. Keenan speaks up first, motioning toward the misty mountains in the distance with his battle-ax. His wide eyes focus on Artagan.

"Riders, my liege! Hundreds, nigh thousands of them! They're coming down through the mountain passes now, flying black standards from their lance poles."

A prickly sensation wends its way up my spine. Black dragon banners. King Iago's Northmen. So the North Welsh army has come. A dim thunder rumbles from the cloud-covered ridges to the northeast, but it is no storm that roars from those heights.

Artagan puts a hand on his sword, his eyes surveying the foggy downs before us.

"What of the Picts?" he demands. "Any sign of them?"

Keenan shrugs. Before anyone else can reply, another set of horse hooves claps up the heath, this time a rider coming from the shore to the west. Arthwys, tall and skinny in the saddle, urges his stud forward. He halts his beast just shy of running us down. The young Prince's cheeks are beet red, his breath fogging his face. He looks right past Artagan and me, addressing his King.

"King Griffith, black sails have been spotted offshore! The lookouts say the sailors aboard have blue skin."

The back of my neck bristles. Blue woad. Queen Sab and her army of Picts will land from the sea, decked in war paint. She means to give us battle for certain. It looks as though I've finally gotten what I wanted, a confrontation with Sab and Iago. Let's hope I've not bitten off more than I can chew.

One enemy army comes from the east and another from the west. They mean to smash us as though between a mighty anvil and hammer. Despite the cold, my brow beads with sweat.

Artagan turns and raises his voice so that all in camp can hear.

"Free Welshmen, to arms! The enemy approaches! Let the bastards hear you roar!"

A deep, throaty hurrah rises from our encampment, loud enough to shake the pillars of the earth. My skin buzzes from end to end. Even the Picts on the water and the riders in the hills must have heard that. The battle draws nigh.

A thin foaming stream full of rocks and small rapids cuts between the mountains and the sea. A narrow ribbon of blue-gray water, it divides our army from our foes. An unremarkable tributary, it nonetheless marks the border between the northern and southern halves of the Welsh Lands this day.

On one bank, rows of green-clad archers stand under emerald dragon banners of the Free Cantrefs. Spear-wives number amongst our rough-looking bowmen while Dyfed spearmen with calfskin shields stand at their side. Farther down the flank, Griffith's men-at-arms march in squarelike formations beneath their crimson flags, looking like a gigantic checkerboard.

Across the river, a mass of horses tears up the muddy earth. A forest of sharp lances towers over the vast cavalcade. Iago's cavalry columns look like a massive creature with a thousand horse legs and just as many prickly spines of pikes. Along the beach, throngs of half-naked, azure-tattooed men and women spill out of the beaks of rawhide ships, covering the land like a black-and-blue plague. My nose wrinkles, smelling the horse manure and the odor of the unwashed warriors from across the stream.

Astride my mountain pony, I turn in the saddle to face Artagan. His dark stallion, Merlin, shifts its weight nervously beneath him. Artagan never takes his gaze off the Picts as I speak to him.

"Should we try to wade the stream, or let them come to us?"

"Neither."

He nods to a Free Cantref soldier, who in turn raises a white linen cloth atop a battle standard. The warrior waves it high overhead for the enemy to see. My eyebrows rise in disbelief.

"You mean to ask for a truce?"

"I mean to parley with them."

"What is there to talk about? We've come here to do battle, not mince words."

"Trust me, Branwen."

I swallow but say no more. Of course I trust him. But it seems like an off-kilter world when I ache for fighting while Artagan argues for diplomacy. But so be it. The child in my womb somersaults. My eyes widen like egg whites, but I keep my composure. Just barely. Times like these make being a breeding woman just about the most damned inconvenient thing in the world.

The North Welsh dip their dark banners in the distance, signaling agreement to the proposed parley. Nothing happens amongst the Picts, but we can only assume they will honor the temporary truce. Or so I hope.

A small group of us rides to the water's edge, a little more than a stone's throw from our army's front lines. Artagan gallops in the lead with me behind him on my mare. Griffith, Arthwys, and even Olwen, of all people, come gallivanting after us on horseback.

An equally small band approaches the opposite bank. Iago rides on horseback with his scantily clad mistress, Ness, sitting just behind him in the saddle. She wraps her arms about Iago's middle. Other than a large fur covering her shoulders, I doubt she wears more than a loincloth from her hips down to her bare feet. She glares malevolently at Olwen and me with a smug, self-satisfied grin. Sab approaches on foot, alone save for her long bone spear in hand. A few more tattoos than I remember have appeared on her face. The Picts certainly have the Devil's sense of beauty.

None of us, save Artagan, have any idea what this parley could possibly hope to accomplish. Does he intend to issue a few threats? Maybe taunt them or try to get inside their heads? I cannot even begin to guess, and judging by the looks Griffith and Arthwys exchange, they too seem equally puzzled. Olwen glares directly at her husband, grimacing until lines form on both sides of her normally flawless face.

Across the stream, Iago shifts uncomfortably in the saddle. Ness strokes and paws at his chest, petting him like a tame cat. As little as I ever sympathize with Olwen, even I would like to put an arrow between Ness's eyeballs. The sultry harlot spares a longing gaze at my husband as well before winking at me. My hand tightens along the grip of my longbow.

Sab speaks first, her voice deep and rough as a hag's despite her almost youthful appearance.

"Blacksword, I never thought you one for much words. More the strike-first-and-ask-questions-later type of man."

"Aye, and so often I am," he replies, grimly staring her down. "But I've a proposition for you."

Ness smiles from behind Iago.

"Come to surrender and join us?" she says with a wicked smile. "My big Blacksword?"

She bites her lower lip, clearly thinking more than she should about my husband, even while she has an arm on Iago. My skin grows hot. I urge my mount forward until I am beside Artagan. Queen Sab's eyes focus on my round abdomen.

"The child comes soon, no? Pity. You've not told him what will happen, have you, Mab Ceridwen?"

I glare back at the savage chieftess, wondering if she even has a heart in which I could embed a dagger. Of all times to bring up my vision of perishing in childbirth! Artagan glances my way, his brows furrowed in thought.

"Told me? Told me what?"

Ignoring him, I keep my heavy gaze squarely on Sab. I don't even blink. Now is not the time to reveal my deepest fears and put one more worry in my beloved's head.

"Let my husband say what he has come to say. If it were up to me, we'd already be raining down arrows on your head."

Sab smirks, clicking her tongue in disapproval. She knows she's gotten under my skin, just like she always has. To think I once sat across from her in a room and talked like we were two human beings. Given the chance again, I'd just as soon run her through with a rusty cleaver. Small wonder the women of the Old Tribes and the Picts were such bitter foes for so many centuries. A Saxon barbarian may try to rape and murder, but a Pict settles for no less than crushing one's very soul. Sab's crooked smile spreads wider across her painted face.

"Very well, speak quickly, King Artagan. I've a war to win."

Artagan draws his long blade, making every soul on both sides of the stream suddenly tense and quiet. His voice sounds sterner than I've ever heard it, his face a mask.

"I challenge you to the ancient rite of single combat. Two warriors in a fight to the death. Our best champion against your best champion, and the victor accepts homage from both armies."

My skin runs cold, my voice deserting me. Has Artagan gone mad? A battle of champions! *That's* his brilliant idea? Everyone on both sides of the brook exchanges glances. King Iago's baritone laughter breaks the silence.

"You honestly expect us to agree to such an outdated custom? Do you take us for fools?"

Sab raises a hand to silence him. Little wonder who really runs the kingdom in the North now. Neither Sab nor Ness are laughing. The Pictish Queen steps to the edge of the stream, looking at Artagan with wide-eyed wonder.

"That is the ancient Pictish way of resolving wars."

"As it was with the Old Tribes, or so my mother always told me."

"And you would abide by the outcome, no matter who won?"

"Just as I would expect you to do the same."

Glancing back and forth between Sab and my husband, I feel everything rapidly spiraling out of control. In another time and place, perhaps Artagan's proposal would not sound so bold, but the more Sab nods her head in agreement, the more my stomach turns over. Every fiber of my being tells me never to agree to anything Queen Sab says. *Never.*

I admit that Artagan's way would certainly reduce the bloodshed, especially with Welshman fighting Welshman on either side of the battlefield. But I've little doubt whom Artagan would select as our champion. He is *my* love, and I'd not sacrifice him for all the Welsh in Christendom. And whom will the Picts select as the best warrior in their army? Artagan may be an unsurpassed swordsman amongst the Free Cantrefs, but does that make him the best in all Wales? I don't want to put such presumptions to the test. Not here and now. Not like this. My head starts to spin as I hold a palm up to my dizzy head.

Sab raises her deathly pale bone spear high over her head.

"We agree to your terms, Artagan Blacksword. Who will be your army's champion?"

Both Griffith and Olwen start to protest, but Artagan silences them with a quick stare. He too will not be swayed from this agreement. I reach out for him, weakly failing to even touch him. My entire body and soul seem sapped of strength. This cannot be happening. Artagan sets his jaw.

"I shall be the champion for the Free Welsh."

Sab's smile forms a deep V. She turns back toward the Pictish mob a few dozen paces behind her, shouting out something quick and harsh in her barbaric tongue. A wave of ululating cries reverberates from the Pictish lines. A lone figure emerges from the crowd of blue-painted savages. Someone with a dark silhouette, towering over every other warrior on the field. Sab lobs her bone-white spear into the grasp of the combatant's hand as he approaches without a word.

My eyes narrow on the huge, well-muscled stranger. I blink furiously in sudden disbelief. My heart plummets within me, sinking like an iron weight. The champion of the Picts twirls the massive bone spear in his hand, his face obscured behind a steel mask with broken antler horns. The mask of my first husband, the Hammer King.

16

A sickening wave of heat rises through my chest. My pony moves back a step, startled by the presence of the Pictish champion. My lower lip trembles as Artagan and I exchange glances. Morgan still lives? The man who once shared my bed, and of late has tried to assassinate my little son, seems to be a ghost no longer. The other members of our small party look equally shaken. Griffith leans forward in the saddle, his voice quivering as much as his bearded jowls.

"The Hammer King? It cannot be . . ."

Across the tiny stream, even Ness and Iago give the Pict champion a wide berth. Only Sab smiles beside her silent warrior. Behind his steel mask, he looks first at Artagan and then at me. The gorge rises in my throat and I can barely keep my breakfast down. Artagan shifts his steed in front of me, the stallion we stole from King Morgan several years ago, no less. My husband aims his long blade across the water.

"The Hammer King perished fighting the Saxons at the Battle of the Bloody Fords, years ago!" he bellows. "I was there when it happened. I never feared King Morgan in life, and I certainly shan't fear his ghost. Show yourself!"

The masked warrior glances at Sab, who in turn nods her head. He removes the iron mask and its antlered helm. A boyish, tattooed face blinks stoically at us. Somehow, I find my voice again.

"Bal? You came to us as Sab's herald when we besieged Dun Dyfed. What are you doing wearing the Hammer King's mask?"

Sab laughs in reply.

"He speaks no Welsh, remember? But surely you recognize him, Queen Branwen? I believe you've met Bal quite often these past few moons . . . at your castle in Aranrhod, on the road to Dyfed . . ."

My mouth opens to reply, but the words stick in my throat. *No.* The assassin who first struck that night in Aranrhod. The one who tracked us into the wilds and would have slain Ahern and me had it not been for the arrival of Artagan's army. My brows furrow in thought. But that was before I had even met Sab, which could only mean . . . Oh, God.

My eyes widen while Sab watches me. She smirks as though she can read my thoughts unraveling the mystery. Her voice sounds haggish and harsh as ever.

"Yes, my little Queen, it was I behind the attacks all along. I sent Bal to strike terror into your hearts, better than an army might have done. What better way to do so than in the guise of your long-dead husband? Bal acquired the mask as a trophy from a raid last year against the Saxons. Fortuitous, no? First he threatens your son, and today your husband . . . I will draw every drop of agony from you, daughter of the Old Tribes, before I am through with you."

I shake my head, still trying to make sense of it all.

"But we parleyed, and talked so often at Dun Dyfed. Why did you not strike us then?"

"You intrigued me for a time, so I called Bal off. But I changed my mind. You and I can never be allies."

So it was not any magic in the boulders at Ogham Stone that kept the assassin at bay. Sab merely toyed with me, like a mouse caught between a cat's paws. My fists shake at my sides as I struggle to reply, my mind still reeling from all she says.

"Why are you doing this?"

Sab's smile fades into a flat, broad line.

"It's an old hate. Your people drove mine into the northern wastes generations ago. Now it's our turn. The Picts shall rise again!"

I eye Sab closely. The manuscript regarding my mother's youth when she lived near the Picts suddenly returns to my mind. Somehow my mother's dealings with the Picts has bearing on Sab's actions now. They must. It's time to know the truth, one way or the other. I aim my index finger at Sab.

"Is this because my mother would not side with the Picts against the Saxons all those years ago?"

Sab's gaze darkens.

"So you've finally figured that much out, have you?" she replies with a hiss. "Your mother betrayed my people! Leaving them to be slaughtered by the Saxons. My mother was the Pict Queen who offered your mother an alliance. Instead of finding an ally, she was abandoned to be slain on the battlefield by barbarians. I was young, but I remember it well. Those of us who survived fled north to scratch out a living amongst the barren rocks where it was too cold for the Saxons to follow."

My eyes widen. Her mother and mine once rivals, then potential allies, and finally enemies once more. Just like Sab and I now. Now the root of Sab's hatred for me becomes all too clear. She plans to avenge her deceased mother by striking down the daughter of her old enemy. But instead of swelling with anger, a flame of hope kindles within my chest. I reach out to Sab, imploring her as earnestly as I can.

"Whatever befell our mothers resulted from their decisions, not ours. We've a chance to start anew, this very moment, you and I. We can choose the same follies all our foremothers made before us in the ceaseless rivalry betwixt the Old Tribes and the Picts. Or we can choose peace. The future is not written, Sab. We can change it, right here, right now."

Sab's lips merely twist into a sickeningly sour smile. The blood runs cold in my veins. There is no compromise, no mercy behind her hard eyes. Her mother is dead, because of a choice my mother made long ago. Our lives have darkly mirrored one another's, each taking up the mantle of our mothers, our fates set on a collision in which only one of us can be permitted to survive. Suddenly, the full fury of Sab's vengeance is so plain to see.

Without another word, Sab backs away from the stream, both Iago and Ness doing likewise. Bal stands alone, twirling his bone spear and flexing his broad, pale muscles. The Hammer King's steel mask rests at his feet. Nothing can stop this contest of single combat now.

Griffith, Olwen, and Arthwys turn their steeds to go. The duel requires only Artagan and Bal. Still, I cannot leave, my mare and I rooted to the ground. Griffith nods toward us as he departs.

"God be with you, Artagan."

Olwen says nothing, her eyes watering as she looks her last on my husband. Even now some small part of her still longs for the young hedge knight who was once her lover. Before he met me and asked me to be his wife.

Artagan dismounts and hands me the reins of his stallion. Our hands meet. I lean down in the saddle, as much as I can with my heavy belly. He presses his lips to mine.

"Look after Merlin." He nods toward the horse. "He trusts no rider other than you or myself."

I plead with him, grasping his hands.

"Artagan, you don't have to do this. They have as many troops as we do, we have an even chance of defeating them in battle."

"And how many Welshmen would die, one killing the other? No, Queen Sab would win either way because of that, and you know it. Today only one man need die, and I intend to make damned sure it's the one who tried to harm our son."

He speaks this last part through clenched teeth. All this time I feared the foe hunting our boy might be Morgan's ghost. Now that my husband knows the assassin is a man of flesh and blood, Artagan only sees red. He will try to take the Pict's head. Or die trying.

I clasp Artagan's hand in mine, not ready to let go. Both armies look on from across the field, an audience ten thousand strong murmuring amongst themselves as word spreads that two champions will duel for the fate of all Wales. North versus South, Pict versus

Welsh, evil versus good. I shut my eyes, the child in my womb shuddering.

Every fiber of my being wants to sink to my knees and beg Artagan not to go. Just run, run away from all of this. We could live happy and poor as sparrows in some mountainside cottage with our family. Deep in the wilds we could simply flee and forget the rest of this troubled world. I know we could.

But Artagan will not yield as an enemy seeks to subjugate our people, and why should he? He is a king, after all, and I am his queen. I will not send him into battle without the blessing of the woman he loves. I squeeze his hand, summoning the last false confidence into my face. My voice barely rises above a whisper as I glance at Bal, then back at my husband.

"Bring me his heart, lover. If he has one. Bring me back his black, bloody heart."

Without a second glance, I lead my mare and my husband's stallion back toward our own lines. All eyes seem to rest on me, but the soldiers give me a wide berth. Only one soul dares sidle her horse next to me. Olwen sits still in the saddle, not saying a word as she waits beside me. We will watch Artagan's fate together, whatever it may be. The two women in all the world who love him most.

Across the greens and the river between us, Sab's black-and-blue figure stands apart from her army. Despite the ten thousand souls who surround us, I know her eyes rest only on me. As though the two of us were alone together, on opposing sides of the same chessboard.

She has outwitted me at nearly every turn, playing me like a child. Me! The Mab Ceridwen who defied a kingdom by forsaking the Hammer King in favor of the man I loved, wedding Artagan and defeating the Saxons despite the odds. My heart thuds faster, my fingertips all atremble. I'd rather face ten thousand Saxons than battle Queen Sab and her plots this day.

At the center of the thin river dividing our armies lies a tiny islet. A grassy spit of land in the shallows, no more than a few dozen ells long. As though previously agreed upon, both Artagan and Bal advance into the waters, wading up to their thighs until they reach the small isle. Something about the knee-high grass and gray silt of the islet reminds me of the scalp of a giant, half-submerged in the river. The top of a mossy skull upon which two men will meet, but only one will come away alive.

Artagan takes off his shirt. Despite the cool air, I know his skin will already be hot and pink just like our little boy's. Unlike some kings, Artagan has never let sitting on a throne soften his physique. Active in the field as ever, the same courage that has gained the adoration of his men has also kept him fit as any other nobleman in Christendom. With taut pectorals and bulging arms, my husband wields his famous longsword with its unusual silver and onyx hues. The Blacksword.

Bal likewise strips until barefoot, wearing only a simple loincloth. His blue tattoos wriggle like snakes across his pallid flesh, bobbing and weaving as he flexes his muscles. Almost statuesque, the silent Pict towers a full head over my husband. Artagan's dark hair flows loose and wild about his shoulders while Bal's short bleached locks stand on end, like spikes greased with lye. Both are warriors, yet the King and the assassin could not look more different.

Artagan takes the first swing. Perspiration breaks out afresh across my temples. Without a word or signal, the fight begins. No decorum. No fancy speeches. Just a battle to the death.

My husband's initial lunges take Bal slightly off balance, the tall Pict teetering on one foot as he leans back. A cheer rises along our lines as the Welsh warriors in our army praise Artagan's aggressive stance. I might smile if it weren't my own love down in the grassy arena. He is brave and was never one to let the enemy take the fight to him. But this is no sparring match where both contenders can merely walk away when finished.

Bal squats down. I cock my head to the side, unable to understand why he bends his legs so. In the blink of an eye, the Pict springs into the air, vaulting well over Artagan's head and landing behind him. Twirling the bone spear like a pendulum of death, he nearly strikes Artagan from behind. The Blacksword ducks and parries with his blade, but only just in time.

My pulse quickens in my throat. This Bal is not human. No Welshman born of a woman can jump like that. He uses some strange Pictish fighting techniques unknown to us. I grimace until my cheeks sting. This is more of Sab's witchcraft. More of her queer Pictish ways. I can almost feel her sneering at me across the divide between us.

Artagan growls loud enough for all to hear, his blood up. Lightning strokes and flashes of steel glint under the gray sun as he puts Bal to the test. Artagan's quick movements would make mincemeat of most men, but Bal does not stay still for long. He dodges and weaves like a dancer. Even while parrying Artagan's blows with his spear, the Pict manages to kick Artagan full in the gut, sending my husband reeling backward. I gasp with a hand to my mouth.

A hush falls over our lines as our enemies across the way cheer their champion. Artagan staggers to his feet, bent over as though he had the wind knocked out of him. Quick to take advantage, Bal pounces with the tip of his white spearhead. Artagan turns aside just in time as the spear narrowly misses him and embeds itself in the dirt.

Pressing my lips together, I look down at my trembling hands. I cannot watch. The clang of steel and bone murmurs from the islet in the stream, both men breathing heavy enough for all to hear. Both armies quiet down. It's so silent I can hear my heartbeat drumming in my ears.

A hand reaches out and grasps mine. Olwen's palm feels cold to the touch, yet she squeezes mine without taking her gaze from the duel. Lost for words, I simply hold on to her long fingertips, forcing my eyes to focus on the two combatants circling one another in no-man's-land.

Both men have drawn blood, each harboring at least half a dozen scars and nicks that show crimson against their fair skin. The two warriors grunt with every thrust and deflection, their breath steaming against their faces in the cool midmorning air. Several ravens circle high overhead. Every man and beast knows that the conclusion between the two titans draws near. I clutch Olwen's palm all the tighter, fighting the urge to look away or charge the field with my longbow drawn. Every moment slides by glacially slow.

Bal growls. He delivers several blows and a roundhouse kick to

Artagan, stunning his opponent in an instant. The massive Pict thrusts his spear into Artagan's side until the scarlet spearhead protrudes through the King's back.

I cry out, clenching Olwen's fingers hard enough to break bone.

Artagan staggers back, he and Bal locked in an awkward embrace. The Pict shoves the spear deeper into my husband's flesh. They glare eye to eye, the entire field of ten thousand onlookers silent as the grave.

Still impaled on Bal's bone-white spear, Artagan lifts his longsword. With a bloodcurdling howl, Artagan brings his blade crashing down on the spear shaft, snapping it in half. Bal has little time to widen his eyes. With the last reserves of his strength, Artagan swings his blade high overhead. A mist of blood sprays through the air as Artagan's longsword whirls in a wide arc.

The Pict's boyish head rolls off his shoulders and into the grass.

Bal's pale face seems almost frozen, still stunned in the last moments of death. Artagan stands upright a moment, looking down at his beheaded foe. In a heartbeat, he collapses in the bloodstained grass, his side still pierced by the broken bone spear. Neither the headless Bal nor my stabbed husband move where their bodies lie. A deathly stillness envelops the moors between both armies.

Tears stream down my face as I reach out, my lips trembling.

"Artagan?"

Before I can contemplate the loss of my one true love forever, a scalding, hag's cry screeches out from the Pictish lines. Sab draws a club in one hand and a bone sword in the other, vociferating in her barbaric tongue. It takes no translation to recognize a curse when one hears it. The Pict Queen turns red in the face, her blue woad flushing purple across her skin. Sab finally speaks in words that both I and her North Welsh allies can understand. Her voice runs hoarse with hate.

"Foul! *Foul!* They've played us foul! Both champions are dead, no quarter! No quarter!"

My eyes dart back to Artagan's still body down on the islet in the stream. I don't understand until the deathly howls arise from the Pict and North Welsh armies. Their warriors advance across the greens toward the riverbank. My eyes go wide.

Sab has no intention of honoring the agreement one way or the other. Now that things have not gone her way, she intends to have a battle anyway. The traitorous witch!

My mind wanders, lost in a fog, water still brimming over my eyes. Artagan, Artagan, *Artagan.* I only want to hold him in my arms. But the blood. There is so much blood. Red grass and red sand.

I clench my teeth, the blood pounding in my ears. Bubbles start to rise down in the narrow stream, the shallow waters gurgling like mudpots as the two armies near one another. The heat rises in my face. I only see red.

Digging my heels into my pony, I move forward more from instinct rather than any conscious thought. Olwen stops me with a hand, her own eyes wide and wet.

"Don't, Branwen! You and the baby must stay safe. That's how Artagan would have wanted it."

I shake my head, only half-understanding. By now our own warriors howl with rage, drawing their swords and bowstrings. But the worries of battle and the chaos that will ensue seem like remote issues, belonging to someone else. Artagan. Only Artagan matters. I must reach Artagan.

King Griffith charges ahead of our troops, waving his blade high overhead. Despite his girth, the old warrior urges his horse forward with the vigor of a much younger man. Tears stream down the fat king's beard as he cries out to the Free Cantref and South Welsh soldiers alike.

"To the Blacksword! The Blacksword, men! Rally around the Blacksword! For the Blacksword!"

My husband's fellow knights join Griffith. Sir Emryus and Sir Keenan sprint headlong toward the enemy with Bowen and Carrick close on their heels. Together they charge the riverbank and into the shallows. Both armies converge in a cacophony of clashing steel and deathly cries, grappling in the water. Like two hornets' nests swarming over the landscape.

At the center of the vortex of battle, Griffith leads our warriors onto the tiny islet where only moments ago two men dueled for the fate of all Wales. Artagan and Bal's bodies disappear from view as the two armies surge over the isle. My heart clenches like a closed fist, pinching so tight it makes me wince through my tears. Dear God, what is happening? Where is my Artagan? *Please, please, Holy Virgin, Mother in Heaven.* My heart is fit to burst. Too much. This is all too much.

I reel from the saddle, falling into a pair of arms. Blinking up into Ahern's face, his one eye squints with concern. Even in the midst of Armageddon, he refuses to leave my side. Some brave warrior-queen I turned out to be. I cannot rise to my feet or stay in the saddle. Cannot even draw my bow and exact vengeance for my beloved husband. I am as powerless as a moth before the flame.

"My lady? Your Highness? Branwen? Branwen!"

Ahern's voice looms over me, but I can do little more than shake my head in my half-numb stupor. Everything seems to happen from very far away now. As though I listened and watched the world through a glass jar.

The hiss of arrowheads scratches the sky. Our bowmen and spear-wives will blot out the sun with arrows for my Artagan. For my love. I shut my eyes. Every one of those arrows shall be my tears. Weep with me, Free Cantref and Dyfed warriors. Weep with your tears of iron arrowheads. Let the Picts feel the steel of your grief.

Olwen and Ahern's voices hover over me, but I can barely manage to listen. Like a mute spectator within my own life. My kinsman sounds grim.

"We have to get her out of here."

"She's in shock," Olwen replies, stifling her own sniffles. "We all are."

"This is no time for a tizzy spell, damn it! Find Rowena and Una. They should have the children in a wagon. We can put the Queen in the cart."

"But the battle?"

"Blast the battle! It'll go on with or without us. We need to get Branwen to safety."

I blink my eyes, but all I can see are gray shapes. My clammy forearms shake, my legs refuse to answer me. I cannot stand. I cannot see. I cannot think. God, God, *God.* Where is my Artagan? Struggling against my own delirium and the roar of battle, I claw at Ahern's sleeve. My voice croaks out, raw as a frog's.

"Artagan . . . You must get *Artagan* . . . his body . . . please, Ahern . . ."

My voice fails me and I collapse in his arms. My brother pats my back, murmuring soothingly into my ear. Did he even understand me? Maybe my words came out as garbled nonsense. I part my lips again to speak, but nothing comes out. My tongue feels dull as a wad of willow fluff.

The creak of a timber axle grinds to a halt beside me. Hands lift me up while the wailing of children echoes in my ears. Gavin? My babe must be nearby. A solid wooden surface materializes beneath me. Una and Rowena's voices argue over me. Even now must they fight?

"Just do it!" Una shouts.

"Fine!" Rowena stammers. "Be it on your head!"

A cold splash of frigid water hits my face, hard as a slap. I suck in a sharp, involuntary breath of cool air, my eyes furiously blinking back the chilled water. Sitting up on my wobbly elbows, the world crystallizes into view again as I find myself laid out in the back of a straw-filled wagon. Water drips from my soaked dark locks. Una, Rowena, Olwen, and Ahern crowd around me with the children sobbing beside us. The deafening din of bloodshed surges closer. We must be less than a bowshot from the fighting.

A beam of sunlight pierces the overcast cloud cover, illuminating the face of my red-haired boy. Gavin nestles up beside me, burying his wet face against my bosom. My boy, my beautiful little boy. You are all of Artagan that I have left. I draw in another deep breath. A steely cold numbness rises up my spine. I can weep later. I have the rest of my days to grieve my loss, but today, now, this very instant my son needs me. He needs his mother, and my people need their Queen.

Clenching my jaw, I sit upright on the lip of the cart, my legs hanging down. My suddenly cool countenance takes my companions aback as I shout out commands. Despite the feigned confidence in my voice, I think almost mechanically. The gears of logic turn even though my soul still seems lost in some fading nightmare. I point a finger at my kinsman.

"Ahern! Are you prepared to risk your life for your Queen?"

"My lady? You are not quite well."

"Your Queen is speaking to you, seneschal. Listen!"

Despite the nearby battle, my companions focus their attention on my voice.

"Ahern, you will lead a sortie into the melee. I want the King's body. Artagan has been a hero to our people. I'll not have what's left of him falling into Pictish hands, to be dishonored . . . or worse."

Ahern stiffens, suddenly the dutiful soldier again. He bows toward me.

"As you wish, my Queen. It shall be done."

"Go."

He leaves without another word, and I do not spare him a second glance. My faithful brother is dearer to me than gold, but I must be a queen now. Hard things must be done, and personal feelings must be buried deep. After this is all over, then we can sort out our mixed love and grief. If any of us survive this.

The battle surges back and forth on either side of the stream, the hardest fighting concentrated right along the isle where Bal and Artagan previously dueled. Pictish warriors scream out their battle cries as Dyfed spearmen and Free Cantref warriors grapple with them. Farther down the flank, Iago's North Welsh riders make charge after charge into the lines of South Welsh swordsmen. Welsh and Pictish bodies mar the stream as its waters turn crimson before spilling into the sea.

Turning to my women, I continue issuing commands. Much must be done. Even if I cannot stand, I must use what wits remain to me.

"Rowena, gather the children. Shelter them behind the wagon. Some of those Pictish slingers probably have us in range by now. And Una, search out another cart, a farmer's wagon, *anything*. We will need another conveyance for . . . for my husband's body."

My two serving women exchange looks before going about their tasks. I am still Queen, and addled by shock or not, they know that they must do my bidding without question. Gripping the sides of the back end of the cart, I narrow my gaze, searching the ranks of the chaotic battlefield for a single figure. My eyes finally stop, alighting on a woman. She stands atop a rock behind the lines of surging barbarians. Sab.

The Pict Queen glares at me across the sea of clashing soldiers. It may be my imagination, but I know she gazes directly at me. Whether or not we lock horns, this battle is as much between her and me as it is between the ten thousand bloodied men. Our armies are equally matched and we'll doubtless bleed each other dry before one side prevails over the other. Sab must be smiling her wicked grin. No matter what befalls us this day, she still wins. Wales will be too weak to resist any barbarians after this bloodbath.

Only Olwen remains beside me, the others going about the tasks I've set them to. She suddenly points across the field. Her voice fights to be heard over the din.

"Branwen, look! Griffith's horse has no rider. The South Welsh King has been struck down!"

Indeed, his steed whinnies and wanders the field without a rider. Not a sign of Griffith anywhere, and he is not a small enough man for my eyes to miss. He is at least wounded, if not worse. My eyebrows rise. With Griffith down or missing, that means his command devolves to another. Across the melee, Prince Arthwys directs his men from astride a white stallion. The teenage ruler pulls his steed back from the brink of battle and inexplicably turns his gaze back toward me.

My heart convulses within my chest. His gray eyes darken, malevolently boring into me from a hundred paces away with his cold stare. An icy hate that I have seen before in only one man. His dead father, the Hammer King. Arthwys has loathed me and bided his time for many years. A cruel half-grin spreads across his cheeks. Without taking his gaze off me, he raises one palm, signaling to his bannermen.

The red dragon pennants waver back and forth, a signal to his troops. All the South Welshmen pull back, giving ground before Iago's northern horsemen. My eyes widen. Arthwys is pulling his men out of the battle. He is ordering his troops to abandon the fight. Jesus, help us.

Across the way, Sab beams at Arthwys, her hands on her hips. Arthwys nods back at her, raising his sword in a brief salute. Lightning shoots through my veins.

That conniving bastard! Prince Arthwys is no stranger to Sab. Somehow the two of them have a prearranged agreement. My sweat-soaked skin sends chills up and down my spine. I turn to Olwen, realizing we have no time to lose.

"We are betrayed, Olwen. Prince Arthwys has sided with Sab. Without his troops we're outnumbered two to one."

"What are you saying?"

"We've lost. If we do not retreat, we shall be slaughtered, every last one of us."

My brave archers have seen the betrayal by now, but they refuse to budge. A hail of arrows from their bowstrings rains down death and mayhem amongst the ranks of Iago's cavalry. But it will stall them only a short while. We cannot battle the Picts to our front and the North Welsh on our flank. Not without Arthwys's soldiers. The enemy is now simply too many.

Turning to Olwen, I try to decide whom to send her to. She must get word to whoever is left in command on the battlefield. Perhaps Sir Emryus or even one of the Dyfed knights. But what can they do in the face of such odds?

Before I can speak, a convulsing pressure surges up inside me. My eyes widen, sweat pouring down my face. Olwen clutches my shoulder, steadying me as I sway in the back of the wagon.

"Branwen, are you all right?"

Hardly able to answer her, I wrap both hands around my swollen stomach.

"The baby . . . the baby is coming."

17

We arrive well after nightfall. Dull stars flicker over Dun Dyfed. The wagon grinds to a halt amidst the chirp of crickets and the dim hush of the nearby sea. I bite my lower lip, groaning as the contractions twist and pinch inside me.

Olwen has pulled off a miracle, urging our steeds all day and into the night to bring me here. The horses slump in their traces, their mouths foaming and their knees buckling. She has nearly ridden them to death in order to bring me to this hill fort. I've plenty of pragmatic reasons for seeking shelter here. Ogham Stone has too few defenses to protect us, and Aranrhod is too far into the mountains. I'd never survive such a journey right now through those winding switchbacks. Besides, Dun Dyfed provides as good a rallying point as any for the survivors of our armies. If there are any.

But one reason above all others has driven me to return to Dun Dyfed. Perhaps my birth pangs have warped my reason, but I was drawn to this ancient castle as surely as a bird flying south in winter. I was born here in Dyfed. If I am to meet my end, I might as well die in Dyfed.

Heaven knows how many hours I've spent jostling in the back of a cart. My joints ache and my bones creak. Rowena and Una help me inside the castle walls. Other than a few peasants tending the grounds, the citadel has been nearly abandoned. After all the Pictish raids earlier in the season, it's little wonder that few settlers were eager to return to this place. And yet, the dull thunder of the surf ruminating through the bones of the old castle comforts me. Flashing a shadow of a grin, I inhale the familiar aroma of smoky peat fires kindled in the chamber hearths.

Long before my serving women get me to a proper bedchamber, I know something is wrong. My birthing pangs surge with ever intensifying pain, burning like fire from the very core of my body. But I do not feel like I can push yet. My labors go ill already, nothing like Gavin's birth. This child will prove difficult to bring into the world tonight. I wonder if I will live to see the dawn.

Olwen takes the children into another chamber, bedding them down for the night. At least I need not worry about an assassin. Bal and his severed head can no longer haunt my son's steps.

Rowena and Una prepare hot compresses for me, filling the room with steam as they warm buckets of water over sizzling braziers. A cool draft through the tower window offers some much needed fresh air. Despite my pains, I recognize the view and the cobblestone walls. This solar was my childhood bedchamber. How long ago it all seems tonight. A shooting star crosses the twilit sky outside. Perhaps my mother birthed me in this very same room on a still autumn night much like this. All those years ago.

Raising an eyebrow, I turn to Rowena.

"What date is today? The exact day?"

"Why, 'tis All Hallows' Eve, m'lady. Your very own birthing day."

I grunt, breathing faster as another series of contractions overtakes me. Una urges me to focus on my inhalations. I try, only halfway succeeding. So today is my birthday. How fitting that it might be the last evening of my life as well. *Dear God, if I cannot live, at least let my babe come forth intact. Let my child share my birthing day too, let the babe live and taste the fullness of a long, healthy life.*

But what life will there be for any in Wales now? The Picts will ravage Wales from the north, and sooner or later the Saxons will overwhelm us in the east. Will my children live free or as slaves? Either way, I doubt I will live to see what becomes of my family and my country.

Wincing with pain, I cry out. The blood rushes through my skull, and I am unable to see or dwell on anything other than the life stirring inside me. Strong tugs and pulls rise and ebb within me, like the waves advancing and retreating along the nocturnal shore. Exasperated, I bellow to anyone who will hear me. My women, the stars, even God.

"Why does the child not come?"

Una ducks under my skirts, examining me briskly with a few prods and murmurs. I shudder as another wave of contractions flows through me, my limbs trembling with exhaustion. I try to steady my mind. All women must do battle in childbirth, sooner or later. I have done this before. Whatever befalls me tonight, I can do it again. As my mother and her grandmothers did before her, all the way back to the Old Tribes. I *know* I can do this. *I must.*

Una emerges from my skirts and glances at Rowena. She frowns, shaking her head. Rowena blanches but says nothing. The child does not come forth. Something is wrong, yet my women try to keep it from me. Amidst my groans, I manage to get a few words out.

"Tell me true, Una. I deserve as much."

"The child has not turned, Your Grace. Without help, the babe cannot be born."

I lean my head back against the cool stone walls. Damnation. Everything in my vision threatens to come true. The moans, the pain, the blood. My doom is nigh upon me. If only the vision had told me whether the child lives or not. Then at least I might have some hope. But I must try and trust in the Almighty's angels of mercy.

A horse whinnies outside. I sit upright, craning my ears. Someone has arrived at the gates. Rowena and Una exchange looks with me. Other than Olwen and the children, we brought no one else with us. We are virtually defenseless in this half-empty castle. Completely at the mercy of any who may come upon us, whether they be friend or foe.

If not for my children, I would welcome death. Then at least I could be reunited with my Artagan. I bite my tongue, trying to blot out any further thoughts. No, not now. I cannot think of him or anything else this night. Bring this child into the world. That is my sole purpose now. After that, I'll have all eternity to dwell on other things.

Footfalls echo off the citadel steps. I clench my jaw, trying to stifle my birthing moans. Rowena and Una each take up a stool as they wait on either side of the chamber doorway. We've nothing in the way of weapons. Whoever the approaching stranger is, he'll meet little more resistance than a pair of broken footstools. May the Almighty watch over us.

"Your Highness?"

We all sigh with collective relief at the sound of a familiar, albeit tired voice. Ahern edges onto the threshold, averting his eyes so as not to intrude within the sanctified female sphere of birthing. The glowing fireplace colors his face, set in profile in the doorway. Rowena and Una rush toward him.

"She cannot be disturbed," Una begins. "Her time is close."

"I'll not interrupt, but I have something to tell her."

"Not now, man!" Rowena whispers thickly. "Can't it wait?"

Ahern frowns, the lines on his face lengthening by firelight.

"I've done as she asked and found her husband. Only he is not dead but still clings to life by a thread."

Almost at my will, my contractions momentarily subside. I lean forward on my wooden stool, calling out to Ahern.

"My Artagan lives? But how? Is he here now?"

"In the next room, my lady," Ahern replies. "But he still has the spearhead in him and is very weak."

"I want to see him."

My pains overtake me again and I shut my eyes tight, trying to breathe in and out as Una instructed. My women-in-waiting shake their heads. Ahern bows from the doorway.

"The King is not conscious, my Queen. I will watch over him myself. As I said, he's in the next room. If he comes to or his condition changes, you will be the first to know."

Without another word, my kinsman excuses himself, nearly stumbling with exhaustion as he descends the stairs. Rowena and Una rush to my side once more, urging me to keep breathing. But my thoughts spin with visions of Artagan. Alive? He lives! If only I could go to him now, hold his hand, be by his side. But if the spear still pierces his side, he must have bled badly. Ahern would have left it in only for fear of making the King bleed to death. My husband's life must indeed hang by a thread. Perhaps tonight we both battle to keep our souls held fast to their mortal coils.

Una places her palms over my stomach, feeling for the child within me. Rowena starts humming down near the crock of my legs, trying to draw the baby with sound. The urge to push overcomes me as a blinding white light flashes against my eyeballs. I bite my tongue until I taste blood. My nostrils flare as sweat runs down my skin.

Unable to contain my anguish, my cries reverberate across the hill fort. Both Rowena and Una urge me to push as my breathing grows sharp and shallow. I clench my teeth, bearing down with all my might. A trickle of blood runs down my legs. Dear God, let this not be the last of earth that I see.

All is darkness. Neither touch nor sounds reach me, as though I lie curled up in the bottom of a deep, deep well. I am alone. So alone, and so cold.

A fragrance of lavender and incense permeates the void. Then the faint smell of woodsmoke and the snap of kindling fills my dark abode. A small fire glow waxes beside me, silhouetting the back of a woman with long, dark locks. She watches over the budding flames. I sit up on one elbow. Just me, the woman, the fire, and the distant chirp of crickets in the dark.

The green-eyed lady turns her gaze on me, the profile of her face lit by the glow of the hearth. She smiles. I blink my groggy eyes.

"Mother?"

"Yes, my little sparrow, I am here."

I forgot that she used to call me that. Little sparrow. Looking at the unnatural darkness, I struggle to keep my voice even.

"Am *I* dead?"

She smiles again, returning her gaze to the fire as she stokes the flames.

"You are . . . *in between,* let's just say. I always liked the dark just before the dawn."

She sits cross-legged, her breathing as calm as the black stillness that surrounds us. A strange tranquility pervades the emptiness, like starlight reflected in a quiet pond. As my eyes adjust to the dimness, the first pinpricks of constellations fill the cosmos encircling us.

Looking up at Mother again, I reach out for her. As though the peace and serenity emanating from her were tangible as a blanket. As though I might wrap myself in her essence and feel complete contentment with all creation.

I call out to her, knowing in my heart that we will be parted once more.

"Mother, help me. I'm all alone against the darkness. Dark winds rising against me."

She beams serenely back at me.

"Haven't I told you before? I am always with you, my child. You are never alone."

"But it's too big, Mother. All of it is too much for me."

She comes close, planting a soft kiss on my eyelid.

"Grace comes not from the will to change things, but to accept what comes, with love in your heart."

Mother and her fire gradually diminish, disappearing into one of the many stars fixed in the firmament. Then all returns to blackness once more. I am alone with my thoughts and half thoughts, adrift in the dark.

Someone calls my name, a woman's voice. Her warm touch seems to breathe life back into me. My eyes flicker open, the room gradually coming into focus. A cozy fire crackles in the grate across the chamber. Warm sheets and pillows surround me in bed.

"Branwen . . . Branwen . . ."

Olwen smiles at me, holding a tightly wrapped bundle in her arms. I try to sit up but find my limbs incredibly weak. Touching my skin, I prod myself to make sure this is no dream. I heave a long sigh. I'm in my old bedchamber again at Dun Dyfed. Olwen leans down beside me.

"Congratulations, my Queen. Meet your new little son."

"Another boy?"

For some reason, deep in my heart, I assumed I would bear a daughter this time. A girl-child of the Old Tribes destined to follow after me, just as Gavin will be Artagan's son and heir. But God placed another princeling inside me this time around. Another heir. My husband will doubtless be beside himself with mirth.

Any pangs of disappointment quickly dissipate as I wrap my arms around my newborn babe, my eyes welling up with water. An unexpected euphoria overtakes me, leaving me awash in warm, buzzing emotions that I neither understand nor have a name for. My tiny pink-faced boy slumbers beside my breast as I gaze down at his perfectly round head.

Olwen grins, her beaming countenance far prettier than I ever recall her looking before. The faint cries of gulls murmur outside over the tide as the sky ripens blue under the first rays of sunrise. She puts a palm to my clammy forehead.

"After the child came, there was much blood. We feared we'd lost you in the night."

"I feared as much myself. I cannot believe it. Last of a noble line, I was born an only child, yet here I am, holding my second son."

Olwen folds her arms, raising an eyebrow.

"Believe it. You had a hard labor as any I've ever seen, and it would've been a death sentence for most women. But you have the resilience of a phoenix, Branwen Mab Ceridwen. I have to admit, whatever life throws your way, you always seem to rise from the ashes."

I give Olwen a sidelong glance, staring at her as though seeing her for the first time. Not some trollop or a petty queen but a woman who has seen no small share of her own troubles and tribulations. An equally resilient phoenix with ash-colored hair who recognizes another firebird when she sees one. I wave her over to my bedside, giving her a quick peck on the cheek. Olwen colors like a child before we both grin at one another. We best not be too nice to one another or it'll go to our heads.

Kissing my newborn child atop his warm scalp, I cradle him against my beating heart. He nuzzles against my breast in his half slumber. A light copper fuzz tops his scalp. *Another* redhead? A grin spreads across my face. My goodness, how the servants will gossip. Artagan and I are dark of hair and yet we seem to produce auburn babies as easily as the Irish.

Olwen leaves the two of us alone, gently closing the chamber door behind her. I lean my head back against a goose-feather pillow. The cares of the outside world seem so distant from the tranquility of my tower window beside the frothing sea.

So did my vision ultimately come to pass? I was near certain I had seen my doom in the scry bowl. But what did I actually behold? The cries, the blood, the difficult birth. I assumed the vision could end only one way, all part of one long defeat. But I suppose I was on a different path all along. Not a journey ending in fear and darkness, but one leading to a shiny bright dawn.

I close my eyes and say a silent prayer, to God, to the angel who came to me in the night. My mother.

Several weeks have passed since the defeat at the Battle of All Hallows. Or so the common folk now call it. Enough blood soaked up the banks of that tiny, nameless stream to fill the Welsh countryside with ghosts for the next hundred years. God help us.

Two storms have already come off the ocean, battering the crags along Dyfed's shores while we huddle close to hearth fires inside the deep stone halls of my father's old castle. A stout reprieve from the storm, a bastion of warmth and peace amidst the troubles that beset the Welsh Lands now. Word of many of Sab's foul deeds reaches our ears here, rumors of burnt villages and tortured peasants. But as of yet, not a single Pict has shown up at our gates.

I tread carefully down the steps in the morning light, my baby sated with milk as he naps in my arms. We turn the key to another bedchamber, where a man wrapped in bandages sits beside a flickering lamp. The window is tightly fastened against the rain and wind. Gavin looks up from his father's cot.

"Mama!"

I shush him with a smile, kneeling down beside Artagan's bed. My husband sits up on his elbows, wincing with pain. He hovered at death's door for nigh over a moon before he finally came around. But he is still wan and weak, his bandages around his abdomen slightly bloodied each morn.

Nonetheless, a smile gradually creeps across his face as he looks down at our newborn.

"What shall we name him, my love?"

Only one name comes to mind.

"Tristan."

Artagan raises an eyebrow, clearly surprised at my giving our child another old Arthurian knight's namesake. He leans over and kisses me. Gavin thrusts his large auburn head between us, peering at his new brother.

"So little," he smiles.

Artagan wraps one arm around our elder boy, the pair of them observing Tristan's small face.

"You're a big brother now, my son. You must always look after him as you would your own mother."

"Och!" I reply with feigned indignance. "As though I need looking after by either my husband or my sons? Amongst the Old Tribes it was the womenfolk who looked after the men."

Artagan puts his palms together in mock prayer, glancing heavenward.

"And may it always be so under our roof, dear Lord."

Gavin chuckles at his father's grin, even if he is too young to understand the humor. I gently paw Artagan's cheek. Hardly a fortnight from his near deathbed, and already my husband speaks as blasphemously as ever. Tristan yawns, unperturbed by all our noise as he momentarily widens his tiny pink lips.

Rowena passes our open door with her girls in tow. Catching a glance from me, she offers to take Tristan and Gavin with her. The children's voices boisterously echo down the passageways as Rowena leads them to the larder. Finally alone together, I press my brow to Artagan's.

"I thought I'd lost you."

"It'd take more than a dozen spears to part me from you."

He grins, trying to make light of his condition. Even as he smiles, his eyes contract when he tries to stifle the pain. The wound from Bal's bone spear runs deep through Artagan's torso, and even now he may still yet relapse and fail to recover. I quickly push such thoughts from my head. No. We will persevere, because we must. Artagan has had his share of wounds over the years, both as a hedge knight and as a king. But even if he regains his health, I wonder whether he will ever wield a sword or ride a horse as well as he once did. A few years shy of thirty, and he has already put his body through so many trials and terrors that he will be lucky if he can still draw breath should he live to see forty. The very though makes my chest smart. I clutch Artagan all the closer.

"I had a vision," I begin, "in which I feared I'd die in childbirth. It has haunted me these many months, but alas, I saw only the pain, not the peaceful conclusion."

Startled, Artagan looks at me with a searching gaze.

"Did you truly see into the future?"

"I saw something," I reply with a shrug. "I have a touch of the Sight, or so Sab said, but I'm reluctant to pursue such awakenings further. I think I prefer living life simply one day to the next, much as you do."

Artagan smiles and rests his brow thoughtfully against mine. I almost mention seeing my mother after the delirium of the birthing as well. But somehow I know my husband already understands the depths of my soul as it is. No words are necessary between us.

We hold one another without saying more, simply content to feel one another's warmth. For a time, I forget all else except Artagan's embrace and the laughter of the children down in the courtyard. All that I care for in all the world are with me now inside the walls of Dun Dyfed.

A man clears his throat outside the lintel of our room. Ahern lingers in the shadows, patiently waiting for me. I help lay Artagan back down on his cot. Within moments his chest rises and falls with the peaceful rhythm of a man fast asleep. Leaning down, I press my lips to his closed eyelids. Rest, my love. Rest and replenish your strength. I cannot go on without you. I *need* you. I love you.

Quietly closing the door, I follow Ahern to the main hall of the hill fort. How many scenes of my childhood passed in this drafty old mead hall? I recall my father, God rest him, deep in his cups before he gave me away as a bride to the Hammer King. And then much later, finding that Pictish Queen sitting on Father's old throne, her barbarians eating and defecating about the hall as though it were a pigsty. The mere thought makes me cringe.

Around a flickering central hearth, Ahern gathers with those few knights who remain to us. Sir Emryus and Keenan steady themselves with a staff or an ax handle, both of their heads wrapped in crimson bandages. The quiet Dyfed knight, Sir Carrick, joins them, his arm in a sling. I nod to each of them before turning to Carrick.

"How fares your brother, sir knight?"

Carrick's gaze clouds over.

"Poorly, Your Grace. Bowen still has fever dreams and the clerics say he will probably lose his leg."

I bite my lip, almost wishing I had not asked. Many brave Dyfed and Free Cantref warriors lie dead or dying. Just one of the many repercussions Wales will doubtless suffer as a result of our defeat at All Hallows. Ahern glances my way with his single eye.

"King Griffith's body has not yet been recovered."

"He should be honored with a king's barrow." I sigh. "His courage on the battlefield led to the rescue of my husband. Without Griffith's valor, Artagan might not be here with us now."

Pacing around the flickering fire, I try to push thoughts of Griffith from my mind. The image of tears streaming down his cheeks as he led men forward to save my husband will remain emblazoned in my memory until the end of my days. I owe the round old king a debt I can never repay. But I've enough grief within me already to burst asunder. The weeping and hair rending must wait for another day. Our country's fate hangs in the balance, and a queen cannot afford herself the luxury of mourning. Not now, not with so much at stake.

I recline upon my father's old throne, the well-worn seat where many of my forefathers once sat. Queen Sab's duff rested here once too, the viperess. She will doubtless return here someday soon to try to reclaim it.

If it irks Ahern to see me in Father's old chair instead of himself, he does not show it. Curse myself, I do my half brother a disservice for even entertaining such notions, no matter how briefly. He has served me faithfully for years since his one betrayal, which we rarely speak of now. Nonetheless, I bet old Sab would promise a man like Ahern the moon if he opened our gates to her army. Then again, with so few remaining under our banners, Sab may not need any further treachery to bring us down. As for Ahern, he would fight to the last drop of blood to keep a villainess like the Pictish Queen from claiming dominion over our birthplace here at Dyfed.

I glance at my four remaining war-captains as they warm themselves beside the hearth.

"Sab will show up here sooner or later. It is only a matter of time."

"The war season has ended." Keenan shrugs. "With the cold weather upon us, no one can wage a campaign. The Picts will wait for spring."

Emryus, Carrick, and Ahern exchange looks, not nearly as convinced. I sit up in my seat, equally doubtful that we will have a reprieve from the fighting. My voice fills the largely empty hall.

"Winter may be coming, Sir Keenan, but Queen Sab is a wily foe. She will not stop merely because of some rain and soggy mud. Her people come from the cold wastes of the far North. They can wage war in any season."

Carrick scratches his sling with his good hand, staring into the flames.

"How many men do we have here now at Dun Dyfed?"

"A thousand, more or less," Ahern answers. "But half of them are wounded, and most of the rest are short on rations."

Emryus frowns, stroking his gray beard.

"Our food stores are nearly exhausted. Many villagers have taken refuge here now that word of Mab Ceridwen's presence has spread. But even with this dun's famously impregnable walls, we won't hold out long with a thousand starving wounded warriors and refugees crowding the citadel."

All four warriors stand silent, lost in their own pessimistic thoughts as they listen to the snap and crackle of the fire pit. With my elbow on the armrest, I put my chin against my fist. When I first arrived here weeks ago, hardly anyone remained in the castle. Now it swells with maimed warriors and scared peasants looking for shelter and protection.

Low on food. Low on warriors. Low on hope. What chance do we stand once Sab's marauding Picts show up on our doorstep? It's a miracle they haven't besieged us already. Only her savages' greed for glutting themselves on the prosperous farms and herds of the Welsh countryside has slowed their progress. The fruits of victory for the invaders.

We need help. We need allies, but from where? Who could possibly come to our aid even if they wanted to? I do not intend to simply rot in Dun Dyfed, waiting for Sab's army to arrive and finish us off. But what choice have I? We seem to have run out of possibilities. I start to think out loud, a dangerous prospect for any leader in times of peril, but we need a plan and we need it fast.

"First, we need foodstuffs, or we are done for in a fortnight. The autumn harvests are in. Surely, the granaries in Aranrhod are full by now. Have we any word there from Father David?"

Ahern grimaces, the firelight lengthening the lines on his face.

"I sent a raven, but it has not returned. The roads between here and your castle at Aranrhod are blocked, my Queen."

"Blocked? By what?"

"*King* Arthwys's army."

Ahern spits into the flames, sneering at having to refer to that teenage monarch as *king*. I swallow hard, realizing that we are in even more dire straits than I first supposed. Poor Griffith may have traded his life to save my husband's, but when the South Welsh ruler died, his throne passed to the Hammer King's son. Prince, now *King* Arthwys. I can still see his hollow gray stare from across the battlefield, betraying us as he sided with Sab. Even in the face of foreign enemies, will the Welsh ever cease fighting each other? Maybe our people do not deserve to be saved.

I shake my head. I cannot condemn my own people for the evil deeds of a few conniving nobles. But I can certainly damn Arthwys and Iago. I clench my fists, racking my mind for any possible solutions.

With Arthwys's troops blocking the roads to the east, we cannot hope to get any wagons of food from Aranrhod. Poor Father David. I left him in charge of the castle months ago, thinking I would be gone only a short while. Now the beleaguered priest has a fortress to look after, and may yet find himself under siege as well before too long. We already drew all available troops from Aranrhod before the Battle of All Hallows. Whom will Father David find to man the walls? Women and children with pitchforks? That will not keep any foes at bay for long.

As much as Arthwys despises me, he has not turned his troops to open battle against me yet. But why? He would not do so by choice, not unless forced to by circumstances out of his hands. The South Welsh followed Griffith when he led them against the Picts and North Welsh, but now they must swear loyalty to the new heir and whomever he calls friend. Although I doubt many relish calling the Picts their allies after so much blood has been spilled. Arthwys treads in dangerous waters, changing his friends and foes so often. I tap the arm of my chair, glancing at Ahern.

"How bad were our enemy's losses at All Hallows?"

My kinsman shrugs.

"Hard to tell. They took the field, but we gave as good as we got, and we lost hundreds, maybe even a thousand men."

"And have just as many maimed and wounded to tend," Carrick adds, doubtless thinking of his brother.

I lean forward in my seat, my wandering gaze lost in thought.

"Then Sab's Picts, Iago's northern horsemen, and even Arthwys's swordsmen will all have suffered equally, maybe losing half their strength."

"Aye, but by combining their forces together, they'll have more than enough troops to overwhelm us," Sir Emryus counters.

A half-grin spreads across my cheek.

"True, but they haven't united their forces, have they? Which means there is discord in their ranks as well. They don't trust each other."

I snap my fingers, rising from the throne and beginning to pace. My knights exchange looks but keep silent, watching me with furrowed brows. I refuse to let their perplexed faces distract me as I follow my thoughts to their logical conclusion, bantering to myself all the while.

"They don't *trust* each other!" I repeat with a smile. "Arthwys and Iago's forces bloodied one another badly, and their troops will sooner see each other in perdition rather than join ranks. So Arthwys merely cuts us off from aid. He guards the roads not only against us but also against Iago and Sab, in case they should change their minds and betray him by marching on the South Welsh Lands."

Ahern nods.

"It makes sense, my Queen. By now the Saxons are doubtless recovering from their bout with the plague, so Arthwys will have to watch his eastern borders as well. He doesn't have the manpower to do more than blockade the roads against us. He cannot march his forces directly against us without taking the risk of leaving his own castles defenseless to Saxons or the North Welsh."

Keenan stokes the fire with a switch, sending sparks into the air.

"But what good does that do us?" The young knight frowns. "So Arthwys won't attack. He has still cut off our food supply, which damns us all the same. There's not a king in all Wales who will come to our aid now!"

I click my tongue in disapproval, still unable to hide my smile.

"Sir Keenan, I've no intention or asking help from any *kings* in Wales. But we might just find an ally amongst their *queens*."

All four knights raise their eyebrows. I could laugh if it wasn't all so serious. Brave as these warriors are, they cannot think outside the narrow confines of battlefields and kingships. They do not see the many other subtle advantages we have yet to press against our enemies as they seek to encircle us. Time will tell whether or not I am right, but for the first moment in weeks I feel a kernel of genuine hope springing to life within me. And yet, our time runs short. I will have to hatch my little plots quickly, before starvation or Queen Sab's armies bring us to our knees.

18

The last of my messenger ravens take to the skies, carrying with them the last hopes for my country. Standing atop a ring of Dun Dyfed's rocky walls, I watch until the dark birds disappear toward the horizon. My windswept hair spiderwebs across my face. The cool breath of the ocean rises off the many whitecaps that dot the western sea. A mist of wet, salty spray dapples my warm cheeks. Una stands with her hands folded as though in prayer, the two of us alone together as she talks over the roar of the surf.

"You're taking an awful risk, my Queen. I hope you know what you're doing."

"Me too."

"If those messenger birds should be intercepted by the enemy . . ."

"I'm more worried about them reaching their destinations at all. The autumn storms have abated a touch, but they will renew their fury before the next moon is out. I can smell it in the air."

I shut my eyes a moment, inhaling the scent of washed-up kelp. Gulls cry out overhead, large whitish-gray flocks streaming inland. A sure sign that another gale forms somewhere far out to sea.

Una paces, her fingers fidgeting nervously. To the east, the open heaths bleed brown pools of rainwater. Half the landscape has turned into a moss-covered bog. It will make travel for our enemies difficult, but not impossible. With the sea on one side and marsh on the other, we seem truly cut off from the rest of the world. Still no sign of the Picts or Iago's army, but that will change. And heaven help us when they do come, for we will be hard-pressed to withstand a siege. A leaden weight sinks in my gut.

Wending my way toward the main hall, I follow the subterranean corridors of the dun until I stop at a chamber near my own. I stand in the doorway, looking in as Olwen brushes back Cadwallon's ash-colored hair. She beams with pleasure as she combs through the toddler's locks, talking to him about their castles in the far North where she hopes he may one day rule as king. I clear my throat, drawing Olwen's gaze.

Una trails me to Olwen's cell. I turn to her, trying to make my voice pleasant yet firm.

"Take young Cadwallon to Rowena's chambers so that he can play with the other children," I begin. "I must speak with Queen Olwen alone."

Olwen abruptly rises to her feet, clearly perturbed at both my interruption and my seemingly high-handed orders, but she acquiesces without a word. She eyes me warily with her violet gaze. Olwen takes a seat on a footstool as Una leads the boy out into the hall. I gently close the door once Olwen and I are alone, waiting until Una's footfalls have dissipated down the corridor. Olwen folds her arms.

"Mind telling me what this is all about, your highness?" she says with a frown.

"I wanted to thank you for all you've done," I begin. "Standing by my side through thick and thin. And most especially, helping with the delivery of my baby."

Olwen blinks, taken aback by my words as her grimace turns into a small smile.

"Thank you, Branwen. Despite our spats, I like to think we've become something like friends."

"That's why I must now ask you to betray me."

Her eyes narrow, the lines on her fair face growing long. I try my best to keep my own face a mask of stoic complacency. What I do now, I do for all Wales. Whatever happens, I must ensure that our people survive, and I'm going to need Olwen's help to do that. She rises from her seat, circling me as though checking to make sure I'm not some apparition or phantom.

"What are you talking about, Branwen?"

"I've set some plans in motion, messages sent to certain parties via my ravens. But I need your help to make these plans work. I need you to betray me, publicly."

"I don't understand."

"It's no secret that you and I have never seen eye to eye, often reluctant allies at best. That's an advantage I plan to use. Our enemies will have little trouble believing that you mean me ill. If you ride into their camp to join them, they will readily believe you've betrayed me, especially if you tell them you and I have been at odds of late."

"*Are* we at odds, Branwen?"

I lower my gaze with a faint smile.

"I don't honestly know, Olwen."

She smirks back.

"A fine answer. I think if you'd said yes or no, I'd not have believed you, but somehow hearing you in doubt, I know what you say is true."

"Will you help me? Will you help save our country?"

"How? By riding into Sab's camp and groveling before my cuckolding husband?"

"I don't want you to go to Sab or Iago. I want you to ride to Arthwys's camp."

Her eyes widen slightly.

"To what purpose? The only reason a deposed noblewoman like myself would ride into a young warlord's camp would be to . . ."

Her eyes widen into full moons as the realization overtakes her. She stomps her foot against the cobblestone floor, aiming her finger at me.

"Oh, no . . . no, no, *no*!" she says, wagging her head. "I'll not do it, Branwen! My God, you've got the devil's own soul to ask me to do a thing like that!"

I put both hands on her shoulders, steadying her with my ivy gaze. "It's only a plot to mislead our enemies, Olwen. One I need you to play as convincingly as any role you've had in your life. You need not actually *do* anything, only give Arthwys the *promise* of what you will do."

Olwen paces the room. Although neither of us has said directly what I'm asking of her, we both know exactly what needs to be done. Olwen is no fool, I'll give her that much. But does she have the gumption to risk everything for the sake of all our kingdoms? Olwen sighs, her shoulders sinking a moment before she stabs the air with her forefinger once more.

"I'll not sleep with him! Even I have my limits, Branwen!"

"I would never ask you to, but an offer of marriage to a landed queen is *not* something a young warlord like Arthwys can afford to dismiss."

"You think he'll use me as an excuse to claim the North, since I am still Queen there?"

I nod.

"And in doing so," I continue, "he will drive a wedge between the fledgling alliance Sab has sought to create amongst her, Iago, and Arthwys."

"But Arthwys should take Griffith's old Queen, Cordelia, to the altar. Fat and boorish as she is, her presence binds South Wales to Cornwall. Cordelia will be livid if she finds out Arthwys is considering wedding me."

"I'm counting on it."

Something in my dark smile must tickle Olwen's own devilish sense of mischief. Her gaze goes blank for a moment as she takes in the full meaning of my plot. A plan I've so far shared only with her and no one else. She flashes a half-grin back at me, clicking her tongue slightly.

"Queen Branwen, I think until this very moment, I've underestimated you."

"Thanks," I reply with a simper.

"When must I leave?"

"Immediately. We've no time to lose."

Olwen nods, sticking her index finger so close it almost grazes my nose.

"Just one more thing, *Mab Ceridwen.* If, *if* I do this, it had better work . . . or so help me I might just betray you for sooth, in order to save my own skin."

I put my hands on my hips, sizing her up as we stand toe to toe.

"Well, Olwen, I can certainly say that I have *not* underestimated you."

"Och!" she replies without another word.

She unbolts the door, hastening into the hallway and toward the stables. Both Rowena and Una see her saddling her white mare. They exchange looks. As the children play in their room, Rowena approaches me with an awkward bow.

"Lady Olwen looks like she's readying her horse, Your Grace."

"Aye."

"Are we going somewhere, m'lady?"

"No, just Queen Olwen. She's betraying me."

Rowena's eyes widen. I keep an aloof expression. Una crosses herself in the corner, neither one of them understanding what has transpired betwixt Olwen and me. Olwen mounts her filly, glancing over her shoulder at me.

"Look after my boy, Branwen. He'll be a king someday, and when he is, he'll remember who was kind to his mother and who was not."

She digs her heels into the steed's flanks, galloping headlong out the front gates and onto the moors. The clack of the mare's hooves diminishes into the distant fog. I draw in a long, deep breath. Godspeed, brave Olwen. Godspeed.

My breasts clench like a pair of tightening fists, and I know I must feed little Tristan once more. Rations are short within our walls, but at least my milk has remained strong for my newborn. Una tends to the other children while Rowena wraps Tristan in swaddling cloth.

Once I recline in my chair within my own bedchamber, Rowena brings my little babe to me. Tristan's eyes close as he suckles greedily, slowly lulling himself into a milk-induced slumber. Rowena whispers so as not to wake the child.

"M'lady, pardon my impertinence, but I still do not understand what just happened."

"That is how I want it for now, dear Rowena. Not just for you, but for *everyone* else. Olwen's part in this plot is between only her and myself."

Rowena's face suddenly brightens.

"But you have a plan, my Queen? A way out of this turmoil that those bloody Picts have set upon us?"

"Aye, Rowena, I have a *plan,* if you'll call it that, and Olwen has a crucial role to play in it. But I've not revealed my full plot to anyone, including Olwen. No more will I say. Not until it is done and the last move made."

"You talk almost as if it were a game betwixt you and Queen Sab, m'lady."

I utter a hollow laugh.

"No, I am done with games, Rowena, although this shall certainly be a fight to the death. Only one of us will prevail, either Sab or myself, and we both might very well be dead before it is over."

Rowena involuntarily sucks in a sharp breath.

"For sooth, m'lady? I'd give mine own life before I let harm come to you."

"You're a better lady-in-waiting than I deserve, Rowena."

I smile at her, my heartstrings more than a little stirred by her unfaltering loyalty. Even though she does not know the details of my plot, the calm confidence she has in me is comforting. She puts her hands on her hips as she gazes out the windowsill.

"Our enemies may have more warriors, more supplies, and more allies than us, but there is one thing they do not have. They don't have Mab Ceridwen on their side."

I press my lips together, unable to think of anything to say. Lovely, faithful Rowena. God bless her.

She smiles and nods before leaving me alone with Tristan. After she shuts the door behind her, I gently rock my young son in my arms. I quietly kiss his tiny warm brow. Hush, little one. Hush. Mother will take care of you. You are still a son of the Old Tribes, and you have a strength within you that you do not yet know. But you will one day, my sweet child. You will know, and be glad.

Ahern's voice rings from the lookout nest atop the battlements.

"Ships! Ships on the water! To arms! To arms!"

I sit up in bed with a gasp, Tristan cradled in the coverlets beside me. He slumbers against my side as my eyes blink back the darkness. It is not yet dawn, only the faintest opal hue lingers on the horizon.

The clack of footfalls on the slick stone steps outside resounds with the tramp of spearmen and archers taking up their positions along the battlements. I doubt Ahern has more than a few dozen warriors to call upon at this ungodly hour. Most are doubtless too weak from wounds or hunger to yet rise. How few of us remain.

My heart pumps fast as Rowena opens the door, one of her daughters half-asleep in her arms. My handmaid's eyes look round as goose eggs, her disheveled nightshift drooping down one shoulder. She whispers thickly into my ear.

"Sails offshore, m'lady. Our foes have finally come for blood!"

"Stay with Tristan, and send Una to make sure Gavin and my husband keep to their chamber."

My little Gavin and wounded husband are the last two people in the citadel who should be out of bed and on the ramparts, but that doesn't mean they won't try. It'll take the strictness of a nun to keep them at bay. Thank the Lord for Una.

I don a robe and pull a doeskin tartan over my shoulders. A quick check of my bow and quiver finds everything in order. I may still have half a stone of baby weight on me, but at least I can draw a bowstring like a proper spear-wife should. Rowena grasps my sleeve.

"Your Grace, you're not going out there, are ye? It's black as the devil's heart outside."

"I won't slip and fall, Rowena. I was born in Dun Dyfed. I know these halls well."

"What if the castle falls, my Queen? What will be the fate of the children?"

I grab Rowena by the wrist, probably harder than I should.

"It will not come to that! Do you understand?"

She nods meekly, and a pang of guilt lances my chest. I shouldn't chide her so, but the thought of what our children's fate will be should we fail is too much for me to contemplate. It simply cannot come to pass. It *cannot.* One thing the Saxons and Picts have in common is that they do not leave the children of defeated nobles alive. The mere thought makes me shudder. I quickly push such nightmares to the back of my mind. I *will not* let it come to that.

Some inspirational leader I've proved to be. I wish I had Artagan's knack for cockiness before a fight. But he will do little inspiring of the troops while lying on a sickbed. God help us, have the Picts already moored their vessels offshore? We've already run out of time.

I race through dim corridors toward the westernmost wall overlooking the dark sea far below. Ahern and a score of warriors squint into the misty fogbanks scattered across the predawn shoreline. Standing beside me, my brother gives me a quick glance. I crane my eyes and ears against the blackness and the wind, trying to glean anything in the blue-gray haze.

Half a dozen sails dot the waters, their ghostly shapes listing heavily in the shallows. Each vessel must be heavily weighed down, but with what? It's still too dark to make out more than the curve of their prows and the canvas of their mainmasts.

Ahern grimaces beside me.

"I'd have bet my last copper that Sab's army would approach by land. She has only enough boats for her Picts, and half of those were damaged at All Hallows. Would she really leave Iago's horsemen behind?"

"I doubt she needs Iago's troops to lay siege to our beleaguered lot."

"What are your orders? Do we loose some arrows? Try to set a few of their ships alight before they make landfall?"

"I'm not sure we have the means to offer even that much resistance."

I frown until my cheeks hurt. This is not how things were supposed to unfold. Sab's tiny fleet alone will upset all my carefully laid plans. Her unpredictability will be the downfall of us all. I clench my bow until my fist smarts. The first rays of dawn pierce the horizon.

A few daggers of crimson sunshine penetrate the thinning fog. My eyes alight on the nearest sea craft as it beaches itself along the strand below the dun. The first sailor hops off onto the sands. My eyes widen, my heart rising against my ribs.

"Look! Those ships are made of timber, not calfskin. Their sails are dun-colored, not black, and their crew wears breeches, not animal skins."

Ahern furrows his brows.

"My lady?"

"Those aren't Picts. They're Cornish ships."

"Boats from Cornwall? But why would they come here?"

"Because I sent for them."

A broad smile spreads across my lips. I shut my eyes and say a silent prayer. Even with all my hoped-for plans, I never expected such a rapid response. My messenger ravens went out barely a week ago. Before Ahern can ask me further questions, I issue orders to his guardsmen.

"Saddle my pony and ready a contingent of spearmen. Mount everyone else you can on the walls and battlements, even the sick and the children. Make it look like there are a thousand of us. I want us to look as well-manned and imposing as possible. I won't have the Cornish thinking we are a few meager defenders standing on our last legs."

"Aye, but we are," Ahern murmurs to himself.

I give him a cross look. He sets about obeying my orders without another word. Although my half brother is a veteran of many battles, he doesn't understand the first thing about diplomacy. It's always better to negotiate from a position of strength, and even potential allies must not see the chinks in one's armor. No one wants to join a lost cause, and we must give our best impression to these Cornishmen if we are to enlist their help. So much do I hope.

By the time the yellow orb rises in the east, half the inhabitants within the citadel line the defenses. Up close, even a blind man could tell they're little more than refugees and walking wounded. But from down on the shore, the Cornish will see what appear to be at least a thousand spears manning the walls of Dun Dyfed.

I ride my mare down the grassy dunes to the beach, letting her dip her hooves in the rushing tide. Ahern and a score of his healthiest spearmen jog behind me with their shields at the ready. Just in case these Cornish sailors are not what they appear to be.

A small gang of Cornish mariners disembarks from their ships, mooring their vessels in the shallows with blocks made of Cornish iron. They wear cutlasses on their belts, each seaman holding a harpoon in one hand. Typical weapons of our distant Celtic kin in Cornwall, the best seafarers in all Britain. Only a skeleton crew mans each craft. So what, pray tell, weighs each ship down so?

Before I can venture a guess, a figure descends a gangplank to the shore, the wooden board bowing under her weight. I sit tall in the saddle, trying to maintain a measure of confidence in my poise, whether I feel it or not. I nod with a smile toward the large round woman, decked out in finger rings and warm-colored skirts.

"Queen Cordelia of South Wales, welcome. My condolences on the passing of your late husband. King Griffith's death pains us all."

"Not as much as his successor pains me," she retorts. "Arthwys isn't half the king Griffith was."

The large Queen sighs, a half-eaten chicken thigh in hand. My goodness, does this Cornishwoman never cease eating? My stomach growls, not having seen so much meat in over a fortnight. My own soldiers doubtless fight the urge to lick their lips. Ahern gives each of them a stern eye. No guardsman so much as budges a muscle.

I bow in the saddle and Queen Cordelia curtsies in turn. I peer down at her from atop my mount.

"You received my raven?" I ask.

"At first I did not believe your letter. Surely, Arthwys would keep me on as queen in order to maintain his mercantile alliance with my cousin King Caradoc's realm in Cornwall. Then I received the news from Arthwys himself, the little *prince*. He means to put *me* aside so that he can wed that exiled Queen from the North. The strumpet."

I repress a satisfied smile. So Olwen has played her part perfectly thus far. I almost feel sorry for Cordelia. Originally betrothed to the Hammer King's brother years ago, she and I might have been sisters-in-law had fate turned out differently. But her first husband, like mine, died at the hands of the Saxons. She wed the next king at Caerleon, Lord Griffith, and likewise expected to have to wed again now that South Wales has a new monarch.

But Arthwys must have taken one look at Olwen and knew he would never take a fat old bird like Cordelia to the altar. Important as the Cornish trade is for South Wales, the chance of claiming North Wales through Olwen's hand in marriage would be too much to resist for most men. And despite Olwen being at least a decade older than Arthwys, she is still a ravishing Welsh Venus. Fertile enough to sire an heir or two. Yes, I'm sure a teenage king like Arthwys had both land and lust on his mind when Olwen rode into camp, offering herself as a wedding present to him.

Cordelia sniffles, dabbing her eye with a handkerchief before using it to wipe the last chicken grease from her lips. In her own way, I'm sure she does mourn Griffith. But she also mourns her former position as queen at Caerleon, with the many comforts that only one of the finest palaces in all Wales can offer. Little did Arthwys reckon the enemy he made in dismissing Cordelia from his court. Cordelia's double chin shakes as she contemplates all her travails.

"It was kind of you to send a raven to my cousin in Cornwall as well," she adds. "King Caradoc was surprised, since the Cornish have little trade with your Free Cantref people, but nonetheless, he sent several ships to collect me from Caerleon. Else Arthwys would have left me to rot outside the city gates."

"And so you sailed here, and we are most glad of your coming to us."

"I've done more than that, Queen Branwen. I've come to offer you what aid I can. Arthwys will pay for what he has done to me. And so I've brought you the one thing he has denied you of late . . . the one thing I never go anywhere without."

She gestures toward the half dozen vessels anchored behind her. I raise an eyebrow, at first not comprehending her meaning. Her sailors roll several barrels and casks onto the sands while others retrieve large chests and crates from belowdecks. My eyes are wide as Ahern and I exchange looks. Cordelia smiles.

"Sacks of barley and flour, barrels of salted meat, a few casks of ale, and dozens of crates of my favorite onions. Have you ever had onion soup, my Queen?"

I lick my lips despite myself. There must be half a hundred vats of foodstuffs aboard her small ships. No wonder their vessels rode so low in the water! Enough supplies to feed a thousand mouths or more. Cordelia has brought us something better than an army. She has brought us life! I'm guessing my people and I will be eating a lot of onion soup in the days to come. I turn toward my soldiers, raising my longbow high overhead.

"Three cheers for Queen Cordelia! The rightful Queen of South Wales!"

My spearmen reply with three throaty hurrahs, their eyes covetously following every barrel and hogshead of rations unloaded onshore. Although they may cheer more at the thought of a full belly than for Cordelia's usurped throne, the deposed Queen nonetheless smiles at my warriors' show of support. Whether the food comes from Cornwall's food stores or South Wales's granaries, it will be a severe blow for Arthwys's cause. His blockade of the mountains roads has not prevented food supplies from reaching my garrison at Dun Dyfed. With real food in our stomachs again, our wounded will recover and our ranks will swell again with healthy, hearty warriors.

Ahern's men help the Cornish sailors break into the first crates, sharing bread and cheeses amongst them. My kinsman graciously offers me a hunk of rye flatbread. I devour it with as much haste as much as I dare in front of Cordelia and her mariners, trying to maintain my manners while still obeying my growling stomach. Every bite tastes like manna from heaven.

Cordelia joins in, tasting more than a little from each barrel as she grabs armfuls of dried goods. Our soldiers and the Cornish sailors haul more crates up to the gates of the fortress, where the inhabitants greet them with boisterous smiles and embraces. Ahern gnaws on a cut of dried jerky, speaking low next to my ear.

"Far be it from me to look down on the miracle you've wrought, but this is but a temporary victory, is it not?"

I smile at my brother, glancing around to make sure none can hear us.

"Brother, you'd see clouds on the horizon during the brightest summer day."

"'Tis my nature. The food will last us a good while, but Sab's armies will still overwhelm us, and gut our bellies no matter how full of food we are."

"And you account Queen Cordelia's support for nothing? We have an ally now."

"An ally? The South Welsh will remain loyal to their King, not her. And as for her royal cousin in Cornwall, the Cornish kingdom is worse off than ours. They've lost half their lands to the Saxons in the last generation alone. The Cornish have no troops to spare us."

"They don't need to. They've already given me the two things we need."

Ahern raises a skeptical eyebrow.

"Two things? Food perhaps, but what else?"

"Their ships. Six solid Cornish ships and their sailors."

"Six ships are not many."

"More than we had before. Besides, I only need a few for what I intend."

I turn to Ahern, my face suddenly serious.

"Brother, I must ask something of you, probably the most dangerous thing I've ever asked you to do."

He rolls his eyes.

"You've asked all manner of perilous things of me these last few years. What more, pray tell, could you conjure up that would be *more* dangerous?"

"I need you to take command of these ships and sail on a secret errant for me."

He blinks incredulously, struggling to keep his voice down.

"Blast it, Branwen, I'm no sailor! I've hardly set foot on a boat in my born life."

"You're the only one I can trust, Ahern. The only one with the will to see it done. Will you do this for me?"

He throws up his hands.

"Do *what* exactly? All I know is that you want me to get myself seasick for some secret plot."

"Keep your voice down, kinsman."

I take him by the arm, faking a smile in case any onlookers in the crowd watch us. He manages only to leer and frown by turns, his face an unmasked cipher open for anyone to read. Fortunately, everyone from Cordelia down to the peasants crowd the unloaded foodstuffs, sharing laughter and drinks as though it were an impromptu harvest festival. Let them have their joys. With so much grief these past few moons, the people deserve a little reprieve. It may be the last break we catch before Sab descends on us for the final siege.

Ahern and I wend our way up to the easternmost parapets, alone together as we stroll arm in arm. We pause, finishing the rest of our bread and dried goods now that no one can see how quickly we eat. It feels like paradise to have a full belly.

Swallowing my last bite, I tell Ahern the details of my plan. He listens without interrupting me once. When finished, he shakes his head.

"What you're proposing has never been done."

"Which is exactly why it will work, why it *must* work," I reply. "Even for Sab, it'll be the last thing she expects me to do."

"I don't like it, Branwen. Not one bit."

I grin sheepishly.

"When has that ever stopped you from doing the impossible?"

He merely screws up his eye in reply.

A horseman gallops headlong toward us on the eastern battlements, one of our green-clad scouts responsible for patrolling the heaths. He neither smiles nor waves at the commoners eating their fill of Queen Cordelia's horns of plenty. Instead, he dismounts before Ahern and me, his steed panting breathlessly. The scout bows slightly, his limbs shaking with fatigue.

"My Queen, our scouts on the moors have just reported back. An army of Picts and North Welsh horsemen marches this way."

A knot forms in my throat. Dear God, we've run out of time, after all. I fight the roiling churn of a half-digested meal threatening to rise back out of my stomach. Ahern and I exchange grave looks. It takes me a moment to find my voice.

"You best depart, brother. There's no time to lose."

He nods and turns to go. He halts halfway into his stride as though contemplating something. He spins on his heel and takes my hand before pressing his lips to my fingertips. Ever the chivalrous guardsman. I wrap both arms around him and embrace my brother, possibly for the last time. Neither of us may live to see another full moon rise over Wales.

Ahern goes without another word. I blink back the water in my eyes so that the messenger rider will not see me weep. As I glance out toward the eastern moors, a dark foreboding wells up inside me, black as poison in my heart.

Queen Sab and her army will be here by nightfall.

19

Artagan stands beside me in the darkness, holding my hand. Torches dot the moors in the distance, snaking their way toward Dun Dyfed like a giant fiery serpent. Sab's army. Thick clouds obscure the moon, but the Picts seems to thrive in the utter darkness. As unhindered by nightfall as a cloud of bats.

Horses whinny faintly on the wind. Iago's northern horsemen must follow close behind the Picts, trailing the glow of their firebrands as they encircle the dun from the landward side. I swallow a heavy lump in my throat. We are cornered, trapped like a fawn before a pack of wolves.

My husband squeezes my palm. He leans against his sheathed longsword, using it like a makeshift crutch. He puts on a brave face but cannot help wincing in the dim twilight. His wounds ail him far more than he will admit. He can barely stand, let alone fight. Our outnumbered spearmen and archers will not have the famed Blacksword to inspire them in battle. I put my arm around him, feeling the faint puff of his breath against my cheek.

"You should not overtax yourself, my love. Your wounds need time to mend."

"I've had worse," he lies with a half-grin.

"You're fortunate to be alive. Thankfully, the bone spear carried no poison. Although it pierced your side, it narrowly missed your vitals. One in a hundred men wouldn't be so lucky."

"I don't need luck. I've the loving protection of the Mab Ceridwen watching over me."

I feign an indignant scoff. Even on his deathbed, my love would still be cocky as a rooster. Does he truly still think himself invincible after all he has seen and endured? Maybe in spite of it.

The two of us stand on the easternmost battlement, watching the enemy loom closer across the nocturnal heaths. I've ordered watchmen to guard every stretch of wall, our spearmen concealing themselves in the shadows. As per my command, every hearth and flame has been extinguished within our walls. I'll not give Sab any advantages tonight. Let her army find me in pitch-blackness if they must. We won't provide a single light to guide their way through the treacherous bogs.

The lookouts give Artagan and me a wide berth, not a single soldier lingering within earshot. The two of us may at least speak in private. With so many demands on our time, I can't recall the last evening Artagan and I were truly alone together. Between being leaders by day and parents by night, I don't think we've spent an evening just the two of us since we left Aranrhod. All those months ago, before the Picts came. And now we stand in the dark, a lone married couple taking stock of what may be their last moments together. The night before our enemies come to wipe us out.

By the silvery starlight, I can just make out Artagan's face. He squints into the misty gloom, eyeing the nearing glowworm of Pictish torches in the east. He pulls me close as I lay my head against his chest, listening to the strong, steady beat of his heart.

"Why do they not attack?" he whispers suspiciously. "The Picts don't seem to mind the dark."

"I bet Iago's North Welshmen do. Sab will wait for daylight."

"But why did Sab take so long in bringing her minions here against us? Even for an army her size, she could have marched the distance sooner. It's taken them weeks to get to Dun Dyfed when it should've only taken days."

I shift my jaw from side to side, pondering awhile before I reply.

"It's no secret that Arthwys's soldiers blocked the roads east of here. Sab would have guessed our rations had dwindled, especially with more and more refugees pouring into Dyfed."

"You're saying she was waiting for us to starve?"

"I've told you that her ways are different, her thinking sideways, her actions indirect and shadowy. Why rush to meet us in battle when by delaying she could arrive after most of us had already starved to death?"

"Thank Providence that Queen Cordelia came to our relief with supplies. I bet Sab was mad as Lucifer when she found out."

"Perhaps. You have to first understand the manner in which a Pictish chieftess like Sab thinks."

"It seems you comprehend her mind better than any of us these days."

A wave of heat rises through my cheeks. Is he comparing me to a savage like Sab? I pull back and face him, starlight reflecting in our eyes.

"To defeat a monster I must learn to think like one, but that does not make *me* a monster. Tell me you understand that."

He smiles.

"You misunderstand me, my love. I was complimenting your cunning, not comparing you to a murderess like Sab."

He caresses my brow with a kiss, wrapping his warm arms around me. I relax a touch under his familiar embrace, yet a new though arises like a splinter in my mind. I was quick to jump to a conclusion Artagan did not intend, but perhaps that's because the same thought has plagued me all along. How different am I really from Sab?

Is she not another version of me, gazing back from the looking glass? The darker side of my very same moon. She fights for her people, defending them and advancing their interests. They are her family. By the same token, I would do anything for my own people. I've suffered plenty of sins and sacrifices for Wales, as have others. How many have I ordered to their deaths? All in the name of protecting my subjects and my family. A shiver runs down the small of my back. Perhaps the real barbarian is the queen who gazes back at me from the mirror each morn.

Closing my eyes with a sigh, I try to wash such thoughts from my head. The din of shuffling feet and clanking shields advances closer across the moors. With every moment, Sab's warriors draw nearer, their forces tightening like a noose around the citadel. The sound of their steady tread sets my teeth on edge. The noise of horses and chain mail clouds my reasoning, constricting my mind like a garrote tightening around my thoughts. If only the clamor from their fiery line of torches would stop. It's enough to unhinge the steadiest of minds.

But something else Artagan said gives me pause. Something that even the cacophony of Sab's savages cannot drive from my mind. If Sab simply wanted to starve us out, surely she could have arrived sooner and laid a siege, just to make sure we didn't try to escape. Even though I can't think of anywhere to escape to. What if not everything has occurred according to Sab's well-laid plans either? All my plots have certainly not played out as I foresaw.

A glimmer of hope kindles within me. Sab's troops have doubtless been pillaging the countryside, scattering themselves far and wide as they burn villages and gorge themselves on the food stores of hard-working peasants. But perhaps in their revels, Queen Sab has not been able to control them. From what I've seen of the Picts in battle and on the march, they are an undirected torrent of fury at best, each a wild, brutish individual, heedless of any commands or restraint. Maybe Sab has unleashed something she cannot fully control. Maybe. But a nagging feeling tells me there is something more to this mystery. Some crucially obvious element that has somehow escaped my notice.

Artagan turns, putting both hands on my shoulders. His serious countenance draws me up short.

"I wanted to tell you that I was wrong," he begins. "When you first brought the children into the wilderness with an assassin on your trail, I didn't know what to think. But you've shown that you're made of stronger metal than any of us. You truly can be both a mother and a warrior-queen. Forgive me for doubting you, my love."

I smile, water welling behind my eyes. It's hard enough for a man to admit the error of his ways, but even rarer for a king to do so. I fondly touch his stubbled cheek.

"There's nothing to forgive, husband. I've more than enough love for you, our children, and our kingdom to go around."

"Not to mention a will of iron." He winks.

I playfully pat his cheek.

A late autumnal breeze makes me shiver in Artagan's arms, winter's breath already thick on the wind. Despite the cold, I cannot retire within just yet. Like a soldier at my post, it seems wrong for me not to stand watch with the others. But the ache in my milk-heavy bosom weighs on me, and I soon retire to my bedchamber.

Little Tristan already cries out for his evening suckle. Still torn between my role as a queen and a mother, my heart already knows which side will win. Artagan was right in admitting that I *can* be both mother and spear-wife, but that doesn't mean it ever comes easy. Was it always thus for the matrons of the Old Tribes? Surely they battled Picts while still having to bear children and keep their menfolk in line. Those women must have been made of sterner steel than I.

Rowena hands Tristan to me. My handmaid smiles before retreating from the room. A leaden weight rises from my shoulders as soon as I sit down with my babe in my arms. He nuzzles at the breast before finding his way. Tristan feeds as quiet as a cat, so different from Gavin, who used to slurp and murmur at the tit. My first boy will always be a prince of my heart, but this second newborn radiates the tranquility of an angel. I gently put my lips to his brow and caress him as I lull him to sleep in my arms.

A pounding comes at the door. Before I can chide the careless intruder, Gavin scampers into the chamber. He stops short when he sees I am with his young brother. The toddler cocks his head sideways as though observing a novelty. He suddenly smiles.

"Little brother." He points at him, before jabbing a thumb at himself. "*Big* brother."

I grin and nod back, keeping my voice low, so as not to awake the baby.

"That's right, Gavin. You're the big brother. You are the brave protector."

Gavin folds his arms with smug satisfaction. He looks like a redheaded miniature of his father. Artagan hobbles in after him, still breathing hard from the stairwell.

"Sorry, my dear. The lad outpaced me on the stairs. He's got the legs of a young colt."

I bite my lip. Never have I seen Artagan so weak, his injury lingering in his bones day after day. When I first met him years ago, he had the strength of a bear and the daring of a fox. It must be doubly hard on him to be invalided so. He puts a hand on Gavin's shoulder, trying to steer the boy out of the quiet bedchamber. I reach out to stop him.

"No, it's all right, Artagan. I'd have my family, my whole family, together this night."

He nods, the firelight from the hearth flickering in his eyes. Neither of us needs to say that tomorrow may be our last. Artagan pulls up a chair beside me, saddling Gavin on his lap. The boy leans his head back against his father's chest, his fingers playing along the leather scabbard of Artagan's famed longsword. We listen to the crackling fire while Artagan hums an old Celtic lullaby that echoes both pleasantly and hauntingly off the chamber rafters. I shut my eyes, rocking my baby against my chest.

I sip in the scent of woodsmoke on the cool evening air, trying to draw out every note of Artagan's song, to make every remaining drop of my life last a little longer. Just a little longer. The first hot tear runs silently down my cheek. If only we had more time. Just a little more time together.

At dawn, a herald from Sab's lines rides toward the fortress gates, blowing on a kinked ram's horn. A line of blue-painted warriors encircles the greens outside the dun. Scalps and polished bones dangle from many of the Picts' spears. Trophies of their latest conquests. And meals, no doubt. The thought makes my stomach churn.

A broad column of horsemen stands arrayed behind them, their black dragon banner snapping in the seaward breeze. Not as many as I feared, but still at least two thousand of Iago's northern cavalry have come. Only a few hundred Picts remain to Sab, but she has relied significantly on the muscle of Iago's numerous troops of late. Setting Welshman against Welshman, gradually reducing my country to rubble.

She has more than enough warriors in her army to defeat the few hundred weary defenders within Dun Dyfed. Many more women and children hide behind our walls. But we are still free Welsh, archers of the Free Cantrefs and spearmen of Dyfed. One free man or woman defending their home is worth ten marauding Picts. Or so I hope. Today's events will prove me wrong or right.

A lone black bird circles high overhead. The creature lands in the castle rookery before a runner jogs down the inner defenses toward me. Artagan and I stand together, clutching our tartan furs close around our throats in the cool morning air. The runner bows and hands me a scrap of parchment from the messenger raven. I recognize Ahern's seal stamped on one side of the page. The crumpled sheet has only one small line scrawled in charcoal: *It is done.*

Artagan raises an eyebrow.

"What does that mean?"

I ball the sheet in my hand, frowning at my own thoughts.

"It means the die is cast, and now we will find out if what I have done was worth the cost."

The Pict herald toots on his warbling ram's horn again as three riders canter out from the enemies' lines. Even from a distance I recognize Sab and her daughter, their fair skin tattooed in azure swaths. They ride pale mounts. Iago trots behind them on his chestnut steed, his armor and plate mail as black as the sackcloth banners his horsemen carry. Artagan gives me a sidelong look, clutching his sheathed sword.

"They want to parley with us? I'd rather answer them with steel and arrows."

"They want to watch us squirm, maybe even beg. But what does it cost us to talk a little? It may buy us some time."

"I'd rather we drop these pretenses and get down to fighting. I've still got enough strength to send a few Picts to the next world, or whatever those savages believe in."

"I don't think a queen like Sab believes in anything at all."

Artagan gives me another glance, but I keep my focus on Sab astride her mount in the middle of no-man's-land. A numbness overcomes me, my face a damask mask, my lips flat and small. Whatever will happen, will happen. It is out of my hands now. Maybe my own fate never really was mine to determine.

I grab my longbow and saddle my mountain pony. Artagan follows me astride Merlin, galloping with me onto the open moors. A third horse snorts and labors behind us. I halt my mare to look back over my shoulder. Queen Cordelia clasps her plump legs around a rust-colored gelding.

"I've thrown my lot in with you against these pagan Picts. I might as well see what the beggars look like up close."

Artagan exchanges looks with me and shrugs. I suppose it can't hurt to have Cordelia along, although I wonder if she has truly grasped the peril we're all in. Grateful as I am to her for saving us from starvation, I doubt that a lifetime of pincushions and feasting at Caerleon has prepared her for a showdown with the likes of Queen Sab. But so be it.

I dig my heels into the flanks of my mare, cantering into the open space between our two armies. Sab, Ness, and Iago wait for us. My hands relax on the bridle as I let my mount slow to a halt. My jaw hangs open, my eyes unable to look away from King Iago.

He sits in his saddle beside Sab and Ness, slumped to one side like a sack of ground meal. The right side of his face sags, one eyelid drooping. Half of his lip curls downward unnaturally.

His right arm is completely missing.

Artagan and Cordelia halt beside me, the fat Queen gasping when she sees the maimed northern King. In the chaos of our battle at All Hallows, I was too concerned with Artagan and the baby to notice our foes' losses. It appears that our enemies have endured tragedies as well.

Iago looks to have suffered a stroke, probably when his clerics had to amputate his wounded arm. His dark hair now has a swath of white running through it. Despite his mangled appearance, he clutches the horse's reins tightly with his one good hand, defying the wind that buffets him and threatens to tear him from the saddle. I almost admire Iago's endurance. Almost. Then I think of King Griffith and all the others we lost at All Hallows. A knot tightens so fiercely within my chest it seems fit to burst.

The voluptuous Ness nudges her mount beside Iago, coiled like a cat in her saddle. She still has Iago in her thrall. I grimace until my cheeks hurt. Whether a commoner or king, anyone who stands with Sab and Ness is an enemy of mine and a foe of all free Wales.

Artagan snaps at Sab. Even in his weakened state he still wants to fight.

"What do you want, Sab? Be quick with it."

"Still alive, Blacksword?" Sab replies. "My, you do have nine lives. Mab Ceridwen's healing prowess lives up to its reputation."

Sab flashes a brittle smile, doubtless thinking of her dead champion. Bal and Artagan dueled to the death at All Hallows. Now Bal lies beneath his burial mound, if his own people didn't eat him. Meanwhile, Artagan has been at death's door for nigh over a moon or more, although one can hardly tell now that his blood is up.

If Sab really meant to honor their duel, she would have acceded that Artagan won and withdrawn her troops. Instead she cried foul, and we've been up to our knees in Welsh blood ever since. My fist tightens on my longbow until the knuckles turn white. My voice is harsh yet firm.

"He asked you a question, chieftess. You're far from home, Sab, what do you want?"

"Why, to spare further bloodshed, of course. I plan to offer generous terms."

"For our surrender?" I reply. "If you want our swords, you'll have to come and take them yourself. One of my archers is worth ten of your mongrels. We'll bleed your army dry."

Sab purses her lips with a wicked grin.

"I was hoping you'd say that. I've two thousand spears that would like to put your boast to the test."

"Come and try it, Sab. Dun Dyfed has withstood a hundred sieges in its long history, and its ancient walls are stout and rocky as ever."

"Aye, but it's fallen to Picts before, and it will again. Once I set my warriors loose, Branwen, there'll be no quarter for anyone inside your walls. Men, women, *children*."

She savors the last word. *Children*. I swallow involuntarily, thinking of Gavin and Tristan. Their angelic faces, so soft and so vulnerable. Only the most heartless of devils would harm such innocents. And yet I've no doubt that Sab is such a demoness, if ever I saw one. Her smile forks into an unnatural V. She seems to enjoy the color draining from my face, watching me squirm.

Artagan nudges his steed forward, his sword hand itching for his blade. He could hardly lift his sword if he tried, but fortunately the Picts don't know that. Sab ignores him, turning toward Queen Cordelia.

"And how about the Cornish Queen of South Wales? Do you wish to fight to the death too?"

Cordelia stutters a few incoherent syllables, her jowls shaking ever so slightly. I edge my steed between Sab and Cordelia. If Sab wishes to pierce our hearts with terror, let her focus on me. Perhaps it's time the Pictish shamaness had a taste of her own medicine. I gently clear my throat as though making a nonchalant comment.

"Queen Cordelia is free to come and go as she chooses. It's not the Queen that should concern you, but her ships."

Sab's eyes narrow.

"What ships?"

"The ones her Cornish kin brought to our aid."

"You got a few foodstuffs, what of it? You'll die with full bellies instead of empty ones."

Now it's my turn to smile. I remove the note from inside my tunic, the parchment Ahern's messenger raven delivered this morning. I toss the balled-up paper at Iago, who fumbles with it in his lap. He raises an eyebrow as he examines the page.

"What is this trifle?"

"A report from my kinsman, Ahern," I reply. "I sent him north with the Cornish ships to attack the Isle of Mona off the coast of your kingdom."

Iago lets the paper fall from his hands, his skin suddenly white as a sheet. Ness and Sab exchange looks as the Pict Queen leans toward me. She no longer sounds quite so confident.

"A handful of ships, maybe a score or two of men, they can't conquer a kingdom."

"His kingdom?" I smile ruefully. "I'm after his *granaries* on Mona. My men burnt half of them to the ground this morning. If they do not receive word from me soon, they shall burn the other half."

Iago blanches, pale as death. I watch him, patient as a cat who has a mouse trapped in its paws. With a word from me, my men could raze his people's winter stores to the ground. A famine would set in.

Gwynedd may be impregnable from the land, but it's vulnerable from the sea. And Mona is the breadbasket of the Northlands, providing most of the foodstuffs for Iago's otherwise mountainous realm. With most of his forces in the South, I gambled that he did not have any troops left behind to guard his homelands. And why should he? Until a few days ago, I didn't have a fleet with which to threaten his coasts.

Iago's curled lips twist into an uneven grimace. It appears that my gamble has paid off. He fumes under his breath, balling his only fist.

"You burn my people's food stores and expect me to capitulate to *you*?"

"No, I expect you to see reason, Iago. Half your people's precious granaries can still be spared, the choice is yours."

Iago shifts his jaw, unable to speak. A deathly silence pervades the surround. Nothing but the whistling wind and the swish of our steeds' tails makes a sound.

It goes without saying that if my men burn down the rest of Iago's grain stores, thousands, maybe tens of thousands, of Welshmen and women will perish of starvation this winter. But how many Welsh have died since Iago joined forces with Sab? How many villages have they burnt? How many widows and orphans have they made? My soldiers on Mona await my orders, but it will be Iago's decision that determines what happens now. The onus hangs on him. Either Ahern's men will set sail in peace, or they will turn Mona's remaining granaries to ash.

Ness sidles up beside Iago, glaring at me as she speaks in his ear.

"She's lying! It's a trick. What proof do we have that any of what she says is true?"

The clatter of a horse gallops across the moors. A white mare, well-bred by the look of her. A smirk plays across my lips as the stranger nears our small gathering. Ness blanches as I point out the nearing equestrian.

"If you don't believe me, ask your own people, King Iago. Ask someone you trust."

Iago furrows his brow before turning to greet the approaching rider. The white filly halts before us, her nostrils dilated and her cream coat shimmering with sweat. A dark beauty of a woman clears the midnight locks from her face, her chest panting as she catches her breath. Iago gasps.

"Olwen!"

Her gaze darts to Iago's maimed limb, but she quickly covers up her shock. Good, Olwen. Good. Don't lose your composure. Olwen nonchalantly looks the northern King over with her appraising violet eyes.

"Hello, husband." She smiles. "It's been some time since you tossed me aside for this trollop. It does look as though she hasn't been any good for your health."

She nods toward Ness, who only clutches Iago's good arm all the tighter. The Pictish vixen sneers at Olwen. I find that I must agree with Olwen myself. Iago would probably have all his limbs had he not sided with Sab and her daughter. The addled northern King stares open-mouthed at his wife.

Cordelia also shifts uncomfortably in her saddle, glaring at the woman for whom Arthwys set her aside. I put a hand to the plump queen's chest to keep her silent. The last thing I need right now is a row between Cordelia and Olwen.

Iago watches Olwen closely.

"Why have you come back to me, then?"

"Because King Arthwys is marching on your lands as we speak. His army has left Caerleon."

Iago unhooks his arm from Ness, staring blankly at the grass. First my raiding party torches half his winter stores and now a former ally intends to invade his lands from the south. He clears his throat, trying to regain his lost voice, but it only comes out in a thick whisper.

"An invasion from Arthwys? Now?"

"He means to claim the North through marriage to me," Olwen replies. "But that was just a ruse to gain his trust. I'm still Queen of the North, *your* Queen, Iago, and I would save our people now if you'll let me."

"Branwen says her raiders have torched half of Mona," he replies.

"She's the devil's own master. If she said it, then she could do it. It's probably true."

Olwen looks me over suspiciously, sizing me up like a wrestler observing an opponent. I know I told her to betray me so that she could drive a wedge between Arthwys and Iago, but how much is an act and how much does she speak true? Sab and Ness exchange furtive glances. Even the two cunning she-devils from the Pictlands cannot tell. Olwen, as always, keeps council only with Olwen.

Sab sneers at the two of us, glaring at me, then at Olwen as she turns to Iago.

"This is a ploy to drive our alliance apart! Can't you see that, you dimwitted oaf?"

Olwen laughs in a singsong falsetto, her confidence unnerving even myself.

"Branwen and I, in league together? The woman who stole my first love, deprived me of my birthright in the Free Cantrefs, and opposed my husband's army in the field?" She laughs again, turning toward me. "What say you, Mab Ceridwen? Should we salt old wounds or retract our claws?"

"You first," I reply through clenched teeth.

I decide that whether or not she is faking her anger toward me, I might as well play the part of her antagonist. After all, how hard do we have to pretend to be foes? Olwen smirks.

"I thought you'd say as much."

Sab ushers her steed between us, snapping at me as though ready to take a blade to my face.

"Enough of this! *I* have no granaries for you to hold ransom, Branwen, and my warriors will feast on your remains when we breach your walls. You've seen your last sunrise this day!"

Sab motions turn her mount to go, but Iago raises a hand to stop her.

"Hold! You will mount no attack today, Sab!"

The Pictish Queen's eyes widen before waning into half-moons. With only a few hundred Picts, most of her army depends upon Iago's two thousand northern horsemen. She cannot besiege Dun Dyfed with her blue-painted savages alone. Her voice rasps out like the hiss of hot coals.

"A backbone doesn't become you, Iago. This army takes its orders from *me*. We attack at once."

"Not with my horsemen, you won't."

Iago straightens his spine in the saddle. Olwen sidles up beside him, linking her arm through his. If Iago takes his cavalry with him, it will deprive Sab of most of her army. A couple hundred Picts aren't enough to conquer the walls of Dun Dyfed, even with only a few hundred able-bodied defenders in my own garrison. My heart starts to beat faster. For the first time, a real glimmer of hope has shined down on me. On all of us.

Ness grabs Iago, speaking softly to him, but the tremor in her tone betrays her lack of confidence.

"Hee . . . Heed my mother, wise King. Let us do away with this pesky Branwen and her kin. Then we can return north and secure our home there."

Olwen pushes herself between Ness and Iago.

"Why not ride north now to defend our kingdom from Arthwys? We could save our granaries in the process. I for one would share my husband even with the likes of you, so long as he takes me back to save my people."

Ness's mouth hangs open, lost for speech for once. Olwen's placating tact has thrown the young Pict completely off balance. Iago smiles at Olwen, putting his remaining hand on her forearm and stroking it fondly.

"You're right, my brave Queen. I should never have let you go."

Iago turns his steed to go, linking arms with Olwen as he calls out to Sab over his shoulder.

"I'm returning north to defend our lands there. If you're wise, Sab, you'll do the same and come with us."

Iago and Olwen depart toward the line of northern horsemen across the fields. Ness looks despondently at her mother, biting her lip. Sab gives her daughter's mare a slap to the hindquarters, starting the animal forward.

"After him, girl! Keep close to him, or that Welsh seductress will turn his head and undo your spell on him!"

Ness departs without another word. She casts one last glance back at Artagan as I glare at her. Go get your own man, little girl. But heaven help you if you return to the north in Olwen's company. It'll take less than a fortnight before Olwen arranges some accident to befall the Pictish enchantress. I would laugh were there not still a few hundred armed Picts within bowshot of my husband and me.

Iago's men dip their black banners as they depart the field and gallop back into the mists. If none of his men return, I'll make sure to send a raven north to Ahern and tell him to stand down. A Welsh queen always honors her debts.

Sab circles her horse, looking fit to pull out every hair on her head. Instead, she draws a bone scimitar from her saddle, hissing like a cat as she bares her sharp fangs. Her dark eyes focus squarely on me.

My pulse leaps in my throat, seeing the unmistakable intent in her face. Even if she had only a dozen warriors left, she would still risk all the perils of hell to come and take my head. Odds be damned.

Queen Cordelia squeals like a sow, her mount bolting back toward the gates of Dun Dyfed. Sab pays her no heed as she closes on Artagan and me. I draw my bow, fitting an arrow to the twine.

Artagan calls out to our soldiers in the bastions behind us, blowing his hunting horn. Our archers and spearmen pour out of the battlements. But there is no time. We might outrun the Picts, but not with Sab only a few paces away. Besides, I've not the stomach for running anymore.

Digging my heels into my mare's flanks, I charge directly for the Pict Queen as her mare bolts toward me. Sab's ululating battle cry pierces the air. She rises in the saddle like an uncoiled spring, a deathly white bone scimitar in one hand and an obsidian blade in the other. Guiding my pony with my thighs, I draw my bowstring to my jaw, never taking my gaze off Sab. I aim my arrowhead for her throat.

All the world seems to slow in the half instant as our mares collide, nose to nose. The cacophony of opening battle between our warriors, the whoosh of arrowheads and slingstones hurtling through the air. Artagan's voice calls out, though whether to me or our troops I cannot tell. My eyes see nothing but Sab. The barbarian foe, daughter of all the Picts who ever opposed all my foremothers of the Old Tribes.

I loose my arrow, deafening myself with my own battle scream. Neither fear nor pain can touch me. My fate and that of my arrowhead lie in God's hands. I am one with that whistling arrow speeding toward Sab's jugular. I am euphoric. I am half a barbarian myself. I am the Queen of Death.

PART FOUR

Winter, A.D. 602

20

Holly and mistletoe hang from the rafters in Aranrhod this Christmastide. The clank of mead horns and the din of boisterous conversations permeate the castle walls, the scent of roasting meat and woodsmoke hanging thick in the central hall. Outside, winter winds buffet the fortress walls, but inside we are warm and dry beside the glowing hearths.

Artagan reclines on his throne beside me. A fit of laughter erupts from his fellow knights as he finishes a joke. Sir Emryus slaps his thigh in mirth while Sir Keenan laughs so hard he shoots beer out his nose. My husband turns and winks at me, probably thinking that whatever he said will prove too bawdy for my tastes. I give his hand a squeeze, gnawing on a leg of mutton from the banquet table. The aroma of sweetmeats and baked bread rises above our many subjects crowded around the long feast tables.

I smile at the peace and tranquility of it all before putting a hand to my cheek. A thin, faded scar along my left cheekbone burns hot a moment before subsiding. It hardly shows anymore, but the memory still stings fresh in my mind. Artagan notices and leans close to my ear.

"Does the wound still bother you, my dear?"

"Bother me? No. But I shall remember it every day of my life."

"A small price to pay, my love. You're still beautiful as ever to me."

He caresses my other cheek with his palm. His azure eyes beam mischievously as he nestles closer. I recognize the familiar look in his eye and rise from my seat with a smile. In the last fortnight we've not gone a day without taking a tumble between the sheets. His war wounds certainly don't seem to hamper him now! I give him a lingering kiss before excusing myself from the throne room.

"I need some fresh air, my love. I'll return shortly."

"Don't wander too far, fair maiden." He grins. "The view does wonders for my health."

I follow his gaze down to my bust. Nursing Tristan these past few moons has made my chest swell more than ever. My dress neckline sags somewhat low. I quickly adjust my gown to show a little more propriety and a little less skin. Artagan makes an exaggerated frown, like a crestfallen pup. My goodness, he would have me sit on his lap in the open mead hall if I didn't rein him in once in a while! Nonetheless, a devilish grin flashes across my cheek. I lean down close to his ear so that he gets one more good view of my shift.

"Patience, my King. Tonight you shall see who is the true ruler in this castle."

I turn without another word, feeling his smoldering gaze following me all the way out of the main chambers. Pulling a fur tartan over my shoulders, I step out into the evening cold. The frosty dusk air hits my warm cheeks, rippling my flesh in goose bumps.

I pace the battlements alone while the golden firelight flickers through the castle's arrow slits. The murmur of the ongoing feast fills every nook and cranny of the castle interiors. In the distance, snow-capped mountains and sugarcoated forests peek through far-off fog-banks swirling around the winter landscape. Mother Nature has taken on her snowy mantle of hibernation, all the world once again at peace.

My feet take me to the one place I already knew they would, but until this moment I did not admit to myself I had any particular destination in mind. I pause atop the parapet above the castle's main gate, the massive wood-and-iron doors closed fast by both the guards and the wintry icicles. High above, dangling from the uppermost tower of the citadel, a small object hangs heavy despite the intemperate winds. I swallow hard, suddenly chilled to the marrow.

From a hempen rope droops the severed head of the chieftess of the Picts: Queen Sab.

Her sunken eyes have long since deteriorated into black holes. Crows have pecked much of the skull clean, but a nest of whitened hairs splays out from her scalp. Some half-frozen sinews still clench her jaw to the cranium, giving her head a lopsided, toothy sneer. I stand still in the frosty evening air, fogging my pink cheeks with my breath. Even dead, the Pictish shamaness still renders me speechless. My fingertips twitch nervously at my sides, feeling for the dagger on my belt. I half-expect her lifeless head to come to life again, a threat from beyond the grave.

A falcon's cry pierces the darkening, overcast sky. I flinch, wondering what bird would still be here in winter. Then I remember, grinning up at my hunting falcon. Vivian descends from her rookery atop my private tower across the castle keep. I pull a leather glove off my belt and thread my fingers through it. Vivian lands on my arm, squawking at the severed head dangling before us.

"Easy, girl. Easy."

I shush my hawking bird, smoothing her feathers. How I've missed her. I owe a great debt to this bird of prey for saving my life and the life of my son the night that assassin first came into our lives all those months ago. Bal, the secret killer sent by Sab to slay my child and strike terror into our hearts. But Vivian descended on his crossbow that evening, marring the shot that would have otherwise killed my child and perhaps me as well. Thanks to this bird, my children and I remain safe, and it is Sab's head who decorates the castle battlements. A grim warning to those who oppose the Free Welsh and their kin.

Finding my voice, I shuffle my feet to keep warm. Vivian remains on my arm as I banter with the dead queen.

"I still bear the scar you gave me outside Dun Dyfed, courtesy of your bone blade," I begin, touching my cheek. "And I see you are still missing the neck that my arrow tore through. I feared you, Sab, as I have feared no man or woman before or since. And yet you are food for crows while me and mine still live. And do you know why?"

The bodiless corpse makes no response, merely rocking back and forth in the fell breeze. It's almost as though she wags her head at me. I look to my feet a moment.

"Everything changed the day Artagan and Bal fought their duel. In an instant, my husband had been wounded, perhaps mortally, a battle had begun, our allies deserted us, and on top of it all my birth pangs came upon me. And do you know what I felt? What I thought at that exact moment?"

Sab's head remains mute, the rope holding her aloft creaking under a draft.

"I felt utterly powerless," I continue. "Weak and insignificant as a bug. All my plots, my scheming, my intricate plans that had made me a queen in the first place all added up to . . . nothing. I realized that despite all my efforts to protect Wales and defeat my enemies, I was not the one really in control. I once thought I was, but now I know better. And that ultimately became the key difference between us, Sab. You were every bit as cunning as me, if not more so. You are very much what in another life I could easily have turned into. A scheming, ruthless ruler of men, heedless of the means it took to justify your own ends. You believe in nothing, nothing but yourself and what you can control. But I am not fate's master. I am in God's hands, or the Goddess's hands, or whatever you choose to call it. The same hands that shaped the history of the Mothers of the Old Tribes and continues to mold my kingdom's destiny now."

I tap my chest, my heart beating fast within me.

"Once I knew that in here, I no longer tried to outwit you at your own game. I simply trusted to God that what was meant to happen, would. Just as my mother did before me. It was *faith* that defeated you. I was only the vessel, the instrument of your demise."

Staring up into her vacant face, I know that this unsightly battle trophy may strike fear into our enemies or give hope to our people, but this image of Sab will fade from my mind in time and I will think on it no more. Instead, the tiny flaw on my cheek will be my daily reminder of Sab, a remembrance of the kind of woman, the type of queen I almost became. The path of darkness I once unknowingly walked in my own arrogance and deceit. I touch the small scar on my face once more, letting my mind drift as the first snowflakes fall on my shoulders.

A man clears his throat nearby.

"Talking to dead people is never a good sign. Particularly on Christmas Eve."

I grin at Ahern. He smiles back before glancing up at Sab's head.

"Wish I could have been there," he says, "when you turned the tables on her at Dun Dyfed. When our people drove those savages into the sea. I wish I could've seen the look on her face."

"In a way, it looked much the same as it does now," I reply.

"Oh, you are harsh, my Queen."

"I'm cold," I retort.

Vivian glances up at my tower, listening to her chicks chirp from their sheltered nest. She vaults from my forearm, ascending to her rookery. My faithful falcon, well fed and nursing a brood of her own. She'll not want for anything so long as I live. Warm hay, fresh field mice, and the freedom to come and go as she pleases. Ahern squints at the spotted falcon with his one good eyeball, still never entirely at ease around my large-clawed pet. I stifle a grin. We best return to the Christmas revelries down in the main hall.

A bugle suddenly erupts from the darkening woods outside the castle. My pulse jumps in my throat. Ahern instinctively reaches for his spear, all of the merriment in his voice changed to gruff suspicion.

"That's a war horn. Who the devil would be afoot on a night like this?"

A second horn blares from the dimness, this one higher in pitch, like a silver trumpet. My eyes widen. There are two separate groups out there in the darkness.

"Ahern, those are two different Welsh horns, but neither is from our kin."

"I fear you're right. Which means two of our former foes have showed up at our gates, the North Welsh and those from the South kingdom."

"Iago and Arthwys?" I gasp. "If they've joined forces again . . ."

I trail off, afraid to complete the thought. Aren't Iago and Arthwys enemies now? Last we heard, Arthwys planned to march against Gwynedd, but only rumors have reached us since. We've had too much war as it is. With Iago's horsemen and Arthwys's swordsmen arrayed against us, our few remaining archers will fall like sheaves to the scythe. Iago's men certainly have reason to be unfriendly. I did order Ahern to lay waste to half their winter granaries with flame and sword. As for Arthwys, he has hated me since he was a boy. I doubt that our differences will ever be resolved but with blood. I bite down on my fist, hard enough to make me wince. Dear God, why now? We've survived Saxon and Pict invasions, only to fall to our fellow Welshmen? Perhaps there's a dark, yet fitting, irony to it all.

Most of the revelers down in the mead hall have not yet heard the war bugles. The clatter of crockery and the music of minstrels still pipe through the vaults within the heart of the complex. Only a few figures come out onto the landing with us in the bitter winter cold. Artagan and his knights peer into the growing darkness beyond the castle gates. Even amidst a Yuletide feast, Artagan's ears are trained for war. He unsheathes his longsword, wielding his weapon with almost as much briskness as he did before his injury.

"Have the lookouts seen anything?" he demands.

I shake my head. Our mingled breath fogs our cheeks. Two more distinct toots sound through the woods.

"But those are definitely North and South Welsh bullhorns," I reply.

He curses under his breath. We both know just how bad this could be, but neither of us wish to say so aloud. We've endured too much for it to end like this. Artagan's eyes narrow.

"Why sound their bugles? Why would they warn us of their coming?"

Ahern and the others shrug their shoulders. Several guards arrive, manning the walls with their bows drawn. Artagan's question lingers in my mind a moment before my eyes widen. Of course! How could I have been so foolish? I hasten toward the guards along the main gateway.

"They normally wouldn't sound their horns," I reply to my husband, "unless they meant us no harm."

I order the nearest guardsmen to open the gates. The warriors exchange looks, glancing up at Artagan for guidance. My husband and my brother look equally taken aback. I shake my head, almost smiling. It's so simple, yet they do not see it for what it is. I put a hand on my hip.

"*Men.* You assume all horns are blown for battle or hunting."

"No knight or king would do otherwise," Artagan retorts.

"Aye." I smile. "But *queens,* now, they are a different matter entirely."

Artagan's eyes wax into half-moons before his features relax. He gives me a peck on the cheek in praise. Ahern still looks as perplexed as ever, but Artagan, catching my drift, leans over the battlements to call out to his guards.

"Open the gates, men! We've some extra guests for the feast."

Reluctantly, the soldiers follow his command. The frozen oaken gates creak and groan as they pry them apart. The clack of horses' hooves murmur down the roadway leading to the castle. The first riders enter the ring of torchlight cast from our warriors' flickering brands. A small retinue of mounted soldiers escorts a pair of riders at the head of their company. A broad smile creases my lips as the two lead riders halt in front of the open gates.

"Queen Olwen and Queen Cordelia." I bow. "Well met. You are both most welcome."

"I hope you've plenty of fare left at table," Cordelia replies. "My men and I are famished."

Olwen and I exchange looks, both repressing smiles and half failing to do so. I doubt Cordelia's men and horses are half so famished as she will prove to be once we get her to the feasting hall. The two matrons enter the main courtyard with their escorts. My guardsmen bar the gates once again against the winter cold and the lingering darkness. Inside Aranrhod's confines, however, everything is warmth and light.

In the main hall, the minstrels strike up new tunes at the sight of our honored, if unexpected, guests. I seat Olwen and Cordelia at the head table with my own family. Olwen's little boy leaps forward at the sight of his mother. My own elder son wraps his arms around my waist as he swallows another mouthful of venison. I smile at Olwen as our boys cling to our skirts.

"To what do I owe this unexpected visit?" I begin cordially.

"Can't a pair of queens visit you just because they want to?" Olwen smiles.

"So you've both managed to become queens again? What of your rival, young Ness?"

"Who?" Olwen replies, pretending for an instant she forgot. "Oh, her. Perished quite mysteriously a full moon ago. Died of a poison arrow, I believe, or so the clerics decided. I, of course, paid the priests to change their minds. A fever sounded more realistic to my taste."

I bury my mouth behind my hand, half-amused and half-astounded by Olwen's brazen use of her newly reclaimed power. I need not ask anything more. Even a blind man can tell that Olwen once again has King Iago wrapped around her little finger. And the whole northern kingdom, for that matter. Perhaps now more so than ever.

And to think I've no one to blame but myself for helping put Olwen back on her throne. I pray that I never live to regret it. I give Olwen a sidelong glance, lowering my voice.

"How are you and Cordelia on such good terms now? And aren't your husbands supposed to be foes?"

"Being queens again has helped mend our differences. As for our husbands . . . well, I might have exaggerated Arthwys's plans for the North. His army never actually left Caerleon." Olwen winks.

Never left Caerleon? Her little fib helped drive apart Sab's alliance, and none of us even thought to question her. It appears I have underestimated Olwen. I'd best keep a close eye on her in the years to come.

Yet she did send me a raven not long ago with some friendly intelligence. When she had him under her spell, Arthwys admitted to having planted the bloody dagger in our door at Caerleon. His father's old blade, covered in pig's blood. I should have known. It was far too clumsy a thing for a real assassin to do, more like a page boy's prank. He took advantage of the situation to sow the seeds of fear in my heart. That I'll not soon forget. A queen always pays her debts. But such comeuppance between King Arthwys and myself will have to wait for another day.

As for Olwen and I, tonight we can stop being rivals for a spell. We can simply enjoy being two mothers celebrating Christmastide with their children beside a warm hearth fire.

Cordelia already finds herself up to her elbows in cheese wheels and a platter of roast duck. Smacking her lips between gulps of mead, she relays a brief description of her reunited condition with King Arthwys.

"He knows which side his bread's buttered on! If he wants to maintain his lucrative trade with Cornwall that has made his kingdom so rich, he'll keep me on as his bride. I'm back where I belong—in Caerleon. I've told the young boy king that if he wants to keep me as wife, he'll need to keep peace with my friends, and that includes the Free Cantref Queen who sheltered me when that little princeling booted me out in the first place."

She winks at me just in case I don't understand that the *friend* she refers to is me. Cordelia finishes her thought as she sizes up a bowl of stew.

"I don't expect a vigorous marriage, but so long as I'm supplied with the life I'm accustomed to, Arthwys and I should get on splendidly."

I bite my tongue, trying not to snort cider out my nostrils. I vaguely manage to picture young Arthwys in the bedchamber with Cordelia's generous girth taking up most of the bed. Few young men in Christendom would envy his position. But he seems to be learning that being king doesn't mean a man can always do as he pleases. For the time being, Arthwys will put up with Cordelia, but for how many years is anyone's guess. Arthwys needs the valuable trade with Cornwall that keeps South Wales rich. So long as the coin continues to flow, he will keep Cordelia as his bride. And so long as Cordelia remains queen, she will keep South Wales at peace with my realm.

A weight lifts from my shoulders as I grasp the full meaning of what has happened. These two queens certainly didn't just come to offer a friendly "well met, hello." They're here to subtly remind me that their kingdoms will remain at peace with mine own so long as the three of us remain in accord with each other. Three queens, together securing a three-way peace for war-torn Wales. I lift a fresh horn of mead to my lips. Such a prospect of enduring peace is the best Christmas present I could hope for.

Rowena comes by the table with Tristan in her arms, my younger son fussing hungrily. I take the child and throw a shift over my shoulder, suckling my babe beneath the folds of my gown. Queen and commoner alike nurse their newborns in the mead hall, a fairly everyday sight that hardly draws a look.

I suddenly notice just how many young ones number amongst the families in our hall. Rowena's two girls, Olwen's son, and scores of small servant children run amongst the long tables while Una and Father David try hopelessly to keep them in line. My toddler Gavin sits on the bench beside me, devouring his meal with the gusto of a growing boy. I've all my children with me, safe and happy, with the real possibility of a bright future ahead of them.

Finally, a long peace in which Wales may bear some fruit. A new generation will come of age, and thanks to Olwen, Cordelia, and myself, we've secured a country for them to inherit someday. Doubtless the Saxons will eventually return when their numbers grow once more, but that will be years from now. Word has it they're still suffering from the plague. As for the Picts, I don't think they'll ever have the strength to threaten our shores again. And if they do, their skulls shall join Queen Sab's outside my castle gatepost.

But what's to stop the Welsh from warring amongst themselves? Olwen, Cordelia, and I won't live forever. We can buy our nation of fragmented kingdoms a few precious years, maybe a decade or two. But what happens after that, when our children come of age? So long as our realms are divided, the greatest threat to the Welsh people will be other Welshmen. One fief threatening to go to war with the other.

Making my way back to the throne, I take my seat beside Artagan.

Tristan falls asleep at the breast, as he often does. I adjust my shift as I let the newborn rest in my arms. Gavin sidles up beside me to get a better look at his little brother. Even after a few moons, he can't seem to get enough of him. He stares and stares, even smiles, but rarely says anything. I cannot help but smile too. My boy seems quite taken with his new ward. He will be a good big brother.

Across the feast tables, the two knights from Dyfed saunter up the main aisle. Brothers, Carrick and Bowen, I can now tell them easily apart by Bowen's limp and his new wooden leg. The clerics had to remove his limb below the knee after the Battle of All Hallows, but he remains as proud a warrior as ever. Much like myself and Artagan, I suppose. Despite losing the big battles, we still managed to win the war. We Welsh are a stubborn people and never give in easily.

Bowen and Carrick have served as loyal allies in our campaign against the Picts, helping to drive the blue-painted savages back to their ships at the last battle outside Dun Dyfed's walls. But something in Bowen's strained face gives me pause. His brother knight grimaces beside him. The two Dyfed brothers halt in front of Artagan and me, standing silent before our thrones.

My husband gives me a sidelong glance. I merely shrug in reply. The crowd gradually quiets down, all eyes turning to the pair of Dyfed knights who have presented themselves before us. My pulse quickens. Both brothers look serious as steel. What ails them so? Bowen clears his throat, tapping the stone floor with his wooden peg leg. The sound of clacking timber reverberates off the rafters like a gavel. Silence pervades the chamber.

"I ask to speak, King Artagan, before you and your subjects."

Artagan raises an eyebrow.

"Speak freely, Sir Bowen. You've stood with us in many a battle and are no stranger here."

Bowen surveys the crowd, speaking to them as much as he does to Artagan.

"I would ask the King of Aranrhod, ruler of the Free Cantrefs, for a favor he owes the people of Dyfed. *My* people. We served as faithful allies when you came to our aid, battling Picts and any Welshmen who joined them. We helped one another and fought as brothers. But we Dyfed men are a proud lot and will not submit to a stranger to rule over us. We ask now that you recognize Dyfed in its own right and the man we wish to declare King of Dun Dyfed!"

Murmurs fill the hall as scores of whispered conversations break out at once. A new *king* of Dyfed? None have been rightful ruler there since my father died at the hands of the Saxons several years ago. I tighten my hand on the arm of my chair. These Dyfed knights have suspected every king and warlord of trying to take over their homeland. Even now, after all we have done for them, they still seem to view us as strangers. Some thanks indeed!

I make a move to rise from my seat, to give these two Dyfed knights a piece of my mind. After all, I was born a royal woman of Dyfed, and I think I still have a right to tell my countrymen what I think. Sensing my rising wrath, Artagan puts a hand over mine to stay my words. He rises from his throne and looks down at Bowen.

"Dyfed makes its own way, and we in the Free Cantrefs shall recognize that. Who would you have as your king?"

"The last living son of the old Dyfed king," Bowen replies for all to hear. "Ahern, son of Vortigen!"

A hush runs over the crowd. My brother Ahern walks alone toward the dais before our thrones, his one good eye staring straight ahead at me. Although bastard born, the ways of the Old Tribes recognize any natural child as a man's heir. Such ways are sometimes neglected in the North and South, but they run strongest in the Free Cantrefs and Dyfed. And Ahern is my late father's only remaining son, even if he is born on the other side of the blanket. I supposed I've always known this day was coming, but I was loath to admit it to myself. After all the adventures we've shared, I simply don't wish to be parted from my dear Ahern.

Artagan turns to Ahern. My brother never removes his gaze from me.

"Do you accept the crown of Dyfed, Ahern son of Vortigen?" Artagan asks him.

"If my lady allows me to accept it." Ahern nods toward me. "I am still her sworn guardsman and seneschal until she releases me from my oath."

All eyes turn toward me. Why have these Dyfed knights asked this of me? Ahern has been with me since I first left Dyfed as a child. We've had our ups and downs, but never did I think I'd have to live without him at my side. And now they want him to sit on Father's old throne. Why should that make my heart twist sideways so? Perhaps because I still see myself as Dyfed's true heiress. Or maybe because I am selfish and do not wish to see Ahern go. I've always slept well knowing he guarded me and my children at night. But now the people of Dyfed need him. A grizzled veteran, a survivor of many trials. He will make a good king.

I bow my head, nodding my ascent.

"I relieve you of your oath, dear brother. Although I shall miss you more than words can say."

Ahern flashes a cordial smile. Why does he look so pleased with himself? Has my brother longed to be released from my service all this time? Have I been so blind?

So he wishes to be a monarch, after all. With all of Dyfed under his sway, will he be a benign neighbor, or will he oppose us? I swallow hard. The people of the Free Cantrefs have endured so much war these past few years. I do not think our kingdom could survive another.

Ahern turns to Sir Bowen and Sir Carrick, his voice resounding and stern.

"Do I have your oaths, then, liegemen of Dyfed? As faithful vassals to their lord?"

"Aye," both brothers reply in tandem.

"Then I agree to be Lord of Dun Dyfed, on one condition," Ahern begins. "That my first and last act as king will be for me to bend the knee to two rulers who are better than I."

Ahern sinks down on one knee before Artagan and me. Sir Bowen and Sir Carrick do likewise. Now I am truly confused. Whatever Ahern is up to, both Bowen and Carrick clearly seem to be in on the same plot.

I hand my sleeping babe into Rowena's arms, standing beside my husband. He furrows his brow, equally as perplexed as myself. Ahern speaks loud enough for the entire hall to hear.

"Too long has Wales been divided by petty kingdoms! Not since the days of Arthur have the descendants of the Old Tribes followed a single ruler. Today we aim to change that. I pledge my loyalty and my Kingdom of Dyfed to the House of King Artagan and Queen Branwen. They came to the aid of Wales when she was in dire need, and I'll pledge my life and spear to their rule."

"I can live with that oath," Bowen seconds, kneeling with his good leg.

"As can I." Carrick grins. "I second the motion."

"Wait!" I interrupt, still trying to wrap my mind around their professed oaths. "You've just made Ahern King of Dyfed and now you wish to pledge your loyalty to us?"

"To join the kingdoms, my lady," Ahern replies. "Not as one realm conquering another, but welded together as equals. You are of the royal line of Dyfed, and King Artagan comes from the Free Cantrefs, but in the days of old they were all *one* people of the Old Tribes. Let us join Dyfed and the Free Cantrefs as one realm once more. Not part of North or South Wales, but a central place united in peace and war . . . a Middle Kingdom."

Dyfed spearmen and Free Cantref archers scattered throughout the hall raise their drinking horns with hearty "hear, hears" and seconded toasts. I swallow, suddenly lost for words. Everything is happening so fast. Permanently join the realms of the Free Cantrefs and Dyfed? Neither realm ruled by the lords of the North or South Welsh Lands. I murmur Ahern's last words. *The Middle Kingdom.*

Every commoner and noble in the main hall stands, cheering their support for Ahern's proposal. We've more than enough mixed company of Free Cantref and Dyfed families throughout the hall, and yet they all seem to raise their voices as one. Only two individuals do not rise quite as rapidly as the others.

Queen Olwen and Queen Cordelia give one another sidelong looks.

They smile politely, but their trepidation is all too clear to my mind. Although I am their ally, my husband's kingdom has suddenly doubled in size, big enough to rival their own holdings in the North and South. Can Wales be balanced so, a third of it under each of us queens and our husbands? Every castle court in Wales will whisper that I've connived for this union from the very first, trying to place half of Wales under my sway. But despite all my past plots and plans, never did I dream so big as this.

Artagan unsheathes his sword as his own knights, Sir Emryus and Sir Keenan, join the others knelt before the throne. My husband's voice rings throughout the hall.

"Here today by common consent, I take the oaths of the people, to make Ahern Lord of Dun Dyfed, and unite all the people of the Free Cantrefs and Dyfed lands into a single nation as our common forebearers once did. From this day forth we are one country, one realm. The Middle Kingdom of King Artagan Blacksword and Queen Branwen the Mab Ceridwen!"

Artagan taps each of his knights on the shoulder with the flat of his blade. They in turn swear firm-sounding "aye, ayes" as they place their palms over their hearts. Artagan bids them rise and takes my hand. The crowded hall erupts with applause, a roar of cheers washing over me as my skin ripples in gooseflesh.

I smile at my brother as he rises to embrace me. I wonder what the women of the Old Tribes would think if they could see all of us now. King Artagan and Branwen the Mab Ceridwen, monarchs of the new Middle Kingdom in a free and peaceful Wales.

The noise wakes Tristan from his slumber, but he quiets his cries once Rowena hands him back to me. Gavin tugs at my leg before Artagan lifts him up with one arm. I plant a kiss on each of their little brows. My two children are now heirs to the largest kingdom in Wales. Heaven help us, we seem to be blessed with both fortune and yet also a heavy burden. There will be many years of work ahead rebuilding this war-torn realm. But the spirit of the people remains strong and united.

With so much of Wales under Artagan and me, we are closer than ever before to uniting all the Welsh under a single banner. It may take years, even decades, but at least we have peace now among the North, South, and Middle Welsh. Best to put aside all other worries for another day. Tonight we have peace and a newly united country to call home.

Artagan kisses my cheek and puts his other arm around me. I rest my head on his shoulder, shutting my eyes a moment to take in the warmth of my family all crowded around me. Each of them safe and sound. For the first time since I was a child, I see a clear horizon ahead of me. Or at least the hope of brighter days ahead.

The flow of cider from newly opened Christmas kegs freely fills every drinking horn. The crowd begins a mantra, not for me or Artagan but for all of us. One people, one tribe, one family. Artagan and I join in with the rest, chanting in unison.

"The Middle Kingdom! The Middle Kingdom! Long live the Middle Kingdom!"

HISTORICAL NOTE

The Picts remain an enigmatic people in the annals of history, and I've certainly chosen to emphasize certain aspects of what we know of their history over others. Just as some of the place names in my book really exist within Wales and some are amalgamations of multiple sites, the culture of the Picts I've depicted relies on a mix of fact and legend. I find both historical and mythological texts to be of crucial value, especially since even a legend conveys grains of real truths.

As for the Welsh themselves, once again, I've chosen to emphasize certain aspects of early Medieval Welsh culture over others, and I've also simplified some people and place name spellings to make them a bit easier for English-speakers to pronounce.

Some of the most influential texts I consulted include the works of St. Gildas, as well as Peter Berresford Ellis' incomparable *Celtic Myths and Legends,* and, of course, the Welsh *Mabinogion.* Portions of the saga are inspired by recorded events, others by folklore and legends, and a touch from my own imagination, but ultimately Branwen and Artagan are creations of my heart.

ACKNOWLEDGMENTS

Heartfelt thanks to my wife, who continues to inspire me in all of my writing, including this book. Thank you to my family and friends whose love makes all things possible

A big thanks to my agent, Rena, who first asked me after reading *Between Two Fires,* "so where's the sequel?" *Dark Winds Rising* has come about due to her hard work and support. Thank you, Rena, for making this sequel a reality.

I also wish to thank Thomas Dunne Books and St. Martin's Press, especially Pete and Jennifer. Your candid advice and attention to detail has been invaluable in making this novel what it is today.

Thank you as well to all of my fellow readers and writers online, as well as my pals from writer's conferences. Each of you continues to spur me on to keep writing and to continually find the beauty of the written word.

And a final thanks to God, who continues to teach me every day.